THE ART OF LOVE

When Anne resumed her pose and began dreaming again, I went to painting the lovely green gown, my brushes guided by the memory of that peerless body which lay beneath the cloth, and as they stroked the canvas it was as if they were my fingers caressing the creamy soft flesh. I was making love to her just as surely as if we were physically joined. My pounding heart, my hard breathing and soaring excitement were not all due to the vigor of my work. The green eyes, looking at me yet not seeing me, told me she knew what was happening and deep inside she was responding, giving herself up to me in an invisible frenzy of delight. My painting was automatic as my mind reached out to her, holding her, kissing her, adoring her, having her. My passion steadily mounted until the painted face on the canvas, beautiful and complete, gasped, "Ah, Jamie, Jamie, no more, no more!"

JAMIE REID

GORDON OGILVIE

AVON
PUBLISHERS OF BARD, CAMELOT AND DISCUS BOOKS

JAMIE REID is an original publication of Avon Books. This
work has never before appeared in book form.

AVON BOOKS
A division of
The Hearst Corporation
959 Eighth Avenue
New York, New York 10019

First Avon Printing, January, 1981

AVON TRADEMARK REG. U.S. PAT. OFF. AND IN
OTHER COUNTRIES, MARCA REGISTRADA,
HECHO EN U.S.A.

Printed in the U.S.A.

Author's Note

Mr. Ogilvie wishes to point out that while the Ogilvie plantation was located as indicated and described in the novel, and was operated by Peter and his brother John (who also later settled in Nova Scotia), the sister Margaret is totally fictional. The actual sister, Anne, married a local man and remained in Georgia.

Chapter I

EVEN THOUGH old soldiers maintain you never hear the bullet that has your name on it, if I had been gifted with the witchly second sight of Anne MacDonald when I painted the now-famous portrait of His Britannic Majesty, King George III, there was a time in his conversation with me when I would have heard the hum of the musket ball that many months later was to knock me arse over the teapot.

It was during the last sitting at Buckingham House. His Majesty was a great talker, once started, especially on the subject of art, an interest that had cost him hundreds of pounds out of his own pocket in his sponsorship of the fledgling Royal Academy. "I've enjoyed our talks, Mr. Reid," he told me, "and watchin' you work with such skill. From now on I'll follow your career with personal interest." His high-colored face smiled. "And I'll let that get about unless you prefer otherwise, eh?"

The portrait and his personal interest would be the capstone of my already considerable success. I grinned. "Thank you, sir. I wouldn't think of preferring otherwise. That would be nothing short of treason."

"Ha," he said with pawky good humor, "I wish your fellow Bostonians were of a similar mind, those pernicious malcontents and democratical anarchists. How d'you think of the liberty they preach, eh?"

Painting in the highlights of the Cadogan puffs of his stylish wig, I answered, "When I left there at seventeen, eight years ago, politics were beyond my understanding and still are, sir. My work takes up all my thinking, time and effort, Your Majesty."

"Not all, I'll wager." His slightly bulging eyes regarded me seriously. "I've heard a bit of your—ah—other work

1

among the ladies, carousin' about the town, sword-fightin' and such. 'Tis time you took a good wife who'll clip your wings, I'd say." He was a solid family man, devoted to his Queen and the more than a dozen royal spratlings he had sired upon her. He said earnestly, "A fellow like you could be tempted into all sorts of mischief or romantical exploits in these times. An American, too. Take yourself a wife, sir, and as for the other, leave it to the Army and Navy. I need you at your paintin'. Great Britain needs you there."

"I'll confess to being partial to the ladies," I commented, "but that's connected with my work because I paint so many of 'em, sir. And as for the swordsmanship, 'tis only daily practice sessions and sporting matches for the sake of good exercise. I assure you, sir, nothing could tempt me away from my easel."

He nodded solemnly. "Shoemaker to his last, eh? I'll hold you to that, Mr. Reid. British artists are jewels in the Empire's crown, don't you know?"

"You have my word, Your Majesty," I smiled. "I can't think of a happier way to serve you than by following my craft here in London."

At that point I might have heard that goddamned rebel musket ball, because at that moment Lord Beauvoir entered the room to speak with the King. A small, slender, middle-aged gentleman, he was a rather frequent visitor to the painting room, slipping in and out like a fragile gray cloud. He always wore gray clothes of elegant cut and sumptuous material, and his communications to the King were delivered in a gray whispering voice, the words inaudible to me. His finely sculptured ascetic face resembled an exquisite ancient cameo. I had no idea of what his official place was, but it was clear that he enjoyed a special confidence with the King. On this occasion His Majesty listened closely, then said irritably, "Damme, why does the man persist? Can he not understand the awkwardness he puts me to? Devil take him! Ha—hum—make the usual arrangements, eh? See he comes to no harm nor gets into trouble. Discreet, eh?"

Beauvoir bowed, murmuring, and as he withdrew he glanced at me with a faint glacial smile. Shortly afterward, I finished the painting and signed it. The King, inspecting the portrait with keen interest, said, "Jolly good, Mr. Reid. Excellent, eh? Not a single false note. Splendid color harmony and remarkable brushwork, I must say. And you've

2

not made me pursy or pouty or so demned treacly handsome as others have done. You must have another exhibition at the Academy soon and this must be shown. I'll be watchin' you, sir, so mind your promise to take a wife and settle down, eh?"

As I strode through the palace on my way out, immensely pleased with myself, Lord Beauvoir, icily smiling, intercepted me. The whispery gray voice said, "His Majesty asked me to settle his account with you, sir." He handed me a clinking purse. "That splendid portrait is worth every farthing of the twenty guineas. A magnificent work of art, sir."

Accepting the money, I said, "Thank you, my lord. I didn't expect payment until after framing."

"His Majesty abhors debts outstanding," answered the little gray man, "and the Household will see to the framing. I'll be obliged if you'll give me a receipt at your convenience. Anytime, Mr. Reid."

"I'd best give it to you now," I told him. "I'm not likely to come onto you again. My sphere of activity doesn't normally include royal palaces and Whitehall."

"Ah," he murmured, "that remains to be seen. If you can spare me a moment I have a matter to discuss with you. I'm not unmindful of the fashionability of your fine work, the demand for your services, and because of the royal portrait that demand will sharply increase. Yet, I wonder—is there a possibility that you could find time for a portrait for me in the immediate future, Mr. Reid?"

He would be interesting to paint. "Of your Lordship?"

The cold gray smile flickered. "Why, no, Mr. Reid. I've three portraits of myself in my house and believe that to be a sufficient display of vanity for any one man. Briefly, the thought has come to me that you have the skill and insight to execute an interesting portrait of Lady Beauvoir." As I opened my mouth to speak, he raised a small, delicately boned hand. "Before you reply, sir, let me say she's hardly a ravishing beauty. To be quite honest, she is plain of face and her manner is not especially vivacious. However, I'm sure you will be able to depict my lady with emphasis on her interesting underlying qualities."

Mildly annoyed, I said, "My lord, I could never paint any qualities into a face that are not in the original. I cannot make a plain lady beautiful for the sake of a fee.

3

My integrity as well as my skill make my reputation, sir, and my reputation is my bread."

"Well and honestly spoken, Mr. Reid," he said, smilingly. "Fear not, sir, your integrity shall remain virginal. I am afraid I did not make my meaning clear. While no dazzling goddess, Lady Beauvoir has a notably strong character overlying a certain inner tempestuousness, qualities I am certain your penetrating insight will lay bare and transfer to canvas in a most delightful fashion. There is no requirement for spurious prettification, sir. And I am prepared to duplicate the King's fee, Mr. Reid."

The payment for the royal portrait was extremely generous even compared with my customary high prices, and this offer was too good to be spurned. In my few seconds of hesitation I visualized Lady Beauvoir and saw her as a withered and bedizened old beauty of decades past, tottering and grunting about in vast billows of silks and satins; sagging, wrinkled face a half inch deep in white lead and wearing on her head a towering wig at least three feet tall, topped with perhaps a wicker cage containing exotic birds. I said, "My schedule is full for some weeks to come, my lord."

"Surely," he remarked, "the price is worth some small adjustment for my accommodation, Mr. Reid."

I surrendered. "Very well, my lord. When can Lady Beauvoir begin posing, and shall the work be done at my house or yours? Also, do you have in mind any specific pose, size, color dominance?"

The cold smile broadened. "Ah, thank you, Mr. Reid. Your kindness puts me in your debt indeed. Your house, if you please. The odor of paint makes me unwell. My lady will call at your house for the first sitting at one o'clock tomorrow afternoon, then, if that is agreeable. I fancy a sitting pose, and the same size as His Majesty's picture. My drawing room is done in white with gilded ornamentation, crimson hangings and rugs. My work places heavy demands on my time, so her brother, Sir Adam Welby, will escort my lady to and from your house. I must also beg that your schedule be further disrupted to permit sittings on each successive afternoon in order to maintain her interest. She has a tendency to be impatient with strangers, therefore I urge you to be patient with her initial high spirits, you'll then find her company enjoyable, I think."

If anybody had high spirits, it was I when I came away

4

from the palace and rode jubilantly through the streets in my elegant carriage behind a pair of matched spanking grays driven by my smartly liveried coachman, Bert. There was no denying it: on that March day in 1778 the world for Jamie Reid was one enormous bowl of luscious oysters.

Arriving at my house on Portsmouth Square, I was not surprised when I entered the library to find Hector MacDonald drinking my best rum and groping under the skirt of Kitty Bumpus, my pretty housemaid, who fled, blushing, toward the kitchen. "Hector," I said, pouring a drink, "London's awash with ladies of proper degree who'd be delighted to entertain your finger or any other append-age you might care about sticking into 'em. You know my house rules. No folderol with my female help."

Red-headed Hector gazed at me with a travesty of inno-cence on his raw-boned Scottish face. "Folderol is it? My good colonial clod, even though I labor at journalism in this festering ulcer of Saxon culture called London, I must remind you that I am a bona fide doctor of surgery and physic and was administering to the poor lassie a bit of an examination in the region of feverish parts, and I shall charge you not a penny for the service. 'Tis a chronic afflic-tion among healthy maidens, her complaint, and 'twill pass without need for medication, but complications may occur if she seeks the rash relief of a lusty young man's donniker. During the hour I've waited here for you, you had two lady callers evidently seeking such relief from yours. God knows how you find the time to daub your pictures, for all the belly-thumping that goes on in your painting room."

" 'Tis labor and research, you Caledonian fishhead," I told him. "A small frolic on the couch with a lady portrait subject is a unique instrument for the revelation of con-cealed character. Tell me, d'you know of a certain Lady Beauvoir? I've been engaged to take her portrait and have the impression it won't be easy."

He shook his head, pitying. "Och, laddie, you'll have need of all your skill for that one. Angels to guide your brush. I've seen her twice, from a distance. She goes out in society very little. I know her brother, Sir Adam, and know a bit of the family history. He's a touch odd, and as for her, she wears a dark scowl on her soul, Jamie. A swarthy, savage wench utterly devoid of charm, with a heart that pumps vinegar."

"How old is she?" I asked.

"Oh, I'd say twenty and three, perhaps," he answered, "though her facial expression says forty. I presume you've met the husband—thank you, I'll take another dram of your excellent spirits, my lad. Here! Fill it to here! That's better. Don't be so bloody stingy with your drink, you Yankee miser. Then the question has risen to your turgid brain concerning the springtime-and-winter relationship. Same boring old story. He had no money to go with his tattered titles and political pretensions, so he married it. She and her brother inherited a mountain of gold and vast estates in Ireland—ancestral Cromwellian loot, ye ken. She was born and raised there in some remote country pile. Beauvoir sniffed out the bucolic heiress, made his offer, and she snapped it up without ever laying eyes on the gentleman, much to the distaste of Sir Adam because his elderly brother-in-law sits high in the councils of George, third Hanoverian monarch and usurper, according to Sir Adam, of the lawful Stuart throne."

"A Jacobite?" I asked. "I thought they were all old men."

Hector chuckled. "He nurses the flame in his bosom, the very model of a Restoration cavalier of olden times. He doesn't quite dare to sport the White Cockade, but favors dark suits, much white lace and wears his hair uncaught down to his shoulders. Not a bad sort, actually, but damned tedious on the subject of the Stuarts."

"He does sound cracked for sure," I commented. "My father—and yours, too—was out for Charlie in the '45, and as long as he lived I never heard him say much about it, except concerning my Uncle John's death."

"Nor does my father," said Hector, laughing. "He sits here in London today counting out his gold to the Anglo-Saxons at high interest rates, getting quietly even for the year he spent in an English prison after Culloden."

"And counting it out to his wastrel son," I observed.

"And whose money," he snorted, "was it that brought you out of that American howling wilderness if it weren't the silver earned by your late sire in Boston? My kettle's no blacker than your pot. Don't come sanctimonious with me, my lad."

It was not exactly true, of course. I'd used my inheritance, a modest one, to support me during my early days in London while I learned my profession. However, I let it slide; my mind was on the prospect of the Beauvoir portrait. "Lord Beauvoir said she had an inner tempestuousness."

"Acid dyspepsia and flatulence, no doubt," he observed. " 'Tis likely a medium-sized fart from her would blow the wee gentleman clear out of bed, and such from her would surely be poisonously sour and gloomily rumbling. This is a dreary subject, Jamie. I say, if you don't have a bedding scheduled tonight with one of your high-born strumpets, come along with me to Mother Allworth's for supper and a few bottles, eh? She's got a new lass in the stable, a handsome dark brown Moor—I've seen her, Jamie!—with an incredible rump and dugs as big as your head, available to regular guests at a special low introductory fee."

I shook my head regretfully. "I've got to joggle my appointment book around to accommodate twenty guineas' worth of uncharming female, write notes to those affected, and go over my investment accounts."

Getting to his feet, he announced, "You, sir, are a penny-pinching drudge with an obscene love for money. Very well, I shall go forth and test the exotic dark lady alone."

"Don't rake her with your spurs," I commented. "I may want to have a romp with her and I don't favor scarified whores."

" 'Tis a good thing I'm taking her first," he said, going to the door, "for likely you'll give her the French pox you'll have picked up the night before from one of your duchesses. Farewell, parsimonious bluenose, and good luck with Lady B."

Good luck indeed. The following afternoon when Lady Beauvoir and her brother appeared in my entrance hall, my quick inspection showed she would be interesting to paint; an easy likeness, I thought, if it were not for the naked hostility that seethed in her cornflower blue eyes as she stared at me during the introductions. Her wigless hair was glossy black and her complexion almost swarthy. Her facial construction was strong-boned, with a wide, full-lipped mouth, an imperiously arched nose and broad cheekbones. It could have been an attractive face had it not given the impression of, as Hector had said, a scowl on the soul. Sir Adam, a solemn fellow of about my own age dressed in severe black, having learned from me that the painting session would be over about four o'clock, told his sister he would return at that time and started for the door.

She spoke to me for the first time in a low, intense, almost grating voice. "If you're now done with looking at me as if I'm a cow to be sold at the fair, get on now with what you've been hired to do."

Her brother halted and said, pained, "Emily, please, I beg you—"

"Trot along to your own affairs and leave me to mine!" she snapped at him, and to me: "Will you stand there forever ogling and leering at me? Get on with it!"

It would be useless to commence the work in the face of such hostility. I said politely, "Perhaps it would be best if we change the appointment to a time when my lady will be more at ease."

"By all means, sir," agreed her brother. "Emily, suppose—"

"Go! In God's name, go!" she exclaimed angrily.

He shrugged in resignation, gave me an apologetic look, bowed and departed. Her husband had counseled patience. I would comply and hope for the best. "The painting room is upstairs, madam. Will you please come?"

As she preceded me up the staircase, her stiffly erect back reminded me of a condemned person marching to the scaffold. In the painting room she silently took the posing chair I indicated, and watched me sullenly. A glass of wine is good medicine for nervous or shy sitters, so I poured her a glass of Madeira. "You might enjoy this, my lady, while I prepare my palette."

She took it and went back to staring balefully at me while I pretended to busy myself. The atmosphere in the room fairly vibrated with her dislike, and the wine remained untasted. Uncomfortable and annoyed, I said vacuously, "This is my painting room, of course."

"I'd not thought it your bogs," she returned acidly.

Irritation fought with patience. "Your handsome crimson gown will be perfect for the composition I've conceived. It sets off your fine shoulders nicely." It had a wide, low neckline, revealing an attractively swelling upper bust. "With your torso turned slightly, the line of your bosom will—"

Her angry eyes blazed and she burst out, "Shoulders and bosom! Isn't it enough that the poor thing is to be done, without your filthy nasty ridicule before it starts? Get on with your dirty joke and to hell with you!"

Dumbfounded, I gaped. "Dirty joke? What in God's name do you mean?"

"Don't play mealymouthed innocent with me, you

8

damned jackanapes!" she exclaimed. "You and Vinny! How the pair of you must have laughed when you planned it!"

Patience fled. I wanted no more of her. "Madam, there will be no poor thing, no dirty joke done here. I have no need of your husband's money. I don't paint shrieking fish-wives, and you may pass that to your husband. I'll order my carriage brought around for you."

She shot out of the chair and flung the contents of the glass into my face, crying, "You damned insulting bastard! Fishwife, is it? Goddamn you for a stinking vile pogue!"

She had to be touched in the head. Mastering myself, I mopped my face with my handkerchief and said with ad-mirable calmness, "I'll show you to the door, madam, and call my carriage."

Dropping back into the chair, she snapped, "Devil you will! You'll get on with smearing your filthy joke and when you're done, we'll see! Yes, by God, we'll see!"

I said coldly, "Madam, the title you bear is no license for disgraceful conduct in my house. I must ask you to leave."

"And I refuse!" she spat. "Earn your scummy money, you . . . you *thing!*"

Puzzlement filtered through my anger. " 'Dirty joke.' 'Filthy joke.' Vinny. Madam, if there's one thing I'm dead serious about, 'tis my work and if any man ever spoke of one of my paintings, in my hearing, as a joke, I assure you he would never do such again. And if Vinny is your hus-band, I never spoke a word with him in my life before yesterday at Buckingham House, when he engaged my services for your portrait shortly after I finished one of His Majesty. I think I'm entitled to an explanation of your strange behavior, madam."

Her face showed surprise and I caught a flash of girl-ishness. "The King? You really took his likeness? And Vinny is not your friend?"

"I'm not given to lying," I answered, "and you'll either explain or I'll have you ejected from my house, Lady Beau-voir. Even if you were the Queen of Sheba I'd not take such abuse from you. I went to considerable trouble to arrange this time for you and had to inconvenience a num-ber of patrons because of it. Well?"

The hostility had gone from her eyes and they studied my face reflectively. She said in a low voice, "I seem to have spilled my wine, sir. May I have more, please?"

9

Her change of mood was dramatic. Warily complying, I said, humoring her, "I hope none spilled on your lovely gown, my lady."

Her tone was apologetic. "Will you forgive me for pouring it in your eye, Mr. Reid? 'Twas my black Irish temper, and I think a sorry mistake." Taking a swallow, she said, "Pity I wasted it, for 'tis good stuff and thank you, sir. The explanation is this: now, you've been looking me over close enough to fairly peel my clothes off with those two-colored eyes you have in your head, and you see no pretty woman with my horsehide-color skin and great frog's mouth. Not the most blessed artist in all the seven worlds could make a silk purse out of this ugly sow's ear, don't you agree?"

"Not at all," I answered, beginning to like this different person. "I see a young lady who goes out of her way to hide a deal of charm behind a bad-tempered pose that's foreign, I think, to her pleasant nature."

There was a wistful girlishness about her now. She sighed. "I feel that way oftentimes, but—" The dourness returned. "My husband does not like me at all. To him I am ugly and stupid. He has a strange humor. He ordered me to come here to have my picture taken and I know he believes it will be a comic thing, like a monkey dressed in silk and satin, for his friends to laugh at. 'Twas in my mind he put you up to it, to make me even homelier than I am, if such is possible."

"A person's opinion of his own looks," I told her, "is an unreliable thing. Certainly yours is utterly wrong, believe me. But if you thought that was his reason, why did you go along with it and come here?"

There was savagery in her eyes. "After the picture was done, hung and well laughed at, I planned to go in the night with a knife and slash it to ribbons, then do the same to each one of his forebears' pictures that he was able to buy back with my money."

"I'd be damned angry if one of my children were hacked to bits," I smiled. "I put a deal of myself into them and 'twould hurt like flaming hell. I'll paint your likeness, my lady, and I pledge you 'twill be no grotesque joke. Your likeness inside and out. My practice is to paint not only face and figure, but what lies in heart and mind, with a glimpse of soul peeping out of the eyes. What of your soul,

10

my lady? I'll wager 'tis a pretty, tender article. What color is it? Have you ever heard it sing?"

A hint of a tremulous smile at the corners of the generous lips. "Ah, that soul of mine. I'd be afraid to have a look at it. Belike 'tis a small shriveled worm of a thing like an infant cast untimely from the womb."

"After we fetch it out to give it a chance to bloom in the light," I said, "I think we'll find it perhaps like a Dutch tulip, a brilliant scarlet cup filled with golden sunshine."

"You have a wonderful slick tongue on you," she murmured, looking down at her nearly empty wine glass, "but I like to hear such blarney even though you're saying it as if I were a child needing soothing." She looked up at me and there was a sparkle in the cornflower eyes. "I'd rather it be a tiger lily. D'you know, I've never met a man like you. A few minutes ago I hated you with all the passion in God's world."

"Passion like that," I smiled, "belongs to love, not hate. More wine?"

Shaking her head, she replied, "No, thank you, sir. Let's get on with digging up that Dutch tulip. How shall you want me to sit?"

Thus we became friends, and as I laid in the groundwork on the canvas we talked easily and without strain. The golden cord formed between us, my name for the mysterious feeling of harmony that sometimes comes into existence between artist and subject-sitter. It has nothing to do with sex, age, social standing or conversation; it is a quiet bond of mutual satisfaction and interest, I think. With it, the work of painting proceeds quite effortlessly, smoothly and with excellent results.

However, with Lady Beauvoir the golden cord was not enough. I could not decide whether she was, in character, a mature woman or artless young maid. As she rattled on from the posing chair about her isolated life in rural Ireland and the differences she found in London, she was first one and then the other, changing with dizzying rapidity. I had always rather disliked painting adolescent girls, with their half-formed womanhood and character, and it seemed to me that beneath her well-shaped womanly exterior, Lady Beauvoir had more than a little of wide-eyed girlishness. If my indecision concerning which she was continued through the portrait, the final picture would be a bland mess, a futile waste of time and effort. The challenge fas-

11

cinated me. She did, also. There was a key with which I
could unlock the puzzle of her character, and I resolved
to apply it to the lady in bed.

At the end of the afternoon when she departed on her
brother's arm, she was almost bubbling with good spirits,
smiling and gracious, which, judging from the expression
on his solemn face, mystified the devil out of him, so different was her demeanor from when she had arrived. That
night I went carousing with Hector in Vauxhall Gardens
across the Thames, but because my thoughts kept returning
to Lady Beauvoir, my dissipation was conducted rather ab-
sentmindedly. The more I mused on the prospect of a romp
in bed with her, the more eager I became.

When she showed up in my painting room the following
afternoon, wearing a different gown but—complying with
my instructions—bringing the crimson one, she seemed
to be yet another woman; silent again but without hostility,
yet with an air of apprehensive tension. She refused my
offer of Kitty Bumpus's help in the changing of gowns in
the tiring room adjoining the painting room. When painting
was resumed she sat stiffly, without speaking, not responding to my jocular efforts to ease her. She did not look at
me. The golden cord failed to appear. I puttered at the
easel, pushing a little paint about aimlessly and feeling a
bit desperate. Then I saw it. She was restless in the chair,
constantly shifting her weight, rearranging her arms and
legs. Her eyes blinked with unusual frequency and the tip
of her tongue often moistened her lips. I had observed such
symptoms many times before, and was delighted. Suddenly
she asked without expression, "D'you see my Dutch tulip
today?"

"A wee glimpse, I think," I smiled. "Enough to make me
want to see more."

"I don't believe you," she said flatly. "There's no such
thing at all. Can you not be satisfied with the woman who's
inside these clothes and never mind what's inside the
woman?" Her voice sounded faintly stifled.

Putting down the useless brush, I said easily, "I suppose
I could start with her. If you'd not mind, there's a special
method that's used when painting exceptional ladies. Many
times the social standing, reputation or splendid dress of the
subject obscures the real person, therefore the pose is un-
dertaken without the interference of covering, you see. Up-

on completion of the painting of the natural person, the posing is continued, clothed."

A touch of color came into the olive cheeks, but the blue eyes studied me unwaveringly. "You'd be wanting me to pose in my pelt? That seems a bold thing for a gentleman to ask and bolder yet for a lady to bare herself for him." She looked at the door. "What if a servant were to walk in? I'd swoon dead away."

"Why were locks invented?" I grinned, and walking to the door turned down the latchlock. When I faced about, she was already working on the unbuttoning of the back of her bodice. Going to her, I relieved her of that chore, wondering what tactic to use to move her without frightening her into the ultimate position on the tiring room couch. Pulling her arms out of the sleeves, she said defiantly, "If you so much as smile when you see what is me, I'll knock your damned teeth out. 'Tis no beautiful thing, but 'tis all I have."

I hoisted the heavy brocaded gown over her head and laid it on the posing chair. Under the gown she had worn nothing but stockings, and she stood naked and proud under my inspection. I had no impulse to laugh at what I saw; her body was sweetly formed and eminently desirable. Old Nick, having briskly risen to the occasion, throbbed in agreement. "You're quite lovely," I said gently, eyeing the pert breasts and smooth belly.

The wide blue eyes looked up at me and I saw what could have been anger. "Ha!" she exclaimed. "You'd paint my picture like this? You damned rogue, I can read in your eyes 'tis no more painting you have in mind than I have!" Hurling herself at me, she seized the bulge of Old Nick in front of my breeches and the words tumbled out with breathless swiftness: "Look at you, all of a boil to have your way with me and didn't I know all the time damn you for a slowpoky jackass of a man why are you standing here like a dummy will it take a whole week for you to come at me and get to it damn it will you move, man move—"

Not all week did it take me. A minute or two, perhaps, to scoop her up in my arms and bear her to the tiring room couch, strip and mount the heated, babbling lady. Nor did it take a week for her to explode into a wild, nearly demented convulsion of thrashing body and limbs, uttering gurgling cries; I had hardly started when that happened.

13

I had discovered her "inner tempestuousness" with a vengeance.

We lay quietly in each other's arms as breathing and heartbeats slowed to normal rate. "So that's what 'tis about," she murmured, regarding me through half-closed eyes. "Dear God, what a great wonder it is! Dear Mr. Reid, a lovely rapist you are, and what do the other wenches you scroon call you—is it Jimmy, Jim, Jamie or James?"

Laughing, I kissed the tip of her nose and answered, "During the action they address me by strange and wonderful names; before and after, 'tis Jamie."

"You know I'm Emily," she said, testing the muscles of my back with her fingers. "Faith, what a big strong lad you are, Jamie. 'Twas a grand idea I had of posing naked for you, wasn't it?"

"Yours? 'Twas my stealthy plan to get at you, love," I grinned.

Her exploring hands went low. "La! What a dear thing. 'Twas my plan to get at this, and I put it in your mind with my talk of me being inside my gown. Wasn't it myself who lay awake most of the night fretting on how to bring your great body to where it is now, my own aching and burning for the hunger for it? When I came here today, 'twas in my mind to have you help me change gowns, but I lacked the courage and then damn near went mad sitting in the chair and thinking on what it would be like to see and touch the great knot of a thing I could see pushing in your breeches. Ah, Jamie, how good it was to have a dear juicy boyo like yourself to fling me down and fill me up with himself! For years I dreamed on it and 'twas a thousand times better than my dreams."

Incredulous, I said, "A virgin? You? What of your husband? And I felt no maidenhead, love."

"Vinny's an old man who scorns my body," she said. "Believe it or not, Jamie, you carried a maid into this bed." She giggled. "I think I took my own maidenhead years ago with . . . with a candle. It hurt like the devil and there was a deal of blood. After, 'twas pleasure, but not anything like the pleasure I have from *your* candle."

I had taken a wife, as urged by the King, except for the fact she was somebody else's, and I liked what she was doing to Old Nick.

"La!" she exclaimed delightedly. "He grows like a

flower! A wee soldier in a fine red hat, standing so straight and—ah, the poor laddie, he's weeping a tear from his one little eye and so I shall kiss him and . . ."

Before the wild flurry that was then begun had finished, Old Nick had thoroughly explored her red tulip again and she was ecstatic in her breathless transformation. She clung to me, kissing my body with avid lips. "Ah, never do I want to leave off doing this, Jamie darling. How long will it be taking for you to paint my picture with my soul?"

"Forever, I think, if this keeps up," I said.

She gave a little squeal of pleasure. "See, he keeps up! You'll be painting at it forever and, God, won't we have a lovely time at it?"

I suppose everybody goes through life wrapped in a cloak of consciously or unconsciously imposed rules that regulate his behavior for the purpose of getting through life with as little unpleasantness as possible. Heretofore I had rigorously followed my rule with women which prohibited any close repetitive relationship. Women are quick to seize a proprietary advantage in a continuing intimate association with a man, I discovered early in my amatory career, and such possessiveness was repugnant to me. Beddable women were, after all, in plentiful supply and I had no desire to be owned by one. Besides, when attraction is ended, disengagement is often as painfully disarrayed as for two armies locked in battle that neither wishes to pursue. But with Emily I broke that rule. Having discovered what her "inner tempestuousness" consisted of and the reasons therefore, I could have polished off her portrait in a few hours and ended our relationship because London was full of prettier women who would enjoy my attentions. The fact is that I had become deeply fond of the openhearted young woman and the unabashed joy she found in her newly awakened sensuality, so I continued to concentrate my attention on her, romping with her every afternoon and deliberately delaying the execution of the portrait in order to prolong the fun.

One afternoon on the tiring room couch, with an arm and leg thrown over me, Emily murmured, "I'll go to my grave thanking God for your spilling of your sunshine into my tulip soul. Will you believe that I love you, Jamie? I do, with all my heart and body, but I know this: never will you love me."

Kissing her shoulder, I said, "I like you as much as a

15

man can like a woman without loving her and it seems to me that's better than loving, being simply dear friends."

She squirmed on top of me to look down into my eyes. "I've had this much joy of you and I'll not complain. Being neither blind nor stupid, I know you took me to this bed so you could paint a better picture of me and also because you simply wanted to scroon me anyway. Well, cushla, you've uncovered and hauled out my soul as you said must be done, and you're welcome to have my soul as well as my body and bless you, Jamie. But in the doing of it I've had a wee peek at your soul, and the pity of it is that one day the tables will be turned and you'll have a great hurting to yourself and maybe others, and then may God give you the strength to bear what will happen to you, Jamie, my darling love."

"Pish," I said, stroking a smooth buttock, "and tush. I'm not the kind who pines and dies for unrequited love. There's always more just around the corner."

"Is there a way of taking your own portrait?" she asked.

"With mirrors," I told her. "Most portraitists do it occasionally for study. One looking glass reflected into another will give a true image."

"Ah, a true image," she repeated softly. "One day you must do what you've done with me, take out your dear soul and have a look at it, paint yourself in true image. Not that I don't know you have a lusty, handsome one, yet a hard glimmer at it might save you from sad trouble when you come over all dizzy and softheaded from love, sweet scoundrel."

"Why am I a scoundrel?" I asked.

She touched her lips to each of my eyelids. "One eye green and one eye brown. In Ireland such men are said to be either scoundrels or geniuses. Being left-handed as you are, too, 'tis likely you're a scoundrel in league with the Devil." Smiling, she wriggled her hips on mine. "Ah, no, 'tis a genius you are, for now I'm feeling a touch of it, nudging away at my tulip down there."

"A touch, is it?" I cried in mock indignation, rolling her over and changing places with her. "I'll give you the full measure of my genius, insulting wench!"

She gurgled with joy as the entire genius invaded her. It was the last tupping of the afternoon and after we dressed and went downstairs we were still chuckling over plays on the word genius. As had been happening often lately, her brother and Hector were in the library drinking and talking, and when we entered Emily was giggling at my latest sally.

Sir Adam, eyeing her merriment, said, for he had some time before guessed at our relationship, "I've more sense than to ask what was the jest, but 'tis a good thing to see in you, Emily. You're quite lovely these days."

"Thank you, Adam," she smiled. " 'Twas about my soul, which we've found is the color and shape of a bright red Dutch tulip, and Jamie's genius opened it with showers of golden sunshine."

"Och," said Hector disgustedly, "will you listen to that hyperbole that comes straight from the provincial head of that wretched dauber? My lady, come and sit by me and let me prove my adoration of your beauty." He half meant it, because he had some time before expressed bewilderment at how wrong his first description of her to me had been, having met her at my house a number of times since her transformation.

It was a pleasant bantering and chaffering gathering and even solemn Sir Adam smiled and made a few laborious sallies. Emily loved these brief moments of good-natured fun in which she could play the fascinating new role of reigning belle, which she carried off with sparkle and grace. As darkness came on outside, indicating it was time for him to escort her home, Sir Adam said, "I say, Jamie and Hector, will you come to my house for supper tonight if you're free? Short notice and all that, but I've got three gentlemen coming in and I must have you to balance the table talk. I promise a top-notch meal and an ever-flowing bowl. I beseech you, gentlemen—what d'you say?"

Hector shot me a quick glance and said to Sir Adam, "Alas, if we had only known! The fact is, Jamie and I are docketed for a rout tonight at some M.P.'s house—what's his name? Oh, yes, Allworth. Avaricious Jamie's all of a sweat to pick up a portrait commission or two from the politicians."

After an afternoon with Emily I was in no mood or condition to go whore-hopping at Mother Allworth's. "Hector, I can't face those back-bencher drunken debates. They're intolerable even when sober. Sir Adam, I can't speak for this Highland cateran, but I'll be delighted."

"Bravo!" said Sir Adam, pleased. "Hector?"

The red-headed Scot shrugged. "I can't brave alone the winds which sweep through Commons with such ripe

17

stench. Aye, count on me, too." He grinned brightly at Sir Adam. "And what dress? Shall Jamie and I wear bonnet, philabeg, sporran and plaidie? If you'd like a spot of proper music and can find me an unlawful set of pipes, I'll give the company a wee tune or two, for I'm a MacCrimmon-trained piper, you know."

Bagpipes and the wearing of tartan and kilts had been outlawed since the last Jacobite rebellion in 1745, the penalties ranging from six months in gaol to transportation for seven years. My own uncle, John Reid, had been personal piper to Lord Ogilvy in the army of Bonnie Prince Charlie and was captured. At his trial for armed rebellion it was proved that Uncle John had not borne arms and the jury recommended clemency, but he was found guilty and hanged at York because the judge ruled that Scottish soldiers never went to battle without bagpipes and therefore the pipes are an instrument of war. The ruling was included in an Act of Parliament. My father had told me of how his brother died.

Hector's facetious remarks offended Sir Adam. He said stiffly, "One day you'll go too far in that baiting, Hector. It does little honor to the history of the MacDonalds, sir. And remembering Culloden and the gallantry of Flora afterward, I'm sure your father will agree with me."

Hector's face reddened and I prepared for a scene of some violence, but my friend said amiably, "Sheathe your claymore, laddie. Neither my family nor my clan needs your defense, though in their name I'll thank you for your honorable intent. My father will agree to that, too, as he does with my position, which is that all the tears have now been shed over that lost cause and the best substitute for useless keening is grace and good humor."

"I'll never see the humor in it," answered Sir Adam, getting to his feet. "Then nine o'clock at my house, eh, gentlemen? Emily, the streets will be filled with Mohock gangs if we don't take our leave now."

After brother and sister had departed, Hector grinned. "By God, did you see the jack-in-the-box, Jamie? You have but to make a sly word on it, and up he bristles spitting fiery indignation! A different song he'd sing if he'd been one of the lads who charged Cumberland's grenadiers with dirk and sword through the sleet and rain, unfed for three days, with the English cannonballs thicker than the sleet. And the damned effrontery of the man, saying such a thing

18

to a MacDonald born and raised on the Isle of Skye who learned the pipes before he ever put a razor to his face! And 'twas my own cousin Flora who ferried flitting Charlie in maid's dress over the sea to Skye! Ah, to hell with it. Fetch out another bottle of your fine bonny rum, Jamie, for we must diligently ready ourselves into numbness for the musty night ahead, thanks to your thoughtless acceptance. Christ, man, you don't have to suck up to the brother just because you've been reaming the sister!"

As I opened another bottle of rum I said, " 'Twas because of her that I've not the mind or capacity for Mother A's buxom stable tonight. A good supper and a conversational drunk appeals to me. After supper, if you've still got a purple bone on we'll break away and go to Covent Garden and there you may reduce it while I empty bottles."

"Ho, ho," he leered, "I doubt even Lady Beauvoir's reduced your lech so low that you'll be able to reject the Moor, my boy. Ah, Jamie, against white sheets her skin's the color of shining, polished walnut, flowing in sweet huge billowing curves over such a majestic body as you've never dreamed of! You can place your head in the deep valley between her breasts, push 'em together, and your head is buried in fragrant warm dark flesh! Her great rump is awesome, phenomenal! When she lies on her back it raises her quim—and that without a solitary hair, lad—so high that you must kneel upright among her thighs to implant the staff of life, and when that's done, Jamie, she moves—aye, Jesus, 'tis like the whole wide earth of the planet slowly shuddering at first, Mother Earth as conceived by the ancients as a goddess to be worshipped. She's a mighty, all-enveloping upheaval, gaining speed steadily and then you become aware of a fantastic inward pulling on you, dragging you into her, the essence of all womankind irresistibly drawing mankind into the mammoth mother body through the tender gates from which we all emerged, the Great Cunt of the human race which—"

Kitty Bumpus, stammering and flushed of face, indicating she had overheard the last of Hector's speech, appeared to announce that a gentleman named Ira Tupper was calling, and before she finished speaking I was off and running to the entrance hall, where I flung my arms around the lanky, poorly dressed man and cried, "Ira, you old clam-digging barnacle of a Down Easter! Welcome, welcome! What in hell are you doing on this side of the Atlantic?"

I hadn't seen him since I was a student at the Latin School in Boston when he occasionally came down from Maine on business, but he hadn't changed much. He was about ten years my senior and his swarthy, craggy face smiled in the easy old way, showing gleaming white teeth. "Ye've growed some, Jamie. Bigger'n your pa, I declare. I was passin' by, close aboard, figgered the famous artist might be to home. Mighty fancy place. I ain't interruptin' anything, am I?"

"You could never interrupt me, no matter what I was doing!" I told him, steering him for the library. "Come have a drink and—God, it's been years! What ever got you away from your lovely wife and that shipyard of yours at Falmouth in Maine?"

"A sorry tale, Jamie," he said. "I'm in London because of it."

Introducing him to Hector, I gave him a glass of rum and he sank wearily into a chair. "By Godfrey, Jamie, my feet are that sore from walkin' I was afraid to look down at 'em for fear I had nothin' left but ankle stumps."

"Take off your shoes, sir," invited Hector, "and don't stint yourself with Jamie's rum, no matter how pale with anxiety the miserly colonial turns at seeing his guarded drink put to proper use."

"Have a care, arse-faced clot," I told him. "Colonials in this room now outnumber you two to one."

Enjoying the rest and rum, Ira asked quizzically, "Sure you two fellers are friends?"

"Our relationship, Captain Tupper," announced Hector, "is more like preceptor and acolyte and beyond belief are the trials I've endured in my dogged, generous efforts to mold this picture-painting barbarian into some semblance of a civilized gentleman. Upon my word, there have been times when—"

"Times when I've been tempted to tie that flapping tongue into a sheepshank," I interrupted. "Ira, what happened up in Falmouth?"

He had been a young shipmaster, recently married, and wanted to swallow the anchor when he came to my father for a loan and credit with which to open a shipyard at Falmouth in the Maine District of Massachusetts. He made an excellent impression on my father with his innovative

20

ideas for ship design and construction and, after the yard was successful, Ira and his wife were often guests in our home during his visits to Boston.

" 'Twas some bad," answered the Maine man, looking at his drink with impassive face. "Good thing I had your pa's loans paid off." He raised his eyes to mine and I saw the glitter of Indian naked hate. "Now I got more debts to pay, Jamie. Never even found Polly's weddin' ring. Wa'n't much left of her to bury." He looked down at his glass again. "That's one debt I'll be collectin'. This is the way it was."

His shipyard, he related, had been the most prosperous one in Falmouth. The Royal Navy liked his workmanship, and as the tempo of the rebellion increased, necessitating more Crown vessels on the American Station, they gave him all their repair and refitting trade on that part of the coast. But down in Boston John "King" Hancock, the merchant-smuggler who had actually sparked the rebellion some years before, issued the word that Tupper's yard was not suitable for patriotic Americans, and Ira's trade with New England shipowners and buyers trickled away. The Falmouth Sons of Liberty, no doubt on Hancock's orders, for he had organized the Sons of Liberty organization, warned Ira several times to end his Navy work or suffer the consequences. The Sons of Liberty in Falmouth was a gang of idlers, drunkards and dockside scum, so Ira ignored the threats, not realizing that the men were a vicious weapon at the disposition of Hancock and his crowd. One night he and his wife were awakened by the din of pealing bells clamoring of fire in the town, and saw by the leaping flames that it was their own yard. By the time they reached the scene, shops, lofts, lumber stacks and the two vessels a-building on the ways were engulfed in flames, while a crowd of townsmen jeered and cheered.

Hoping to salvage plans and business papers, Ira and his young wife rushed into the main office, and there the flaming roof fell in on them. A loyal shipwright managed to drag Ira out, but his wife could not be reached. Her charred, fragmented bones were uncovered two days later when the ashes had cooled. He stared at me with eyes like knives and said, "They owe me, Jamie. They owe me a tolerable lot, them Liberty Boys."

Horrified, I exclaimed, "The senseless bastards! That sweet woman!"

"Ay-yeh," he said, drinking his rum, "ye might say that.

21

Wa'n't no use goin' on, not with Hancock runnin' the merchants from Thomaston to Block Island. I come over here, hearin' that the Crown might make up losses in such cases. Been here near a fortnight, gammin' about and around the Gover'ment offices. Take an Act o' Parliament, says the office folk, and money's scarce on account of us Yankees causin' so much trouble. Why, says I, I'm goddamn sorry I went and got my wife killed and my yard burned down to cause ye so much trouble. I done a cruise in the Royal Navy as a lad and I'm a shipmaster now, I says, will ye give me a proper rate in the Navy so I can fight them rebel sons o' bitches? They says, we can find a berth for ye there if ye'll take bosun or sailmaker or such."

"You should be lieutenant, at least!" I exclaimed.

"To hell with it," said Ira. "I've got enough silver to take me back home, if ye can call New York town that. The New York region and Philadelphia's the only places clear o' rebels, seems like. Figger mebbe I can land a master or mate's berth in the sugar and rum trade." He wriggled his shoeless feet. "By Godfrey, I'm some rimracked with it all."

"Rimracked?" repeated Hector. "Odd word."

"Ye might call it Down East talk," explained Ira. " 'Tis the feelin' that comes over a man when he's about to fetch the turf on a lee shore, stove in bad, the wind risin' and glass fallin', rudder gone adrift and the seas buildin'."

Nodding, Hector commented, "After what you've been through, I don't wonder. Down East—may I ask where that is?"

I grinned, knowing what was coming. Non-New Englanders invariably asked that question. Ira answered, " 'Tis Maine and Nova Scotia, if the rebels ain't moved 'em southerly."

Hector wrinkled his brow thoughtfully. "As I recall from the maps, those provinces are northward of the others. Shouldn't that region be called Up North instead? The only thing to the eastward is considerable salt water till one brings up against Ireland."

"Ay-yeh," said Ira, "a body'd think so, lookin' at a chart. But ye see on account o' prevailin' winds, when ye sail from Boston ye cruise down wind nor'easterly clear to Halifax if ye like. Ye've never been to them parts?"

"I've never been abroad except to a German university for a degree after taking one at Edinburgh," replied Hector. "America interests me, however. Since coming to know

22

Jamie Reid I'm curious to have a look at what manner of country would have the damnable audacity to foist such a hapless rogue on the innocent rest of the world."

"That's a tolerable unkind way to speak about him," remarked Ira mildly.

"On the contrary," said Hector, refilling his and Ira's glasses and ignoring my empty one, " 'tis a kindness. It has a way of keeping him to some decent extent in his place and less the cock of the walk, especially when the drink is at him. In his cups his preening arrogance and smug self-satisfaction are unbearable. As his guardian and mentor, 'tis my duty to insure he holds his drink like a gentleman, in proper grace and humility. Surely in the past few minutes you've noticed a certain rising impetuosity in his manner, the danger signals, and therefore I must turn his tap to—no more drink for the undisciplined lout, which will mean all the more rum for you and me, Captain Tupper, because in his miserly bluenosed Boston habit this is the last bottle from yon cupboard. The remainder of his cellar is contained in a subterranean vault, guarded by five savage mastiffs which he feeds only at high noon on St. Michelmas Day."

"They're Irish wolfhounds, you Hebridean idiot," I said, "and 'tis on St. Patrick's Day I feed 'em, which is only two days off, and 'tis in my mind to give 'em a special treat this year of raw chunks of red-headed Scottish physician-turned-scribbler."

Hector said to Ira, "The dolt is mad with jealousy for my Caledonian birth and breeding, you'll notice. The wretched sod's a generation removed from the Highlands and it gnaws at his soul. Ashen with envy he turns when he hears my fluent, melodic Gaelic because he has none, his late honorable father being an Angus man, where the true tongue has not been spoken in five hundred years, give or take a few rainy days."

I struggled to dredge up from memory some appropriate Gaelic sentiment as heard from my mother, and said haltingly, *"Trod chairdean is sith naimhdean, da rud nach coir feart a thoirt orra."*

Hector stared at me with incredulity. "Well, by God, here's a miracle!"

"Sounded some like Hindoostanee," commented Ira. "Gaelic, was it?"

Translating, Hector beamed, " 'Friends quarreling and

23

enemies agreeing—these are things of which one should take no notice.' Jamie, I'll withdraw the proscribing of your drink, sir, and will even pour it for you. Where in god-damned creation did you ever learn such a marvel, laddie?"

"From another man's wife," I told him, "in whose arms I spent my most happy hours, a remarkably pretty, sweet and tender lady who loved me dearly."

"Losh, man, I never met that one in your company," said Hector. "The only Scotswoman I've ever seen in this house was the Aberdeen jeweler's wife who got so merrily drunk and swung from the drawing room chandelier, nakeder than a shorn sheep. I'll not believe you ever took time to learn Gaelic when you had a lass in bed, Jamie."

Ira's dark face smiled. "I mind that lady well, nor will I forget them fine hot buttered scones she built to go with tea at your house, Jamie."

"In Boston, was it?" asked Hector. "I've heard colonial maids are vigorous bedmates once they're scoured clean."

" 'Twas my mother, fog-wit," I said. "She was a Gaelic-speaking Hebridean, even as you. Ira, how is old Boston these days?"

"Not fit for human livin'," he answered. "The big sport there is Tory-huntin', tarrin', featherin' and ridin' on rails. You're well gone from there, Jamie."

I nodded, "So sayeth His Majesty. He told me Bostonians are malcontents and democratical knaves and said I showed good sense in leaving. But I didn't leave because of its politics—I didn't know politics from a ploughshare and still don't. I came here to get rich as an artist and I'm in a fair way to bringing it off."

Ira raised black eyebrows. "Ye've clum high, Jamie."

" 'Tis a carefully kept state secret," declared Hector, "that Old George Hanover and Old Jamie Reid are boon comrades and the Empire would topple in ruins if Geordie were deprived of Jamie's advice on how to rule it. The gullible public believes Lord North's hand is on the helm, but strictly between us 'tis the stealthy hand of our devious friend here, and may God help, apart from save, the King because of it."

I said to Ira, "Did you ever hear a man so uncommonly full of shit? And his capacity increases the drunker he gets, for then he goes at it in Gaelic. The fact is that I've only met His Majesty while painting his portrait and he turned out to be a rather nice fellow. A bit on the stuffy side, but

24

what can you expect of a man who sits on top of an empire?" The clock in the hall melodiously chimed the quarter hour. "Damn, I'd clean forgot! Ira, Hector and I are to have supper at a friend's house. Why not come along? Nothing fancy, no ladies, only a few stags eating and drinking."

Hector said, "By all means, Ira. One look at you and Welby will run to don a wig to hide his flowing locks for fear of scalping. If you don't mind, you have the look of what I fancy a Red Indian chief might be."

" 'Twould be some strange if I didn't," remarked Ira, "seein' as how my pa's mother was a full-blood Abenaki whose pa was a chief. No, thanks, boys, t'wouldn't be polite. I'll just cruise on back to my lodgin's and you stay on course."

None of us was actually drunk at that point, though we were steadily moving in that direction, and I had taken enough to make me feel nostalgically affectionate toward Ira and sympathetic sorrow for his tragedy. I said firmly, "Nonsense! You'll come with us, sir! Sir Adam need only set another plate and he should be damned glad to have at his dull board a genuine American Indian of the blood of chiefs to spice the usual London blather. We shall eat, drink and then fly to a perfumed cavern of houris where dwells, according to this red-headed windbag, a dark lady who is the eighth wonder of the world."

Stroking his long chin, Ira said, "Waaal, now ye've got my attention. Ye sure this salty old suit o' clothes won't put nobody out?"

After convincing him his attire was satisfactory, I ordered my closed coach brought around and we bowled through the night streets to the event which, taken with the Lady Beauvoir affair, was to propel the three of us into blood and battle beyond the seas.

Chapter II

IT HAD BEEN an unmitigated, dolorous mistake, I brooded fuzzily, sitting at Sir Adam's table and trying to follow the droning conversation. The food had been good and the drink copious, but the evening had become an empty hole carved out of my life. The three gentlemen—Brown, Parker and Winton—were elderly, solemn and tediously didactic regarding their subject-in-chief, which as far as I could gather, was some sort of encyclopedic dissertation on the cause and effect of governmental revolution from ancient times to the present. For some years they had been researching material throughout the archival repositories of Europe.

But there was nothing scholarly about their drinking. They attacked the bottles with singular gusto, particularly Brown whose scarlet-veined face revealed him to be a veteran of many such skirmishes. He had clearly once been a handsome man before the sags and pouches had melted his visage. We three tried to be helpful to the scholars, who queried Ira about the struggles of the New England tribes against the encroaching English settlers during King Philip's War, and when Sir Adam pointed out that Angus Mac-Donald and my father had been taken at Culloden in The '45, the scholars zealously quizzed us about our fathers' actions and attitudes. I was of little help because my father had said but little to me on that score, so a great deal was asked of me concerning my career, the recent Royal portrait and related matters.

More than half drunk and drinking steadily, I pondered woozily on how to pass a signal to Hector so we three could exit with some semblance of courtesy, and then became aware of him having some sort of argument with Sir Adam on the other side of the room. At that point my memory becomes fragmentary. The room was suddenly filled with noise, the howling and skirling of bagpipes, and there was Hector marching around the table with them, his face red with blowing and his fingers dancing on the chanter. I remember lurching to my feet and crying something like, "Man, you'll have us all in Old Bailey!"

Sir Adam, grinning owlishly, waggled a finger at me and clapped his hands in applause to Hector, whose face bore the look of a happy man as he huffed and strode around the room, making the rafters ring with the wild, blood-stirring challenge of the pipes. The scholars watched him. I have a blurred image of Brown's face, which seemed to be falling apart.

The next thing I remember is the cold March night air striking my own face like a bucket of ice water, partially clearing my head. Ira and Hector were at my side at the top of the portico steps. The air was sweet and held a suspicion of snow that might come. The side lamp of my coach gave off a dim circle of radiance, and in its light I saw Bert, my coachman, suddenly raise his whip and point.

" 'Ware the blokes by the steps there, Mr. Reid!" he called.

Beside the steps there was an entry below the level of the sidewalk and in the darkness there I saw a movement. Still dazed from drink, I whipped out my smallsword and heard Hector draw his. Ira muttered, "Three of 'em. Careful."

We went slowly, carefully, down the few steps and faced the entryway, and I snapped, "You, there! Come forward!"

To this day I am not quite sure what happened next. Perhaps the strangers came forward too quickly, as in a rush. I vaguely recall one of them speaking, but I don't know what he said. The London night in those days crawled with footpads, gangs and lurking cutthroats, and no prudent gentleman could afford to open a debate with them. In any case, there was a rush and flurry of movement in which my sword came up instinctively and I gave it a long hard thrust. For the first time in my life I felt my blade bite through flesh, muscle and bone, and that I remember as clearly as if it happened yesterday, for no man ever forgets his first killing of another human being.

It was over almost before it started. Two men lay sprawled and silent on the tiles and the third lay groaning in pain. "Bert," I called, "fetch the coach lamp here!"

By the light of the lamp, Hector hastily examined the men. "Two dead and so will this one be if he isn't treated soon." He tore strips from the injured man's shirt and applied them as dressings to the arm wound.

The event had shocked me into near-sobriety. "Bert," I said, "see if you can find the watch. Try the nearest alehouse and have them get a cart to take this bleeding villain to the hospital."

But, attracted by the coach lamp and activity, a pair of ancient city watchmen appeared quickly enough without being summoned. I explained to the best of my ability what had happened, and one of the old codgers said, "Aye, summat like it 'appens an 'alf dozen times a night, seems like. We'll get 'im to an 'orspital, sir, and make the report all Bristol fashion, sir. Good-night to you, sirs."

Mother Allworth's no longer appealed, so we went to my house for a nightcap and post mortem on the evening's action. In the library I said, "There's no sense in inviting more of that. You two must stay the night. Plenty of empty bedchambers."

They both agreed. Hector, frowning in thought, said, "I thought that fellow said something about the Crown. 'Tis an old thieves' trick. At least I hope it was."

"What would Crown agents be lurking there for?" I asked skeptically.

"Keeping an eye on Welby's guests, I suppose," he replied.

Ira stroked his chin. "Not us," he murmured reflectively.

"Not us," agreed Hector. Catching my puzzled expression he smiled without humor and said, "My hat, Jamie, were you that taken in? We've just been honored with the company of the chief of all Jacobites, you colonial ignoramus, and the chiefs of two of Scotland's greatest clans."

I stared at him. "You're still drunk."

"I wish I were," he answered wryly. "Would you think that Brown, with his wisp of an Italian accent, was Polish Sobieski on one side and Stuart on the other? Did you see his face come sagging and the tears rise when I serenaded him with 'Lochaber No More'? 'Tis Bonnie Charlie's favorite tune down in Rome where his house is, they say, and now I believe it."

"You're out of your senses!" I exclaimed. "That broken old man Bonnie Prince Charlie?"

He shrugged. "I've seen his likenesses often enough to know the man, and for days there's been a rumor about the city that he's in England on a stealthy visit from Rome.

And there's Welby who wears the White Cockade on his heart. Never fear, gentlemen, tonight we've supped and drunk with King Charles III, unthroned, uncrowned and a fugitive with a price on his head yet—I think—of five thousand pounds."

Unimpressed, Ira said, "I'd have taken him for a schoolmaster married to the bottle."

"I'll not believe it," I protested. "Why would Welby want us there if that were the case?"

Hector shook his head sorrowfully. "Poor innocent Jamie. Look you, lad: your American rebellion is siphoning off much of our treasure, troops and ships. 'Tis almost certain now that France will side with the rebels, and then Spain will jump in to have a whack at twisting the lion's tail, too. France and Spain have an interest in Stuart aspirations. If Great Britain were soundly whipped we could look for the House of Stuart to replace the House of Hanover. Charlie's beating the bushes for support, financial and otherwise. My father is rich and supported the fellow last time out. You, God save the mark—I choke on the words —are a popular figure about London with perhaps a sizable following if you wished to raise it, as well as being the son of a hero of Culloden and nephew of a gallant martyr to the cause. And Ira, the noble Abenaki Indian, was an unexpected chance to take American soundings."

"You're damned sardonic toward the man who could have and might yet be our lawful king," I said, "if that all came off. What kind of Scots patriot are you?"

"A cautious one," he returned. "About thirty years ago that gentleman stepped ashore at Eriskay and gathered clans to him at Glenfinnan, and my country has not recovered to this day from the fury of the Germans in Buckingham House. Scotland's medicine is not spelled Stuart, Jamie, 'tis the moving of Scots into high places to make policies and carry them out, and the Saxons will awake one morning to find England a southern province of ancient Alba, with the government moved to Edinburgh along with the Stone of Scone to accommodate the royal arse."

"And haggis will replace Sunday roast beef throughout the land," I said. "But, see here, if those men were actually Crown officers we could be in a hell of a stew."

"They come at us, Jamie," observed Ira.

"True," said Hector, "we only defended ourselves." He frowned. "How did that second man die, though? I missed my man and only got his arm, and Jamie took his with a clean thrust through the chest. There was no mark on the other but he was dead."

"Come chargin' at me like a bull," Ira explained, "so I gave his head a twist as he come by. Ye might say he done it himself in a manner of speakin'. Jamie, I'll be obliged if ye'll show me my berthin' space. I've had a moderate long day."

At breakfast the next morning I asked Ira what his specific plans were, and he said, "There's a packet leavin' Blackwall next Monday to join a fleet o' sail for convoy to New York. I've got just enough silver left to buy passage and victuals for the v'yage, as well's pay for my lodgin' till Monday."

Hector said to the maid, "Kitty, darling, will you refill my tankard with that lovely cool ale and put a finger in it to sweeten it? Ira, my brain moves slowly this morning, but it moves. You've heard of the MacDonald Company?"

"Most have," agreed Ira.

"The Company is my father," Hector told him. "Angus MacDonald."

"Ye don't say," said Ira.

"Good God!" exclaimed Hector, exasperated. "Can you spare us from that Down East manner of speech this morning? It hurts my head! Now, there's no need for you to cross the bloody ocean to get a ship. My father owns them by the score, and many in the West Indies trade. He can find a place for you and pays better wages than the East India Company, which annoys them. I'm to see him this morning. Come along with me and meet him."

Pleased, I interjected, "Angus is a wise and good man, Ira, and I'll never know how he came to be afflicted with a son like this one. He's a great deal like you in his thinking and you'll get along well with him."

Ira nodded. "That's some nice o' you, Hector. I know West Indies waters like the back o 'my hand."

"And on the way back," I said to Ira, "pick up your baggage at your lodging and move into this house. Don't argue. My home's your home. And don't gibber about money. I'm a rich man, for God's sake! The money from painting comes in so fast I have to invest it instead of spending it, and then it comes in even faster."

"I ain't arguin'," said Ira. "I'll do that and thank ye,

Jamie, but I'll keep an account so's I can pay ye back when my cows come home."

Later in the forenoon my swordmaster, Captain Gailliard, arrived at the usual time for our daily spirited sessions with épée and saber, but only to regretfully inform me that he was no longer on half pay from the French Army and had been summoned to active duty in a newly raised regiment of foot. He was effervescent with pleasure at the prospect, and as I bade him farewell and Godspeed I wondered what peculiar madness it was that made an otherwise intelligent gentleman so eager to die or be crippled for life on some gory battlefield.

In the afternoon, on the couch in my tiring room after our first romp, Emily confided that her husband had sent for her brother at his house and there had been rather a dustup between the two men. Sir Adam had evidently slapped Beauvoir's face with great force before he flung out of the house, for Beauvoir's usually pale cheek was angry red when she saw him just afterward. Beauvoir made no comment to her other than to icily smile and ask about the progress of the portrait, to which she had replied that it was coming along slowly but well, though being the subject she was hardly a judge.

That evening Angus MacDonald, that genial gentleman, spent the evening drinking and talking with Hector, Ira and me in my library. As I had hoped, he was greatly taken with Ira and Ira's sharp knowledge of maritime affairs and thoughtful concepts of new ship design. They talked of post-rebellion trade with America. "No matter who wins the bobble," declared Angus, "those restrictive trade acts will be gone, forbye, and if my guid friends in Parliament can halter the John Company, MacDonald Company will carpet the sea with ships betwixt here and North America." He had that morning given Ira a master's place in a ship then refitting at Liverpool, and Ira was a very happy man behind his calm, dark and rugged face. I had my sketchbook by me as usual and as I drank and talked with the others I filled several pages with drawings of my good friends at their quiet pleasure, and I was never to forget that good evening, for it was the last good one I was to have in Britain for a long time to come.

The first of fate's bludgeonings occurred the following afternoon. The weather outside was cold, wet and blustery, and in my painting room fireplace a cheerfully glowing sea-coal fire made the adjoining tiring room snugly warm, so much that Emily and I, naked on the couch, were moist with perspiration as a result of almost an hour's continuous frolic. My reservoirs were quite exhausted for the moment, while Emily was eager to continue. Testing wilted manhood, caressing it affectionately, she murmured, "Jamie, you simply aren't trying."

"The spirit," I told her, "is willing but the flesh is weak. Rest and be patient. Caesar's soldiers fell in battle only to rise and fight again, and Old Nick is the noblest Roman of them all."

"The poor dear needs only loving inspiration," she said, and thereupon arranged herself to give full and close inspiration. After a moment, exquisite little tremors within my body gave evidence of some rising success to her delicious efforts, the sight of which was blocked from my vision by her sweetly looming buttocks and full-fleshed thighs. Her diligent ministrations produced in me a desire to plant a kiss on the hairy cleft presented to me. I stroked it with light fingertips, enjoying her wriggle of pleasure.

"Ah," said the whispery gray voice of Lord Beauvoir from the doorway, "so there you are."

My heart stopped. Emily and I became instantly frozen statues, unable to move. His lordship stood with one hand on hip and the other atop his long walking stick, the cold thin face regarding us without expression, sharp eyes inspecting us. I recall thinking that his stick would contain the currently fashionable long thin rapier with which he could, if he moved quickly enough, skewer us both like sausages on a pin. But he neither moved nor said anything further, remaining motionless in the doorway.

Evidently it was up to us to end the tableau. Patting Emily gently on her haunch, I said, "It appears that we have company. We'd best get dressed."

She silently got off the couch and proceeded to dress, leisurely, without a glance at her husband, who stood unmoving, watching. I set about putting on my clothes and the oppressive silence coupled with his eyes made me say absurdly, "My lord, if I'd been apprised of your coming I would have welcomed you in courteous style."

"The error is mine, sir," he answered. "I took the liberty of telling your servant I was expected and could find my

33

own way. I had no wish to interfere with your work, only to look in on it to satisfy my curiosity concerning the progress of the portrait."

So this was the way of an elderly man who finds himself cuckold. I adjusted my stock and buttoned up my waistcoat. Emily, gowned, passively watched me don my coat, and I said to Beauvoir, "Will you take a glass of Madeira, my lord?"

The glacial smile appeared. "Thank you, no, Mr. Reid. I've an important appointment at Whitehall after I escort our lady home—if you're quite through with her for the day."

Emily's voice was dry and metallic. "Are you, Jamie?"

The entire scene struck me as comic. I smiled at her and said, "Even the noblest Roman of them all must rest between campaigns."

I could see her fighting to suppress an hysterical giggle. "Then I'll go, and say a Roman prayer for Caesar's soldiers."

We moved out into the painting room and her husband nodded toward the painting on the easel. "It seems finished, Mr. Reid, and I must say I'm immensely gratified. At first glance when I inspected it in your absence I noted what seemed to be, knowing my wife, a spurious charm and sensuousness which I thought you might have added in an attempt to prove you had uncovered the inner tempestuousness I mentioned. However, a moment later I saw the characteristics being fully demonstrated and my confidence in your professional skill and integrity was happily restored. It lacks only your celebrated signature, sir. Please deliver it to me in person tomorrow morning between the hours of ten and twelve o'clock and I shall make settlement."

"Very well, my lord," I said. "If you're satisfied, so am I, but as a rule I don't release a painting unframed."

"Like His Majesty," he smiled, resembling a deaths-head, "the pictures I acquire are framed at my direction according to my taste, which is considerable. My lady, I shall see you home. Mr. Reid, tomorrow morning, eh?"

Left alone, I poured a hearty drink and pondered. I could be named correspondent in a suit of divorcement, but it was unlikely that Beauvoir would take that step, because he had married Emily for her money, not her affection or body. Yet he struck me as the sort of man who would not let such a contretemps pass unchallenged. He was a politi-

34

cian, and as such would seek to turn affronts to himself to advantage. Then again, he was an impotent old man, according to Emily's report that he had never come to her bed. It was not unheard of for limply aging gentlemen to make a discreet arrangement with their wives' young lovers in order to keep domesticity and dowry monies safely in hand. With my affair with Emily obviously terminated, however, as far as I was concerned, I celebrated by going with Hector and Ira to Mother Allworth's hummum that night and amazed myself by indefatigably bringing the Great Earth Mother, the fabled Moor, to shrieking volcanic eruption. She was everything Hector said she was.

Chapter III

THE BEAUVOIR HOUSE on Grosvenor Square was more of a Palladian palace than a dwelling house. Admitted to its polished marble and gold leaf interior magnificence, I felt a twinge of awe that my sprightly bedmate had the riches to provide her husband with such a thing and still have mounds of gold left over. A liveried and unusually good-looking manservant carried Emily's portrait as he ushered me up a broad Italianate marble staircase to the second floor, then down a long corridor lined with portraits of past Beauvoirs to the room where the present one awaited me.

It was a vast high-ceilinged chamber, so elegantly decorated and furnished that it would have dazzled a Doge of Venice. Facing the door, Lord Beauvoir sat in a large upholstered orange chair, wearing an orange silk robe with a swirling pattern of purple. Dainty orange slippers were on his feet. The contrast between the brilliant rig and his normal muted gray dress was startling. The carefully composed arrangement would have made an interesting portrait, and it crossed my mind that it had been planned for that effect on me.

"Good-morning, Mr. Reid," said my host, icy smile going. "You're looking fit. Fergus, lean the picture against the fireplace andiron so I may see it and you may go, my boy. Thank you, Mr. Reid, please be seated. A drink for restorative purposes? Your diversions last night must have been taxing, though I must say it doesn't show on your face. The resilience of youth never fails to astound me."

From our first meeting I did not care for Lord Beauvoir. Through Emily, I had come to enjoy him even less. Now I began to actively dislike him. "Thank you, your lordship. I never drink in the morning. It isn't necessary for you to put spies on me—if 'tis evidence against your wife and me

37

you want, you got it yesterday. I'll thank you to pay me my fee so I may return to my work."

The cold smile widened. "Divorce spies? My dear Jamie —I shall use our Emily's form of address, since we three share a unique relationship—you wrong me to impute such petty motives to me. But then, you may not be aware of my official duties. Few people are." Rising, he swept to a desk littered with papers, selected a document and handed it to me. "As an American you may have some interest in this."

It was a letter dated some five or so days earlier at Passy, France, addressed to the Continental Congress of the American rebels. It stated that except for some minor issues, the terms of the French-American Alliance had been agreed upon and signing could be expected at an early date. It was signed for the Commissioners by Benjamin Franklin. Handing it back to Beauvoir, I asked, "How came you by this, my lord?"

"My agents in France took it before the ink was fairly dry," he murmured, watching my face. "I have many of them, you know. Some are assigned to watch resorts such as Mrs. Allworth's. You would be amazed and amused at what is often said in that place. Please deliver my congratulations to your friend Captain Tupper on the occasion of his employment by Mr. Angus MacDonald; the chap's had a most disappointing time thus far during his visit to London, I'm afraid."

A prickle of apprehension grew. I said slowly, wondering what I had gotten into, "I'll not try to guess your position. You tell me."

The smile was without a trace of warmth or humor. "It must not be mentioned, Jamie. I often think of myself as a spider, sitting here in London in the center of my efficient web, a godlike spider perhaps, who observes the sparrow's fall. An absorbing occupation, you may be sure, dear boy."

The gentle whispering murmur and delicate gray fragility suddenly symbolized menace and my inward eye caught a glimpse of awesome, towering power. I said, "I fancy it must be, my lord." I wanted to flee. "I really must be on my way—"

He raised a small-boned hand. "You've only just arrived, my dear sir. Surely you can spare me a few short minutes of your valuable time. No doubt the little affair of yesterday bears on your mind. Dismiss your cares in that respect, Jamie. I intend no divorcement or even recriminations. I must say that our Emily has improved considerably in demeanor since coming to enjoy your—ah—friendship."

A wholly feline man, he was playing cat-and-mouse, I decided, and with anger rising in my resentment I said, "If you have a point to make, my lord, reach it and have done with it, and I'll thank you for my twenty guineas so I may go."

A steely glint appeared in his eyes. "I fear you give that paltry sum undue importance in your conversation, Jamie. My reports on your financial affairs indicate it to be comparatively trivial, thanks to your man Bartram's astute management of your investments. Nevertheless, you shall have your fee in hand, but first, would you be interested in painting a picture for me for—say—one hundred guineas?"

It was a remarkable sum for the work of a living British artist. I asked cautiously, "What sort of picture?"

His chuckle was like rustling paper. "I expected that would unbend you a bit." He rose. "Come, I'll show you some examples of the type of work I have in mind and which will surely stimulate your creativity." Leading the way to a locked door at the end of the room, he murmured as he unlocked and opened it, "Not even the servants are permitted in here, Jamie, only my very particular friends, for the collection's monetary worth is incalculable."

There was no furniture other than large silken cushions scattered about on the deep-pile rugs. Light filtering through beautiful stained-glass windows gave the place a cathedrallike atmosphere—until I saw the paintings, etchings and drawings that covered the walls from top to bottom, and I caught my breath as I recognized by their styles the works of near-legendary masters; Dutch, Flemish, Italian, French, German and Spanish.

But it was the subject matter that stunned me. It was a riot of carnality, depicting not only men with women, but men with men, women with women and some of either sex with animals, all performing sexual acts and many of them defied imagination. Subject aside, each picture on its artistic merits could be considered a masterpiece, and in the subject the genius of the artist was implicit in the atmosphere of the room; I could smell the reek of sweating bodies and pungent sperm, hear the panting, grunting and groaning of unbridled lust. Despite myself, my loins stirred.

A red chalk drawing caught my eye. Two males were engaged in contorted union. One was a plump fellow, balding in middle age, and the other was a graceful youth whose pretty face was that of a lascivious madonna. Beauvoir, so close to my side that he brushed me, murmured, "The Bishop was rather a love. Would you believe that my figure has hardly changed since then, Jamie? If you should like to compare it, you may. I wear nothing under this robe, dear boy."

It would be the understatement of the age if I said I was staggered. Man-lovers were no novelty in London society and I was distantly acquainted with several, whose private preferences I regarded with indifference, so the revelation that Beauvoir was thus inclined did not shock me of itself; it was the horror of finding myself a target for his grotesque desires and the fact that such a man occupied such a position of power and trust so close to the Throne and the top levels of government. I looked down into his face, upturned to mine with an expression of breathless anticipation on it, and shame and revulsion swept me. I plunged out the door and strode rapidly toward the stairs, desperate to remove myself from the sight and sound of Beauvoir. He called out in a harsh, brittle voice, "Stop! I have not dismissed you, sir!"

Discretion overcame disgust. The man was dangerous and powerful. I halted, turned and said, "I have no further business with you. Keep your twenty guineas."

"You'll find you have more business with me than any other person alive," he said coldly, sitting down at his littered desk, "unless you think your own possibly imminent death to be no business of yours. End your childish petulance and be seated, sir."

There was nothing gentle in the whispery gray voice. I was reminded of a snake's hissing. Returning to the desk, I sat down and asked slowly, "What further nastiness have you?"

The glacial smile turned on. "I beg you erase that fearful frown, Jamie. 'Tis horribly disfiguring on your charming phiz. The matter of your danger can wait a bit. I have more pleasure in relishing the picture I should like from you. I'm sure you noticed that no British artist is represented, eh? My desire for what I have in mind is so great that I shall remove a number of the works in order to provide space for your grand life-size composition, Jamie, so it

40

may dominate the room and inspire the viewers into immediate emulation on the spot. I visualize an arrangement similar to that which I intruded upon yesterday, dear boy, placed in a sylvan glade. Glorious Adonis supine on a mossy bank while Venus bends with classic grace to render homage to the virile pillar of masculine strength, and Adonis shall be your self-portrait and Venus will be Emily's likeness. Exciting, eh, dear Jamie?"

"You're insane," I said.

"Nonsense," he smiled. "I'm merely devoted to the joys of human sensuality, the wellspring of all beauty and pleasure. You will have to confess that you could not have painted Emily with such consummate perception had you not often plunged your admirable pintle into her hospitable quim. And, by the bye, in addition to the hundred guineas you may enjoy Emily's favors at will during the painting of the picture."

"I'll paint no picture for you," I said.

"Think it through carefully, Jamie," he warned. "Apart from other considerations, I will grant you unimpeded access to her in this house or yours, dear boy."

"You offer her as if you were a whoremaster," I said, feeling a little ill with nausea, and added coarsely, "Would you reserve the right to watch me fuck your wife, my lord?"

He only smiled again. "Only at your invitation, Jamie."

"Can you speak of anything other than your perverted filth?" I demanded. "What is this danger to me you mentioned?"

"Perverted filth?" His tone was silky. "Dear boy, I pray you not to scorn honesty of heart, regardless of its form. Accept my sincere love with compassionate affection, I implore you, my sweet."

My stomach heaved. Mastering it, I said, "Emily. You used her as bait. The portrait was for this."

"Of course," he smiled. "When you first delighted my eyes in the palace I was suddenly smitten as a schoolgirl. Until yesterday I had only anticipated some splendid romping with you, but when I saw the magnificent perfection of your naked body and your utterly marvelous staff I knew you were the great passion of my life, my darling, and I was transfixed with adoration. Let me say that I know you do not understand this higher kind of love now, but once you have been lovingly initiated you'll find all prior experiences with common females mere wasted time. I am an exceedingly wealthy man, Jamie—Emily's substantial money aside, my position brings me rather massive emoluments—and my power is nearly limitless. You may be sure these are no idle boasts, dear love. I offer you the sharing of my riches and the protection of my power if you will accept my devoted love and embraces."

It was, I decided, a form of madness. Angry contempt would get me nowhere. I said with an attempt to reason, "My lord, you mistake me. I'm attracted only to women."

He sighed. "Dear stubborn boy, how can you reject that which you've never known? As an intelligent man with the sensual skills developed over a lifetime, I will give you unending pleasure and joy beyond comprehension. Women are slobbery beasts, capable only of responding to animal instinct in the procreative act. They are solely for childbearing, my dear. Powerful as I am, I shall be your adoring slave and you will exult in the unparalleled pleasure of my exquisite body, which even at my age is mindful of Cellini's sculpture of Perseus."

It was too much to be borne. I gave up pretense of humoring him and said harshly, "The only cock and balls that interest me are my own, and the only sex they'll ever touch will be female. I do not like you, my lord. I will not paint your obscene picture for any amount of money, and if your body is so goddamned alluring, I suggest you fuck it yourself."

As I started to rise he brought his open hand down on the desk with a loud slap and his eyes glittered. "You severely test my patience which I am endeavoring to maintain, because for all your charm you're still an impetuous ignorant young calf. We shall now discuss the next aspect of your position."

I said, "I'll listen to no more enticement to sodomy."

"And I'll tolerate no more degrading allusions to my sincere affection and hopes for you," he said in a new crisp tone as he picked up a sheaf of papers from his desk. "Here, my love, I have enough evidence to see you and your two present close companions hanged at Tyburn for murder and treason."

I gaped. "You *are* mad!"

"Mad in love with cruelly insensitive Jamie, perhaps," he murmured, glancing through the documents, "but never mad in connection with my official duties. Jamie, on a certain evening of recent date, you and your two companions went to the house of Sir Adam Welby, a notorious Jacobite, and then and there did meet and conspire against His Majesty, with Welby and three other known criminals who have been under sentence of death for some years, having been tried and convicted in absentia for treason and armed rebellion against the Crown. The leader of the three, who styles himself Prince Charles Louis Philip Casimir Stuart, entered the United Kingdom by stealth for the sole purpose of soliciting others to their treasonous cause and recruiting monetary support from wealthy secret Jacobite sources. Indeed, while in France en route, those three conferred with officials of the government of France and with emissaries of the American rebels with the intention of joining the imminent French-American alliance against our King and country. At Welby's house, rebellion and revolution against constituted government were thoroughly discussed. In addition, Mr. Hector MacDonald played bagpipes, a separate offense. Jamie, my memory is sharp. You were with His Majesty when I reported to him the presence of the Pretender in this country. The court may assume you warned the Pretender of that." He smiled. "Impressed, Jamie?"

Overwhelmed, I said desperately, "There was no conspiring, no treason! The men were introduced to us as Brown, Winton and Parker! They were writing an historical treatise and we discussed that! Sir Adam will confirm it!"

"The only thing he has confirmed is his guilt," smiled Beauvoir, "by his flight to the Continent a few hours ago. Yesterday morning I offered him my protection in return for his—shall we say kindness?—and he rejected it with some violence."

Emily's report of the face-slapping leaped to mind. I stared at the creature. "Do you mean to say you invited him to pederasty as the price of his safety, your own brother-in-law?"

"Ah," said Beauvoir softly, "such darkly serious young men are furiously passionate once aroused. You've had the sister—fancy, if you will, the violent transports of her brother. I could have had him arrested at Dover, but have no further interest in him since seeing you yesterday afternoon, Jamie." He scanned his papers again. "Ah, 'murder most foul.' This evidence reveals that you and your two fellows savagely fell upon three officers of the Crown, my

43

agents who were then and there in the performance of their duty in His Majesty's service. You murdered two and grievously maimed the third; he has furnished this deposition against you, as have the two city watchmen who came to his rescue against your assault."

"They attacked us without provocation," I said, wishing I could remember better, "and it was I who summoned the watch and gave complete information about the incident!"

"I have found," he smiled, "a small gratuity distributed here and there sometimes brings about keener recollection on the part of witnesses."

"Blackmail for sodomy, bribing witnesses," I said. "Suborning of perjury. 'Tis unbelievable that a monster like you can hold a position of the highest trust close to His Majesty who is such a decent and honorable gentleman."

He murmured, "Actually, he's a garrulous and rather fatuous fellow. However, he's taken an extravagant liking to you—you are a charmer, dear boy—and when he learned that you were taking Emily's portrait he insisted that he must have first viewing. Of course, he'll be dreadfully shaken by your treachery toward him. Even in these enlightened days the anger of a king betrayed by a friend can be a fearsome thing, Jamie."

"He'll never believe this outrageous shit," I growled.

"His belief is immaterial," said Beauvoir. "In criminal matters the justice court rules, not the Royal, and these papers contain a complete case for the prosecution in that court, every little legal nicety neatly tied, all defense loopholes tightly blocked. I have never sent a case to the Crown that did not result in conviction and the sentence I recommended. I pride myself on my thoroughness."

"You have little enough to take pride in," I muttered.

"I have many prideful things," he said, "which you shall share without restraint if, having considered this depressing legal affair, you choose to reassess your attitude toward my affectionate protection, bearing in mind that I might well discover some ingenious way to dispose of these charges without prosecution."

I shook my head. "All the trumped-up evidence in the world could not force me to become your pederast or catamite."

The antique cameo face was solicitous. "My dear boy, do you speak as attorney for your fellow murderers and traitors? Would you have them pay with their lives for your wilful stubbornness?" My startled face showed my reaction to that new attack. He smiled softly behind the ice. "Ah, there's the true gentle heart of my beloved Jamie reaching out for his friends." His voice became brisk. "The outside world demands my presence now and I've detained you overlong from your work. I urge you to discuss this regrettable matter with your associates at the earliest possible time. In view of the legal ramifications I shall require an early decision, Jamie, so I shall call at your house tomorrow at precisely eleven of the morning to receive the good tidings."

The horrible reality of my situation was beginning to sink in. Numb, I said, "There'll be no good tidings for you."

"Dear foolish Adonis," he smiled, "do you suppose your friends will offer their lives to keep you from my tender embrace? Ah—in your discussions, remind your companions that what I have revealed to you concerning my position is not to be further revealed, it being secret, and as I have said, I watch the sparrow's fall. You will also impress upon them that I have many alternatives at my disposition, while you have but two: Tyburn or acceptance. Until tomorrow, then, eh, dear Jamie? I shall count the minutes."

Ira was frowningly thoughtful and Hector was violently incredulous. Hector exclaimed, "Director of the secret service! Holy God, a man like that! He could topple the Throne, turn Parliament into a shambles, shatter the Empire! Christ, he should be turned off! I know a few fellows who would cheerfully do him in for a pound note! He'd look lovely floating arse-up in the Thames among the rest of London's turds!"

Ira stroked his long chin. " 'Twon't do, Hector. Considerin' his spies, we'd still end up hangin' at Tyburn. Looks to me like he's boxed us in some good. Like Jamie says, the man's thorough and he ain't foolin'."

"I've heard of men going to extraordinary lengths to nip off a woman they had a bone on for," Hector said, "such as King David and poor old Uriah with his Bathsheba, but this"—he gave a twisted grin—"this is going too far. Jamie, I never realized your charm was so impressive."

"I'll have no goddamned witless jokes about it!" I barked angrily. "Jesus, I'm sick to my stomach! 'Tis shameful, vile, and if that son of a bitch wasn't who he is in the Government I would have fed him two and a half feet of steel!"

45

"Steady as ye go, Jamie," counseled Ira calmly. "We know that. Cool down and let's sort her out. We ain't got a chance in the courts, right?"

Hector and I nodded dolefully. "Right."

"We can't corpse him without corpsin' ourselves, right?" went on Ira.

"This is a waste of breath," I said, despairing. " 'Tis because of me you both are in peril. I refuse to subject you to any more of this nonsense. I'll take the little bastard on and work it out from there. When I kill him I'll be the only one hanged."

Hector leaped to his feet and shouted at me, "You're crazy! We're in this together and who the hell are you to say what's to be done?"

Ira said, "Set down, Hector. I ain't through talkin' yet. Instead of thinkin' about what that feller says he can do, we'd best be thinkin' of what he thinks. As seaman and shipmaster, I seen boy-lovers in my time. There's two kinds: them as likes to ram their donniker into another man's backside—them boys'll scroon anything with a hole in it, man, woman or beast—and them as likes it done to themselves or like to play the old skin flute, ye might say. Them last kind ain't whole men. They think like women about the feller they're smashed on. This Beauvoir, I figger, is like that."

I shuddered inwardly at the recollection. "You're right. A lot of the time he talked to me like an old trollop with a ravenous cunt, a kind of bitch in heat."

Ira nodded. "If he wa'n't a power in the Gover'ment, didn't have a hold on ye, ye could kick and beat him, rub his face in the backhouse hole, and he'd come right back crawlin' and beggin'. He ain't goin' to see ye hanged, Jamie, till he's tried everything. Maybe not even then, but I wouldn't want to wager on it. Ye can't tell about them cur'ous fellers. I misdoubt he's goin' to give up easy, and ye can lay to that."

"Alternatives," I said, musing. "He said he had lots of alternatives."

"Of course," commented Hector. "Ira's right. Disabuse your imbecilic mind of giving in to the man. That would satisfy nothing but his revolting lust. He'll still have his criminal case against us when his passion is sated. Blackmail's a sorry thing to surrender to. By God, the man's bluffing! He's bluffing!"

"That's a wager I'd not take," remarked Ira. "Them she-males is more unpredictable than the real item, from what I seen of 'em."

"Well," I said, "if 'tis agreeable to you both, I'll call his bluff and we'll play the game from then on as the cards are dealt, and tell him my attitude has not changed, so say we all, and he may do as he likes about it."

Ira, nodding, said, "But I got an idee he'll haul out somethin' real interestin' in place of it."

"Tell him, Jamie," advised Hector, grinning, "that he may satisfy his pleasure by sticking his evidentiary documents, neatly rolled up, up his arse, and I'd like to be present when you say it."

Ira's craggy dark face smiled faintly. "I'd like to be aboard for that, too."

Indicating the closed sliding doors that separated the library from the drawing room, I said, "You'll be able to hear from here with the doors open a crack. His performance—I beg you, don't vomit—will be best when he's alone with me. If you think I've drawn the longbow about his conversation, you have a revelation coming."

And so it was that promptly at eleven the next morning, Lord Beauvoir appeared in my drawing room, an elegantly delicate gray moth. I did not invite him to sit. He said with his icy smile, "There you are, Jamie, a celebration to my senses. I hardly slept a wink last night for yearning for this moment."

Looking down on him from my six feet and one hundred and eighty pounds I could have picked him up and broken him as if he were a bundle of twigs. He was hardly five and and a half feet tall and weighed no more than a hundred and ten soaking wet. "Go on yearning," I advised him. "Our committee has convened and adjourned with a unanimous recommendation that you soothe your yearning by rolling your papers concerning us into a cylinder and then sticking said cylinder into your itching arsehole, my lord."

With a smile colder than ever, he murmured, "A schoolboy's crudity. 'Tis hardly flattering that you would prefer the gallows over the pleasures of my person, dear boy."

"The thought of such pleasures turns my stomach," I said.

"That is not an unusual reaction for the uninitiated," he smiled. "A fear of a new experience as in the case of a

47

timorous virgin. Jamie, you must be convinced that my determination to have you as my lover is inflexible and you must not make the mistake of thinking my passion for you is a passing fancy that will in time be diverted elsewhere. I am prepared to be patient, for I desire you to come to me of your own volition, freely and without reservation."

"I'll say this freely and without reservation," I answered. "You are a mad, villainous son of a bitch and a vicious disease festering in the heart of government."

Something akin to delight appeared on his face. "You think to hurt me with such reckless insults, but instead you delight me even more. I adore your brutality, dear boy. It inspires me with delicious urges. Someday you will castigate me, berate me marvelously, all the while you paddle my tender little bare rump."

Controlling myself, I said as calmly as I could, "I think our business is concluded. I suggest you leave my house before my boot makes violent contact with your goddamned rump."

"Beautiful, beautiful," he murmured, smiling. "How your lovely eyes sparkle in your temper, my sweet. But we have not yet concluded our business. That we shall never do, heart of my heart. Naturally, my disappointment at your decision is great, but not wholly surprising considering your two boorish companions. And it should not be surprising to you that I have no intention of delivering you to the gallows without first exhausting alternative remedies. I intend to hold in abeyance any formal action in the charges against you, pending an opportunity for you to revise your stubborn resistance to my entreaties."

Ira's analysis had been correct. I said, "That's decent of you, my lord."

"Sarcasm ill becomes you, Jamie," he smiled. "With your boyish directness you lack the necessary subtlety of inflection. To go on, I have in anticipation of your coyness arranged an education experience for you, during which I expect you will learn that I am firm in my resolve and that I am your master." Grotesquely, he cackled with mirth like an old crone. "Or perhaps mistress would be more apt."

I wondered if Hector and Ira, listening from the library, were as sick in the stomach as was I. "Get to the point and be quick about it, your ladyship."

Flicking a glance at the front of my breeches, he smiled, "I should adore getting to your point and doing with it what

48

I burn to do, dear boy. But that must wait, alas. Though the prospect pains me, for I shall languish in your absence most cruelly, I have arranged a sojourn abroad for you, during which I fully expect you to come to your senses and come to me with open arms."

I was thunderstruck. "Abroad!"

"Abroad indeed, love," he murmured. "In an austere world of spartan comfort and modest privation, far from your London ladies and admirers and sycophantic pleasures, where you will learn your essential lesson that survival in this chancy world demands compromise with your selfishly childish principles of narrow-minded morality. Success has spoiled you, dear boy. London's comforts and luxuries have become indispensable to you, and deprived of them you will quickly realize that life with me is infinitely preferable to that dismal environment."

"I'll be damned if I'll let myself be forced to go anywhere," I said.

His eyes glittered. " 'Tis your only alternative and is final."

Again Ira had been right. Beauvoir's face and tone of voice made it clear that this was no bluff. It was not a threat; it was a promise. I loved life far too much to risk further challenge to the powerful madman. "Where? Paris, Rome, St. Petersburg? You insane bastard."

The cold smile again had that curious delight. "I told you your insults do extraordinary things to me, darling. Unless you desist I shall surely spend in my breeches. No, not Rome nor any other Continental fleshpot, Jamie. Your retreat will be where the King's arm—mine—may reach you if I decide you are beyond learning. And speaking of His Majesty, you are reminded that you will be unable to send a written communication to him without it being first read by me. To proceed: in anticipation of your unhappy decision—I know you better than you realize, my love— yesterday afternoon I arranged with the Admiralty to expedite your departure from England and furnish you with a swift and reasonably safe transport over the sea to America—"

"America!" I exclaimed, dismayed.

"Where you will dwell," he continued smoothly, "in rude colonial inconvenience and discomfort until you send me a letter admitting your error and fully accepting my affec-

49

tionate protection. It should not take long, given your addiction to the good things of life in London, my sensual dear."

"And what guarantee will I have that you will not go forward with your false case in any event?" I demanded.

His thin shoulders shrugged. "Why, none at all. However, I promise that when you come to my arms, eager for my kisses and caresses, those documents will be destroyed and all witnesses silenced quite conclusively."

That meant he would have the unfortunate men murdered. "The King told me he would personally follow my career and spoke of an early exhibition at the Royal Academy. How will my absence from England be explained to him?"

"I expect he'll inquire about it," answered Beauvoir, "and likely will address his inquiry to me. He will be told you've been called home to Massachusetts on urgent family affairs—illnesses or such like." Taking a folded piece of paper from his pocket, he handed it to me. "This is your authority to travel in a King's ship with your two associates. It states that you three are members of a secret Royal Commission appointed to look into certain aspects of the suppression of the rebellion. A necessary bit of fiction for the use of a naval vessel and you will not enlarge upon it to any person, Jamie, except at your peril, for you will remember that I watch the sparrow fall anywhere throughout the Empire. Deliver that document to the captain of the ship upon boarding at Plymouth. The vessel is a courier ship and will sail directly you are aboard, the dispatches it will be carrying being important ones directed to the commander of British Forces in North America."

"And when," I asked heavily, "will this take place?"

The glacial smile was almost amused. "Rather sooner than later, Jamie. A special Admiralty coach will call here for you and your company at about seven of the morning on the day after tomorrow and will carry you with all speed to Plymouth."

Aghast, I cried, "For Christ's sake, I can't even begin winding up my affairs by then!"

"An inconvenience," he murmured silkily, "but not insurmountable. Reflect on the alternative, dear boy."

"The gods have a painful end in store for you," I said bitterly. "Tell me, you uncunted bitch: why didn't your spies enter Welby's house that night and arrest us all on the

50

spot? Where was your service to the King then, you crazy pogue?"

"Oh!" He clutched his breeches front. "You naughty boy, those delicious names nearly made me spoil my clothes!" He regained composure. "His Majesty has some respect for his foolish cousin and wishes to avoid the shame of a Royal execution. I find the fellow's furtive visits to England a convenient snare for catching individuals whose use to me may be of some value."

"For your private obscenities," I said, "through blackmail."

He smiled, "A fruitful source of quiet revenue as well as one for an occasional frolic. I think now, Jamie, our business is temporarily at an end. I have a meeting with Lord Germaine within the hour. I know you'll not kiss me farewell, my love, but will you not at least take my hand?"

I growled, "I'd rather dip my hand in liquid shit."

He sighed, then bowed, showing a fragile, well-shaped leg. "America will richly mature you, Jamie. *Au revoir et bon voyage, mon coeur.*"

After I heard the front door close behind him, I went into the library. Ira and Hector sat regarding me silently as I poured myself a stiff drink of rum and said, "No need to discuss the poisonous turd. I hope you agree with what I did. I see no other way out."

"We dissected the stinking cadaver yesterday," commented Hector. "Consider it buried. America's air will be sweeter, without that hideous monster breathing it. I'll enjoy the holiday."

Ira said, "Waaal, I was on my way to New York before this ruckus started."

"But," I objected, "Angus has given you a ship, Ira. You'll be well out of it."

He shook his head. "That little old wench with balls don't leave no stone unturned, Jamie. He'll have a hawser on Angus to get at you through me and Angus, and there ain't any sense in gettin' Angus a-foul o' this hurrah's nest."

"That's a fact," agreed Hector. "There was talk at Welby's house about my father and the servant, or whoever it was, would have reported that. Beauvoir could twist that for his own purpose."

Full awareness of the imminent upheaval came over me. "My God, I've got portrait sittings scheduled clear to June!

51

And my house, servants—I can't turn them out without decent notice!"

"As for the portraits," advised Hector, "send out notes; you've had a family emergency that requires your presence at your home in America. In my father's company there's a department that handles the sale, leasing and custodial care of estates for absent owners. Make over a power of attorney to MacDonald Company and they'll take care of it, staff and all."

"Hector and me," said Ira, "can do a deal o' squarin' away and securin' Irish pennants for ye, Jamie, we bein' idlers. Let's turn to."

It got done somehow, and in the frantic rush I had no time to brood over the bizarre circumstances of my exile. I drew enough cash from my bankers and a sizable letter of credit for their New York affiliate to insure comfortable living in New York for at least a year. I packed only two trunks of clothes, and those, with my collapsible traveling easel and other painting gear, consisted of my baggage. By the time everything was ready I found myself actually looking forward to returning to my native land.

Chapter IV

THERE WAS another passenger in the big red Admiralty coach when we climbed into it that blustery March morning, a thirteen-year-old boy in naval uniform who clutched in his lap the red leather box inscribed with the gold royal cypher which contained the dispatches. Eventually we learned that while reporting at the Admiralty for his first Navy assignment as a midshipman, Tom Stokely had been entrusted with the dispatches for delivery to the courier vessel which was to take him to America for posting to a man-of-war on the North American Station. It was evident that the contents of the box were of some importance; I could see no other reason for the headlong rush of the coach behind six galloping horses which were changed at stages during our brief pauses for meals.

We had brought along a copious supply of rum for the long ride and as we made inroads into it, we talked about every conceivable subject except, by unspoken agreement, Beauvoir. America was a recurring topic, especially for Hector. "I'm looking forward to meeting my half sister for the first time," he remarked. "Ira, would that wretched rebellion prevent me from visiting Georgia?"

"Ay-yeh, most likely," answered the Maine man. "I didn't know ye had kinfolk over yonder, Hector."

Hector explained to Ira what I already knew. He was born to Angus's first wife who died when Hector was very young. Leaving his son to be cared for by a spinster sister, Mary, Angus went to the southern American colonies as a factor and quickly got into mortgage banking in Georgia, South Carolina and the Bahamas where most planters affected a ducal style of living which kept them perennially in debt. With his fortune burgeoning, Angus married again. By all accounts the lady was exceptionally beautiful and

53

Angus built what he called a jewel box for her, a splendid house on the best of all the plantations he had acquired. A daughter was born to them, but while the child was still a toddler the mother was carried off by a fever and Angus imported his sister Mary from Scotland to rear and educate the girl, Hector by that time being away at school. Not long after that, his banking interests having become too complex and far-flung to manage in the colonies, Angus moved his headquarters to London with the idea of returning to his Georgia plantation to live after a fling at doubling his fortune in the London financial center. But having gotten into it, his mercantile empire grew to such enormous proportions that he couldn't let go, so he sent for his sister and daughter to come to London to live.

"Aunt Mary was willing enough," said Hector to Ira, "but that Anne—she's a bullheaded wench, it seems. She writes sweet and clever letters but refuses to go to London even though she loves her father. It isn't that she loves Goodowns more, she claims, 'tis because she must remain until she no longer may." He frowned. "Frankly, I think she's a bit fey. When she last wrote—my father is deeply worried about her presence in the middle of the rebellion—she told him not to worry and that she'd see me soon when church bells are pealing and potatoes are peeling."

Young Tom Stokely giggled, and Ira chuckled, "That's some comical. Ain't ye got a sense o' humor, Hector? She carrot-topped like you?"

"That's more feyness," replied Hector. "She's never laid eyes on me, but a while ago she sent a lock of her hair and said she believed it was a yellower red than mine."

I said sagely, wise with rum, "A young woman isolated in the wilds of Georgia would be prey for unusual fancies, and as your half sister she no doubt shares your propensity for rattlebrain ones."

"Why, you damned colonial lout!" he exclaimed indignantly. "Who was it steadied your rattlebrain the other day? Who soothed your panic and with cool aplomb guided you into sensibility? Who—"

"Ye sound like an owl with all them who's," interrupted Ira. "Pass the bottle and bear off a p'int from the wind— your mains'l's flappin'. Mister Stokely, have ye ever been to sea?"

"No, sir," answered the boy, grateful for the attention, "but my father's told me all about it. He commands the

54

Poseidon frigate on the Mediterranean Station now, sir. I wanted to be posted to his ship and he wouldn't have it."

"Can't say's I blame him," commented Ira. "A ship's company's a tight balanced thing and 'twould come skewgeed if they figgered the cap'n's son was gettin' special favors, even if he wa'n't. Bein' a born Navy man I s'pose ye already know chart, lead and log, riggin', navigation and such."

"No, sir," the boy replied, somewhat abashed. "Papa was never home long enough to teach me." He confided with the great earnestness of a boy impressed by important events, "I'm to receive instructions in those duties during the voyage to America, sir."

"Nothin' like startin' early as ye can," said Ira, "like right now. D'ye want to, Mister Stokely?"

"Yes, sir," said Tom eagerly.

"Waaal," drawled Ira, "the thing ye start with is the ship. Now, what's a ship? She's a plank-built bucket with p'inted ends that floats in water and carries folks and cargo from one place to the other, bein' pushed along by the wind. What catches the wind is the sails, which're hung onto masts. The masts won't hold straight nor can ye move the sails without proper riggin', standin' and runnin', so let's figger that riggin', eh?" He talked easily and plainly and in almost no time had a fascinated audience as he probed into the highly complex art of ship rigging and the science of wind propulsion. As a man born and raised in the port of Boston I had thought I knew a lot about it, but Ira's quiet lecture proved the depth of my ignorance.

But two weeks later at sea, fighting seasickness in the first real gale since departing Plymouth, I cursed His Majesty's armed schooner *Jason* for being a tiny plank-built bucket with pointed ends and swore that someday, somewhere, I would crush the life out of Lord Beauvoir with my bare hands. The *Jason* was hardly sixty feet long from stem to stern, a yachtlike little pisspot with enormously tall masts which, while they allowed her to carry an astonishing spread of canvas, caused her to roll and pitch in a comparatively smooth sea. In a full gale her motion was brutal.

The only way plates at meals would stay on the cabin table was by the cook's mate's wetting down the tablecloth with seawater. There was no fresh water except for drinking and cooking, and it wasn't fit to drink. Shaving and bathing were accomplished with seawater, cold and sticky. When our clothing got wet, which was constantly, it remained wet, for there was no fuel to be wasted on warming fires. With the ship's bow swept by huge green seas, the head could not often be used for nature's needs and one was forced to empty his bowels into a bucket; unless you were firmly braced, the action could turn into a foul disaster on the violently plunging deck. Our sleeping quarters consisted of canvas stretched on wooden frames built against the ship's side in the great cabin.

The food was atrocious—seldom even warm because in rough weather the galley fire was doused—and it was usually unrecognizable. The only two ship's officers, Lieutenant Lindsay, captain, and Passed Midshipman MacNeil, had to divide the watch on deck between them and that, coupled with other duties, made them always tired and short-tempered. Only the private stock of good rum we had brought aboard made life partially endurable.

Out of boredom, Hector volunteered his physician services, so long neglected, to relieve the captain of that chore, which pleased Lindsay. Ira made himself useful in assisting with ship's work and sharing the instruction of Tom Stokely with MacNeil who was also grateful for the reduction of his burdens. Being neither surgeon nor seaman, I spent much of my time with my sketchbook, roving about the *Jason* making drawings. In reasonably calm weather, at my insistence, Ira obligingly gave me lessons in the arcane skills of his Oriental style of murder and mayhem, joo jitsoo, which he had learned in the Far East while his ship was laid up for extensive refitting after being dismasted in a typhoon. It was good exercise for me, though bruising and bone-jarring until I learned to use my opponent's aggressive movements against himself.

All told, however, it was a miserably uncomfortable voyage and I was forced to agree with Beauvoir insofar as I had been spoiled by London's creature comforts. After nearly six weeks of plunging and pitching, smelling the stink of unwashed bodies, being always cold and wet and eating maggot-ridden sea biscuit and repulsive gray slumgullion I was horrified at myself one day as the *Jason* drove south off Cape Cod to find I was actually contemplating surrender. With rising gorge I smothered the thought in infancy.

The sea torture ended one balmy evening in May when

56

the *Jason* arrived at Ambrose Shoal off New York. Because of adverse tide and currents in the Narrows, Lindsay put the ship on a small triangular holding course under shortened sail to await the morning tide, and as a precaution in those rebel-infested waters, doubled the watch and brought the crew to sleep at battle sations. He also ordered all lights dowsed, and in the darkened cabin Ira, Hector and I drank the last of our rum and discussed, in high spirits, our plans after landing the next day in New York town. During the voyage Hector had made a momentous decision: he announced that he was returning to his profession as physician and surgeon and would hang out his shingle as soon as he could locate suitable quarters. That pleased me, of course, and I suggested that we acquire a decently commodious dwelling in which space would be allotted for his surgery and for my portrait work.

"My dear oaf," said his voice in the dark, "did you imagine for a single minute that I would abandon my responsibility for guarding you against the temptations of those rustic fleshpots that beckon us now from the shore? Of course we shall share the same roof. We shall hire a formidable housekeeper-nanny who will severely regulate your conduct and comings and goings."

"Considering the frustrated ache in my balls right now," I remarked, "even if she looked like the *Jason*'s bosun I'd give her my comings until her arsehole whistled 'Rule Britannia'."

Hector snorted, "And you're the one who kept his London housemaid in a chastity belt. Ira, you'll move in with us, naturally. Don't hem and haw, man. We know you're rack-rimmed. Damnation! This dark—who's got the bottle?"

"Comin' at ye," said Ira's voice. "Got it? Ye mean rim-racked. Nope, I'm some jizzicked instead, bein' so scanty o' money. I ain't one to hem nor haw—I'll move right in with ye and thank ye, but the costs'll be set down in my account book for later settlin'. 'Tain't goin' to be easy findin' that dwellin' house. When I was at New York last winter she was full up with Loyalists come in from upcountry, along of God knows how many Redcoats, Germans, provincial and militia regiments. Hundreds of folks livin' in marquees, tents, and a lot sleepin' in the streets."

"Hell's fire," I grumbled, "I can't paint portraits in a goddamned tent."

Hector's voice said, "I suppose the place is civilized enough to have inns. If we can't find space in one, Jamie and I have enough money to buy the owner out, eh, Jamie?"

"If it comes to that," I answered, "we ought to buy a whorehouse with a full staff laid on. Ira, how are the women in town?"

"Thick as ants at a 'lasses barrel," he stated. "With all them soldiers on hand, the gals've been pourin' in from the farms and villages to turn an honest shillin' or two by lyin' on their backs. I'll tell ye, though, the feller to see for a dwellin' is the barrackmaster, an Army officer under the quartermaster general. The Army keeps tabs on houses for quarterin' reasons, ye see. Rents, leases and sellin' has to be registered with him."

Hector laughed. "Good! We'll commence our careers in the New World by bribing the quartermaster general."

An idea struck me. "Maybe, but you forget we're a mysterious Royal Commission and have a paper to prove it. We'll barge right in on the good Q.G. and take the best he has available, in the name of the King."

"Jamie," said Hector's voice in tones of awe, "you've outdone yourself, you dishonest, devious, most excellent of rogues."

The comfortable rising and falling glide of the *Jason* as she rode the offshore swells, combined with the soporific effect of the rum in the dark cabin, sent us yawning early to our canvas berths and I went quickly to sleep.

I had my first dream of the roads.

Once again I was a little boy in Boston, pushing sea-rounded pebbles through the sprinkling of clean white sand on the scoured kitchen floor. My mother, young, pink-cheeked and pretty, appeared and took my hand. "Two have woe and one is blessed," she said, and we walked straight through the kitchen wall, then I was a grown man running swiftly down a road in a murky, greenish light. Strange faceless men suddenly sprouted from the ground and came at me with swords. Unarmed and filled with fear, I ran with mad perversity directly at them and they became shadows through whom I passed. The road before me branched into three, and on one of them a cloaked figure appeared, saying in a sweet woman's voice, "Come to my road."

I ran to her and we were naked, embracing, her lips soft on mine. We sank to the ground and I entered her body.

Mine convulsed and my loins emptied into her in great shuddering spurts while I passionately kissed her, and then to my horror the flesh on her face decayed, rotted and sloughed off in stinking clots, the body in my arms becoming a moldering skeleton. In panic I fought my way up to the surface of sleep to find the dark cabin full of shouting, shoving and cursing seamen.

On deck somebody was roaring, "Repel boarders, repel boarders!" There was a great scuffling sound and confused shouts. Fully awake, I realized the seamen in the cabin were taking cutlasses and pikes from the normally locked racks on the forward bulkhead.

Fear works in strange ways. I was honestly petrified with it for a few seconds, and then it was overwhelmed by a desperate wish to fight for my life, which catapulted me out of the berth. Dressed only in the small clothes I had slept in, I found a cutlass and charged out onto the *Jason*'s waist, directly into the thick of a moiling, shouting, flailing mob so quickly I had no time to reflect. Hacking, thrusting and parrying against what seemed a great crowd of strange, half-naked men I wondered if they were pirates; then as I heard their shouts and saw them in the gray dawn light, I recognized them as my fellow countrymen and rebels. With my concentration centered on the enemies before me, I became vaguely aware that a large sloop with a mammoth mainsail was lashed alongside the *Jason* and the boarders from it heavily outnumbered our people. The odds, however, were gradually evened by the dogged discipline of the highly trained *Jason* crew against the wildly milling and flailing of the rebel ploughboys. One of the latter appeared in front of me swinging what looked to be a scythe blade lashed to a broomstick. I shall never forget the expression of bewilderment on his young freckled face when my cutlass removed his right arm midway between shoulder and elbow. As he went down, another man took his place, and so it went. It was hot, sweaty and bloody work. Time and again I switched my weapon from one hand to the other as my arm tired, one of the benefits of being left-handed while being forced to acquire dexterity with the right hand in this right-handed world, a circumstance which had made me, to a great extent, ambidextrous. I saw Passed Midshipman MacNeil go down, impaled through the body by a pike. Almost absently the thought passed across my mind that young Tom Stokely, as the next senior in rank in the *Jason,* would become Lindsay's mate.

Though it seemed much longer, the furious hand-to-hand combat lasted about a half hour and the first rays of the rising sun bathed the locked ships in an appropriately blood-red light when the rebel privateer struck her colors and the surviving rebels hoarsely cried for quarter on their own deck where we had carried the fight. There was a great deal of blood on the planking and dead and wounded lay everywhere. Blowing hard and leaning on my cutlass, I wiped the perspiration from my eyebrows and saw Tom Stokely beside me, his wet young boy's face grinning jubilantly and his cutlass as red as mine. He panted, "That'll teach the scoundrels to attack a King's ship!"

"How did you ever learn to handle a cutlass like that?" I asked.

"My father had me learn from our gardener at home, sir," he grinned. "Dickon was an old sailor."

"Dickon knew his trade," I smiled. "Your father will be very proud, Tom."

We were standing under the huge mainsail boom on the enemy ship's deck, and Lindsay came rushing up to us, also sweaty and out of breath. "Mr. Stokely, we've lost Mr. MacNeil and you're now ship's lieutenant. Take command of this prize and follow *Jason* into port. Captain Tupper has volunteered to act as sailing master and pilot for you. I can give you but four men for prize crew. Surgeon MacDonald will attend all wounded in your great cabin. I'll take all prisoners into the *Jason*'s hold. Get a Union Jack from my flag locker and run it up above that Yankee gridiron rag, clear your grapnels and get under way quickly; the tide's nearly at flood. Bear a hand, mister!"

A thirteen-year-old boy being given his first naval command is a sight to see. Tom's chest visibly swelled, his shoulders went back, chin high, and the struggle to keep from shouting with glee was plain on his face. His hand came up in a smart salute and he cried proudly, "Aye, aye, sir! Thank—"

The crack of the pistol shot in the now quiet morning air was like the clap of doom. The child's face melted into hurt surprise and the saluting hand went to his chest where a large blotch of blood had suddenly appeared. I reached out and caught him as he slumped, but I think he was dead before he reached the deck. Looking around to see where the shot had come from, I saw a rebel crewman, with the still-smoking pistol near his hand, lying dead with a peculiar growth sprouting from his face. Ira Tupper appeared, walked to the body and wrenched his big Abenaki hunting knife from the dead man's eye socket, saying in a choked voice, "Burn in hell forever, you yellow stinkin' rebel son of a bitch."

I knelt over Tom and for the first time since childhood wanted to weep. Lindsay's hand touched my shoulder and, using my first name for the first time, he said quietly, "Thanks for leading the fight, Jamie. We'll bury Tom ashore. Come away now and help me take the *Jason* into port."

Chapter V

WE DIDN'T GO to the barracksmaster underling. We took our "most secret" travel authorization directly to the Army quartermaster general, a corpulent brigadier who was adequately impressed though puzzled, and his puzzlement changed to amiable obsequity when Hector and I produced a sizable confidential gratuity for him. As a result, we had to put up at an inn for only one night and then moved into, under lease with option to purchase, a splendid large house in an excellent neighborhood. It had been confiscated outright by the Crown, having belonged to a wealthy Hudson River patroon who had taken high rank in the rebel army. It was elegantly furnished and surrounded by lovely gardens, and because of the crowded state of the town we had no trouble in quickly hiring a servant staff. Horses and carriages were in short supply, but there again our cooperative quartermaster general, with a bit more silver, filled the void. Hector chose a pair of rooms on the first floor near the front door for his waiting room and surgery, while I set up my easel in a large, airy room on the second floor where floor length windows opened on the north to give me a fine cool light.

Neither of us had to advertise in the New York *Gazette*, for that newspaper published an extraordinarily high-colored article on our part in the capture of the rebel privateer *Sea Ranger* just outside the port, embarrassingly extolling my gallantry in leading the fight to the enemy decks and creating such carnage among the attackers. In addition, the *Gazette* discovered that I was the James Reid whose portraits were all the rage in London, royal portraitist and dashing fellow-about-town, so requests for portraits poured in from wealthy Loyalists and higher ranking Army and Navy officers.

University trained surgeons and physicians were few, and in no time at all Hector had more practice than he could handle, particularly in his treatment of nervous complaints in which he had been trained at the University of Göttingen. I was astonished at the change in him. While in moments of relaxation over drinks he was the same old Hector, toward his profession he was sober, intense and indefatigable in his efforts to serve his patients. It pleased me, because while I had always made carousing and dissipation a part-time activity that had no part in my daily labors, Hector in London had made it a round-the-clock occupation which seemed destined to lead him to an early grave, much to his good father's despair, not to say mine.

New York women, I found, were even more frolicsome than those of London and seemed to be much more plentiful. A curious difference, however, was a general sense of tentative prudery among them, a sort of superficial reluctance to abandon chastity without first going through a show of virtuous indignation. However, once that convention was disposed of, so was all else except the hearty, single-minded pursuit of fleshly pleasure in my bed. Beauvoir could not have sent me to a happier exile.

On the other hand, Ira had a poor time. Merchant shipping along the coast hardly existed due to the incursions of rebel armed vessels and their effect of driving up insurance rates. That and the flooding into town of Loyalist shipbuilders and shipwrights made employment in the yards, such as they were, impossible for him. As the days wore on, Ira became increasingly silent and darkly glum. He had long since spent his last farthing and his dependence on Hector and me was galling to the proudly independent Maine man. We worried about him.

Late one afternoon after my last portrait sitter had gone, I was sitting in the comfortable library having a quiet drink, staring out at the pretty garden and musing on Ira's unhappy lot, when Hector, who had been downtown, came bustling in radiating high spirits. "By God, man," he exclaimed, pouring himself a glass of rum, "why do you sit mourning in the gloaming? 'Tis a time for lights and laughter, cheers and toasts!"

"Strike all the lights you want," I said. "I'm not mourning, just meditating. What's got your homely Caledonian arse in an uproar?"

Going about with the flint-and-steel, lighting every candle, he chuckled, "Laddie, you and I are going to buy a yacht and spend holidays cruising the New York Bay with a wriggling cargo of lusty wenches and drink!" He flung into a chair, beaming. "And as we sail o'er the face of the deep we'll all go naked as we were born. Och, Jamie, think of the friggin' in the riggin' and the belly-button matching in the lazaret, the scrooning on the poopdeck and lovely buttocks backed against the mast!"

"You're crazy," I said. "After sailing in the *Jason* I've retired from the sea. The next and last vessel I'll ever sail in will be the packet that takes us back to London."

" 'Tis different on the bay, you idiot," he answered. "Steady as a rock, sunshine and balmy breezes, perfumed tits, and eager quims laid out on cushions on the deck. And she's a downright steal, man!"

I said, "Who is?"

He exclaimed triumphantly, "The *Sea Ranger!* The rebel pirate you singlehandedly—says the *Gazette*—captured, my boy, you gallant, magnificent heart of oak and lion of courage! And a damned untidy mess you made for me to clean up, sawing and stitching, I must say. One of my patients, a Navy lad at Howe's headquarters, told me the Navy's not going to take her in because money's so tight, thanks to parliamentary concern about the cost of suppressing this rebellion of yours—"

"Not mine, my fart-faced friend," I interrupted.

"You," he declared, "are definitely coarsening in this rude insular milieu. The chap explained to me that the sloop rig on her was designed for Hudson River work and is useless for the deep-sea general purposes for which the Navy would need her, you see. She'd have to be rerigged as a brig, schooner or ketch. So she's to be auctioned for the *Jason*'s prize money, but there again is a financial impasse—with the conditions for sea-borne cargo the way they are, no sensible merchant in town will invest a single shilling in her. Result: Mssrs. Reid and MacDonald pick her up for a jolly song."

"What made you think I'd be interested in yachting?" I asked.

" 'Tis an elegant way to drink, eat and diddle," he grinned, "and apart from your paint daubing, what else have you ever been interested in? The thought also rises that when the way is clear for our return home she can bear us homeward. She's bigger and beamier than the *Jason*.

Fancy that, Jamie! Crossing the Western Ocean in our own yacht!"

I looked at him. "We'll buy her, Hector. Save your persuasion for that young widow you're trying to fit on your whing-whang."

"Good lad!" he exclaimed. "The auction is to be at Navy Quay near the Battery on the day after tomorrow! Ah, the sport we'll have, humping the lassies in the bright sun and healthful salt air! Of course, we'll not have her with that great beast of a sail and 'twill cost a few pounds to make a decent schooner of her. If you're reluctant to part with your ill-gotten gold I'll pay the whole cost, you skinflint."

"I'll share the cost," I assured him, "but we'll have sport of a different style. What we shall do, if you can get your mind off your balls, is charter her over to Ira Tupper on contract. He'll supervise the refitting and take her to sea as master and agent, paying us a small percentage of any profit he makes above costs. He'd want that for his own conscience."

He stared at me for a moment, then broke into a broad grin and exclaimed, "Damn you for a stealthy dog, thinking of that before I did! As the curate said to the lady organist, I didn't think you had it in you! Shall we keep it a secret and surprise the old shellback?"

Shaking my head, I answered, "He's been going through hell. All he has left is his pride and that's shot to tatters. We'll give him the job of bidding at the auction, and being an old shipmaster experienced in such things as well as having a personal stake in it, he'll know how to get the ship knocked down to us cheaply enough."

We were already eating supper when Ira came in, dark and dour after another fruitless day of tramping the waterfront, and when we gave him the news he laid down knife and fork, looked from one grinning face to the other, and said quietly, "That's some nice o' you boys. I'll not forget it." He bent his head and it was almost a half minute before I realized he was silently praying. Raising his head, he smiled gently at us and said, "Had to have a word with the Skipper for puttin' in a good word with ye." He resumed eating. "Now ye best tell me about that auction."

Thus it was that Hector and I became shipowners, and at Ira's insistence we had a lawyer draw up the contractual papers and after they were signed he lost no time in moving the big sloop to an East River shipyard not far from our

66

house, had her hauled up on the ways and commenced the work of making her into a schooner. From the first day it was evident that he was deeply in love with the vessel; swept off his feet by his truly lovely wooden mistress, for up on the stocks her sweetly modeled underbody hull lines were marvelous even to a landlubber like myself. We saw little of Ira from then on. He came home only to eat and sleep.

With Hector chasing after Alice, the pretty young widow who refused to exchange her virtue for anything less than matrimony—to which Hector was adamantly opposed—and Ira absorbed in the ship, I labored hard each day at portraits and each night on a different woman in bed, just as I had done in London. Sundays, however, were free days— free of portraits and social or sexual engagements—which I spent strolling around the town making sketches in my sketchbook, or tallying accounts and generally being lazy. Though I had long since given up regular attendance at church, I rather enjoyed the Sabbath atmosphere in the town, when folk appeared in their best clothes to promenade and visit with friends to the sound of church bells.

One bright blue Sunday morning in June, armed with my sketchbook, I came on a tangle of traffic in an intersection not far from our house. It was amusing, a drayman and a farmer violently arguing about the locked front wheels of their vehicles and, as happened often in New York, a crowd of jeering onlookers quickly gathered. The farmer's wagon was loaded with potatoes and a woman, probably his wife, sat on the load. She wore a traveling cloak with the hood pulled up to protect her hair from road dust. I took out my pencil and began to make a hasty drawing of the scene, and as I started, the woman turned her head to look at me. The motion caused the hood to fall back, and my whole world jolted to a sudden stop.

Over the heads of the crowd I saw the most beautiful woman I had ever seen. The sun made her hair a burnished helmet of red-gold. Even from my distance, I saw her eyes were green and they gazed straight at me so intently I felt a strange shock of recognition. She turned and said something to the shouting farmer, who paid no attention, then she carefully climbed down by a wheelhub to the street, pushed through the catcalling spectators, and walked directly to me. Her cloak and the gown under it were worn and a bit frazzled here and there. The closer she came, the more perfect I saw her face, which was serenely composed. "Good-day, sir." Her voice, incredibly, matched her beauty. It was rich crystal, full and round. "You would be Jamie Reid." It was no question, a statement of fact.

"Yes," I breathed, awed. The green of her eyes, close up, was like the depths of the sea, the sun's rays striking deep into fathomless depths as her face turned up to mine. Her nose was flawless, lips exquisitely sculptured.

"I'm Hector's half sister," she said simply, "just come from Georgia."

"You aren't real," I said feebly. "My mind just invented you."

The lovely voice said, "Oh, I'm real enough, Jamie. The soreness of my poor rump from riding those potatoes is truly real. New Jersey potatoes must have sharp edges, for I fear they've peeled my hide."

Even as I was envisioning the most perfect rump, memory jarred. I half-gasped, "Church bells pealing and potatoes peeling! You are! You're Anne MacDonald!"

"He told you of that, of course," she said. " 'Twas a little half-joke, and don't the bells make a grand sound? I knew you from Papa's description of you as Hector's friend. There couldn't be two artists in New York who are left-handed and have two-colored eyes."

"You're the most beautiful creature I ever saw!" I blurted.

"I'm pleased you think so," she commented, "but my looks are none of my doing nor any virtue of mine. Besides, 'tis only my outsides; inside me there's a great empty stomach crying for mercy. I'm hungry and weary and fearfully dirty, Jamie. Will you take me home?"

Taking my arm, she walked beside me and I couldn't take my eyes off the marvelous face. " 'Tisn't far," I said. "You haven't smiled. Do you ever smile, Anne MacDonald?"

"Aye, Jamie," she answered, looking straight ahead.

"Then smile for me and light up the world," I said.

She walked in silence for a few paces, then said, "You'll be finding me a vexing nuisance sometimes, Jamie. I beg you not to ask me to smile for you and not to take it amiss. 'Tis not unfriendliness, because you and I will always be friends. 'Tis something I cannot control, Jamie."

"I know enough about you from Hector," I told her, "to

guess that you have the gift of second sight. My mother had it. Has your unsmiling something to do with that?"

She avoided a direct answer. "The second sight is no blessing. 'Tis a curse in many ways. Will Hector be at home?"

"Yes," I answered, "he sees a few special patients on Sunday mornings. Why does your second sight forbid you to smile on me, beautiful seeress?"

Turning her head, she looked at me and I went swimming in her eyes. "Please, Jamie, don't speak more of that. This is my happy day, for I've met you and now I shall meet my brother for the first time. Will you say something happy?"

Giddily, I smiled, "My benison to you, bonny Anne: fair be thy pathways and sweet be thy stepping, always and forever. This is surely a happy day for me."

"That was a happy benison and I wish the same to you, Jamie," she murmured, then exclaimed in silvery delight as she saw Hector's physician sign on our gate, "La, isn't that a wonder? My doctor brother! And what a huge lovely house! The flowers—Aunt Mary would have wept with delight!"

I said as we walked up the graveled drive, "I'll not show you off to Hector till you've had a chance to primp and be refreshed. I want to see him dissolve into mush like me. Where's your baggage?"

"Strewn about a New Jersey bramble patch," she answered. "There was a battle and a deal of shooting, and that scared my horses so they ran away, then the general's carriage got upset and spilled me into the brambles, and the shooting was so close I ran away as fast as I could, with the stuff from my bursted valise hanging all over the briars. Will you get me a nice gown for greeting Hector in, Jamie?"

"Battle, shooting, general's carriage," I said. "Bonny Anne, you're—no, I've run out of superlatives. Our housekeeper, Mrs. Quimby, will either find you a proper gown quickly or I shall send her back to keeping a boarding house."

In the house I came upon our efficient Quimby counting bed linen in the closet under the front staircase and I introduced the two women. "Miss MacDonald lost her baggage. Will you see to settling her in with a hot bathe and locat-

69

ing a decent gown for her to wear as soon as possible? I know 'tis Sunday, but . . ."

Mrs. Quimby emitted a little shriek of concern, embraced Anne and exclaimed, "You poor beautiful lamb! I've a dressmaker friend just down the street! While you're having a good soak I'll run out and see her! Come, dear, and I'll put you in the Green Room that will match your lovely eyes!" They went upstairs, with Mrs. Quimby, enthralled, talking a blue streak, clutching Anne as if she were a precious, breakable item.

Hector emerged from his surgery, adjusting his coat, and looked upstairs where the women had just disappeared into the hallway. "Who's Quimby gibbering at? I thought the house was falling down."

"I just brought home a lady houseguest," I answered.

"What's remarkable about that?" he demanded. "If you didn't pop in with a lady t'would be surprising, but I don't recall Quimby ever being anything but sniffy over your playmates, as well she might, considering the pecker tracks you leave on the sheets and the stiff spots in the towels." Mrs. Quimby, bonneted and shawled, trotted down the staircase and through the front door, her face intent. Looking after her, Hector said, "I've never seen her move that fast. What the hell's set her behind afire?"

"She's gone to get the lady something to wear," I explained.

He eyed me curiously. "She hardly sounds your style, Jamie, a poorly dressed woman. Are you dipping into tinkers' wives now, or fishwives?"

I said, "She's not my lady. She happens to be kinfolk and has lost her baggage."

"Kinfolk?" He raised shaggy red eyebrows. "I didn't think you had any living kin in America."

"I haven't," I replied.

His face showed sudden alarm. "Jamie, what are you saying? I'm fond of Ira, but don't tell me we've got another rim-racked and jizzicked Down East Tupper in the house! After all—"

"She's none of Ira's, either," I said, and couldn't restrain the grin.

His jaw dropped. "Then . . . then . . . my God, Jamie, d'you mean—that woman upstairs is . . ."

I laughed. "The church bells were pealing when I found her and she claims the load of potatoes she had been sitting on peeled her rump. Oh, 'tis her, Hector, and no doubt of it, second sight and all."

But before I had finished speaking he was hurtling up the stairs, and I heard him pounding on a bedchamber door and crying, "Anne, Anne! 'Tis Hector! Let me in, d'you hear? Let me in!" There was a pause, then: "But I'm a physician! Naked ladies—stop laughing, damn it!" A pause. "All right, Anne, but do hurry, please! No, not starkers, for God's sake! Quimby will be back soon!"

He came downstairs beaming. "That voice! God, Jamie, what a marvelous voice! Like the setting sun and seven rainbows seen through pure crystal! Oh, lovely day! Let's have a libation, old clod!" As we went into the library he asked with a note of anxiety, "Is she pretty, Jamie?"

I shrugged, pouring rum. "Wholesome. Healthy. One might say a strong young woman."

His eyes narrowed and he said apprehensively, "You're evading. Damn it, man, is she pretty?"

"Well," I said, hearing Mrs. Quimby rush through the front hall and up the stairs, "she's not exactly blighted, crippled in any physical way."

There was woe on his face. "You're trying to let me down easily, I know. An ugly duckling. No wonder she refused to come to London. A big hard frontier wench with a face like a sun-beaten brick wall." He rambled dejectedly on about the unhappy quirk of nature that often thrust into the best-looking families a strangely unlikely freak, and the more he droned on the wider was my grin. He noticed it finally and grumbled, "That's right, sit there and laugh at me. This puts you one up on me, doesn't it? Well, sneer, damn you! I'll care for her, the poor thing, because she is my half-sister even if she does look like a scalded cat."

Anne appeared in the doorway behind him and for the second time that day the world ground to a halt. Washed clear of the travel film, resplendent in a magnificent low-cut gown of two shades of green that went like symphonic harmony with her green eyes and glorious red-gold hair, she was superb. She said to Hector's back, "Come greet your scalded cat, Hector."

He shot out of his chair, wheeling, and froze. "Holy God. Jesus—"

Then I saw her smile and it did light up the world. "Ah

71

well, you might say a prayer for our coming together at last, brother."

He flung himself at her, embraced her, kissed her soundly, then stepped back to look at her. He whispered, "If you aren't the—" He turned and stabbed an accusing finger at me. "Swine! That's what you are, Jamie Reid, swine! I'll even up with you one day for that foul joke!"

"Did I lie?" I laughed. "Anne, I only told him you appeared healthy and unblighted. The scalded cat was his own idea. Hector, this lady has been through battles and carriage wrecks and is near starved."

"Starved?" He was solicitous. "Anne—good God, you're beautiful!—I can have something brought for you now, or would you rather wait until dinner in about a half hour? We'll be having salmon, squab, roast beef with—"

She gasped and flung up a hand. "Please, please, Hector! I'll wait, but say no more! Those words make my poor stomach rumble and wring its hands. I'll risk a small glass of wine, sherry or Madeira,, though don't be offended if I lurch and belch silly giddy."

"In this house," Hector told her, giving her a glass of Madeira, "you may do anything you like, Anne, because none of it will be wrong. Where did you come from? Where have you been? Where's Aunt Mary? How—"

"All in good time," she said, smiling at him. "After we've eaten, please?" Glass in hand, she went to the open doors looking out on the garden. "Oh, the sweet darlings! What a fine garden for them to play in!" She looked toward the little pond where the ducks were paddling and said in a muffled voice, "Oh." She came away from the door looking slightly embarrassed.

There was nobody in the garden. I asked, "Who are the 'sweet darlings'?"

"Oh, drat," said Bonny Anne. "I'm sorry. I've been trying not to do it. There were some children playing and I didn't know they weren't real until I saw Jamie over there near the ducks painting my picture. 'Twas all not real."

To bewildered Hector I explained, " 'Tis the feyness you once mentioned. Highland second sight. You've got a beautiful witch in the family."

He nodded. "I should have known. A MacDonald tradition that sometimes skips a generation. Bells and potatoes pealing and peeling. You saw that, Anne?"

"I did," she replied, "and it came out that way. Jamie,

72

you're thinking that you don't want to be pushed into taking that picture of me just because I thought I saw it." Her bottomless green eyes were looking into mine. " 'Tis but the way things are and there was no thought in my mind of your doing it till I saw it being done. I've never seen an artist, let alone seen one at work, and 'twas a curious thing. I want no picture of myself, yet there will be someone else who shall be pleasured by it, I think."

There were small moving shadows far down in the green depths. I suddenly felt lost and afraid. "I . . . I will paint you, but . . . when there's time," I finished lamely, wondering what I had meant to say.

"You must know me better, mustn't you?" she asked. "There will be time and when the time comes 'twill be perfect and we'll know it to be the time."

I hardly recognized my own voice. "Shall I ever know you better?"

Her eyelids dropped and she turned her face away, breaking the spell. "I think you're making me out to be more complicated than I really am, just because of this dratted second sight. I'm but a simple country maid from Georgia backcountry and don't have the arts of the London ladies Papa wrote me that you and Hector enjoy so much. 'Tis not in me to be coy and play with words of two meanings, making artful conversation with gentlemen. You'll know me better and then know the truth of what I'm now saying, Jamie."

"But your second sight does complicate you," I argued.

Shaking her head, she said, "Only what's around us and what is to be, not you nor Hector nor me." She sighed. "I'll tell you this once and for all: I cannot speak of what I see to the person concerned. I'm not the sharpest wit in the world, but I've sense enough to know my sighting could be only an empty fancy with no truth in it at all and knowing of it would cause something to be done that might be harmful. If the sighting is true, then 'twas ordained by God and telling of it would be interfering with His work."

"Gad," commented Hector skeptically, "a simple uncomplicated country maid."

"Of course," I agreed. "Any normal, average simple country maid would travel alone for hundreds of miles through a country at war to find a combination of church bells and potatoes, then walk up to a man she never laid

73

eyes on before and say, 'Here I am. Please take me home.' No, there's nothing complicated about that."

Bonny Anne showed a flash of irritation. "You're poking fun at me, both of you. Well, one day you'll have a hard look at yourself, Jamie Reid, and you'll see who's complicated! Now, stop talking about me and that wretched second sight or I'll pour wine all over you, because I *am* getting silly giddy on my empty stomach."

Ira, home for dinner, walked into the library giving off the pleasant smell of tar and cordage, stopped short to stare at Anne and made an eloquent speech. "I vow. By Godfrey. Great Jehosaphat."

I laughed and Hector said, "Precisely, Ira. Furthermore, thunderation and land of tunket. Anne, allow me to present Captain Ira Tupper, mariner extraordinary and the embodiment of Christian conscience for depraved Jamie Reid, and my diligent assistant in my efforts to uplift Mr. Reid. Ira, this lady is an example of what my father can do when he puts his mind to it, my half sister Anne MacDonald from the end of the world, Georgia."

Her smile to Ira was dazzling as she extended a hand. "How d'you do, Ira? You're exactly as I pictured you, strong and dark."

Making a courtly bow, Ira bent over her hand and said, white teeth gleaming in the widest smile I'd ever seen on him, "Ma'am, until I come in here just now I figgered our schooner was the prettiest lady afloat. Now I know better. What 'mazes me is how a homely mug like Hector could be such close kin to ye."

"Ha!" snorted Hector. "Hear big Abenaki chief speakum, him who gottum nose so long and sharp him cleanum fish and shell clams with um."

Anne said to Ira, "Thank you. Your schooner? Oh, when may I see it?"

" 'Tain't an it, 'tis a she," smiled Ira. "Ye'll see her soon enough. What I was goin' to say when I come in, before my breath was took away, was that the refittin' is done and I'm goin' to put her to the brine tomorrow."

Our maidservant appeared and, staring openmouthed at Anne, said, "Sirs, dinner's on." She fled in a whirl of skirts, obviously breathless to inform the kitchen staff of the spectacularly beautiful red-haired lady dinner guest.

As we went into the dining room and sat down, I commented on that, and Anne, digging into the food with un-

74

abashed relish, said, "I think you're all being silly about people's looks. There's no helping that. 'Tis what's inside that's important and needs helping, if we can find out what's in there."

"Listen to the simple, plain, uncomplicated country lass," I remarked. "Anne, 'tis all very well for you to be modest about your looks, but there isn't a man alive who'd not be staggered by 'em, and as for your insides, I'll wager that your liver is as lovely as your face. You have no business expounding philosophically on the condition of the human spirit; your sole object in life, surely decreed by God when you were born, should be to gladden the hearts of men by simply being visible and audible."

"Oh, fish," she retorted. "You expect me to be some sort of coy simpleton, fluttering my eyelids and fan and saying feeble-witted things."

"Disregard Jamie's dissertation, Anne," advised Hector. "With his limited intelligence he has a towering suspicion of wit in beautiful women, for in his view 'tis an obstacle to seduction. He likes 'em stupid. If he ever comes at you with lust in those beady particolored eyes, fend him off by saying something profoundly wise and he'll recoil in confusion." He cocked an eyebrow at me. "And if I ever hear of you making such an advance to her, Jamie, I'll consider opening you up with my dullest surgeon's scalpel to have a look at *your* unpretty liver, my boy."

There was some truth in what Hector said. Early in my womanizing career I had learned to avoid strikingly beautiful women, not because of fear of their intelligence, but because as a rule they were so obsessed with themselves they had nothing to give. In bed they tended to be passive, sheeplike, devoid of lusty passion. When I had confided that to Hector once in London, he said sagely, "True, and no matter how beautiful they may be, you'll find they always have pimples on their arse." But though I had known Anne for hardly two hours, I knew she would never have blemishes on her behind, other than welts raised by lumpy potatoes, and I could see no trace of vanity in her. Another thought struck me: until Hector had mentioned it just now, the idea of seducing Anne had not been in my mind, which was decidedly odd, for never had I ever met an attractive woman without immediately considering her fair game for a frolic in bed. Even now, looking at her at the table, marveling at how her beauty remained intact as she tucked away the food like a laborer, I had no urge to bed her. Perhaps, I reflected, it had something to do with her refusal to give me the wonderful smile she bestowed on the others, a peculiar and disheartening indication that some mysterious barrier existed between us. On the other hand, every time our eyes met I felt an equally mysterious bond that confused and daunted me.

"Now will you tell why Aunt Mary didn't come with you?" asked Hector.

" 'Twould be best if that waited till we finished, Hector," answered Anne.

"No, now," he ordered. "Before she raised you, she raised me on Skye like a mother."

Anne sighed. "Very well. She's dead, Hector."

Shocked, he exclaimed, "My God, Anne! What happened? That dear woman!"

" 'Twas a gang that came down on us one morning last month," she replied. "There are many gangs, mostly night riders, who range about looting and burning and killing, ravishing the womenfolk and driving off stock, but mostly they went against the farms and plantations far apart from neighbors. They call themselves Liberty Boys—"

Ira growled, his dark face savage, "Liberty Boys."

She went on, "Or Loyalist partisans, whichever suits them for what they've done to the people, you see. We think some of them are hired by rebel planters to drive out landowners so the land will be confiscated as enemy Loyalist property and can be easily got at auction."

"You crazy stubborn wench!" barked Hector, furious. "You refused to come to London to remain in such a damned country? And got Aunt Mary killed by it?"

She laid down her knife and fork and looked at Hector with heartbreaking sorrow on her lovely face, the green eyes moist with tears. In a faint voice she said, "Don't. Please don't. Aunt Mary didn't want to go away either. We were happy, though we knew we would have to leave one day. Hector, she was like my mother, too. She . . . she died in my arms."

I wanted to reach out and hold her and comfort her, for I could see the pain was deep, and Hector said, "I'm sorry, Anne. Go on."

"They had always left us alone," she explained, "because the three plantations—Jenks Town, Goodowns and Elderbank—are close together and we all guarded together, our

76

superintendent, Mr. Barstow, Abraham Jenks and the Ogilvies at Elderbank, but that morning they rode right in and while they were herding off the riding horses from the paddocks they shot and killed poor Mr. Barstow. Aunt Mary and I ran out of the house and while we were running through the peach orchard on the way to the woods the men saw us and shot at us. That was when it happened. She . . . she had no pain, I think, Hector. It was quick. I ran into the woods and hid in what had been my secret cave when I was a little girl, and the bandits came after me. They knew me, because they called me by name, promising all kinds of dirty things when they found me. Finally they went away and I went to Elderbank. Marg is my best friend, and her brothers Peter and John run the plantation. They're Loyalists, but have to keep it secret. We buried Aunt Mary that afternoon, along with Mr. Barstow, in the peach orchard where Mama lies. I knew 'twas time to go and I must not stay, so I turned Goodowns over to Brutus —he's the Negro Papa sent to England to be educated, and helped Aunt Mary educate me—and Peter took me to Savannah where I took a boat to Charles Town."

Hector groaned, "Jesus, what next! Anne, you're—"

" 'Twas fine from there on, Hector," she smiled. "At the inn I met a family and went with them all the way to Philadelphia. The gentleman was taking his invalid wife—she was from Philadelphia and the fevers of Charles Town made her ill—to their old home in Pennsylvania. 'Twas a large, comfortable coach and the servants were armed. The inns were dreadful, though, full of bedbugs, fleas and drunken wagoneers. At Philadelphia nobody would hire out a rig to me for the journey to New York because they were all afraid of losing it to Washington's rebel army which was supposed to be darting about all over the place in New Jersey, so I went to see General Sir Henry Clinton at Army headquarters."

"Who no doubt operates a livery stable on the side for beautiful distressed red-haired maidens from Georgia," commented Hector. "What made you do that?"

"Why," she said, "I thought he might be a friend of Papa's." Her smile was glorious. "And he was! They belong to the same club in London! He knew about me and about Papa's American property because Papa had told him not long after General Clinton got orders to come to America. Sir Henry was most sweet, and he had dispatches to send to New York, so he loaned me a splendid carriage and off I went to New Jersey with a handsome company of dragoons to guard me and the dispatches."

"And who," asked Ira, "was to guard ye from the dragoons?"

Her silvery laughter pealed. "I declare, you men! If I were afraid of ravishment I'd still be in my secret cave in the piney woods behind Goodowns! Oh, the dragoons were dears, waiting on me hand and foot, fussing over me as if I were a helpness baby or a porcelain doll. At any rate, all went well until late yesterday afternoon. The captain told me they'd reach the Weehawken Ferry just after dark and we'd all be in New York by bedtime. Then all of a sudden there was all this shooting from behind stone walls, horses rearing and screaming, men shouting. My driver fell off the box and the team ran away, mad with fear. I climbed over the dashboard to stand on the tongue where I was trying to pick up the reins that were trailing under the whiffletree, and that's when we turned over and I went sailing into the brambles."

I said, "When I first laid eyes on you, I said you weren't real. I stand by it."

"Oh, stuff," she said. "Those damned thorns pricking me were real, and so was all the din of the fighting just down the road, and so was my fright. I was scared to death. I ran for dear life as fast as I could until I couldn't move another step, then I hid in some underbrush by the highway and went to sleep. The potato farmer's wagon rattling by early in the morning woke me. He was a good friendly man, told me all about his family and why he was taking his load to New York on Sunday morning. New Yorkers pay terribly high prices for produce and Sunday's the best time because most farmers won't go there on the Sabbath, only to church. The rebel soldiers are very angry at the farmers for being greedy instead of patriotic. I went to sleep on the potatoes and then the church bells woke me up and I knew 'twas going to happen as I saw it because the potatoes were skinning my rump, and suddenly there he was, Jamie Reid, drawing in his book and looking at me."

"Just looking at you," I said, "not drawing. 'Tis a complete occupation in itself, looking at you."

Frowning, Hector said to Anne, "Before you go to bed tonight, you'll write a full account of that to Papa. Aunt

Mary's death will be hard on him. I'll try to get it off to London on the next sailing."

"I might be able to have Lieutenant Colonel Campbell send it in the Army dispatch box," I volunteered. I'd painted Campbell's portrait, which he wanted as a gift to his wife in Scotland, and we had become good friends.

"Do that," agreed Hector, "though a man of that name will bear close scrutiny in any matter of trust concerning MacDonalds. The Campbell militia fought for Stinking Willie Cumberland at Culloden." He caught my glowering look and grinned sheepishly. "Sorry, Jamie. I guess we've had enough of that Jacobite song."

Anne, eating her savory of candied pears and whipped cream, said, "I'll give you the letter in the morning, Jamie. This is wonderful! The whole meal was perfect! I'm going to get fat here and enjoy every pound. You gentlemen have a fine cook. As a matter of fact, I didn't expect such a neat and well-regulated household. Papa's tales about your wild ways made me look for something, well, different."

"Jamie and Hector's kind of belayed their carousin' some since London," Ira told her. "Nobody gets drunk here before nine of the mornin' and scarlet women ain't allowed to stay aboard till breakfast, nor can they run nekkid through the hallways unless they got shoes on."

She had a rich, throaty giggle. "You're joking, but I know you gentlemen are fond of drink and ladies. I'll be embarrassed if you change your ways for fear of offending me. I'll be no spoilsport."

"Ira and I," said Hector, "are sober, continent men, he wedded to his ship and I paying steady court to a virtuous young lady, but you must guard yourself otherwise. What goes on in a certain painting room in this house besides painting is unspeakable."

"Bah," I said, annoyed at the second of such references to me.

Anne regarded Hector without a smile. "Jamie's private affairs are his, and so with all who dwell here so far as I'm concerned. Take your pleasures and joys as you find them along the roads you must travel, for there's more than enough of the other."

She was not looking at me, yet I knew the words were addressed to me. I asked, "And will the pleasure and joy I find there be you, Anne?" I was smiling and not serious.

But the green eyes were serious as they turned to meet

79

mine, and there was a shadow of pleading on her perfect face. "Ah, Jamie, will you leave off asking things that have to do with sightings? But to keep from asking that again, it must be answered so I'll tell you that will be for another man in another place in a different time, and his pleasure and joy will be mine."

I saw the small, dim moving shadows in the depths, fathoms down. "You know," I said, not knowing what I meant myself. "You know. Why is it? You must tell me."

"Leave off, Jamie, please," she said.

" 'Tis my right to know," I persisted, confused.

The green eyes were enormous and again I was swimming in them. "No, no, you mustn't, Jamie!" Her face winced. "There's a hurting there! Stop, I beg you!"

Hector's voice broke the eerie spell as he snapped, "Stop whatever the hell you're doing, Jamie! Didn't you hear her? What's hurting, Anne?"

I said, still puzzled but back to normal, "Her potato-bruised lovely behind, of course. You should have given her a cushion to sit on at table."

There was a general chuckle which included Anne, and she said, "I wonder why folk laugh about behinds? No other part of a person is thought to be funny. Aunt Mary always called it a 'sit-down' and was shocked when I called it a rump."

"Around here," Hector informed her primly and un-truthfully, "we call it the posterior."

"And you're talking through yours," I grinned. "Anne knows better, you idiot."

"That's what I meant a few minutes ago," agreed Anne. "You mustn't come over all genteel just because I'm here. I come from a rough country and know all the words men use, like arse for rump, and sometimes I swear and curse as good as any field hand or overseer." She looked at Ira, smiling, and said, "You've been just sitting there thinking and watching me, Ira, and thinking about your lovely ship, too, haven't you?"

He nodded. "I have." He glanced at Hector and me. "I was thinkin' if there ever was a ship and a lady that could be twins, ye wouldn't have to seek far. The schooner's a bonny, elegant lass, with lines so sweet ye can near see her tremblin' with joy to be put back into the sea she was made for. She's a new vessel, she is, and lacks but one thing."

"Ah," I said. "Bonny Anne, will you look my way?"

She did, and I nearly drowned in the green eyes. The rich crystal voice said, "Thank you, Jamie. You'll not know how honored I feel, and so proud."

"You knew it," I accused. "When Ira walked in at noon, you knew it. And you knew Ira was sitting there thinking of it, so you spoke to him because of it."

"I'm not shamed of it," she answered. "I'm proud and honored and happy, and hope I can live up to it."

"What the devil are you two going at now?" asked Hector with resignation.

"I think," said Ira, "our schooner's got herself a new name."

Anne looked down at her hands and there was a touch of high color in her cheeks as I said, watching her, *"Bonny Anne.* What else?"

Hector cheered and Ira grinned, and amid Hector's pleased exclamations Anne said, "This is the most happy day of all my life, I think. I told Jamie I was proud of the naming, but I'm humble, too. You've raised me high and I pray God I'm worthy of it and won't get a swollen head. May I watch my sister's wedding tomorrow, Ira?"

"Weddin'?" he echoed, puzzled. " 'Tis a la'nchin', Anne."

She shook her head. "You said she was trembling with joy to be where she was made for, and for any *Bonny Anne* that can only be in the arms of her bridegroom. Isn't she the bride of the sea? And won't her launching be the wedding?"

"By God!" Hector stared at his half sister. "When I was a boy on Skye the ship launchings at Portree were celebrated as weddings just exactly like that! And here's this lovely witch of a sister of mine who's never been away from Georgia, putting it all together in the ancient way! Aye, a wedding-launching 'twill be! Ira, may we have a platform under the bow, bunting, flags, a band of musicians, refreshments? Is it too late to arrange? I don't care what it will cost! Anne must christen her with . . . with a bottle of rum, for we're all rummers! Can you do it all, man? Don't stint on money—we'll give Anne the second happiest day of her life!"

" 'Twill take some doin', " said Ira, getting to his feet, smiling, "but 'twill be done, ye may lay to that. Don't need help, so don't fret; I've rigged many a la'nchin' on shorter notice. "By Godfrey, Jamie, how'd ye know I had that name in mind?"

81

"You may not believe it" I said, "but I read it in a green-eyed newspaper. I thought it was my own idea and now I don't know who thought of it first."

He smiled at Anne, saying to me, "I hope that newspaper don't look too much farther into my thinkin'; it might turn some red for blushin'. Good day to ye all. I'm off to the yard." Unshakable, imperturbable Ira took Anne's witchcraft in his stride as if the reading of his thoughts was no more exceptional than hearing them voiced.

Since Hector had a patient to see after dinner, I showed Anne our gardens and stable, kitchen and carriage house, introduced her to the servants and then we went to sit on the marble bench by the duck pond, one of my favorite spots. Watching the waterfowl glide over the glassy surface, Anne said, "Aren't they pretty? Do they live here or just visit?"

"I think they were here before the house was built," I answered. "You're going to live here and not just visit, aren't you?"

Without looking at me she replied, "We're all just visiting, but we're living, too, every minute. I have no other home to go to now and you can't know how happy I am to be here."

"After what you've been through," I commented, "I've a good idea." Her profile was flawless, adorable. "Anne, we're going to have trouble, you and I."

"No matter what happens, Jamie," she murmured, "you must remember that I'm your friend and nothing you ever do will change that. And be honest with me—always be honest and speak the truth to me, and the trouble between us will be less than it could be."

"That should work both ways," I said. "Will you tell me why you won't smile at me?"

"The honest answer is no, I won't," she answered gently, "because I have clear knowledge why it is. It isn't because I don't like you for I do, very much, and my feeling for you is—oh, Jamie, 'tis no good to talk about it!"

"What's happened to that honesty and truth?" I asked, annoyed at her attempt to run for cover. "Here's mine: I've only known you since this morning but I think I fell in love with you the moment I first saw you. I can't seem to see enough of you, hear you speak enough, and when I look into your eyes I get dizzy and sometimes have a strange feeling like dread instead of joy. What's happening to me, lovely witch?"

She still refused to look at me. "You're not in love with me, Jamie. Forgive me, but I doubt you've ever loved anybody, at least knowingly. You like my looks and you've never met a person like me before—I know I'm different from most people and often 'tis a dreadful nuisance to me as well as to others. Are you working toward seduction of me, as Hector warned me you might?" There was an amused inflection in the crystal voice.

"Honesty again," I answered. "That puzzles me too, because while you're the most beautiful woman of my life and would beyond doubt be an incomparable partner in bed, I have no urge to seduce you. It's never happened to me before. Instead, I have the urge to fling myself at your feet and worship you, and at the same time I resent you for being so untouchable, as if you were some kind of goddess or vestal virgin."

Surprisingly, she reached over and took my hand in hers. "I'm for another man as I said, in another place at another time, Jamie. I'm far from being a goddess, for Heaven's sake, though I'll admit to being a virgin. As for me being such a partner in your bed, I'm afraid you'd have more pleasure in coupling with a tree, though I think myself a normal woman where my body is concerned. I can speak of these things to you that I'd speak of to no other man because I know as well as you do there's a . . . a strange close thing between you and me, closer than brother and sister, yet different from lovers. And in a way, you're right: I know that when the man I love—I've never met him, but will know him when I see him—takes me to his bed, I shall be such a partner. There are times in the night when I think of him that my body fairly burns and aches and my mind"—there was a flush of color on her face—"does perfectly wicked things. Are you shocked, Jamie?"

"Only astonished that you confide it to me," I answered, "as if I were a priest in the confessional or a eunuch in a Turkish harem. I'm not, damn it! This fellow of yours, the thought of him rolling into bed with you, despoiling you, violating you, makes me see red! I'm jealous, by God!" I was suddenly furious. "He has no right! And you're a fool for dreaming such dreams about him! And telling me—did you think I'd leap with joy at the thought of another man slaking his filthy lust in your lovely body, drooling and

83

grunting on you like the animal he is?" I raised the hand she held in mine and kissed it. "How can you say I don't love you, you marvelous, glorious witch?"

Gently withdrawing her hand, she said, "I can say it because of what you just said, Jamie. I spoke of my happiness and you—no, Jamie. In a little while you'll go your ways to travel your roads—please don't look at me like that! I have no pleasure in saying these things!—and on the way you'll meet and love a woman who will love you and then you will know what it means to love, the endless joy of giving and giving. And you'll look back on me and laugh."

"Laugh?" I was still angry. "Weep is more like it! And what d'you mean I'll be off in a little while to travel my roads? The only road I'll travel is over the sea back to London when Hector and I have had enough of New York, and you'll come with us. Your father will be overcome with joy, and you'll be the toast of London as Mrs. Jamie Reid."

"Oh, God," she said with almost a moan, "will you leave off, Jamie, will you leave off? That cannot be, it may not be, don't you understand?"

"No!" I exclaimed in exasperation. "I don't understand, but I know you do, somewhere miles down in those damned green beautiful eyes, and for all your preaching of honesty and truth you hide behind your second sight witchery and refuse to tell me what this bloody mystery is all about! You prate of love as if it were some kind of spiritual uplifting like religion instead of what it really is, a deep affection that gives a man and woman greater pleasure when they bring their bodies together! Giving! 'Tis a mutual taking of joy, not giving, for God's sake! Why don't you quit the preaching, the philosophy and talking in riddles and be the wonderful woman you appear to be? Come to my bed and I'll rid you of those burnings and achings and awaken you with all sorts of fine wicked surprises!"

She got quickly to her feet and faced me, her lovely face angry. "I'll not take such abuse from you, Jamie Reid! You're not the man who'll do the awakening, do you hear? Don't come at me like a spoiled brat who's been refused a bowl of pudding! And don't ever again try to tell me what I'm to do with my body or what true love is, because I know! I *know*, you great overgrown child!" She whirled and fled toward the house, leaving me to moodily ponder why her arrival in our midst had raised such havoc with my heretofore merrily tranquil way of life.

Chapter VI

IN THE MORNING I took Anne's letter to Army headquarters and gave it to Archie Campbell. At first a little reluctant to accept it because of regulations against inclusion of personal letters in the official boxes, he accepted the letter when he saw the name of the addressee; Angus MacDonalds' name was a magician's wand. Studying the graceful script, Archie said, "A lady with a fine hand. May I ask who she is, Jamie?"

"You may," I answered, "and if you think the handwriting is beautiful, you should know that it's a wretched scribble compared to the maker of it. She's Hector's half sister, newly arrived, and her looks will have all New York standing on its ear very soon." I told him about the last stage of her journey from Georgia and the Whig ambush.

He whistled. "So that's who it was, eh? And you say she's unharmed? Excellent! The carriage was recovered by the escort and used to carry the wounded into town. The captain commanding has been worried about her. Hector's half sister? We'd all been thinking that perhaps Sir Henry had found a Mrs. Loring of his own. A pretty woman, you say."

"Good God, Archie," I said, "that's like saying Guy Fawkes had a mild disagreement with Parliament. In my trade I'm used to beautiful women and I'd thought I was hardened to them, but Anne MacDonald—you've never seen anything like her. She's an incomparable feast for the eye."

"She must be a remarkable package," he said, "to have impressed Jamie Reid to that extent. I can hardly wait to meet her. By the bye, you might be interested: a Royal

Commission has arrived to talk peace with the rebels. I doubt much will come of it, nor does the rest of the Army. We're working some things out in case the talks fail."

"Talking is futile," I said, "now that France is in it."

"So say we all," he agreed, and gestured to several London newspapers on his working table. "These came in the commission's ship. It appears that a certain Jamie Reid is a new British hero, a famous and romantical artist become gallant warrior against the King's enemies in a ding-dong sea fight. There's a curious discrepancy among the various versions of why you left London. On the one hand you're here on some sort of secret Royal Commission and on the other you're in America because of illness in your family." He eyed me quizzically.

Evidently the quartermaster general had not let it out, good man, but being an intellectually lazy man I didn't like being under the necessity of maintaining a lie. Since the question had arisen in Campbell's mind, so it would form in others'. Campbell's primary duty post was as commanding officer of a Highland regiment of foot, but at present he was filling in a high place on the staff of the commander of British Forces in North America and therefore an official to be reckoned with. I gave him a wry smile and said, "That's embarrassing. The fact is, Hector MacDonald, Ira Tupper and I accidentally stepped into an unpleasant situation that might have been a major scandal if we hadn't left London for a while until the dust settles. Speed was of the essence, so an acquaintance of mine in a high place at Whitehall arranged for us to travel in the next King's ship for America, using the commission which he invented to get us aboard. 'Tis still a delicate matter, I've heard, and I'll be obliged if you'll say nothing about it. You have my word of honor that we have done nothing dishonorable, disloyal, shameful or criminal."

He nodded. "If half what I've read in these papers is true, 'tis a marvel such a matter didn't happen earlier. You should get a wife—your own—and make babies instead of making cuckolds from whom you must flee across oceans." He smiled, "A bonny wife in your own bed will save you a deal of lost sleep, wasted money and hairbreadth escapes. I was a bachelor once."

I said, "I'll wed soon enough, I expect. Incidentally, if you should like a peep at Hector's marvel of a half sister, come and see the launching of our new ship this noon.

We've renamed her the *Bonny Anne,* and the live, very bonny, Anne will do the honors."

"Even though I can stay but a few minutes," he said, "I'll be there, prepared to be spellbound. And you might give my suggestion serious thought—perhaps you won't have to search far for that good wife."

"I doubt it will be Anne MacDonald," I said. "For all her splendor, we seem to mix like oil and water."

At the end of the morning I was delayed by my boot maker, who insisted on measuring my feet three times for a new pair of riding boots, and I was nearly late for the launching, arriving at the shipyard with not more than two or three minutes to spare. A good-sized crowd was on hand, for there was nothing like a ship launching or a public hanging to draw men from their labor, women from kitchens and children from the schoolroom. Towering in the timber cradle on the railways, surprisingly huge out of water, loomed our ship, proud in her gleaming fresh black paint above the waterline and her underbody glistening like ivory with a smooth thick coat of tallow. Her two new masts of buff-painted pine speared the soft blue sky, and brightly colored signal flags fluttered from her stays, fore and aft.

Under the high arching cutwater of the ship's bow was a platform decorated with gay bunting, and on it stood Anne and Hector. She was a breathtaking, stunning figure in her green gown, and crowning her red-gold hair was a saucy little bonnet with three long blue-green plumes. Making my way through the crowd, I noticed the people were watching her with open admiration. When I stepped up on the platform, Hector said, "I had you down for drunk and fallen in a gutter, Tom Tardy."

"You should rid yourself," I told him, "of the habit of visiting your own shortcomings on your betters. Anne, you're ravishing. The mob is about to fall prostrate in adoration. Where's Ira?"

"They're admiring you, now," she said. The rays of the sun struck deep into the green eyes and I had a dizzy sensation. "You appear quite like a prince. Ira's on the ship. He told me that when the noon gun sounds from the Battery he'll strike the ship's bell twelve times, and on the twelfth stroke the men will knock out the chocks that hold the ship. Then I must quickly break the bottle." She showed me the bottle of our best rum, its neck swathed in a towel.

Her eyelashes and brows were rich chestnut. Her exquisitely modeled lips were slightly parted and the tips of her teeth were in perfect alignment and gleaming white. We stood silently looking at each other, and it seemed as if important things, which I could not comprehend, were being said. With an effort I broke the lock of our eyes, took out my watch and snapped open the cover. "Five seconds. Place yourself and see you have room for a swing, quickly, Anne."

She moved to the ship's cutwater and tested the arc of her swing. The crowd was hushed. A gull circled overhead and gave a laughing cry. Then the cannon at the Battery boomed, and the ship's bell began clanging the noon hour, twelve brazen strokes in pairs, the last ones almost drowning out Anne's voice as she cried in her clear crystal voice, swinging the bottle, "Go to your bonny bridegroom, *Bonny Anne,* and may you ever sail the bonny road that's forever blessed!" The fragrant rum sprayed and bits of broken bottle shimmered through the bright air like diamonds. Sliding sternward, the vessel swiftly gathered speed in the heavy cradle and when she plunged into the placid surface of the East River there was a mighty splash. She floated clear of the cradle and drifted out to the length of the snubbing lines, and the yard laborers began hauling her in, to work her alongside the adjacent pier. Ira stood with quiet pride beside the helm on the poop.

Anne was transfigured, and exclaimed with joy, "See how she floats! What a beautiful, beautiful thing! No wonder men love ships! A woman could be jealous!"

"Dear lady," said a silky murmuring voice I had never wanted to hear again, "surely the ship must be jealous of her sponsor, about whom it would say if it could speak, 'What a beautiful, beautiful person!' Jamie, Mr. MacDonald, how good it is to see you."

Hector said in a suffocated growl, "Well, damme—"

I stared at Lord Beauvoir, who had stepped on the platform, impeccable in his gray suit, smiling his glacial smile. Archie Campbell, at his side, said, "Lord Beauvoir expressed interest in these proceedings when he learned you gentlemen own the ship."

"A splendid little ship, gentlemen," said Beauvoir. "May I be presented to this extremely charming lady?"

Hector was glowering and clearly on the point of snarling, so I quickly made the introductions, adding, "Miss MacDonald is half sister to Mr. MacDonald."

"I don't wonder Mr. Angus MacDonald has kept you hidden away, Miss MacDonald," said Beauvoir, frostily smiling at her. "The arrival of your beauty in England would be the greatest conquering of the land since that of William the Norman. Your home is in some remote southern province, I think?"

"Georgia, my lord," she said, gravely inspecting him. "I'm presently visiting my brother and Mr. Reid."

"And finding it a notable relief, no doubt," he said, "to be away from the dreadful Whigs, and a notable pleasure to be in the company of these two excellent gentlemen." He fixed me with sharp eyes. "Jamie, I've heard no end of your popularity and success since I arrived. You appear to be duplicating your London triumphs. And now a shipowner, of the very ship you helped capture. London went quite mad when news of your gallantry arrived, if you haven't heard."

His nearness made me almost nauseated. "Are you a member of the Royal Peace Commission, my lord?"

"Quite so," he answered, making a slight expression of distaste, "and a drearier waste of time cannot be imagined. I couldn't refuse His Majesty, however. By the bye, he took the report of your reckless exploits with some displeasure, and made some comment about your disobedience. Don't be alarmed, my boy—I soothed him with some talk of your true British courage, and suggested that an artist of your standing who met and overcame the King's enemies by force of arms may be worthy of special recognition." He smiled thinly. "I left him pondering that, Jamie."

"My lord," I said, losing the struggle to be coolly polite, "I do not desire your intercession. My position has not changed."

"Tut, my dear fellow," he murmured. "I had hoped that by now you would have learned that we live in an uncertain world, full of unexpected events, and highly placed friends are to be prized, but it would seem that New York is not the schoolroom for that lesson. Nevertheless, however much you may object, I shall continue to have your best interests at heart in London. And speaking of hearts in London, Lady Beauvoir asked me to convey her most affectionate regards. I must say, Jamie, I was most disappointed at not having had a letter from you."

He was turning the screw. I said, conscious of Anne's eyes on me, "I've had no news worth writing you, my lord."

"Possibly you'll find some later," he said, "and Lady Beauvoir will be delighted. She still hopes you will one day paint that special picture she asked you to do for her. You remember? The one for the gallery in my house?"

The incredible little clot was referring to himself. I said, "My specialty is portraits, my lord. My regrets to your lady, sir."

"She'll be disappointed," said Beauvoir, "but she'll not give up hoping. Don't underestimate her desire, Jamie." He said to Anne, "Miss MacDonald, forgive me for rushing away; nothing but the most urgent Crown business could tear me from your charm. Jamie, Mr. MacDonald, we must get together and have a talk about old times in London, eh? Colonel, if you're ready?"

Turning away to accompany Beauvoir, Archie grinned at me and said, "An incomparable feast, indeed, Jamie. Goodday to you, Miss MacDonald, Hector."

Ira had to remain at the yard for work on the ship, so Hector, Anne and I walked home in a pall of silence, Hector and I gloomily pondering the appearance of Beauvoir, and Anne lost in her own thoughts. The servants were setting the table for the noon meal when we entered the house and there was a delicious smell of food, but I had no appetite. Anne said, "Something has happened to us. I expect you'll have a drink of rum. I'll get it for you and have some myself." As she poured it, she said, "I've never tasted rum. The ship launching was beautiful, but the little lord spoiled it and my appetite."

Hector drank deeply and muttered, "That slimy dog!"

Anne tasted the rum with the tip of her pink tongue. "It tastes like medicine, but if you gentlemen like it, so must I. That man is a danger to you, isn't he? To both, but mostly to Jamie."

I said, "He's an infernal nuisance. He was, in London, and he is the same here. There's no need to go into details. Let it go that he's an unpleasant swine. Anne, you were perfectly glorious when you christened the ship."

"You'll not turn me away, Jamie," she said gravely. "I saw what I saw and heard what I heard and felt what I felt. Will you tell me it's none of my affair if I ask you if the matter concerns his wife who sent you her affectionate regards?"

90

"Yes," I answered, "I'll tell you that. It's none of your affair."

She put down her glass and the green eyes locked with mine. "A danger to Hector and you *is* my affair. I shall tell you: you made love to his wife, Jamie, and he found you out. Now he has a hold on you, and on Hector, too, because Hector's your friend. Probably Ira, also. That was why you left England so suddenly. Is it true?"

"Nosy wench," I said, trying to be light, "stop rummaging about in the attic."

Hector said, "Anne, it's none of your affair, as Jamie told you."

She had not removed her gaze from me. "It is true, isn't it? And is it true that the King knows you?"

"Slightly," I said. "I painted his portrait and he's interested in art. We talked about it."

"If the other thing weren't so important," she said, "I'd ask you all about the King. It's exciting to know someone who's a friend of the King." She was silent for a minute or so, then said, "It was the way he looked at you, Jamie. I couldn't understand what it meant. Now I do. There was a woman hidden inside of him, peeping out at you."

"Bah," grunted Hector, frowning.

"No bah!" she retorted. "I'm a woman, and if I ever saw a woman look at Jamie the way that little gray moth did, I'd know what she had in mind! And now I remember I saw something else: when he said the ship should be jealous of me, his eyes said *he* was jealous of me!" She stared at me in alarmed surprise. "Can such things be? And the wife he was talking about—Jamie, what kind of man is he?"

Hector said, "He's a kind of evil witch, Anne, and doesn't bear talking about, just as you're a sweet, adorable, beautiful witch who must be talked about by weak mortal men upon whom you've placed your weird."

I was anxious to leave the subject of Beauvoir, so I said heartily, "And who has now placed our good vessel under her thrall. Bonny Anne, you gave your sister a sweet blessing, but there you were bubbling of roads again. A ship follows a course, not a road, though I hope as you said, hers will be blessed."

"And so 'twill be," she said firmly, "for I saw the great joy in her when she splashed into her lover's arms, then nestled deep in his embrace. A course or road are one to me in my meaning and my heart will go with her wherever

91

she sails. Oh, what a wonderful thing it is to have such a dear sister suddenly on top of just finding my dear brother! And coming on Jamie, too, though you're a worrisome, difficult man, Jamie Reid, but having Ira for a friend means there's hope for you."

"Very funny," I said sourly.

"You and Hector are always joking like that," she retorted. "May I not also make a silly remark with a bit of truth in it? You put me off a moment ago to change the subject. Hector said Lord Beauvoir is an evil witch. The man is a warlock, the woman a witch. I myself saw——" She broke off and something like horror came into her eyes. "It can't be! How can it be? Jamie, tell me!"

The Beauvoir affair was shameful enough without Anne projecting herself into it. I said harshly, " 'Tis none of your business."

The green eyes studied me. "It is. What harms you harms us all."

Hector said to her, "Stop prying, Anne. Jamie's right."

Walking to the open door, she stood gazing out into the garden for a moment, then said, "I'm done prying. I've seen it now. The wee gray man is quite mad, isn't he? About that, I mean, and Jamie. It makes my stomach sick. Jamie, did you ever——"

God knows what she was going to ask because I blew up then. The combination of Beauvoir's appearance and Anne's persistent intrusion into the beastly matter sparked my anger. I snapped, "It makes *your* stomach sick? It wouldn't be sick if you kept your nose out of my affairs! I've known you for scarce twenty-four hours and you act toward me like a nagging wife and the Oracle of Delphi! You moon around talking of roads, spouting fuzzy philosophy about love, truth and honesty, acting as if you own me!" She raised her eyes to me and I went plunging down into them, but kept on raging. "Look at you sitting there with those great reproachful green eyes mourning at me as if I were some damned monstrous tragedy, as if I were your child born with two heads! Who appointed you to supervise my life? 'A bowl of pudding,' you said! Madam, to hell with your bowl of pudding!"

Hector was on his feet, indignant. "That's enough, Jamie! What she said doesn't merit that kind of diatribe, sir!"

Anne said, looking down at her hands in her lap, "No,

Hector, Jamie's right. I have no business interfering in his affairs."

That only made me more furious. "Ho, so speaks Miss Meek-and-mild now! You walk all over me without giving me so much as a smile, and now you——"

"Goddamn it, Jamie!" shouted Hector. "I told you, enough! You'll not berate my sister like that! I demand you apolo——"

Anne let go an anguished wail. "No, no, no! Stop, both of you! You're not to quarrel over me, d'you hear? Not another word!"

I flung out of the library and stamped upstairs to my painting room where my rage slowly cooled. A portrait sitter had postponed an appointment and I welcomed the opportunity to go ahead with my marine painting, a spirited depiction of the battle between the *Jason* and *Sea Ranger*. Taking up my brushes, I walked out of the MacDonalds' life and into blood-red morning off Ambrose Shoal where once again I could smell the sea, tar and cordage, hear the clash of steel on steel and the shouting din of the struggling men. I lost track of time and reality. Anne's voice, behind me, brought me back with a start.

"Oh, Jamie," she whispered, " 'tis the most beautiful thing! I never——I mean, I knew you're an artist, but to make a thing like that is like being a god! I hear it and smell it—— and I'm frightened at what's happening there!"

Her loveliness, the wide startled eyes, wrenched my heart. I adored her. "I smell and hear it as I paint it, and once again I have the fear of God in me. All viewers of my paintings should be witches who feel my feelings."

She raised a hand and pointed to a small figure in the swirl of fighting men. "That boy beside you——oh, dear God, Jamie, no!" Tears welled in the green eyes.

My pleasure departed and anger revived. "D'you think I'm that much of a god of pictures that I can change that? Isn't second sight admission of predestination? You'll tell me nothing but mumbo-jumbo as to myself, and yet you can look at Tom Stokely and know he's going to die again in a few minutes in my painting of him and weep for him! What the hell are you doing, snooping around in my memories now? Isn't my present and future enough for you? How did Tom die, eh? Tell me that!" I was dimly aware that I was weeping, too. "Spit it out, witch! How did Tom die?"

Her face was full of hurt. "He was shot and you caught him in your arms. I know you did, Jamie. 'Tis written all over you and never mind second sight. Will you stop being angry with me? I came here to ask you to forgive me for upsetting you. What must I do to prove I'm your dear friend?"

"For a start," I answered brutally, "you may peel out of your gown and spread yourself out on that couch over there, like the beautiful bowl of pudding you are, and I'll humanize you, O sacred Oracle."

"If I didn't know you better," she said, "I'd pick up that stool and beat your head in with it. You know damned well that couch isn't the crucible that will make what's ailing you go away." She raised her sweet chin defiantly. "If I thought it would I wouldn't hesitate for a second and the devil with saving my maidenhead for that other man, for he won't care, but 'twould only make matters worse for you because to you it would be a battle to be won, not love, and the thing you'd do it with is your weapon that you'd thrust into me like a sword, just as are the men—and you there with your back turned—in your painting. Jamie, please be my friend and stop worrying and fretting about love, because I do love you in a . . . a strange way and you're making me unhappy."

No longer angry, I told her the truth. "I don't know what's happening or how to handle it, Anne. I feel this thing for you that must be love, but then a minute later I almost hate you, and with all this within a full day after meeting you, how shall I stand up under it after weeks, months or a year? I was a happy man till you came and now everything's changed. What in God's name are you doing to me?"

"I don't know, Jamie!" she exclaimed despairingly. "I'd give anything if it weren't happening, to make it stop! If I were a real witch instead of an unhappy wench with second sight I'd cast a spell and send it away, I swear! But will you stop and think that maybe it's not caused by me at all, that it may be what's inside you? This I know, that a long hard road lies ahead of you and you may already be walking it. The time of change is on you, just as it came on me last month at Goodowns when I knew 'twas time to go from there. There are strange things waiting for you on your roads and there is nothing we can do to change it."

"Tell me then," I said, "shall I survive this dire experience? At the end will I find the pot of gold under the rainbow or whatever will be my reward, O Witch of Endor?"

She said resentfully, "You're poking sarcastic fun at me. I don't know. I can't see all the way, and even if I did I couldn't tell you. Will you be over sulking by suppertime? Hector wants us to celebrate the launching with a little party. His lady friend will be here and he's gotten bagpipes from a Highland regiment for the music. We'll have a gay time and you men may get merrily tiddly. I'm wonderfully excited because at Goodowns after Papa went off to London when I was a girl Aunt Mary and I never had parties, nor were there any gentlemen in the house except Mr. Barstow visiting with his family sometimes and he was a sober, serious man. Jamie, will you come and laugh and joke and be merry? 'Tis like a birthday for me, my sister's wedding day."

"I'll be at supper," I answered without enthusiasm, "because I have to eat, but likely I'll still be sulking over being refused my pudding." I nodded toward the couch. "Unless you've changed your mind. There's plenty of time for a maidenhead to be disposed of."

She gave me a scornful look. "You've got a deal of growing up to do before you get any kind of such pudding from any woman. You'll see what kind of a man you are when the growing pains are on you, Jamie Reid." She dropped a quick curtsy and flounced out of the painting room.

A party. I opened a bottle of rum, moodily thinking I might as well prime myself with a good headstart, and went to drinking as I resumed painting. In Salem about three generations back, Cotton Mather would have had her hanged for her supernatural pretentions, I reflected, yet there was nothing really witchlike in Highland Scottish second sight. I knew it existed and accepted it as a matter of course, having been born into a household to a mother who had the gift.

My mother's first language was the Gaelic of her native Isle of Lewis, where second sight was common, and the careful English she had learned from my father made her second sightings explanations to me a little bewildering, such as, "Jamie, the toys at you away must go not later than one minute. Not a good day has had your father and the walking of King Street he is taking to home now is not happy making." Which means simply that she had seen my father leave his counting house in a disgruntled mood and was coming home by King Street, and I should clear up

95

my toy-clutter lest he be further disgruntled by an untidy house. He never was, but my mother used her gift to better serve him and me.

Now, thinking back, I remembered her last words to me as she lay dying of a fever and I felt a slight shock. I had been twelve years old, and she had said, holding my hand, "God's blessing be on you, Jamie. The good, strive to, and the bonny road will be at you. Woe have the others." The dream I had on the *Jason* rose in memory and my skin prickled.

Now here was Anne MacDonald babbling about roads to me, dangling her beauty and exquisite body before me and withdrawing it when I reached for it, somehow bonded to me yet walled off from me, delighting me one minute and infuriating me the next with her mystic nonsense. Our acquaintanceship was measured in hours, but it was as if we had known each other for years on a maddeningly intimate level. Insofar as roads were concerned, I could see the one ahead with us under the same roof was going to steadily worsen. I wondered if I were coming down with some sort of nervous breakdown; my very nature, normally buoyant and pleasant, seemed to be changing to glumness and anger. There was the fit of rage and weeping over her sighting of Tom Stokely; I had not wept since small boyhood. Hector treated patients with nervous complaints—something he had learned in his German university—but even as I thought about taking my troubles to him I rejected the idea; he was too close to me as well as to Anne. I knew him well enough to expect that his prescription, if the woman were not his half sister, would be something like, "Take her to bed, man, and get it out of your system." Yet despite my coarse invitations to her I still had no genuine inclinations to bed her, and that in itself was enough to make me think I was going crazy, because never had I met a more desirable woman.

Drinking, brooding and painting through the afternoon, when the supper chimes sounded from the lower hall I went downstairs unsteadily, fuzzily determined that the only way I could live henceforth in the same house with Anne was to ignore her completely as if she were not there, which was an absurd impossibility. The dining room was brightly lighted, noisy and full of merriment. Besides Anne, Hector and Ira, Hector's cute and buxom young widow, Alice Tunns, and Meg Barr-Pettit, were at the table. Meg was one of our neighbors, an attractive woman in her late thirties whom Hector was treating for some curious nervous affliction; her husband was an Army colonel who had been for some weeks absent on a temporary duty posting to Clinton's headquarters at Philadelphia.

My appearance was greeted with hearty welcomes, to which I responded with a lame attempt to be affable, and I sat down in the vacant chair beside Meg, on Hector's left. He sat at the head, Anne at the foot, Alice and Ira across the table. Both Hector and Ira were in rare form, Hector expansively jolly and Ira behaving as though it were his wedding day which, in a sense, it was. The ladies, including Anne, were kept in almost constant gales of laughter by Hector's sallies and Ira's outlandish anecdotes. I ate silently and kept the maidservant busy refilling my wineglass, drinking more than eating and trying not to look at Anne's radiantly smiling face, and ignoring the fact that I was advancing swiftly into drunkenness.

Ira told a story about a ship launching custom he had once encountered among the natives of some island in the Great South Sea, where a ship was subject to a curse unless a virgin maid were sacrificed by being crushed under the vessel as it was pushed into the sea. There were cries of horror from the women and Ira, smiling laconically, confessed he had just made it up to see what silent Jamie might have to say about it. The company looked at me expectantly.

I said owlishly, "You may not be aware of it, but such a practice was actually the origin of our present-day custom. Nowadays, the virgin breaks a bottle on the stem of the vessel, properly a bottle of red wine to symbolize her pure life's blood, and 'tis a cowardly degeneration of a once-noble ceremony. Our good ship would have been more effectively blessed today if we had flung our immaculate virgin under the keel as would have our more sensible Celtic forebears."

The men frowned and Alice looked startled, but Anne said cheerfully, "The ship would have stopped sliding instantly rather than harm her sister. Anyway, Jamie just made that up, too."

"The wish is father to the thought," I muttered, staring into my wineglass.

"No matter, Annie darlin'," said Ira, "I love ye both, lady and ship, my pair o' bonny Annes."

"Ah, will you not love me, too, Captain Tupper?" asked Meg. "Jamie's ignoring me." It was only then that I realized that under the table not only was her near leg pressed firmly against mine but her hand was on my thigh.

Hector, looking past me at her, said, frowning slightly, "Jack loves you, Meg, and you know I do."

"Don't be stuffy, Hector," Meg smiled. " 'Tis only a bit of fun." The hand under the table inched slowly up my thigh and Old Nick stirred.

I said to her, "I'm sorry. I didn't mean to be rude. I'm preoccupied by a painting I'm working on, I suppose."

The hand rested near my crotch. There was mirth in her eyes. "May I have a peep at it this evening?" The hand slithered to my crotch and halted on the bulge of Old Nick, tentatively fingered, then grasped. "Is it a big one?" Her hand stroked, measuring length.

"You may see for yourself," I answered, enjoying the groping and wordplay.

Anne spoke enthusiastically from the foot of the table. "Oh, 'tis beautiful and exciting, Meg!"

"I'm sure it is," remarked Meg, giving Old Nick an affectionate tweak. She wore a gown that left her shoulders bare and had no modesty piece covering the tops of her breasts. Her skin was milky white. The smile she turned to me was that of an excited, anticipatingly aroused woman. Drunk as I was, I was tempted to take her from the table that very minute and rush her up to my painting room for a resounding introduction to Old Nick, but that would have to wait until a withdrawal could be made with some grace. I leaned over and whispered in her ear, "Stop that before something happens that will make you sorry. Be patient."

The hand departed and she laughed as though I had told her a joke. "Jamie, you rascal! I'll hold you to that!"

Vaguely I became aware that there was no more food on the table and there were bottles of port, rum, brandy and whisky, with platters heaped with nuts, sweets and fruit. I was drinking, it seemed, brandy. The rafters shook and the air vibrated to the skirling of bagpipes. Hector marched around the table, his face red, cheeks puffing and fingers dancing on the chanter. The scores of candles in the chandelier reflected on the polished table surface. Faces appeared and disappeared, laughing, showing great expanses of teeth. Besides me, Meg was standing and singing, displacing the pipes, a cloyingly sad ballad about unrequited

98

love and tragic death on a battlefield. I spilled a puddle of brandy, refilling my glass.

A clear, bell-like crystal flood of sound washed over me and my blurred attention centralized on Anne. She was standing and singing. The unreal beauty of her face and voice clutched me, and my heart swelled so that I could hardly breathe. I worshipped her, adored her. Her eyes were on me, drawing me into them. The tune was sweet and slow, and gradually the words filtered into my understanding:

> *And see ye not yon braid, braid road*
> *That lies across the lily leven?*
> *That is the Path of Wickedness.*
> *Though some call it—*

Lurching to my feet, I erupted like a raging volcano, insanely torn by sudden fury and an overwhelming, confused sorrow that was somehow crumbling me into tiny despairing bits. I shouted at her crazily, "Shut up! Hold your damned carping, mooning tongue, you silly jade! To hell with your goddamned roads and your bloody preaching of 'em! Smile on me, damn you, smile on me! Who sent you into my life—"

Then it was my turn to be interrupted. I never saw Hector spring from his chair, but I felt the solid punch to the point of my chin that made the world disappear. When I came to, I was stretched out on the sofa in the library and Hector was bending over me, scowling fiercely into my face. He growled, "Ha, come around, have you? Pity."

I sat up. My chin was beastly sore and I seemed to be quite sober. The dim memory of what had happened came over me and I felt ashamed. "Hector, I made an ass of myself. I'll apologize to her. I think I'm going mad."

"If you ever do anything like that again to her I'll kill you," he said. "She wept! She stood there with tears pouring down her cheeks while you showered her with your filthy insults!"

I wanted to crawl into a hole. "I'm ashamed to face her," I muttered.

"You'll face her and you'll apologize to her, by God!" he declared. "But go somewhere and pull yourself together decently first." He stalked out of the library.

I gingerly felt my sore chin and as I told myself I deserved it, Meg came in, her face anxious, and when she saw me on my feet she smiled with relief. "I was afraid Hector might have broken something. 'Twas a fearful blow but you deserved it, you know."

"I know," I answered, and I remembered where she had left off under the table. "I'm afraid to go back and face her just yet. Would you like to see the painting?"

"Oh, yes, yes!" she exclaimed happily.

I had left the lamp burning in the painting room and as we entered, I said, "There's the picture on the easel."

"After," she breathed, coming to me, "after."

Her kissing was stormy, frantic, and she nearly ripped the buttons from my flies in getting at Old Nick and dragging him out. "Beautiful, beautiful dolly," she panted, stroking him, and then she dropped down to her knees and the warmth of her mouth and tongue was too much for me. I quickly hauled her to the couch and, flinging up her skirt, she spread her legs and whispered so rapidly I could hardly follow the words, "I want my dolly, I want my dolly, give me my dolly fuck me fuck me fuck me hard papa give me my dolly back—"

She gave out a groan as I mounted her with my breeches at half-mast, and her legs and arms coiled around me in tight embrace when Old Nick went all the way. When the rhythmic motion commenced, her face distorted strangely into a gargoyle's grimace and from her gasping mouth there issued a torrent of the most astonishing obscenities I had ever heard a woman utter, but she was a splendid performer, heaving and thrusting with superb vigor. Holding back my own climax, I felt hers approaching with remarkable quickness, and she made noises of sputtering gurgles and grunting whimpers. Then she exploded, her body arching, straining in mighty heaves, crying, "Unh, unh, unh, unh!" I let myself go and spasmed, driving deep, and in the middle of it the corner of my eye caught a movement elsewhere. Bouncing away, I turned my head slightly and saw Anne MacDonald standing in the doorway staring at us. Then she stepped back into the darkness and was gone.

It happened so swiftly that I doubt that I missed a stroke, and even if I wanted to stop I couldn't, not at that stage, in the middle of coming. With her eyes closed in that climactic expression of agony that many women show in their peak of transport, Meg had not seen the visitor, and her peak was an extraordinarily long one which I pleasurably obliged

100

by continuing to plunge into. Suddenly she went limp, her legs and arms fell away from me and her face looked up at me with a mask of horror. Then she began pummelling me, screaming, "What have you done? What have you done? You've raped me, raped me!" And she set up a frightful blubbering.

I withdrew and removed myself from her in some haste, pulled up my breeches and protested, "But, Meg, you wanted it! You asked for it!"

She got up to swing around and sit on the edge of the couch, and there she glared at me. "Bastard! You ravished me—" Her face became piteous and she went back to weeping while I stood openmouthed. She left off sobbing, looked up at me with a curious lopsided grin and whispered, "Did you give me my dolly, my new dolly? Papa sent my others back to the maker because he said they were broken. I didn't break them. I was a good girl."

She was out of her mind, loony. Hector was treating her for "nervousness." I said, "I'm sure you'll have a fine new dolly, Meg. Would you like me to call Hector?"

That frightened her. She exclaimed, "Oh, no, Hector will punish me! You mustn't tell Hector, please, please!" Then she changed again and smiled slyly as she whispered, "I don't want him to see me. Nobody must see Meg or they'll take her new dolly away. I'll go down the backstairs and go home." Then she beamed and said in a bright voice, "Unless you want to fuck me again?"

Uncomfortably, I answered, "Well, no, not at this time, Meg. Some of the others might come here and that would be embarrassing if they saw us."

"Like your red-headed woman did," she said vaguely, and I was stunned. She had seen Anne in the middle of our climax. "Jamie, will she tell Jack? I'll die if she tells Jack. I love Jack. . . ."

The blubbering was about to commence again, so I quickly helped her to her feet, saying, "She'll tell nobody, Meg, and she's never met Jack. Go home, there's a good girl, and have a nice night's sleep."

She gave me a peculiar hunted look and rushed out of the painting room. I followed, saw her disappear down the back stairs, and gave a sigh of relief. Sounds of laughter and conversation drifted up from the front of the house, but I was in no mood to rejoin the group and face Anne after

101

what had happened so I went to bed where, after a period of uneasy reflections, I went to sleep.

The nauseating dream of the roads and making love to the rotting corpse came back and I came awake sick to my stomach. The night was past and the pre-dawn gray light was brightening with imminent sunrise. My head was foggy from the drink of the night before. I dressed, washed, and went down to the stable, backed my favorite mount out of his stall, and as I was saddling him for a head-clearing gallop, Anne MacDonald appeared. She watched me cinch the belly band in silence, then said, "Good-morning, Jamie. May I ride with you?"

She was wearing a handsome new dark blue riding habit and the first rays of the rising sun touched her brilliant hair with fire. Unshaven and sour, I felt like a grub, and grunted, "We don't have a sidesaddle for you yet."

Raising the bottom of her skirt, which I saw was oddly divided, she displayed legs encased in deerskin-fringed leggings. "Ladies in the back country of Georgia wear these and ride astride."

There was no getting away from her. I brought out the chestnut mare that Hector used for his visitation sulky and sometimes rode a-saddle, and prepared her for Anne who quietly watched, then lightly vaulted into the saddle. I had never seen a female sit a man's saddle before; it was generally considered indecent, but Anne made it look exactly right. "I've ridden horses since I was a baby," she said, "and never a coach or carriage before leaving Goodowns."

I mounted my horse and we rode through the streets at a brisk canter to the town common, a parklike expanse of natural countryside, and there set about galloping over the greensward and hurdling the sheep meadow fences. My malaise passed and good feeling revived. In the early sunlight the colors were intense, the air sweet, and dewy cobwebs in the grass glittered with thousands of diamond droplets. The horses were spirited and clearly thankful for the exercise, and constantly sought to break into a gallop on the way back home when we were walking them to cool them down.

Anne spoke for the first time since departing the stable. "I was a fool again for going to your painting room, Jamie. I wanted to make things better for you. I'm sorry."

"Perhaps now you'll have learned to stay out of my life," I said.

102

"Don't start that again, you ass," she answered tartly. "That's impossible and you know it. There are things that must be said this morning and I'm going to say them. You hurt me last night when you broke into my singing, but I know the hurt you had was worse and nothing can help it. I felt your pain and that was why I wept, not because of mine, though Hector cannot understand that."

"Nor can I," I said dourly. "I was drunk and made a beast of myself. I apologize. Spare me your talk of feeling my pain."

"I shall," she answered lightly, "and to hell with your childishness. Are you thinking me shocked by coming on you with Meg? I'll disappoint you. 'Twas interesting, and the only reason I left quickly was because I didn't want to cause you embarrassment. 'Twas curious and quite funny, all those arms and legs, bodies thrashing about and the odd sounds." She sighed. "I suppose it isn't funny at all when you're doing it, and when I come to do it with my lover I won't think it funny at all. I've seen our livestock doing it all my life, for good breeding of stock is important, and it seems there's no difference in the way of it for humans except 'tis face to face, no doubt for kissing, and there should be love in it which is beyond you, Jamie."

"That," I said, "is the most enlightening lecture on human copulation I've ever heard and the personal footnote was right on the mark. Did you rise at the crack of dawn to badger me?"

"You big surly nit," she said, "I rose at the crack of dawn because I had a nightmare about you and it frightened me so much for you that I couldn't go back to sleep. I heard you pass by in the hallway, so I came after you."

"What was the dream about?" I asked.

"I can't tell you," she answered, "because you'd only be angry with me again. Jamie, if I promise not to badger you and that I'll be quiet as a mouse, may I ride with you again each morning? I always rode before breakfast at Goodowns."

It would be an unsettling way to begin my days, but on the other hand I was forced to admit we had had a good ride and she was a joy to watch, galloping her mount over the grass and taking the fences in effortless perfect form. "As you like," I grunted.

Chapter VII

IN THE AFTERNOON of the day following the launching party, my last sitter of the day had departed and I was cleaning my palette, idly wondering how Anne expected to join me mornings at the stable unless I called her—which I didn't intend to do—when Hector walked in, grave-faced and silent, and sat down.

"Look here," I said, "if you've come to bite another piece out of my arse over last night, you'll be wasting your breath. I've apologized to Anne and I'm still ashamed."

"I want to talk about Meg," he stated. "You had her last night, didn't you?"

At first I thought Anne had told him, then I realized the question was interrogatory, not accusatory. "Why, yes, I did. What about it?"

He frowned. "How did she behave?"

She was Hector's patient and he should be made aware of her bizarre conduct, so I told him the details, from the groping under the table to her departure via the back stairs. "Balmy as a March hare, in my opinion," I finished, "but a damned good piece of tup."

"Three stillborn children can produce a disturbing effect on an excessively maternal woman," he said. "It chronically unhinged her, particularly immediately after her monthly flow, making her indiscriminately promiscuous though she was really a very moral woman who loved her husband dearly. She blamed herself for the stillbirths, and I had just about convinced her that it was God's fault, not hers, and He had taken them back because of His poor workmanship. Her remorse after one of those compulsive sexual episodes was a terrible thing to see."

His use of the past tense struck me and apprehension grew. "Hector, why are you talking about her like this?"

He said woodenly, "She hanged herself in her attic last night."

"Oh, my Christ!" Stunned, I stared at him, then recollection of the early morning nightmare of making love to the rotting corpse burst on me. My stomach clutched. Meg had been dead when I dreamed it. "But how could I have known? I thought her only a lonely wife with a powerful itch!"

"I'm not accusing or judging you, Jamie," he said. "Perhaps I'm at fault. When she left the party she told me she was going directly home and I should have escorted her. Instead she went to you. In my examination of the corpse I found the vagina full of spunk and reached the probable conclusion."

"The hell you're not judging me!" I exclaimed. "You're telling me I as good as killed her! That's utter horseshit and you know it! It could have been your so-called treatment that did it! I'm shocked and grieved because I liked her, and sorry her mind was ill, but I'll take no responsibility for her death."

He shrugged. "Suit yourself. I've only given you the facts. And while I'm here I may as well tell you that Ira and I are concerned about your behavior toward Anne, including —but not limited to—last night. I've never seen you behave so poorly." He was grim. "Whatever you've got in mind, hands off, Jamie, d'you hear?"

My old friend was suddenly a stranger. "She's in no danger from me. If you want the truth, I don't much care for her though I admire her beauty."

"You're acting strangely," he said. "Something's gnawing at you and maybe I can help. Want to talk about it?"

"There's nothing to talk about," I told him, going back to cleaning my palette.

He walked out without another word. As I finished my cleaning chores I glanced out the window and saw Anne sitting alone on the marble bench in the garden. She had had an alarming dream, too. My skin prickled with gooseflesh. I went downstairs and out to where she sat watching the ducks on the pond. Sitting beside her, I said, "You've heard about Meg."

"Hector told me," she murmured.

"When we went riding you knew," I declared. "You dreamed it. That was what you wouldn't tell me."

She gave a little sigh. "I was on one road and you on

106

another, and you were making love to her as you did last night, and I could see she was dead and you didn't know it, so I called out to you to stop but you couldn't hear me, and then her skin began falling off—"

Horrified, I exclaimed, "That was *my* nightmare! My God, Anne, now you're even into my dreams!"

"Don't blame me for it," she said quietly. "I didn't do it on purpose. When I woke, I knew something awful had happened to Meg and you had something to do with it without meaning to, and I wanted to be with you. I nearly told you so I could comfort you, knowing you'd blame yourself."

Exasperated, I snapped, "I want none of your comfort or any part of your cursed second sight! Is there no part of my life you can't stick your nose into?"

She leaped to her feet and said angrily, "You big ninny, can't you see I can't help it? I'm sick of your evil temper and tongue-lashings! You're a big damned spoiled brat, an overgrown child, and may God help you when you come to face yourself!" She marched away, and I reflected sardonically that between the pair of them, the MacDonalds' major aim in life now seemed to be the reconstruction of my character. I sorely missed the old carefree Hector. Doctor MacDonald was beginning to come on rather too heavily, and the holier-than-thou hat fitted him oddly.

The day was not improved by the arrival, shortly before dinner, of a servant bearing a note from Lord Beauvior asking me to have a late supper with him at Fraunce's tavern. It was worded innocuously, courteously, and I flew into a towering rage, cursed the messenger, and shouted at him to tell his lordship where he could stick his supper. Then I threw on my hat and coat and went to the best bawdy house in New York, the American equivalent of Mother Allworth's, got drunk, had a good meal, and slept the night with a pretty mulatto whore from Haiti who spoke only French and performed remarkable feats.

New York society discovered Anne and the drawing room seemed to be perpetually mobbed with aspiring military and civilian swains, worshipfully adoring Anne who reigned over them in regal grace. Every night she was off to some ball, rout or supper, escorted by some drooling jackanapes, with Mrs. Quimby trailing along as dragon. I couldn't bear being in the same room with her and yet I couldn't bear her being gone from my sight. I gave up my morning rides and

Hector took my place as her riding companion, grumbling mightily about having to rise so early but nevertheless enjoying the unusual, for him, exercise.

By then I was drinking more or less steadily through waking hours, spending my nights with the dusky trollop who had conceived the notion of teaching me, among other things, the French language. Women of higher degree no longer attracted me. I grew careless in my drunken fog about acceptances or regrets in social invitations and often found myself at a party without knowing how I got there or whose it was. And always I brooded about Anne MacDonald, the immaculate virgin, prying seeress, holy oracle who was the most beautiful woman in the world.

Surfacing one evening from alcoholic amnesia, I found myself jovially present at a masquerade ball, though I wore no mask. By the look of the elegant place and the sumptuous dress of the guests, it was being held in the Governor's Palace, where I had been before. A large company of musicians played diligently and the masquers were also diligent in their drinking and dancing, swirling about in the light of thousands of candles in the huge prismed chandeliers. Several masked people smilingly greeted me by name as they passed by. A lady nearby, standing alone, eyed me, fluttered her fan and gave me a faint smile of invitation. The exposed portion of her face around the mask seemed pretty. On the petite side, she had an interesting bust, though it was disappointingly covered by a modest neckline. Her face and neck were liberally covered with fashionable white lead. Stepping to her, I bowed and asked, "May I have the pleasure, madam?"

She nodded and we joined the dancers. My equilibrium was good despite the drink and my partner was graceful. I decided I would have her, and when the music for the dance ended, I said, "Will you take the fresh air with me on the balcony?" Wordlessly she took my arm and on the outside balcony where three or four other couples were billing and cooing I went directly to the point. "If you'll part from your escort, madam, and come with me, I promise you a merrier dance."

She whispered, "You are my escort, sir, and I'll hold you to the promise." Standing close, her hand touched my breeches front. "La!" she murmured. "The dance will be merry indeed with that, sir. Let us hurry away!"

But my blood had congealed with shock. The murmur

108

was gray. Unbelieving, I reached and tore the mask away. In the light from the ballroom, Lord Beauvior's painted face smiled at me and said, "Darling Jamie, I thought you'd never arrive. Am I not lovely tonight for you? Let us go quickly to our merry dance and we shall dance all the way back to London, my sweet boy."

Paint and a stuffed bosom! Had it not been for the messy white lead I would have kissed the supposed woman on arriving out on the balcony. Revulsion brought nausea and I struggled against vomiting. I found my voice. "You horrible bastard. You obscene shit! I've a mind to break your filthy neck!"

He cackled a crone's giggle and as he reached to embrace me I turned and fled from the Governor's Palace and, neither knowing nor caring if my carriage had brought me, strode as fast as I could to the bawdy house, my head filled with confused thoughts of murder, suicide and overwhelming revulsion toward myself. Later, in the arms of my naked half-caste when my thinking processes became more orderly, I conjectured that Beauvoir had somehow arranged the incident, carefully planned it. Though I grimly explored the possibilities of murdering him, common sense told me that he never left things to chance and I would never get away with it. It had been fortunate that his lust had driven him to speak, for otherwise if I had reached under the skirt and found male instead of female organs I would have surely slain him on the spot.

It was all Anne's fault. If she had not driven me to such swinish drunkenness I never would have been in such a filthy predicament. She had poisoned my life, made it intolerable, sending me to the depths of degradation, while she floated about like some inhumanly chaste goddess far above me, smugly pure and untouchably beautiful. The idea took root. She had humiliated me, made me sick with self-revulsion. I would turn the tables on her. I would strip and mount that flawless body, savagely invade it and pour into it the seething accumulation of bitter acid that was destroying me and make her share my humiliation and self-disgust.

My pocket watch showed half past two in the morning. I got out of bed and dressed quickly and, oblivious to the pleas of the whore, left the house and headed for home, half drunk and raging with anticipation. The house was dark and quiet when I let myself in. In my bedchamber I stripped, donned a robe and went to Anne's door, which I opened stealthily, but I was momentarily taken aback by the sight of her sitting up in bed, a lighted candle on the bedside table, her eyes dark pools, watching me. She wore a white silk bed gown, low-cut and sleeveless for the warm summer night. The red-gold hair, uncaught, tumbled in gleaming, lustrous waves to her creamy shoulders and framed her lovely face. I walked to the side of the bed and looked down at her as she returned my gaze, her face expressionless. "You're too bloody perfect and I'm going to flaw you," I said. I could see her sweet breasts. The glimpse of her body and anticipation of my imminent insane action caused Old Nick to rise. "I'm going to humanize you."

"I think we should talk, Jamie," she said.

The calmness of her voice made my anger flame. "There's been too much talk, especially yours!" I ripped the sheet off her. "Pull off that gown, quickly!"

In the candlelight the eyes were dark jade green and they regarded me for a moment, then she removed her bed gown in silence. The blinding magnificence of her whitely gleaming nakedness shook me. Even her pubic hair was beautiful, a warm chestnut color nestling between two perfect thighs. The aureola of her nipples were delicately pink. I had an impulse to fall on my knees and pray forgiveness, then flee, but mad perversity drove me on. I dropped off my robe and pushed stiff Old Nick at her face, saying, "This is what a man is! A human man! Kiss him!"

She leaned forward and I felt the touch of cool lips. She looked up and said, " 'Tis a strange, powerful-looking thing."

I had planned for panic, fear and revulsion, and there was only the rich cool crystal of her voice. "Lie down and spread your legs," I ordered, and as she obediently did I climbed onto her, settled between those marvelous thighs and rested my upper body on my elbows, feeling Old Nick nuzzling against the hair.

"Should I do something?" she asked.

"Guide my pizzle into you!" I growled.

Her fingers grasped Old Nick and I felt his nose touch softness. There was no expression on her face but a sort of blank absorption in the task I had given her. Old Nick probed the entrance, her hand still on him, and I started the victorious impalement thrust with my hips, but her eyes, a couple of inches from mine, were huge dark pools

110

of surprise and she murmured, "Jamie, I think something has happened down there."

Awareness burst over me like a flood. Instead of a mighty battering engine of her humiliation, Old Nick had become nothing but a lump of flaccid flesh ineffectively touching her crotch. I disintegrated inside, and great sobs wrenched out of me, tears poured from my eyes, dropping onto her face. Stroking my cheek, she whispered, "I'm sorry, Jamie."

I rolled off her, trying to control my outrageous self-pity and, doing a poor job of it, donned my robe. She reached out and caught my hand, drew me back toward the bed and covered herself with the sheet as she said, "Stay a bit. Neither of us will sleep for a while. Sit down."

Wanting to run from those merciless green eyes, I obeyed and muttered, "Now I've really done the unforgivable."

"No, only if you'd finished," she said, "and then 'twould be your own unforgiving of yourself. As it is, no harm was done and maybe some good. I told you 'twould be like a tree, Jaimie."

I forced myself to look at her. "You were lying here waiting for me."

She nodded. "I've been doing that often lately. Do you think I haven't been watching you, feeling your unhappiness and knowing where it was aimed and that sooner or later the storm would come. But why did you speak of making me human? Before God, Jamie, I'm the most human woman who ever was! I'm a virgin who's never seen a man's thing all swelled like that, let alone touched one, and I have no desire to be raped or scrooned before marriage, but there was excitement and desire in me just now despite the poor way of it! But I knew 'twas not to be, for I'm never to be taken without the giving."

I said dully from the ashes of my shame, "I thought to hurt you, degrade you, and succeeded only in doing it to myself. Never have I gone limp with a woman before. Never have I not wanted to have an attractive woman before. Never have I been such a scurvy, cowardly dog before, drunken and vicious. You make me furious, yet when you're no longer in my sight I feel empty and abandoned. Anne, for God's sake, tell me what's happening to me!"

The sheet had fallen to expose one exquisite breast but

111

neither she nor I cared. "That I cannot tell you, Jamie, for 'tis for you to find out as you go your ways. If I knew and did tell you, 'twould be for no good, not now. After you've come to the woman you'll wed, who waits for you now though she doesn't know it, you'll find some answers."

"Have you seen that woman in your sighting?" I asked.

She hesitated, then answered, "I've seen her. Earlier, before you came here tonight, I drowsed a bit and dreamed of you and her. She's—no, I'll say no more, save that you and she will love each other dearly."

"It wasn't you by any chance?" I asked.

"No," she said slowly, "not by any chance at all, Jamie." Her eyebrows knitted. "Damn you for a stubborn loon, worrying over you will be near the death of me before I find the man who's to be my only lover!"

"I guess we're friends again if you can curse me," I smiled.

"We were never nor will we ever be anything less," she declared.

Glancing at the lovely bare breast, I joked, "Then maybe we should have another try at unfinished business."

"Stupid, stupid idiot!" she flared angrily, and pulled the sheet over her head. Her muffled voice exclaimed, "Go away before I throw a chair at you or rouse the house, you . . . you goddamned dim-witted clown!"

Getting up and feeling better, I said softly, "Thank you and good-night, Anne."

From under the sheet her voice said faintly, "Good-night, Jamie, and God bless you."

It was only when I snuggled down in my own bed that I realized that her benediction was sobbed. Anne had been weeping under that sheet. And well she might I told myself bitterly in self-disgust, after the terrible thing I had done to her.

But in the morning as I, first up in the household that morning, sat eating breakfast, she came into the dining room to have hers and said cheerily, "Good-morning, Jamie. Did you sleep well?"

"No dreams of coupling corpses," I answered, adoring her. "How can you be so beautiful fresh out of bed?"

"You need spectacles," she answered. "My eyes are baggy. Jamie, will you ride again with me? Hector's too lazy to get up anymore."

I laughed. "Only if you promise not to throw chairs at me."

Hector bustled in, dressed and shaved, a far cry from his London habit of sleeping until noon. "Well, well! A stranger at the table! Clear-eyed, combed and smiling. What wonder is this? Decided the human race couldn't get along without you, eh, Jamie?" He grinned at his sister. "God, you're the loveliest marvel of the seven worlds, Anne! Why am I your brother? The glorious sight of you gives rise to mad thoughts."

Her smile to him was dazzling. "I had a wonderful dream last night. A dear friend I love came home again."

He stared at her for a second, then cocked a bushy red eyebrow at me. "And high time, too. What caused this pleasant miracle, or shouldn't I ask?"

"You shouldn't, you blabbering Caledonian quack," I said.

Bursting into laughter, he slapped my shoulder. "That's our old Jamie! I won't ask, then! But I know damned well my clever witch sister had a share of working the magic. Welcome back, Jamie, and God love you. Oh, what a perfectly splendid day! Anne, I warn you: I intend to get lovably drunk at your garden party this afternoon and lovably insult your Redcoat Sassenach guests and as in fond days of yore my fellow Scot, one generation removed, will enthusiastically help me."

Spreading a muffin with currant jelly, Anne said, " 'Tisn't a real garden party, 'tis just a few of the garrison officers in for drinks and talk, boys for whom my calendar for going out with had no room and I want to make it up to them. If Jamie will be there 'twill be a special day indeed."

Her eyes raised to mine and once again I sensed that something important was being said. Relations had definitely been changed between us, but exactly how I was not sure except there was an absence of tension in me and I felt a pleasant warmth. "What better way to spend Sunday afternoon than by watching you?" I asked. "Will the day be special enough that I may expect a smile from you, Anne?"

I saw the faint moving shadows in the green depths. "It will be special, this Sunday afternoon," she said, then her gaze broke away and she went to bantering with Hector about his lie-abed slothfulness on riding mornings and in-

113

formed him that he need bother no longer, for I was to be her companion again.

The afternoon in the garden was one of those bright, clear, still and warm times when every object is sharply defined, colors are intense and sound carries far in the tranquil air. Ira had come home from one of his short Army freight-hauling cruises up the Long Island coast, the *Bonny Anne* having been chartered for that purpose now, and he and Hector lounged with me on the grass, drinking rum punch cooled with last winter's Hudson River ice as we watched Anne, sitting on the marble bench, laughing and chaffing with five young Army officers. She wore her lovely green gown, and with the brilliant scarlet coats of the soldiers in the sun-dappled shade, the scene was delightfully colorful. In all the shades of green of her gown and foliage behind and above her, her beautiful face and glorious red-gold hair seemed suspended in a mystic cavern of a dreamworld.

Lieutenant Colonel Campbell, splendid in his kilted Highlander regimentals, came striding around the corner of the house to where I was, and said, smiling appreciatively toward Anne, "Good-day, Jamie, gentlemen. I seem to have intruded on a party reigned over by the Queen of Elfland."

"A new way of getting drunk," I explained. "We take a drink, then look at her and get the effect of another. See your young men sprawled at her feet, casualties all."

Bowing to Anne, he called, "Good-day, Miss MacDonald! I call quarter! Your beauty is destroying the Army!"

" 'Tis they who are destroying me," she answered, smiling. "Spoiling me rotten, the rogues. Save me, I beg, sir!"

"Too late, too late," he grinned. "Your magic has robbed me of the strength to order retreat." He turned to me and said, "I've only a minute. I'm slaving away down to headquarters. Couldn't even spare the time for church. There's a matter I'd like to discuss privately with you tomorrow. I'll buy you a cracking good dinner at Fraunce's, eh?"

"Delighted, Archie," I said. "Any dinner at Fraunce's is good. About noon?

Nodding, he said, "At twelve. Don't be late, old boy." Then he bowed his farewells and left as quickly as he had appeared.

Hector said lazily, "I could learn to like that lad, even with his name."

114

"Hear tell," murmured Ira, "them fellers is nekkid under the kilts. Drafty in winter time, ain't it?"

Hector launched into a lecture on Highland dress and I watched Anne with a sudden rising excitement as the idea sparked and caught alight. That was it. I'd been a blind fool. It was as an artist her beauty had enthralled me and I had confused it with simple sexual attraction. Instead of raping her to get her out of my system, I had to paint her —immediately, as she was right now. I sat up from my lounging position and stared at her, weighing shapes, tonal values and hues, assembling the composition in my mind, seeing the final result, a nearly life-size portrait of her in that leafy, sun-dappled grotto under the trees. Her face turned to me, looking at me over the heads of her coterie of admirers, and regarded me intently. Then she said to the officers, "Excuse me, gentlemen. Mr. Reid has need of me." She got to her feet and called to me, "I think 'tis time, Jamie."

One hand came to her breast and she took a graceful, hipshot pose. It was exactly as I had wanted it. The exquisite beauty sent a sharp thrill clear down to my groin, and I cried, "The bonnet with the plumes!"

"I know," she said. "Have it fetched when you get your painting things."

I heard Hector say, "Damme, I remember—the first day she was here, she said it."

"A body'd best pay attention when she says what she says," murmured Ira.

The officer guests, though I paid them scant notice in my exuberance, regarded the preparations for the impromptu portraiture with fascinated interest. Fortunately, I had on hand a stretched canvas of the right proportions already primed and stained with my favorite ground color and as soon as my easel was set up with the canvas on it, I said to Anne, "I won't be doing the expression on your face for some time but you must wear it from the start so it weaves through the picture and no matter what has been said about it, I want no smile on your outside now, rather a reflection of inward joy if you can feel it. Do you understand?"

She nodded, her face grave. "A wee dreaming and maybe seeing." She took the pose, fixed her vision on me, and in a moment I saw her gaze was fixed on infinity, looking through and beyond me. With no smile on her face, a

115

radiance of dreaming ecstasy seemed to surround her like an aura and I felt the impact of breathless happiness coming from her, then a nearly overwhelming sensation of joyous sensuality that gripped my loins. It was as if she were telling me: *the beauty of my face and body is matched by the strength of my love and passion for the man to whom I will give myself like this.* The officers, who had moved to one side apart from her, and Hector and Ira, watching her silently, saw only a remarkably beautiful girl posing, I knew, and were not included in the message from her. This was the real Anne MacDonald, demanding that I paint the subtle but seething fire she promised her future lover.

I flung myself at the canvas, furiously scrubbing in pigment, slathering, scraping, wiping out, using both hands, losing myself in a world that contained only the two of us, frantically covering the surface in my eagerness to finally come to that marvelous dreaming promise on her face. When the large shapes had taken general form in the composition I told her to take a few minutes of rest and it took her a few moments to return from where she had been. The eyes came into focus and once again she was the gracious hostess to her guests as one of them presented her with a glass of wine, saying with a smile, "I have found you out, Your Majesty."

Accepting the wine, she gave him a slow smile. "Ah, have you now? I thought my secret was safe." It crossed my mind that she was aware of what she had exhibited of herself in the pose and was concerned that anybody other than the artist had seen it.

"You didn't keep it safe from Thomas the Rhymer of Ercildoun," he grinned, "after he mistook you for the Queen of Heaven when you appeared to him on Huntly Bank on your horse whose mane was hung with fifty silver bells and nine. If I may kiss your lips you may bear me off to your Elfland where I'll gladly stay for seven years."

Her crystal laughter pealed. "Oh, my soul! My dear sir, that bonny ferny road is not for a soldier of the King! Think of the promotions and glory you'd miss during those seven years!"

The conversation became general on the subject, which was the ancient Scottish ballad she had sung on the night of the ship launching and which had sent me into a fit of insane rage, but now I experienced nothing but supreme joy in the sudden recognition that it was as that I had

116

envisioned her for my painting: the Queen of Elfland, beautiful, wise and mysterious, caught casting a spell while posing for a normal portrait.

When she resumed the pose and went into her dreaming again, I went to painting the lovely green gown, my brushes guided by the memory of that peerless body which lay beneath the cloth, and as they stroked the canvas it was as if they were my fingers caressing the creamy soft flesh. The conviction grew. I was making love to her just as surely as if we were physically joined. My pounding heart, my hard breathing and soaring excitement were not all due to the vigor of my work. The green eyes, looking at me yet not seeing me, told me she knew what was happening and deep inside she was responding, giving herself up to me in an invisible frenzy of delight. My painting was automatic, proceeding without conscious awareness as my mind reached out to her, holding her, kissing her, adoring her, having her. She rested occasionally, but I continued to paint during the intervals, maintaining my high passion which steadily mounted until the painted face on the canvas, beautiful and complete, gasped through parted lips, "Ah, Jamie, Jamie, no more, no more!"

I dizzily emerged from that delirious world to realize the real Anne had said it and she was sitting on the marble bench breathing hard with an air of exhaustion as she watched me with huge eyes. The sun was near setting and the Redcoats had departed. There was a clammy wetness in my breeches and with some embarrassment I knew what had happened; I was glad I wore my painting smock to cover the dark stain on my front. It had been a mating in more sense than symbolism. Clearing my throat, I said, "Thank you, Anne."

She rose and came to stand beside me in front of the easel, her breathing still fast, and looking at the painting said, " 'Tis like a looking glass. You've put in the beauty I was seeing and feeling, Jamie. You call me a witch. You're a magician!"

Inspecting the picture myself, I was astonished, for it isn't easy to complete a nearly life-size portrait in one sitting of about three hours. It was done and it was a truly beautiful job of work. My furious brushwork, slashing and slicing, made it a confused jumble at close range, but from six or more feet away the Queen of Elfland in her ferny grotto, marvelously beautiful, regarded the viewer with fathomless green eyes that cast a spell of delicious unknown promise.

Hector commented, "By God, Jamie, you are! You've caught the bonny witch red-handed at casting her spells!"

"If she was ever to look on me like that," commented Ira, "I'd leave home and mother and never let her out o' my sight. Jamie, 'twas some interestin' watchin' ye do that. Ye done a fair day's work there." He looked me over. "Noticed ye was kind of out o' breath and don't wonder. You're sweatin' like a horse."

I laughed, pleased with myself and exhilarated. I felt somehow freed of a heavy burden. "Now you've seen how I get my exercise. Anne, will you accept it as my gift of thanks for the pleasure it gave me in the painting of it? Perhaps the man you'll marry will like it."

She raised her face to mine and in her eyes I saw clear awareness of what had happened to me. "Thank you, Jamie. The giving was both ways. Whenever I look at it I'll remember the joy of this happy afternoon."

That night at supper I found I could accept without resentment her lack of smiling at me. The strange coupling that afternoon had purged me of something in a way that no rape might have done. I regarded her with tranquil friendliness, reflecting that I must never again make the mistake of interpreting the artist's compulsion with that of my churning masculinity. Nevertheless, the sight and sound of her beauty still enthralled me and I suspected that this new calmness was comparable to the post-copulation contented lassitude that the French aptly call "the little death" and my former furor would soon return to create another crisis between us.

Chapter VIII

AT THE FOOT of the steps in front of the three-story brick Queen's Head tavern on Broadway, popularly called by the name of the genial host, Mr. Fraunce, a curious apparition blocked my path, a short, scrawny Redcoat whose Brown Bess Tower musket was nearly as long as himself. Blinking nearsighted eyes at me, he said uncertainly, "Nah then, sir, 'old up. 'Ave you go' a pass, sir?"

"Since when do I need an Army pass to go in here?" I demanded.

"Harmy hoffices it is nah, sir," he answered apologetically. "Hit tykes a pass to pass." He grinned, showing a gap in his teeth. " 'Les you're a lass for a glass or a bloody—' "

"I haven't got a pass," I said impatiently. "Lieutenant Colonel Campbell is expecting me for dinner."

"Can't 'elp it, sir," said the sentry. "Hif you was to be tearin' a bloater wif 'is Majesty 'imself you'd not get by wivvout a bloody pass, 's'truth, sir."

"Call somebody with whom I may speak, then," I told him. "You do have a superior officer or somebody, don't you?"

He was apprehensive. "I'll catch bloody damn all 'ell if I 'oller for the cawpril, sir. Cor stone the crows, sir, 'e's got a bloody sharp tongue, 'e 'as, sir, and that's a bloody fact, sir. One time 'e says to me, 'e says—"

"For God's sake, stop yapping and call him!" I exclaimed. "I have an appointment!"

He blinked at me, then threw back his head and bawled, "Cawpril o' the guard! Post Number One!"

A burly noncommissioned officer emerged from the front door, glared down at us and barked, "Filkins, what's the bloody row this time?"

"I'm the row, Corporal," I said. "My name is Reid and I

119

have an appointment with Lieutenant Colonel Campbell in this fortress, and I don't have a passport or whatever the hell is needed."

"Right you are, sir," he responded heartily. "Got it right down in my orders of the day. Filkins, you flamin' prick o' misery, I told you—"

The sentry blanched, wincing, and I said, "He was only doing his duty. Now if you'll be so kind . . ." I went up the steps and entered the tavern.

The corporal, following me, said, "That bloody Filkins, a man's got a right to be stupid but he abuses the privilege. If we wasn't so short rank and file he'd be back where he belongs in the regimental stables shovelin' regulation horse-shit into regulation piles. Disgrace to the Colors, he is. The colonel'll be up them stairs, sir, first door to the right."

It was a good-sized room in which I had eaten and drunk several times before on festive occasions. Now it had a severe martial appearance with maps pinned to the walls and a long businesslike table surrounded by a number of chairs. Campbell greeted me and ushered me to a dining table near the windows, and I was no sooner seated when a soldier entered, pushing a tea cart bearing our dinner. As the soldier served us, I said to Campbell, "This kind of Army occupation will go down hard with Fraunce's regular guests. Whatever made you people do it?"

"Circumstance and necessity," he smiled, pouring the wine, "the twin handmaidens to Mars. New York will be crowded even more when General Clinton's headquarters and regiments arrive from Philadelphia one of these days."

"Ah," I said, "I'd heard that rumor. Then you are giving up Philadelphia to the rebels after all. Is that the doing of the Royal Peace Commission?"

"It has nothing whatsoever to do with peace, old boy," he said. "On the contrary. We've got a few interesting irons in the fire. Why else did you think I was with my nose to the grindstone yesterday, on the Lord's Day?"

I eyed him suspiciously. "You have the look of a canary digesting a cat and I have a fee-fi-fo-fum feeling. This whole business is odd. Why aren't we in your regimental officers' mess as before?"

"Don't be shy with the claret, Jamie," he encouraged. "This joint of beef is exactly right, isn't it, rich crust outside and running with gore inside. We kept Fraunce and his staff of cooks on, you know."

"You," I declared, "are hiding. Come out, wherever you are, Archie, and answer up. There's more to this than meets the eye. Why am I here, apart from the pleasure of my sparkling company?"

"The last is always enjoyable and if you accept our little proposal it will be sorely missed for a space of time," he said seriously, "but your friends' loss will be our King's gain, Jamie. Frankly, there's a job of work needs doing and it's been recommended that you're the laddie who can bring it off. I heartily agree."

"What in God's name are you talking about?" I asked.

"Some months ago General Clinton received certain instructions from Whitehall," he answered. "If I remember correctly, you came along with 'em in the *Jason* and we're all thankful they didn't fall into enemy hands. We're going to launch some new campaigns, Jamie, and certain preparatory work must be done to insure success. We need your help in that."

"You're daft," I said. "I know nothing of soldiering and less of politics."

"Your occupation and ignorance of those things," he told me, "are your best qualifications. The less you know, the less you'll be suspected."

"Jesus!" I exclaimed, taken aback. "You're talking of spying?"

"We prefer to call it field observation intelligence," he replied wryly. "Some of your other qualifications are your loyalty, proved courage, good health and a fair set of brains, Jamie."

"Who the devil recommended me for such absurd nonsense?" I demanded.

"Your friend Lord Beauvoir," he answered calmly. "I'm told he has a heavy official interest in the political aspects of the planning apart from his membership on the Peace Commission. Knowing you, I saw his point and agreed—I say, Jamie, what are you—"

I brought my fist down on the table, raging. "That little son of a bitch is no friend of mine! Find yourself another idiot! I'll have nothing to do with anything that man's a part of, aside from the insanity of it!"

Campbell, raising his eyebrows, said blandly, "I have a definite opinion of him, too, which under the circumstances I shall not divulge. For the sake of the Crown, I ask you to withhold final decision until you learn what is involved.

121

Listening will not commit you. You're not being pressed, forcibly 'listed. The work is essential to victory and will take but a few weeks. Will you listen?"

It would be interesting to find out what grand plans were in the offing and rather than run the risk of offending Campbell with nothing more than an emotional rejection of the proposal first crack out of the bag, it would be better to hear him out and then give the unqualified refusal as any intelligent man would do. "I will, but 'tis a waste of time, Archie."

"There's a conference after dinner," he told me, "and you'll meet some of the others who will be associated with you. I'll rely on your good sense to keep these discussions secret. Have more oyster and orange dressing; you'd never get anything like that in my regimental mess. Well, look you: I'll give you the general picture. The new campaigns, to be started this winter, will be aimed at splitting off the southern colonies from the northern provinces. General Augustine Prevost, commanding in East Florida, will ram up into Georgia. At the same time an expedition from New York will strike at Savannah. When that province is recovered and established as a base for operations, the provinces northward will be successively reduced."

"That's a big bowl of chowder," I commented. " 'Twill take a lot of soldiers to do that and at the same time hold what you have here, and with France at war you're not likely to get many more troops from over the water because Great Britain itself must be defended. I think you're biting off more than you can chew. When the news gets out, American Loyalists will despair even more than they do now."

He gave me a keen look. "You've hit the nail on the head, Jamie. Military strength is our chief problem. However, Whitehall has finally seen the light and now knows that the job cannot be done without marshaling the power of the Loyalists who are able and willing to bear arms for the King. Our best soldiers will be used for storming and assaults and there won't be enough of 'em for sustained campaigns in the field unless they have reserves and support. Rear bases must be maintained and defended, too."

"Right," I agreed. "I want to be kept safe here in New York against rebel incursions."

"When you return from Georgia," he smiled, "so shall you be, and honored by a grateful Crown. The ultimate de-

122

cision to execute the plans will be largely dependent on your findings, Jamie."

"I'm trying not to laugh," I informed him. "Great God, my gardener would be better fitted for this than I am! I'm nothing but a portraitist, man! And not to boast, but a rather well-known one. The rebels down there would hang me out of hand!"

" 'Tis the end of the world as far as you're concerned," he assured me. "The land is more than half wild, primeval, and the folk remote from the capitals of the world. You'll be equipped with a false identity and forged papers. As for the political adherence of the people, we have reason to believe that most of them are Loyalists. The other rebel provinces had to threaten blockade and sanctions against Georgia to dragoon it into the confederacy. I doubt you'll be hanged unless you openly invite it."

After dinner we moved to the large table and Campbell sent the soldier-waiter to inform the others it was time for the meeting. Two officers came in after a few minutes, a Regular major named Mark Prevost, representing his older brother, General Prevost, and wiry sun-browned fellow named Captain Hugh Wallbrook of an Irregular Loyalist regiment called Browne's East Florida Rangers. As the introductions were finished, Lord Beauvoir drifted in, a gray delicate cloud, smiled icily all around, and took a seat. "Good-day, Mr. Reid," he rustled. "Such a pity you were unable to remain to the end of the Governor's rout when we last met."

"I found the smell unpleasant, my lord," I answered stiffly.

"Lord Beauvoir, gentlemen," said Campbell, "Mr. Reid has not yet accepted the assignment. He withholds decision until the whole proposal is known to him."

Prevost nodded. "Sensible. So would I."

"I'm confident that he will accept," murmured Beauvoir's gray voice, "when he becomes aware of what is at stake and the unpleasant alternatives." A twist of the screw.

Wallbrook said nothing, his face impassive and dark brown eyes studying me. He wore a green coatee with red cuffs, collar and facings, white deerskin breeches and black riding boots, and had a ruthless look about him. I wouldn't desire him for an enemy. Campbell droned over the bare bones of the project. I would be taken to Georgia in disguise, and using my artist's occupation as a means for get-

123

ting about, would make an evaluation of the Loyalists, noting their degree of adherence to the Crown. It would take me through the late summer and early fall, and then I would be withdrawn and returned to New York. The Rangers had made a similar appraisal by numbers, but it was believed that I could acquire a more accurate account because, unlike the Rangers who were native to the region, I was by my manner and speech a clear indication to Loyalists that London meant business this time. In other words, I was also to be a symbol of hope to despairing people.

The projected campaigns were to be launched in late fall and early winter, Prevost moving up into Georgia in November and the Savannah expedition leaving New York in October in a loosely coordinated joint operation. Campbell would command the troops from New York and hoped to reach Savannah, weather permitting, early in December. There would be other Crown agents scattered through Georgia and South Carolina and all their reports had to be complete by the middle of September, when they would be collected by East Florida Rangers for delivery to General Prevost.

Campbell moved to a wall map and circled an area with a forefinger. "This region is crucial, Mr. Reid, and it will be yours if you undertake this task. The line between Savannah and Augusta will be our base line, you see, and your section of evaluation will be between Briar Creek bridge, here, and Augusta, here, along the Post Road."

Going to the map, I peered at the indicated area. Plantations, farms, hostels and mills were shown by the names of the owners. I saw the three described by Anne: Jenks, MacDonald and Ogilvie and had a queer feeling of being nudged by some invisible force. "That place is owned by Mr. Angus MacDonald of MacDonald Company," I remarked.

Beauvoir's whispery voice murmured, "Ah, better and better. It should be a most comfortable dwelling, Mr. Reid, eh? Has your beautiful houseguest said that it is free of . . . er . . . rebel encumbrance, confiscation?"

Wallbrook sat up alertly and exclaimed, "Beautiful houseguest! Mr. Reid, would that be Anne MacDonald?"

"It would and is," I answered. "Her half brother and I share a house here and she's living with us. D'you know her?"

His lean grim face split in a grin. "Man, I know everybody in that region and who there doesn't know bonny Anne! I've knowed her since she was no higher'n a chigger's knee! We been a sight worried since Peter Ogilvie loaded her out for Charles Town. By Jesus, I got to see her!"

Campbell said, "Sorry, Captain. There won't be time, for you and Major Prevost will be away for St. Augustine on the evening tide tonight."

"Oh, hell," grumbled Wallbrook. "Well, will you give her my greetings, Mr. Reid? Tell her Goodowns is in good shape and Brutus is handlin' it real well. The place ain't been taken up by the rebels yet on account of Abraham Jenks; he's still after it, tryin' to take it some easy way. Old Angus ain't been named as an enemy Loyalist so far. Lordy, I'd like to see that gal!"

"I'll deliver your message, Captain," I told him.

"Better that you should not at this time, Mr. Reid," said Beauvoir silkily. "This meeting is confidential and the presence of this . . . ah . . . partisan gentleman in New York must be kept secret. My information sources indicate there are nearly as many rebel spies in this town as there are foot soldiers in Washington's gaggle of bandits. However, Colonel Campbell, my thought in connection with the MacDonald estate is that, it being more or less central to Mr. Reid's zone of responsibility, it would provide him with a comfortable lodging during his sojourn in that rude wilderness.

"Have your clever penman include an authority from the Continental Congress for Mr. Reid to occupy it, and since the redoubtable Doctor Franklin has been ever interested in sharp land dealings, indicate in the Franklin document that he has been given an option to purchase the holding by Mr. Angus MacDonald; that should deter that . . . ah . . . Jenks fellow from pursuing his greed in that direction, if I understand the situation correctly. I happen to know that Franklin is interested in acquiring some lands owned by distressed Loyalists throughout the colonies here.

"In order that Mr. MacDonald not be surprised to learn through advices from friends that he may sell his estate in Georgia to an enemy of the King, when I return to London I shall personally inform him of this arrangement. Unless, of course, Mr. Reid declines the task being offered him and wishes to return to London with me, which he may do rather than risk his neck in various ways." His glacial smile was for me alone, as was the implied threat. He was show-

125

ing me his power and once again enticing me away from danger for his own purpose. The entire business, based on his recommendation of me for the job, was arranged to bring me to heel. He had gambled that I would refuse the prospect of hardship, danger and possible hanging for a spy, and might conceivably surrender.

I said to Campbell, "What of the documents His Lordship just mentioned? Are they to be my passports?"

"They are," he nodded, and went on to explain. As Robert Allston, my birthplace was Boston—as it was in truth—but my artist's training was obtained in France where I continued to work and live. When I painted Franklin's portrait in his house at Passy, he was much taken by my skill and patriotic rebel fervor. He then conceived the notion of my painting thirteen great canvasses, one for each of the rebellious provinces, depicting something typical of them at the time of the new nation's birth. He then submitted the idea to the Congress with the urging that the resulting pictures become a national treasure, a patriotic shrine, and that Congress underwrite the plan. Not surprisingly, a forged approval was executed by the British Army penman, directing me to return from France and commence the work immediately, starting my field work in the south and working northward, enjoining all loyal citizens to give me assistance. I was also exempted from military conscription into the Continental Army.

It was a magnificent concept. My blood stirred. Why stop at the mere thirteen provinces? Why not paint the entire marvelous continent, from Hudson's Bay to Mexico, from the Atlantic to the Pacific? America's plains, mountains, rivers, Indians, beasts, birds, endless forests—'twas my country as much as it was the rebels'. America needed artists. There should be an American Academy of Art. Graduates would fan out across the land into the wilderness with brush and pencil, and the Academy would be mine. The mammoth, fascinating task became real in my mind, not a spurious tool for a skulking spy. It was that which decided me, reinforced by the desire to once again flout Beauvoir and the need to get away from the bewildering presence of Anne MacDonald. I said to Campbell, "I'll do it."

"Good lad," he commented, unsurprised, but with a trace of a smile around his mouth, and I knew then that the historical paintings had been his clever idea to ensnare me. I decided to never again underestimate the imagination of that officer. "Then we'll begin your preparation tomorrow."

Beauvoir, unsmiling, said, "If you have reservations, Mr. Reid, I strongly suggest you not undertake the work. I'm sure another chap may be found here. It might be better not to commit yourself, all things considered, and return to London in my ship. His Majesty, as you know, has certain opinions regarding your activities."

"I have no reservations, my lord," I answered, "and as far as His Majesty is concerned, I hardly think he can object to a subject accepting an important service to him. Colonel, what of these preparations?"

"We can't run any risks of your being caught up in some small slip," he told me. "Your region is fairly well populated and some of the residents, I understand, are educated men, so you must receive a grounding with reference to your French background, the political and real geography of Georgia and so forth. You'll report here each afternoon for that purpose and be prepared to depart New York secretly in about a fortnight. Needless to say, you must discuss this with no person beyond these walls, not even with your closest friends. To explain your daily visits here you might tell them you've been engaged to take the portraits of high ranking officers here."

Major Prevost said to me, "If things should take a dicey turn for you on station down there, run for the Florida line and make your way to St. Augustine where our headquarters are. And I think you should bear in mind that all the while you will be under the command of General Prevost much as though you were an officer of the Army."

"Rangers'll be lookin' in on you now and then," added Wallbrook, "includin' me. If the dicey turn comes on real dicey, we'll get you out. And while I got the floor I want to say that we been in there steady since the troubles started and Colonel Browne's give the general straight figures on what you're goin' to do all over again." He looked disapprovingly at Campbell.

Major Prevost said to Wallbrook, "We're familiar with Colonel Browne's work and his opinions on the subject, Hugh. You heard what Colonel Campbell told Mr. Reid at the outset of this discussion, why an outsider is being sent in there. The efforts of your Rangers are not being belittled."

"They most certainly are not," agreed Campbell. "The

Rangers have our great respect as does Colonel Browne. Gentlemen, unless you have further business on this subject, I think we can adjourn." To me, he said, "Stay a moment. I have something personal to discuss with you."

Beauvoir, cold and unsmiling, bowed, murmuring, "Should you change your mind, Mr. Reid, please send a note to my house, otherwise I wish you every success and an eventual safe return to London." He wafted out the door without waiting for a reply.

Prevost and Wallbrook shook hands with me, wishing me well and promising all aid to me during my mission, and after they left Campbell said to me, "It isn't personal at all, Jamie. The matter is too secret to mention even in front of trusted men from that part of the world, because it concerns the identity of a gentleman in most sensitive circumstances in Savannah. To begin with, you will have another task, that of rendering Savannah as defenseless as possible at the time of my attack."

"Oh, for Christ's sake, Archie!" I exclaimed. "Isn't that piling it on too rich? Who the hell do you think I am—Joshua? And Savannah, Jericho? Enough is enough!"

"Patience, patience," he smiled. "The fact is, as you pointed out earlier, my expedition will be necessarily rather small, perhaps a brigade of about three thousand men. To have a chance of success in a ship-to-shore assault on a contested objective, the assault force must outnumber the defenders by at least three to one. The attackers are completely vulnerable, you see, during the transit to shore and prior to forming up. Our latest advices show the enemy's nearest sizable force in an army at Fort Sunbury, some miles well south of Savannah, commanded by a fellow named Robert Howe. I want him to stay there and be there when I strike at Savannah in December. Now, at Savannah is a man named Alexander Cameron. He's a most influential chap—leading member of the Legislature, wheelhorse of the State Safety Council, magistrate and God knows what else. Here's the secret, if there is one: Governor Wright has told Lord Germain privately that Cameron was one of his most loyal supporters as a member of the Royal Council, and Wright has reason to believe that Cameron is still loyal despite his elevated rebel status. You'll be taking your life in your hands, but you must somehow approach him, and if he proves the governor's opinion of him, put him to the job of keeping Howe at Sunbury for me."

"Archie," I said, "there are limits even to my idiocy. I won't agree to do that, my friend."

Campbell's face became flinty. "As Beauvoir said, you may back out if you like, but if you're in this you'll obey orders, and this is one of your orders. Your two jobs, the head count and this, are vital to the entire scheme of the southern campaigns. Without Loyalist support and without a chance of taking Savannah, we might as well pack up the lot and leave America to Washington. I don't expect you to march in on Cameron, identify yourself and give him his instructions. I expect you to approach him warily, intelligently, without giving yourself away unless you are completely assured he is our man. Spend a bit of time at Savannah before you go up to the backcountry. You might take a few likenesses to establish your credentials. Try that out on Cameron and in the course of it you might find out where his real sympathies lie; you're a glib fellow when you're at your easel. If you hadn't painted my portrait for my wife I wouldn't be one of your friends."

I laughed. "And I wouldn't be here, mixed up in this mad affair. All right, I'll give Cameron a try, but remember I'm no hero and don't be surprised if it comes to nothing because of my timidity."

"Timidity?" he snorted. "Oh the contrary, if I know you, it may come to nothing because of your rashness. Jamie, in that occupation rashness is fatal. Go warily. Weigh every move with great caution. And whatever you do, do not become personally involved. Objectivity is the watchword for you. If your security is threatened, and by that I mean the Crown, you must be prepared to take either flight or instant, brutal action against the person who poses the threat, and if you haven't been careful, that person could be someone you have come to like. But you must kill him if there is no other way out.

"Your life is expendable, Jamie, but your service to the Crown is beyond personal considerations. By the bye, while on this duty you'll have civilian rank equal to that of major in the Regular Establishment, with pay accordingly. And upon completion you'll be reimbursed for reasonable out-of-pocket expenses after filing your claim memorial."

I said, smiling, "If this honorable service to the King begins with making me a liar to my friends and later includes my murdering a friend, there's no wonder the occupation of spy is thought to be dishonorable among gentlemen."

"When your battle is joined, as yours will be shortly," said Campbell, frowning, "it will be like all other battles, and in this dirty business we all have our share of throats to cut, and betrayal is a general weapon. Peacetime moral strictures go out the window, Jamie. If you pause to philosophize on right and wrong when you're in a tight fix, you'll be a decent gentleman but very shortly a rather dead one."

My housemates accepted my story of painting the bigwigs at Fraunce's and each afternoon I went there to be immersed in my new identity of Robert Allston and the study of Georgia. The Army caused French tailor labels to be sewn into the clothes I would take, and provide me with a French smallsword to wear in place of my English one. They also presented me with a quite pretty French pistol of superlative workmanship. An Army officer of French origin coached me in conversational French and loaned me prints of Parisian scenes, from which I made drawings in my sketchbook as if I had drawn them in place.

Thus it came to pass that one night I sat in my bedchamber, packed and waiting for a hackney that would come to the back gate in the lane behind the garden at midnight to spirit me off to my ship. I had written a note to Hector, explaining that I was off on secret business for the Crown and asked him to notify friends and portrait sitters that I had been called away unexpectedly to Nova Scotia on an imperative investment matter. There was a sort of land rush going on in that province. It would be strange to be separated from Hector. There had hardly been a day in all the years we had known each other that we had not been together, however briefly. In a sense he was my family and very like a brother.

My door opened, and in came Anne, fully dressed though I knew she had gone to bed hours ago. She gazed at me, at my trunk, traveling easel, roll of canvas, and then sat down in a chair. "I woke up and knew," she said, "so I came to say good-bye, Jamie."

"I'll be away for a few weeks," I said.

The green eyes were steady on me in the candlelight. "Longer than that, Jamie, much longer. You've long roads to travel."

Lighthearted with the excitement of my imminent adventure, I felt myself free of her enchantment and laughed. "But not one of them will be your ferny bonny road to

Elfland, Your Fairy Majesty. They'll be of my own choosing."

"Don't be a fool," she said. "None of our own choosing. Listen to me, Jamie Reid. You'll not tell me where you're going, but I know you're going into something I wish to God you didn't have to because I may never see you again. There will be roads and there will be roads, but there is only one you must follow to the end and you will find that one only after you've met another man and made him your friend."

I grinned, "Ah, you're second-sighting like a house afire tonight, aren't you, my lovely witch? Who is that man and what will be my wonderful reward when I reach the end of that final road, O mystic oracle?"

"He's a man I've never seen but dearly want to meet," she declared, "and you'll know the reward when you come on it, whatever it may be, for you shall have earned it—if you yet live then. Jamie, I'll pray for you. Stop laughing at me, Jamie, or I'll turn you into a great goggling green frog this instant!"

"Smile back, Anne," I grinned, "and I'll turn into a one hundred piece regimental band and saluting battery."

"Your wife will do the smiling on you, Jamie," she answered, "and I'll be only a tiny memory in the corner of your mind. You're on the road to her now and I'll bother you no more." She looked down at her hands folded in her lap. "When 'tis done, I may be in London with Papa or in Rome where 'tis said the sun is warm like Georgia's. You and your wife must come to visit with me if ... if ... oh, Jamie, be kind to her, be kind to her! Never hurt her, never!" She raised her face and I saw tears glinting in her eyes.

"If I ever love a woman enough to marry her," I said, "what the devil would I be hurting her for?" My ears caught the faint sound of wheels. "My hackney is here."

"Let me carry your painting things," she said.

Boosting my small trunk on my shoulder, I led the way through the dark and silent house and through the garden to where the hackney bulked darkly in the starlit night, the driver sitting silently on the box. I dumped my gear into the carriage and Anne said, "Will you kiss me good-bye?"

"Since we're not lovers," I told her, "I'll give you a brotherly kiss." Gathering her into my arms I did, but never having had a sister it became something else and with

131

astonishment I felt her responding, openmouthed, her tongue curling to meet mine. Passion sparked and I broke the embrace. "Anne, never kiss a man like that unless you want to be raped on the spot."

Her face was a dim oval in the night, and her words came to me in a faintly heard breathed whisper. "The road to the benns, the road to the benns." Then in her normal crystal voice she said, "Good-bye, Jamie Reid, and may God guard you."

"Good-bye, Anne," I answered, and was no sooner in the hackney when the driver clucked at his horse and I was off on the King's service.

Chapter IX

THE CARRIAGE DROVE onto a quay where I could vaguely make out the shape of a vessel moored. The driver wordlessly took my baggage and set it on the ship's deck, then drove away. I stepped from the quay to the bulwark, down to the deck and peered about. The ship was no Western Ocean packet, that was sure. A man's dark figure moved to me. "Be you Mr. Robert Allston?"

"I am," I replied.

"I'm Lucius Noble, the mate," he said. "I'll show ye your berthin' and ye can stow your gear in the mornin'. We'll be gittin' under way now and ye might's well git to sleep, for there ain't nothin' to see, us bein' dark ship till we git to sea. This way, sir."

He guided me into the after cabin and to a small stateroom, left me, and after undressing I crawled into a surprisingly comfortable berth where I listened drowsily to the thudding of bare feet on deck, the creak of blocks and slatting of sails being hoisted. The work was done without audible command. The ship heeled over, gathering speed in the light breeze, and the sound of water rushing past the hull was like a soothing lullaby. Good-bye, dolorous green-eyes, witchly second sightings and most beautiful wench who ever lived, I mused, and slid off into sleep.

In the first moment of waking I thought I was back aboard the *Jason,* feeling the ship rising and falling as she plunged over long, easy swells. I used the chamber pot, dressed, and washed at an elegant little washstand, the water coming from a water breaker set on brackets above the stand. The appointments were a far cry from the *Jason.* Stepping out into the main cabin, I nearly collapsed at the sight of Ira Tupper at the table, busily tucking away breakfast. He gave me a mildly startled look, grinned, and said

133

amiably, "Mornin' to ye, Mr. Allston. Set down and have a bite."

I said, looking about at the splendidly paneled cabin, "This . . . this is the *Bonny Anne!*"

"Aye," he nodded, "and ye'll find her some comfortable, Mr. Allston. She's fast, sound and pretty, she is. Her owners put a sight o' money into her. I'll guarantee ye a fast comfortable v'yage to New Providence Island."

I sat down. "Ira, belay that. I am me. Remember me?"

Jerking a thumb upward toward the poop over our heads, he whispered, "The less he knows, the better. Same with the crew. I trust 'em but don't want to tempt 'em. I never laid eyes on ye before." In usual conversational tone he went on, "Ye'll find the vittles good. Plenty o' fresh meat and produce, kept in ice in the hold. I calc'late to pick up a few pennies when I sell that ice ballast down to Nassau. Maine river ice is best, but them island folk won't care about quality. Hudson River ice'll cool their drinks good enough and keep table fruit from rottin' untimely. I'm Ira Tupper, master, and if ye don't know it, my ship's under charter to the Army for this errand, Mr. Allston."

"But New Providence?" A man appeared and laid a heaping plate of ham and eggs in front of me and poured me a mug of hot, black coffee. When he left the cabin, I told Ira, "I'm supposed to be going to Savannah."

"Bonny Anne takes aboard her disguise at Nassau," he explained. "I've got a special-writ log that says we come there from Le Havre. At Nassau she'll load the cargo that's supposed to come from there, along with a proper manifest and French customs clearance papers. Savannah'll be some joyful to greet us, just like old St. Nick with a sleigh-ful o' hard-wanted sugarplums, seein' how close that coast is watched by the King's Navy."

I had never been to sea in the *Bonny Anne* before, and now I could see why Ira loved her. Yachtlike, fast and graceful, she exuded an exuberant joy as she flung herself up and over the long rolling, foam-crested seas, rollicking jubilantly in the arms of her lover, the ocean. Sometimes, sitting in the comfortable cabin that was paneled in bird's eye maple and Dominican mahogany, and feeling the surging happy buoyancy of her beneath me, I'd think that this was how the flesh-and-blood bonny Anne will revel when she finds that man of hers; then I would have the eerie feeling that if I turned quickly enough I would see her standing

134

behind me. To get away from Anne MacDonald I had made a poor start.

One day when Ira was forward by himself, inspecting the lashings of the bower anchors, I joined him and said, "There's no denying it. She was right, Ira. The ship's her twin."

"Ay-yeh," he grunted, "ye might say that. Jamie, take a glim under the bowsprit and tell me what ye think."

Leaning over the knightheads, I saw the cutwater slicing cleanly through the deep blue Gulf Stream waters, throwing up on either side a roll of creamy white foam that reminded me of Anne's skin. I thought of how delighted Anne would be to stand at the bow as I was and watch the ship's pleasure, her own mingling with it, and then I understood. "She needs a figurehead of bonny Anne, Ira."

He nodded. "Been on my mind since she swung that bottle at the la'nchin'."

"Don't hire a carver to do it," I ordered. "When I first went to London I got my first artist training in the Signmakers' Guild and learned wood-carving. I was good at it. When I'm finished with this Army errand I'll give your ship a figurehead that will be a portrait of Anne, and by God what a smile I'll put on that face!"

"Figgered ye might lash onto it," he said.

I laughed. "One of the reasons I'm here is because I wanted to get away from her, and now look at me."

His black eyes surveyed me. "You're a moderate big idjit sometimes, Jamie. Waaal, I got to spell Lucius of the watch. Good-day to ye, Mr. Allston."

Despite my quiet apprehensions about French men-of-war and rebel armed vessels, we never sighted another sail until the *Bonny Anne* rolled down the North West Providence Channel and then we only raised a few local fishing boats. The smoothness of the passage, I thought as we sailed into Nassau harbor, was a good omen and I hoped it would set the standard for the rest of my task. As soon as the anchor dropped through the clear water to rest on the sandy bottom, Ira had spare sails rigged as awnings over the poop deck and forecastle, and ordered the longboat lowered. As he prepared to leave the ship, he said to the mate, "Lucius, keep them bumboat bawds out o' the *Bonny Anne*." From the shoreline, crowded with moored small island craft, a sizable flotilla of dugout canoes and decrepit

135

pulling boats was advancing on us. "They're rotten with the French pox and crawlin' with crabs. Nor do ye let any o' that monkey rum aboard—'twill drive the lads blind or crazy. Let 'em have all the fruit they can pay for, but keep 'em turnin' to, readyin' for sea; likely we'll be haulin' arse some soon." He ordered the boat crew to shove off and they rowed him briskly toward the beach.

The bumboats arrived, loaded with fruit, bottles of spirits, carved coconut shells, palm frond baskets and mats, bangles carved from bone, and women. All the merchants were women, crying their wares, and the noisiest of all were those whose merchandise consisted of themselves, smiling invitingly and calling, "Eh, mon, you want jigajig? I show you plenty fun, mon! One way, anyway, fuck, suck, up behind, all same price! Eh, jigajig, mon, jigajig, firs'-class virgin maid!" In truth, to men who had been at sea for a time they were quite appealing, young, vivacious and for the most part voluptuously curved, ranging in color from blue-black to café au lait. As the hands bought fruit from the other vendors they engaged in exchanges of good-natured obscene jokes with the whores.

The town of Nassau consisted of a huddle of buildings stretching along the landward side of a road that ran along the curving bay shore. The smell of the land was heavy with flowers, sour swill and ordure, an oppressive mixture that seemed to accentuate the broiling heat of the sun. The pitch in the deck seams bubbled and the tar from the stays dripped from aloft. Despite the poop deck awning and my drink of iced rum, my shirt was soaked with perspiration as I occupied myself by sketching the bumboat women from my seat on the cabin skylight. Down the harbor several British men-of-war lay at anchor and, somewhat apart, was a Dutch merchantman. I yearned to go ashore for some convivial drinking and have a try at some acquiescent island lady despite the risk of being noticed by rebel spies.

The besieging bumboat fleet thinned out as the jigajig wenches, held at bay by Lucius and the boatswain, gave up in disgust and paddled away, leaving the more prosaic vendors to a skimpy trade and friendly chatter with the crew. Evidently the women enjoyed the sociability as much as making sales. I noticed one of them, a rather pretty brown girl with piles of golden and pink mangoes in her pitpan, lay off somewhat apart from the others, kneeling quietly and occasionally dipping her paddle to keep the craft from

136

drifting away. It occurred to me that she might be the daughter of one of the older women who were bantering with the crew and she was patiently waiting for her mother to leave off unprofitable visiting so they could approach a vessel with a more affluent crew. I lazily sketched her and was annoyed to find that sweat from my hand and wrist wet the paper so badly that drawing was becoming impossible, so I gave up and walked to the ship's side to look down into the water.

The sandy bottom could be seen clearly about three fathoms down, the water like glass with a faint tinge of green. There were fish down there, their artful natural coloration making them nearly invisible and their location was betrayed by their shadows cast on the bottom sand. When they swam into the large bulking shadow of the *Bonny Anne* I could see them. The flitting shadows in the greenish depths made me think of Anne's eyes.

A long, slender shadow appeared and it was only when the girl spoke that I became aware that it was caused by her pitpan coming alongside. "Sah," she said, looking up at me. "You want a good ripe mango, sah?" She was standing and held a pretty mango up to me. At close range she was extremely attractive, with well-formed features, smoky eyelashes, glistening black hair and a coppery skin with the flush of vibrant health beneath. Her lips were full and soft, and the teeth revealed by her smile were gleaming white. She wore a simple white cotton shift, sleeveless and knee-length, which revealed rather than concealed her lithe body. The lovely girl, mango and pitpan against the blues and greens of the harbor waters made a striking arrangement, stimulating both artist and man. Gazing directly down at her I could see the front of her body below the valley between her breasts. Old Nick stirred restlessly.

Smiling, I said, "You're the mango I'd like. You're very pretty."

Her eyes were liquid brown, large and soft. "I ain' in that trade, sah. Take my mango I'm givin' you for no money. Reach you hand and take it, sah."

I took it and said, "Thank you, love. Now I'm in your debt. If you give me that other mango I'll settle the debt by paying you well. Nobody could say you were in that trade if a man pays you for a mango."

Now she was serious. "Mon, I saw you makin' a picture like you was writin'. Show me."

137

I went to the skylight where I'd laid the sketchbook and passed it down to her, opened to the right page. She studied the drawing, then said in an awed voice, "Hooee, Ol' Diggory, he plenty right!" Her face turned up to me again and I saw it was wreathed with delight. "You give me this picture, mon, you got all my mangoes!"

Glancing around the deck, I saw none of the crew within earshot or watching, so I told the girl, " 'Tis a bargain, love. Haul around to the rudder and come in through the transom widow."

She stood motionless for a moment, her eyes moving from one of my eyes to the other, then she knelt and began paddling aft. I went below and by the time I reached the transom windows she was tying her canoe to the rudder chain. Taking my extended hand she came quickly boosting through the window and into the cabin to stand looking at me with a brightly glowing smile. "My name, 'tis Nancy Harris. What's yours?"

"Robert Allston," I answered, taking her in my arms. There was no resistance. On the contrary, her body fairly melted against mine and her arms went around me. Her pretty face shone as if something wondrously happy was going on.

"Maybe you got another name," she smiled.

That smacked of experience she denied. As a rule, a British gentleman would not give his proper name to a casual trollop. "Of course I have." Old Nick was pressing, nudging her as I held her close. "Come to my stateroom and show me my special mango."

She came with me, holding my arm, and in the small, hot and dim space she said, "Rob, you want me bare for you?"

"How else may I see my lovely mango?" I answered, peeling off my clothes.

She flung off her shift and piled onto the berth to lie on her back. With the louvers of the door open, I could see her body was superb. She was a dusky goddess of some barbaric island tribe and her white teeth flashed, her arms reached out to me. "Come, hurry, you kiss me, make love like you husban' and me wife!"

She was no whore. The passage was tight, and her response no professional counterfeit. Her kiss was sweetly and curiously maidenly until feverish transports brought on wildly avid abandonment, and her coming was marvelously

spectacular. Our perspiration-drenched bodies slapped and
slid together and our kisses tasted of sweat. When it was
over and we lay panting in the wet berth, she ran a hand
over my body and said, "You one good mon, Rob. You like
me?"

"Very much," I answered truthfully. "Tell me, who is
Old Diggory?"

She rolled onto her side and kissed my wet chest. "Obeahman at home. What you call lookman. He makes magic,
sees things that ain' happened yet."

"Oh, Jesus," I muttered, "more second sight."

"True," she confided. "Like seein' twice as good. You
think I make jigajig with you because you give me picture,
eh? I played a trick on you. Ol' Diggory, he tol' me, go to
Nassau town, Nancy, fin' you man you goin' love all you
born days, no other man only him."

Despite the heat and sweat, my skin prickled. Apprehensively, I asked, "How were you to know him when you saw
him?"

She lay half on top of me, squirming with slippery pleasure. "Ol' Diggory say he white man, got two different color
eyes, lef'-handed, makes pictures for money and he ain' got
his right name with him."

"You," I said, "are making this up. You knew all
those things before we got into bed, Nancy."

"Nancy never spoke no lie in her life," she murmured.
"Ol' Diggory say one more thing about you, Rob. I don'
know, you tell me if 'tis true. He say you draw a picture of
King George, he's you friend."

I felt clammy. This Old Diggory could have read about
me in some old London newspaper and filled Nancy with a
lot of superstitious fancy, and our meeting like this was
simply coincidental, a million-to-one shot that came off. I
said, "Well, I don't like lies, either. But, how many friends
will you tell about being with me like this?"

"I live alone," she told me, "don' like Nassau girls.
Nancy's business is Nancy's business, and you my husban',
Rob, jus' like we wed. I don' ever take other man now. You
goin' have plenty other wenches, marry in a church, maybe,
but Nancy don' care, she foun' you for good and all. Ol'
Diggory said true, eh?"

"About the King?" I asked. "Yes, but he could have read
all that in an English newspaper."

"Ol' Diggory can't read or write, like everybody at

home," she said, "and he nearly blind from bein' old." She giggled. "Don' you like Nancy lovin' you, all that talk maybe Ol' Diggory do that, do this, fool me?" Her hand was insinuating, coaxing, caressing. "Rob, come fill me full again."

The second time was extraordinary. When I was fully home, she whispered, "Don' move. I love you from inside." I lay quiescent on her and then an exquisite interior stroking began, a dark and secret flexing. "You feel?"

It was excruciating pleasure. I gasped, "Oh, yes, yes!"

Her hands stroked my wet back. "I love you inside and outside, Rob. I never have jigajig before. First time I don' know how to do it." Her breathing rate increased and her body was trembling, as was mine under the soaring tension of unendurable pleasure. Just when I felt I couldn't stand another second of it a whimpering cry burst from her and her body shuddered and convulsed, strained and thrashed in a mighty climax, and my body gave way in a powerful explosion that matched her ecstasy. I was vaguely conscious of her interior still stroking, drawing out of me every drop of spurting spunk, greedily sucking me dry.

After that the heat and perspiration were too much for either of us, so we dried off as best we could with one of my towels. She asked me for a kerchief and I was amused to see her stuff it into herself. Out in the cabin the slight breeze coming in the transom window was a blessed cool relief. Her thin shift clung to her lovely body most interestingly, for she was still perspiring. She smiled, "The kerchief, 'tis yours for me to keep and now it keeps you good juice in me."

"Ladies have babies that way," I pointed out.

"I ain' no lady," she smiled, embracing me. "I'm only a silly nigger wench crazy for love. Rob, I know you ain' stayin' Nassau long, else you'd go ashore. Maybe someday you come back, look for Nancy's bumboat on the quay near the Bourse where they sell slave niggers."

" 'Tis unlikely I'll be back, Nancy," I told her, enjoying her clearly genuine affection. "My home is over the ocean. And you're no nigger wench. Looking at you I see a beautiful blend of European, Indian and African. I like you most extravagantly. What you must do is put me and Old Diggory's nonsense out of your mind and find a good man to settle down with. You're much too pretty and sweet to be running about loose."

She shook her head. "I ain' runnin' about loose. I find my good man, you. Maybe I don' ever see you again, no matter. You want me to go with you in this boat, I go. When you go home over the ocean, you want me, send and I come. Don' have to love me, I work for you, do anything. Ol' Diggory, he said 'twould be so, now I know 'tis so."

I had not heard the longboat come alongside. Ira came down the companionway ladder and said, looking at us as we stood with arms about each other, "By Godfrey, ain't that a friendly picture? The way her clothes is stickin' to her, ye might have hauled her out o' the brine, Mr. Allston. I see you're some wet yourself."

I laughed. "Miss Nancy Harris, Captain Tupper."

She made a dipping curtsy gesture. "How do, Cap'n Tupper." Her smile was radiant.

"Pleased to meet ye, Miss Harris," he said. "Now, h'ist that pretty tail o' yours out the window and into your pitpan I seen moored to the rudder. 'Tain't I don't appreciate ye, because you're some ornamental, but the hands might be surly about missin' a tumble if they was to know ye was servin' the afterguard."

"Just a minute—" I began.

Then Nancy exclaimed indignantly, "I ain' no whore! Rob and me, we got wet makin' love and you know it plenty well, but that's what we was doin'—makin' love! I ain' shamed! Me, I'm plenty proud I come on Rob this day! If he tells you about me, you'll know why!" She said to me, "Nancy's goin' now. Remember what I tol' you, darlin' Rob."

There was pleading tenderness in the large soft eyes. I kissed her long and hard, then she climbed through the transom window down to her canoe and paddled away without a backward look.

Ira said, "Didn't mean to hurt her feelin's. She didn't have the look of a whore about her but ye can't tell about these island wenches. Pretty little piece and smashed out of her mind on you, as usual." He dropped his voice to a hoarse whisper. "Goddamn it, Jamie, that stiff joint o' yours could be the death of us one day! Them rebels use women for spies!" He bawled up the ladder, "Lucius, lay below!" When the mate came clattering down, Ira said to him, "Takin' on cargo tonight and sailin' in the mornin'. Soon's it's dark, buoy and slip the cable. Tow with the longboat

141

to the Dutchman. No lights, muffle oars. Put the ice aboard the Dutchman; I've sold it to him and he'll sell it at Surinam. Take his French cargo aboard, then we come back for the rest o' the night at this moorin'. Clear for Savannah after sunup."

Lucius nodded. "There's a power o' sawdust with the ice. I'd best git some hands to work sackin' it." He went above and Ira said to me, "By the new papers we got, we're homeported at Alexandria in Virginia. Bein' you're by way o' bein' an artist, will ye paint her in place o' New York on the stern tonight?"

"At my going prices," I grinned, "I doubt you can afford the fee."

"I'll bill them tightfisted young scoundrels who own the ship," he said. "Hope ye can do it in the dark. Feller ashore told me there's so many Whig spies watchin' this harbor that a seaman can't pick his nose without the Continental Congress hearin' about it before he can wipe his finger on his britches. A deal o' trollops are on Whig pay, too."

"She's no trollop," I declared, "and there was nothing here of any value to a rebel spy, anyway."

He said solemnly, "Spar dimensions is of value, such as the long and thick o' your bowsprit. What in tarnation was she talkin' about, about you and her? Seemed a moderate big fuss to make over bein' caught at a frolic."

I told him about it and he commented, "Ain't that a caution? That feller Old Diggory puts me in mind of a red-headed lady. I calc'late he's one o' them voodoo priests, maybe, what they call a conjureman for the spirits and visions they conjure up. The good ones has second sight, I figger, like that red-headed lady, only they color it up with a deal o' whoopteedoo and fires, dancin' and chantin' magic words nobody can understand. I don't put 'em down. As the feller said when he fell through the backhouse seat, there's more to it than meets the eye. Waaal, if ye ever wander back to Nassau, ye got a lively warmin' pan for your bed."

"Well," I said, "if we're sailing in the morning I won't see Nassau ashore, now or ever again. What's it like over on the beach?"

"Bedlam," he answered. "Everybody's mad on each other. There ain't room for all the Loyalists to settle, so they settle anyway on the big plantations. The big planters raise hell and the governor gets it from both ways. There ain't enough of anything except mad. The governor hollers to London for help, but London's got other things to worry about. Damn pity. Most o' them refugees lived in America a long time, their pa's and grampa's, too, sweatin' and bleedin' for every foot o' ground they cleared six days a week and fightin' off Indians on the seventh. The Crown owes 'em a hell of a lot for givin' it up because they're loyal."

"It seems to me," I said, "if they had so much to lose they would have done better to stay and fight for it instead of running away here, expecting the British Army to do it for them."

"Mr. Allston," he said, "I once met a young Boston feller in London a while back who was havin' a hell of a good time wenchin' and drinkin', livin' in a grand comfortable house, while most of New England was turnin' into a shithouse for rebels. Called himself a Loyalist, too. I didn't notice him rushin' home breathin' fire and shoutin' damnation to the Whigs, cryin' for a musket and bayonet."

"He no doubt had his reasons," I said.

"Ay'yeh," answered Ira dryly, "like a cellarful of the best grog and bedrooms full of pretty women."

"Oh, balls, Ira," I said. "If you'd been in his place, you'd have done the same."

He swiveled his head and looked squarely at me. I saw the pain in his eyes and wished I had not said it. "Not likely," he said. "I've got a fair-to-middlin' size bone to pick with them rebels. Well, I s'pose I'd best get to plannin' our moorin' shiftin' with Lucius." He swallowed the rest of his rum and went above to the deck.

After sunset, night descended with the suddenness of a lamp being turned out, with hardly any time for twilight. The warm darkness seemed to intensify the heavy tropical smells from the land, and the sky was an inverted bowl of bright stars that were mirrored on the glassy harbor water. The *Bonny Anne*'s anchor cable was slipped, buoyed to mark its location. With eight men pulling on muffled oars in the longboat, the schooner was slowly towed to the Dutch packet and moored alongside. With orders passed in whispers, the hatches were quietly opened, and using the Dutchman's cockbilled mainyard as a derrick, bales, barrels and chests were lowered into the *Bonny Anne*'s hold after the big cakes of ice and their insulating sawdust were transferred. Meantime I went over the taffrail, lowering

143

myself in a boatswain's chair, and in the faint light of the stars painted out New York and gave my ship her new home port under her name which loomed insistently before my eyes. "Bonny Anne," I whispered, "get out of my life and leave me alone!"

When I finished I went on deck where the two ships' crews labored silently. It could go on for hours, I saw, so I went below to my stateroom and to bed. The berth was still clammily damp from two persons' sweat and as I drifted off to sleep I thought fondly of the island girl; she was sweet, honest and naive—and one of the most remarkable performers I had ever tumbled. That flexing trick had seemed to be pulling all of me into her body. Confused, senseless dreams swept by in the panorama of sleep, then one focused, clarified, and I was peering out the transom window down at Anne in her green gown standing in the pitpan and reaching a hand up to me. Her eyes were no longer green; they were soft brown. She said with Nancy's voice, "Eh, mon, we two goin' whistle for a wind."

"Get out of my life!" I shouted angrily.

She became entirely Nancy and smiled happily, "Can't do that, mon. All peoples you take in you life, they make a part of you."

Reaching for Nancy's hand, I awakened and found the early sun streaming in through the stern transom windows, and Ira was stamping out of his stateroom calling, "Ahoy, Lucius, heave up and lash up! Let go your root and grab your boot! All hands! No breakfast till we're clear o' soundin's!"

Chapter X

"YONDER COMES TROUBLE," remarked Ira, studying the distant sail through his long glass as the *Bonny Anne* ghosted over a nearly glassy sea off the East Florida coast. "And there ain't enough wind to blow out a candle. King's Navy brig with stuns'ls set, everything hangin' out. 'Heave to,' she says. Lucius, put the hands to wettin' down the dimities."

As the mate went off to set the crew to work throwing buckets of water from the ratlines on to the sails I said to Ira, "We've got nothing to fear from our own people. Why run?"

Closing the glass, he answered, "You ain't goin' to last long as a spy if ye don't use what's betwixt your ears better'n that. With all this French cargo and fancied up log, clearances and all, they'll put a prize crew aboard and us in irons and take us into Augustine. By the time we get through explainin', the rebel folks in Georgia'll know more about us than we know ourselves. Then what's goin' to happen to them great plans the King's Ministers cooked up?"

The brig, a pyramid of canvas, bore steadily toward us before the faint northwest wind on its stern, displaying one of the few advantages of a square-rigged ship over the fore-and-aft rig of the *Bonny Anne,* whose sails, though close-hauled, scarcely bellied with the wind on her beam. Even with the naked eye, I could see the tiny colored signal flags flying in the brig's rigging. Another flag hoist went up. " 'Heave to or open fire'," commented Ira. He looked up at the chain of men in the shrouds passing up buckets of sea-water. The sails were wet, but *Bonny Anne* still lazed, almost drifting. "I could out sweeps, but 'twould only pick up a half knot, maybe." He surveyed the sea and sky, the cloudless calm. "If ye can whistle, Mr. Allston, ye best

145

pucker up and call us a wind or else git ready to do a lot o' talkin'."

Memory of the dream in Nassau harbor came to me. A puff of smoke blossomed at the bow of the oncoming man-of-war, followed by a faint thud. "Long Tom bow chaser," observed Ira. "'Tain't often ye see a brig carryin' a twenty-four-pounder. About twenty minutes and he'll have the range. Wal, I ain't ready to see *Bonny Anne* knocked to splinters. Might's well break out the Union Jack and heave to."

"What tune is best for raising a wind?" I asked.

He gave me a quizzical grin. "Any one except the one the old cow died of. If you're of a mind to fetch a miracle, make her a good one. I want about a ten-knot breeze— more if ye can strain a bit—on the port quarter. Whistle your tune on that bearin', Mr. Allston."

Feeling silly, I said, "What can we lose?" Facing the port quarter on the poop, I puckered up and whistled the first melody that came into my head, the song Anne had sung, "The Ballad of Thomas the Rhymer." I heard Ira order the hands to belay the sail-dowsing. Another cannon shot sounded. The schooner continued to loaf under slack sails. I closed my eyes and imagined Anne beside me; we two will whistle, she had said. The Royal Navy fired again. It is hard to whistle when you're tense with desperation. No longer feeling silly, I put my heart into it and in my mind I heard her whistling clear and true.

A wisp of moving air touched my face, then another. I heard rigging creak. I whistled on. Incredibly, the breeze steadied, increased. The deck canted and over my whistling I heard the sound of a burbling wake under the stern. Ira shouted, "Lucius, leave them sheets be! She ain't goin' to capsize! Brace the fore-tops'l! Take the slack out o' the jib sheets!" He said to me, "Reckon ye can belay the concert, Mr. Allston, and thank ye kindly."

The wind had shifted from northwest to southwest and was blowing at all of twelve knots, and the *Bonny Anne* was fairly leaping through the no longer glassy sea. Far away, well abaft our beam, the Navy brig was clearly outdistanced. Laughing with relief and pleasure, I said, "She chose her own song."

"I'm surprised ye remembered it, considerin'," commented Ira, and he shook his head, rubbing his long chin. "I'll tell ye this: all the years I been to sea, man and boy,

146

I been hearin' about whistlin' for a wind and never seen it done before this day."

"Well," I said, "you've never before commanded a ship who had a witch for a sister. I'm going below and have a drink. I need it."

"Ye ain't alone," Ira declared. He called forward to Lucius, "Splice the main brace for all hands, Lucius. A gill apiece. Mr. Allston, I'll jine ye in a dram and a toast to them sisters."

Wind and weather stayed good, and a few days later the *Bonny Anne* lay off Tybee Island in the mouth of the Savannah River, flying a flag request for a pilot. The offshore breeze brought with it a strong smell of swampy vegetation and tidal mud. The July sun was broiling and the heat moist. Nervous on the brink of my immersion among the King's enemies, I paced the poop deck.

A smart little ketch flying the rebel gridiron flag came scooting out from shore, shot past the *Bonny Anne,* came briskly about and eased neatly alongside. Two men climbed over the *Bonny Anne*'s bulwarks, and we were in enemy hands. The pilot was an elderly, taciturn fellow who immediately took over the helm and grunted orders to Lucius after perfunctorily shaking hands with Ira and the mate. The other man, a sickly looking young man in what I learned was the uniform of a captain of the Continental Army, introduced himself as Captain Roche, Army representative of the Collector of Customs and Searcher. After carefully inspecting the ship's papers and finding them satisfactory, he turned his attention to me and my business.

For the first of what was to be many times, I displayed my letters from Congress and Doctor Franklin and explained the historical pictures enterprise. Roche appeared mildly impressed but not enthusiastic, saying, "Coming from France and all, Mr. Allston, I don't know what you expect to find when you get ashore, but I'll tell you it isn't much for making pictures of. And I'll say this, too: there won't be any great new nation to make pictures of anyway unless we get more men who'll 'list for service long enough to learn to soldier instead of just long enough between crops. But I see you don't have to be concerned about that—says here you're exempt from soldiering while on this work of yours."

Patriotic zeal was indicated. "I'd not be concerned even if I weren't exempt, Captain," I declared fervently. "I'm as willing to fight for my country as any man alive. I'm no coward, sir!"

He gave me a sick man's wan smile. "Your pardon, sir. I didn't mean to question your courage. I was only blowing off about the Army's troubles." We were in the cabin and Ira was restowing his ship's papers. Roche said to him, "Sir, you're the first merchantman to call at Savannah from abroad in a long time. Likely you'll sell everything on your manifest before your mooring lines are fast. And for outbound cargo, the storehouses under the bluff are crammed full of goods waiting for a shipmaster like yourself, with guts enough to chance the enemy, to come in here and take the stuff out. You'll be a ring-tailed solid gold hero in Savannah, sir."

"That's some good to hear, about that outgoin' cargo," said Ira. "My owners was worried about sailin' out light, what with profits bein' cut into by them high insurance rates nowadays."

"Those owners!" I exclaimed disgustedly, and to Roche I said scornfully, "Captain Tupper's told me about them, a pair of avaricious young scoundrels who scheme how to get rich out of this struggle for liberty, while soldiers like yourself and sailors like Captain Tupper risk their lives against Royal tyranny!"

Roche shrugged and said mildly, "No matter what happens, lots of folks are going to get rich out of it. I used to get pretty fair mad about it myself. But look at it this way, Mr. Allston: if those owners weren't greedy enough to send this shipload of goods to Savannah, would that have helped the folks who need the stuff?" He grinned weakly. "Now I'm a little older and been shot at, racked up with this fever, gone hungry and barefooted some, if I die and get reborn and run into another war, I'm going to be one of those greedy young scoundrels and let somebody else have a whack at the soldiering."

"Ye know damn well ye'll do it all over ag'in," said Ira with his easy grin. "There's some who does and some who sets, and you ain't a setter, Cap'n. Well, there's eighteen miles o' river ahead and I ain't even seen a chart of it. You gentlemen rest easy here and help yourself to what's in the spirits locker and welcome." He went up the ladder to the poop.

I opened a bottle of port that had come with our French goods and Roche sipped it with obvious pleasure. "Ah, that's the real thing. There's not much of it left in Georgia. You'll find Savannah not much like Paris. Georgia's an overgrown poorhouse, no money, everybody trading or bartering. For drinking there's a poor choice. Rum, home-brewed ale, whisky cooked off behind a cow barn, peach brandy—oh, lord, the peach brandy! Everybody has a peach orchard and everybody fancies himself the highest master of brandy making."

"I'm partial to good rum for serious drinking," I told him. "In warm weather like this I like a strong and bitter ale with a chill on it."

"You'll find that ale at Peter Tondee's tavern," he said. "Peter has comfortable lodgings and sets a good table. If you like, I'll steer you there when we reach town."

"Why, thank you," I answered. "I was wondering where I would stay."

He was shivering from head to foot, his hand shaking so badly that his glass was in danger of spilling. Catching my concerned look, he said, "Don't worry about me. 'Tis only St. Mary's fever, comes and goes. We chased a mob of Tories from South Carolina down there last month and ran 'em into the swamps on the Florida line. Nearly caught that bastard Browne—found his shirt, by God! I came down with the fever, along of a lot of other boys, and Bob Howe sent me back to Savannah for light duty with the garrison, so that's why I'm boarding officer now."

I knew who Browne and Howe were, but I was a new-comer from France, so I asked him who they were. "General Robert Howe, commanding the Southern Department from Fort Sunbury. Browne, he's a Loyalist son of a bitch who heads up a gang of murdering, raping, looting savages called the East Florida Rangers. He was an officer of the British Army before he took up a big plantation above Augusta. When Governor Wright and his royal crowd got thrown out in '76, Browne skedaddled too and got Tonyn, he's royal governor in East Florida, to let him recruit those worst scum of Georgia." His eyes had become bloodshot, his face ashen. "This goddamn fever—nobody in their right mind does any soldiering along this coast in the summer."

With some astonishment at my concern for this enemy soldier, I said, "Captain, my stateroom is there. I insist you lie down in the berth and rest."

His teeth were chattering with chill, though the cabin's steamy heat was nearly unbearable. "I won't fight that.

149

I'll thank you to roust me out when the port comes in sight."

After seeing him into the berth I went above to the poop deck. The *Bonny Anne* sailed quietly on the broad sweep of the river, helped by the incoming tide against the current. The air was oppressively humid and smelled of decaying plant life. The wooded banks shimmered in heat waves rising from the river. Conversation was desultory, the heat seeming to stifle small talk. The crew stood by the sheets and braces, for each bend in the river required a new bearing. A seaman forward took soundings steadily, calling out the depth. The afternoon oozed slowly by, and at length some buildings and a couple of piers came in sight. The pilot said, "Stand to your heavin' lines."

I went below and gently touched Roche's shoulder. He shot out of the berth and was on his feet before his eyes were open, tense and in a sort of crouch, then he came all the way awake and grinned wryly, "Thought I was somewhere else. Savannah?"

His face had regained its normal color and his eyes were nearly clear. I said, "I presume so. The crew's standing by the lines."

The *Bonny Anne*'s arrival was a momentous event. Judging by the crowds that filled the piers, riverfront and the bluff above, the news had traveled upriver a lot faster than the vessel. A smiling knot of officials came aboard, exclaiming welcomes and shaking hands. Roche left my side to speak to a tall, well-dressed man to whom Lucius Noble was talking, then went ashore. The tall man nodded to Lucius, said something, and came to me with his hand extended. "How do you do, Mr. Allston? I'm Alexander Cameron. Captain Roche just gave me a hasty report on your purpose in our fair state."

Feeling slightly numb, I shook his hand. He was the dominating figure present, exuding power and influence. "I'm honored, sir," I said.

"I've asked the captain and his mate to have supper at my house tonight, sir," he announced, "and hope that you will join us, Mr. Allston."

"Delighted, Mr. Cameron," I said.

He smiled, "Excellent, sir. At nine, then. I live on Bull Street in the most pretentious house in sight. The palace is only loaned to me—I have a modest home at my plantation up the Ogeechee more suitable to my unregal taste."

150

Someone drew him away amid cries of pleasure over the cargo manifest and Roche reappeared on board accompanied by a pair of Negro men. "Mr. Allston, these niggers will carry your traps. We can walk, for 'tis a short way, unless you want a chair."

I laughed. "I'm dying to stretch my legs on solid ground. I'll walk."

Following him up the path on the bluff, it was borne home to me with some force that the solid ground under my feet was enemy-held soil and I was now in constant danger of being strung up to the nearest tree. Thrusting such defeatist vapors from my mind, I became Robert Allston of Boston and France in every pore and walked away from Jamie Reid, resolved never to think of that name again until the task was done.

Chapter XI

TONDEE'S TAVERN was a two-story frame building on a brick foundation. The ground floor was largely taken up by the public room which was almost comfortably cool thanks to a small Negro boy in one corner who, through a rope and pulley rig, kept a large ceiling fan moving to circulate the air. On the upper floor were several large, high-ceilinged chambers with floor length windows fitted with jalousies to shut out the sun. Peter Tondee was a quiet, small man with a slight French accent and turned out to be a Swiss, one of those men who appear destined from birth to be an innkeeper and are good at it. After showing me to my room, he sent up a laundress to collect my soiled clothing, a tub of hot water for bathing and shaving, and a jug of his own peach brandy which I found to be superb.

Bathed, shaved and dressed in my lightest weight London suit, I enjoyed a good light meal of sliced meats, cheese, bread and fresh fruit at a table in a corner of the public room, where a dozen or so townsmen drank ale and carried on a murmuring conversation, occasionally glancing at me in not unfriendly curiosity. I noticed the men favored light linen suits and none wore wigs, a sensible dress in that torrid climate. I wondered how many of them were secret Loyalists.

Having washed down my food with ale, I was having another tankard of the good cool stuff when Captain Roche returned and joined me at the table. He was looking much better and buried his nose in the ale I ordered for him. "Ah, by God," he said, coming up for air, "the best ale in Savannah, that. I hear you're to sup with Mr. Cameron tonight."

Nodding, I said, "He seems an important gentleman and I'm looking forward to it."

"Nothing much goes on in Georgia without his approval," remarked Roche. "Good man, knows politics better than anybody. He was on the Royal Council before the troubles, a Redcoat colonel on half pay who took up a good-sized grant up on the Ogeechee. When the time came to switch, he came right over to give all his education and experience to our side, but he's not the kind to switch easily like some others around here I could name. I swear to God, if you scratch one of these moderate fellows you'll be drawing blood from something that looks close to a damned Tory! I'm a South Carolinian myself and maybe prejudiced, but I'll bet an English pound to a Spanish Joe that if Clinton and his army were to come marching down the street right now, most of Savannah would rush out to cheer their heads off, and if half an hour later our boys ran the Redcoats out the same people would huzzah and throw flowers. It took a lot of pulling and shoving to move Georgia into the Confederation, believe you me."

It was delightful news. I frowned and said severely, "That doesn't speak well for the patriotism of Georgians. I sincerely hope you're wrong."

"Wait till you've been here awhile," he warned. "You'll see these summer patriots, like that fellow Paine wrote. Another thing—every son of a bitch and his idiot cousin here thinks himself a better general than Alexander the Great. When we went off to bag those Tories down south and Bob Howe thought to take a crack at Prevost and Browne while we were there, the people here shouted that 'twas a great stroke of military genius. When it didn't come off they said it was stupid and ill-advised from the start."

"Who is Prevost?" I asked, knowing the answer well enough, but wanting a rebel's opinion.

"He's the British general commanding the King's forces in East Florida," explained my enemy friend. "He's fixing to start something. There's a deal of moving around going on around Fort Tonyn and St. Augustine. Ships going back and forth from New York. We watch 'em. We've got as many spies as they have."

I made an expression of disgust. "It must take a scurvy beggar to accept such employment, regardless of the cause. How can you trust such people?"

"If you'll excuse me, Mr. Allston," he answered, "you've got a lot to learn about this affair. 'Twould be different if we were fighting Spanish or French where language and

154

country are different. This is a damned dirty mess where brothers and cousins are fighting brothers and cousins for what they claim is their own land. I call it no rebellion, I call it a civil war and there aren't any gentlemanly rules in civil war. Our spies are brave and gallant people running more risk than any soldier on the battlefield and I respect 'em. Don't ever look down your nose at spies, Mr. Allston."

I said apologetically, "My ignorance is appalling in these matters and you must forgive me. I'm sure you're right, yet I could never bring myself to accept such work. I would not be satisfied with anything less than meeting the enemy face to face in open struggle."

My enemy looked at me with a trace of amusement. "That's never what it's made out to be, Mr. Allston, mark my words. Well, your great pictures will be remembered in this country, I suppose, a long time after we soldiers and spies have been forgotten. What are those French folks saying over there about the Alliance?"

Fortunately, my indoctrination at Fraunce's had included a course of sprouts in the background of the French-American Alliance, so I held forth in satisfactory fashion, so satisfactory that several of the other guests joined us and we had a rousing rebel discussion in which I received new insights of some value. The ale and ideas flowed freely and by the time I had to depart for Cameron's house I had established myself as a thoroughgoing, earnest patriot, short on hard reality but long on fiery enthusiasm.

One of Tondee's servants guided me to the Cameron house on Bull Street and in the dark I couldn't see much of the exterior but the inside was surprisingly lavish, almost baronial, in a style more suited to an English country manor than Savannah. The night was hot and muggy, and despite the smoking punks that were supposed to discourage flying night bugs, each candle had a circling host of moths and assorted other pests. At the handsome supper table, served by white-gloved, liveried Negroes, everybody's face was shiny with perspiration, especially Lucius Noble's whose plump and florid features ran with it.

Mrs. Cameron was a large-boned, rather plain lady with an air of quiet competence about her, a characteristic I later found universal among the wives of the more prosperous planters. Her father had been a shipmaster and she and Ira discussed that common ground at some length, but

155

Cameron dominated the conversation in general, expounding endlessly on the blooming of Georgia that was to come when the successful rebellion would also bring forth the glorious flowering of the rights of man under a just democratical form of government. I saw my hopes go glimmering. The man was a rabid rebel. The supper was excellent, though I would have enjoyed it more if I had not been so damned hot and sweaty under my fashionable London clothes. Toward the end of the meal Cameron said to me, "I'm told you have taken the likeness of Dr. Franklin, Mr. Allston, and he was eminently satisfied. Mrs. Cameron has been coaxing me for years to bring our only good portraitist in this part of the country, Mr. Theus of Charles Town, down here to take my likeness. Do you plan to do any of that work while you are here, sir?"

"Yes, sir, I hope to," I answered. " 'Tis my bread and butter. Congress won't lay out a penny until the contracted work is finished. At the risk of seeming presumptuous, I brought along tonight a few drawings and rough chalk portraits I made during the voyage from France, thinking you might be interested. I left them on your hall table."

"Excellent, excellent!" he smiled. "After we gentlemen have our port, Mrs. Cameron will rejoin us and we shall have a showing." The servants were starting to clear the table and Mrs. Cameron, chiding her husband about not talking to us too long because she was anxious to see my work, dropped a curtsy and withdrew. A servant brought in the port and glasses on a silver tray, and when the wine had been passed and the servant gone, Cameron said to Ira, "I understand that not only have you sold and discharged your cargo, you've already taken on an outbound cargo."

"Ay-yeh," answered Ira, " 'twas fast hot work and I ain't particular happy to leave Savannah so quick, but my owners don't get happy when the *Bonny Anne* lies idle in port, eatin' up wharfage fees and such. They're goin' to be some happy this time, I expect, over them fancy prices my French cargo went for."

The rebel politician was benevolent. "I must say you certainly merit those high prices, Captain Tupper, for running the risks you did to bring the stuff to poor threadbare Savannah."

Savoring the fine port, Ira remarked, "The risks wa'n't so steep. We only come on one o' the King's ships, down

156

off Florida, and showed our heels to her. The *Bonny Anne*'s some fast, a real blockade runner, and I figger—"

Lucius Noble, his face livid with anger, smashed his fist down on the table, making the wineglasses jump. He exclaimed loudly, "Mister Safety Council Cameron, this gammin's a-wastin' time! You're settin' around swappin' horseshit with this pair o' traitor sons o' bitches when they ought to be already dancin' in air! Git to your business or by God—"

"Treachery!" I shouted, leaping to my feet and whipping out my smallsword.

Ira was up, crouching warily, his big Abenaki knife in hand, eyes flicking from furious Lucius to calm, urbane Cameron and back. "Steady, lad. You take Lucius and I'll take the other. Do it clean."

Cameron, who had not moved, said quietly, "Don't be hasty, gentlemen. My house is well-guarded and there are men within my call."

"Then for Christ's sake, call 'em in," barked Lucius angrily, "and haul these fuckin' Tories off to gaol!"

The heavy knife in Ira's hand changed position and I knew he was going to throw it at Cameron; the man would be dead before he knew what hit him and would have no chance to summon help. Cameron saw it, too, and said, "Captain Tupper, I have no doubt you can kill me with that weapon from where you stand, but my ball will return the favor." He slowly removed the covering napkin in his lap to reveal a pistol held in his other hand, pointing at Ira. He could kill Ira even as Ira could kill him.

But he couldn't kill both of us. I shifted my weight in his direction, tightened my grip on the sword, and selected the upper left pocket of his flowered silk waistcoat as my target. Poised, I said, "If 'twill make your death more pleasurable to you, I was sent here on His Majesty's service."

"Pray don't be impulsive, Mr. Allston," he smiled. "Hold, I beg." He looked at seething Lucius who was on his feet with his own smallsword drawn. "Mr. Noble, the times are invidious and I'm truly sorry. You see, I too am His Majesty's servant."

Lucius let out a bellow like a maddened bull and drove at Cameron with his sword. Ira told me afterward that I apparently sprouted wings, because I sprang and soared over the table before Ira could shift his aim to launch his

157

knife. The force of my flight drove my sword clear through Lucius up to the handguard and the man was dead, I'm sure, before we landed on the floor with me on top of him. I had to put my foot on his body to withdraw the weapon, and as I wiped the bloody blade on Lucius's coat, Ira said cautiously to Cameron, "Ye bought about ten seconds with that. Talk."

"Put up that meat cleaver, sir," said Cameron. "I have been waiting for an agent of the Crown too long to enjoy being killed by one." He laid the pistol on the table. "However, if you must, you must. I shall not shoot this pistol. The shot would bring out the town and impede your escape to your ship. That much I can do to serve my King."

I sheathed my sword. Any man who could offer such an invitation while looking into the sure death that showed in Ira's slitted Indian eyes was not bluffing. I said to Cameron, "Governor Wright told Lord Germain that he believed you still loyal despite your rebel appearance."

"His Excellency should have," answered Cameron, "because I told him of my plans when we parted." He smiled. "I suppose my rebel role subsequently became convincing enough to create doubts on the King's side."

Ira put his knife away, sat down and drank off the port left in his glass. "That's tolerable good port, Mr. Cameron, too good to waste on a feller who was already drunk when he come here to supper."

Cameron eyed him alertly. "Ah. Of course. The Crown should have had more sense than to send a spy to Savannah incapable of holding his drink like a gentleman, eh? 'Twas fortunate he betrayed himself in his cups."

"My boyhood shipmate," said Ira sadly, shaking his head, "my own ship's officer I trusted like a brother, a dirty Tory spy."

Joining the charade, I said righteously, "The moment he opened his mouth and showed his true colors as a royalist spy I saw red and couldn't control myself. I'm sorry now. He would have been better hanged."

"Seriously," said Cameron to Ira, "how well did you know the man? Had he a chance to communicate to any others about what he knew concerning you and Mr. Allston?"

"Like I said," answered Ira, "we was boyhood shipmates together. I know his family at Thomaston. I was short a mate for this v'yage right up to the day o' sailin' and he

158

come aboard lookin' for a berth, so as old friends I signed him. He didn't have a chance to go ashore from then till now."

"The rest of the crew?" asked Cameron.

"All reg'lar Loyalists," Ira assured him. "Been aboard since I was made master o' the *Bonny Anne*."

"Good," commented Cameron. "Then I shall summon the town bailiff to remove the late Mr. Noble. Tomorrow morning there will be a coroner's inquest and I shall testify as we have agreed. Due to my position it will be unnecessary for either of you to appear, gentlemen. The fewer the versions the better. One more thing, Mr. Allston. After the bailiff and his men depart, we shall resume the evening as planned. You will exhibit your samples and my wife will ask you to take my likeness. You will accept, naturally. Whatever your business here in the King's service, you will need my help. Now let us remove to the less gory atmosphere of my library, and proceed."

It all went off as he had said—better, in fact, for my standing as a fire-eating rebel was nicely confirmed. The bailiff and his men shook my hand soundly, congratulating me enthusiastically for slaying the Tory spy. Mrs. Cameron was delighted with my samples and it was arranged for me to begin the Cameron portrait in the morning, immediately after Cameron's appearance at the coroner's inquest. After hearty good-nights, Ira walked with me to Tondee's tavern, where the public room was closed for the night. He was taking the *Bonny Anne* to sea on the early morning tide and I felt vaguely desolated at the prospect of being left alone without him. "What will you do with that rebel cargo?" I asked.

"There ye go," he said, "countin' up your owner's share. Wal, don't count too high. 'Tis prize cargo, same as if we captured it. 'Twill be auctioned off at St. Augustine where I'm to go on orders. After the King gits his slice, we git ours. Jamie, for God's sake walk easy in this country. Ye seen tonight how quick things happen when ye least expect 'em."

"Don't worry," I replied, "I'll walk on tiptoes from now on. D'you know, I'm scared, but I've never been so excited in my life."

"If ye want to keep that life," he remarked, "don't ever git over bein' scared, but cool off that excitement. By

Godfrey, Jamie, there's folks who are some fond o' you and no matter what ye say, they're goin' to worry till ye get free o' this mess."

"Including myself," I laughed.

"I was thinkin' of some others," he said soberly, "includin' myself and—well, that red-headed lady. Ye treated her poorly, Jamie and ye know it well enough. While you're diddlin' around here ye'd do well to think on her."

"Be damned if I will," I answered. "One of the reasons I'm here was to get away from her and even on shipboard she was all around me. When you get back to New York tell Hector I miss his ugly mug."

"Ay-yeh," he said, and took my hand. "I got to get back aboard. Good-bye, ye loon, and try to keep your mouth shut and your bowels open."

"Good-bye, noble Abenaki clam digger," I said, slapping him on the back.

He walked away and I went in to bed.

The next morning at Cameron's house, after I had set up my easel and started the portrait of the man, I said to him, "The inquest went off all right, I gather."

"You're something of a hero," he commented. "The proceedings only lasted about ten minutes. I'll be obliged if you'll tell me your mission here, Mr. Allston."

Producing my forged documents, I let him read them and when he finished I ran through my instructions, ending with, "The hope is that you can do something about keeping Howe at Sunbury."

"If I had a laurel wreath I'd properly crown you as a hero," he smiled. "That is marvelous news. In December, eh? I'll see Howe remains at Sunbury, never fear." He was thoughtful. "Let me see—ah, of course. Drunken dying Mr. Noble cursed us and declared we would all hang after General Prevost took Fort Sunbury at the end of the year."

"But," I suggested, "suppose Washington sends down more troops because of that, and the legislature here decides to rebuild and strengthen the city's fortifications?"

"Washington doesn't have enough men to divert on the basis of a rumor reported by a drunken man," he told me, "nor does this legislature have the money to patch up these dilapidated defense works, and even if there was money I'm in a position to defeat any such wasteful appropriation. As for your other task, I'll give you a letter that will keep the county safety committees from interfering with you, particularly Burke County's, since you'll be staying at Angus MacDonald's Goodowns. How did that come to be inserted in your excellently forged documents?"

" 'Tis conveniently located for me," I answered, "and Miss Anne MacDonald had told me about it. I'm a friend of her father and her half brother Hector is my closest friend. She's at this moment living in the house I share with Hector in New York."

"You," he said, "are full of wonders, sir. Thank Heaven she got through safely. A number of people, not only Loyalists, have been deeply worried about her. I knew Angus well and have known Anne since she was born. A remarkable young lady. I hope she was not harmed during her travels."

"She's as flawless as ever," I told him.

"That's a blessing," he commented, then frowned. "It occurs to me that your feat in killing the Tory spy will set your purpose to nothing. The people of the backcountry are suspicious by nature and I doubt you will be able to gain the confidence of any secret Loyalist with your notoriety as a rebel hero. I suspect that your credibility has been destroyed. Perhaps you should withdraw and have them send in another agent or let them accept Colonel Brown's Ranger figures."

"The time is being shaved as close as possible now," I pointed out. "There won't be time to place another man in here, and they won't accept Browne's count without confirmation. I must stay and do my best."

"If I had the authority," he said, "I would forbid you to stay. Your risk of betrayal has become great and you possess information of great importance the other side can extract from you. However, since you refuse to withdraw, you must agree to accept help from someone who is known and trusted by the Loyalists. Adjoining Goodowns is Elderbank plantation, owned by a pair of brothers named Ogilvie. They helped Anne away to Charles Town, by the way, and haven't the remotest notion, I'm sure, that I know. I know many things that go on among the Loyalists, but in all the world, sir, you are the only one who knows my true adherence, so please guard it well.

"The Ogilvies, for instance, do not know that I have saved their plantation from confiscation several times and themselves from banishment through my position on the Safety Council. You must find a means of convincing them of your true identity and if they're satisfied they'll help you, I know. They know every person between Ebenezer and Augusta, I think. But be very, very careful in your approach; they are wary, intelligent men who can be ruthless if convinced you're double-dealing them, a rebel spy in disguise. By the way, your true name is James Reid, is it not?"

I nearly jumped out of my boots. "How the devil did you know that?"

"All of us here have old friends on the royalist side," he answered, smiling at my surprise, "and some are in London. The outgoing post is carefully watched, but incoming letters slip past the watchers. One of my correspondents supplies me with a potpourri of London gossip to reassure me that the civilized world is as dizzy as ever. Your activities are considered gossipy plums and your sudden departure for America puzzled the entire city, evidently. When I learned that your French background was false and I saw the excellence of your sample drawings, I began to suspect.

"As the son of famously wealthy Angus, Mr. Hector's doings are similarly noted by Londoners and since he is known to be your inseparable companion, one puts two and two together. I'm flattered at having the celebrated portraitist of the King take my likeness, but I must warn you not to swagger here in Georgia. Be ever modest, discreet and retiring. Efface yourself, Mr. Reid. There may be others who are familiar to some extent with your London standing, and a slip of the tongue could give you away. And above all do not try to cut a swathe through the ladies here as I'm sure you could do, judging from my wife's private remarks to me and my own observation of your appearance and manner. The men of this country take an astonishingly stern and often fatal view of gentlemen who interfere with their womenfolk, especially outlanders."

I laughed. "I pledge you that I have no intention of despoiling Georgia wives and maids. My sole desire is to get my job done and be gone from here back to a place where my every third thought won't be worry about being hanged."

Chapter XII

I SPREAD THE WORK on the Cameron portrait out over a
week in order to better make myself known around
Savannah, in which I was successful enough, being constantly invited to dine by the leading citizens. The price
of such popularity was stiff, though; through each meal I
was forced to listen to interminable lectures of rebel sentiment and on the paradisical future of the great state of
Georgia. The crushing heat of Savannah evenings didn't
encourage socializing to all hours, however, and I was
usually in bed by half past ten o'clock.

The night before I was to give the portrait a few more
swipes with the brush and end it, I was lying awake thinking of the saddle horse and pack horse I was to buy the
next day from a dealer on Cameron's recommendation.
The Post Road, he said, was the graveyard of wagons—
full of holes, ruts, boulders and fords of unreliable depths.
A woman's voice penetrated my musing, coming from the
next room. Her voice was low, to be sure, but the wall was
thin.

"But a week here won't make me any more of a lady
than I am now," she said. "Besides, all our friends are
gone."

A man's voice said, "Buy yourself a nice gown, shoes, a
pretty bonnet and gewgaws. That ship that was here
brought some good things, I hear. Needles and thread,
ribbons, yard goods. Tondee'll take good care of you and
you'll have a fine rest."

"Good glory," she grumbled resentfully, "you could buy
what's left from that in five minutes, Tondee said. Damn
it, I don't want to stay here! You need me for that next
herd!"

"It's time we had a lady around the house instead of

another cowboy," spoke up another man's voice. "Forget about MacGillivray's next batch of critters. Peter and I can fetch 'em down to the pens ourselves, which is why we're riding back tonight."

She said defiantly, "I'll ride back myself alone in the morning, you wait and see!"

The first man growled, "If you do, and if you arrive home alive and unraped, my girl, I promise that you'll never work the stock again at Elderbank."

Amazing. The two men had to be the Ogilvie brothers and the woman their sister Marg, Anne MacDonald's friend. She sounded damned thorny to me.

"Any man tries to force me," she declared, "I'll open him up and carve my initials on his liver."

"Maybe you could do that with one," said the first man who was apparently Peter, "but they travel in twos or more. No more argument, hear? Papa was set on you being a lady and 'tis high time you began looking and acting like one."

She retorted, "Elderbank needs another strong back, not a damn simpering female clotheshorse!"

"Well, as head of the family, you'll do as I say, young lady," said Peter. "Now if you need anything, tell Tondee. John and I've got to ride. We'll be back to get you next week. Simmer down, now, and enjoy your town visit."

I heard them leave, and after a few minutes the bed creaked and she muttered, "Men. Goddamn men. Do this, do that, I'm head of the family. One of these days . . ." And the rest, as Shakespeare wrote, was silence.

A female cowboy man-hater. Lady-hater, too, for that matter. Anne MacDonald had an odd taste in female friends. Then again, to give Anne the benefit of the doubt, on her remote plantation she wouldn't have much choice among girls of her own age. I liked the timbre of this one's voice, but the words spoken by it conjured up a vision of a leathery-faced, muscular Amazon with callused hands. Nevertheless, I was going to have to cultivate her acquaintance because I needed her brothers. What price His Majesty's service, I mused grimly.

I didn't see her about when I had breakfast in the public room, and at Cameron's house as I completed the portrait I mentioned her presence at Tondee's. "They left her here for a town visit, did they?" said Cameron. "Well, they may not know it yet, but they'll not be driving the second

164

herd to Savannah. I met Mr. MacGillivray on the street this morning and in the course of conversation he told me he had decided he could save money by slaughtering and skinning at his cow pens up there on the Beaverdam and rafting the meat and hides down to Savannah, starting with the second herd the Ogilvie brothers are to deliver."

"If she knew that," I remarked, "she'd not stay a minute after her shopping is done, except that her brothers have forbidden her to travel alone on the road."

"Interesting," he said. "You might consider the ramifications. You would do well to have a guide when you start out tomorrow and her brothers are quite right. A woman should have an armed escort on the Post Road."

When I arrived back at Tondee's around noon I was mounted on my new horse, Prince, towing a shaggy, hammerheaded pack horse equipped with a curious contrivance called a packsaddle. One of Tondee's stable hands took the animals in charge, and as I started to leave the stable I noticed somebody currying a horse in one of the stalls. From his dress, he was no Tondee servant. He was dressed in a linen hunting shirt that came to the knees, buckskin-fringed leggings, moccasins, and on his head was a low-crowned, broad-brimmed black hat. He worked industriously with his back to me, and there was an odd grace in his movements that gave me pause. Unless another lodging guest had arrived during the morning, this person could only be my next door neighbor. I said casually, "Good-day. Why don't you let the stablemen groom your horse?"

The person straightened up and turned to look at me and I had an agreeable surprise. From under the man's hat a pretty woman's face regarded me out of level gray eyes. Her face was a smooth oval, nose faintly acquiline and her lips were full on a generous mouth. There was a trace of dimple on her firm chin. She was tall for a woman and her hair was light brown. "I care for my own stock." The eyes inspected me from head to toe, studying the London cut of my suit. "I can see why you don't, sir." She turned her back and resumed work.

The stableman had left and we were alone. I said, "Miss Ogilvie, my name is Robert Allston. I'll be leaving Savannah tomorrow morning to ride to the MacDonald place, Goodowns, where I'm to stay for a few weeks."

She faced me again and there was no good humor in her expression. "I heard about you in the shops this morning, you and your letters from Congress and killing that . . . that Tory spy." A large and vicious-looking knife suddenly appeared in her hand. "Stay clear of me, mister, or I'll open your craw!"

"Honeycake," I smiled, "if you were to do that, Anne MacDonald would be terribly distressed."

The gray eyes widened. "What's that supposed to mean?"

"The green-eyed witch," I answered solemnly, "sees all and knows all. At this very moment, hundreds of miles away, she's probably watching us in a dream and saying, 'Marg, quit being an idiot. 'Tis bad enough that he's one for being where he is at this moment'."

The veil of hostility dropped for a second and I saw a bright flash of delight, then she went behind her guard again. "What have you to do with her? Where is she?"

"She's well and happy and living in the house I share with her half brother Hector," I told her. "In New York. Look, I tell you this in peril of my life. I'm an agent of the Crown, here on His Majesty's service."

Her knife was at the ready and it made me nervous. "You have the smell of a Patriot spy, mister. Likely your people have her in some prison." Her eyes searched mine and she gave out a startled, "Oh!" Then she recovered and demanded, "If you're a Crown agent why did you kill another one at Mr. Cameron's house? I heard about that. Everybody has."

Reluctant as I was to give away Cameron's closely guarded secret, there was no way out. "The man was a rebel spy, trying to betray the captain of the ship and myself to Mr. Cameron. Mr. Cameron is one of us and now that secret is known in Georgia only to you and me. Your brothers owe him a debt of gratitude for his keeping your plantation from being confiscated long ago."

"A pretty story," she said skeptically.

I took a long chance. "If you don't believe me, then turn me over to the authorities and you'll have a chance to be a rebel heroine. Put that damned knife away, please, and be sensible. I need your brothers' help. I learned this morning that they won't be returning to Savannah with that second herd, that the cattle buyer has decided to accept them at his pens on Beaverdam in order to save money. If you like, I'll escort you home. I'll be leaving here in the morning and could use a guide."

"That could be a trick," she said. "Who told you that?"

166

When I explained, she nodded thoughtfully. "That could be so. The driving to Savannah causes the cattle to lose weight and many go astray. If you're telling the truth about Anne, tell me this: who schooled her?"

I smiled, seeing the battle being won. "Her Aunt Mary who was killed by the raiders in the spring, and the English-educated Negro Brutus, whom she called Boodoo when she was a little girl. And you were her fellow pupil whenever you could be persuaded to leave the work at Elderbank."

Warily, she asked, "What is it you're supposed to do here?"

"I'll tell your brothers," I answered.

She gazed at my face, thinking, for a long moment, then said, "If my brothers don't believe you it will be a poor day for you. I'll saddle now and ride to Mr. MacGillivray's cow pens and if 'tis as you said, I'll ride with you in the morning." She looked me over again. "Under those popinjay clothes is there a man who can fight if needed?"

I said, laughing, "Under these clothes there's a man who can fight well enough as well as perform other interesting feats."

She was not dull-witted. Color heightened in her attractive face. "That's slick city talk for something else. Mister, if you so much as lay a hand on me you'll be dead."

"Perish the thought, ma'am," I smiled. "How long will the journey be?"

"It takes two and a half days of moderate riding in good weather," she told me, setting about saddling her horse. When I moved to help, she said shortly, "I'll do this. I'm not helpless, even if I am a woman. Can you lash a pack-saddle?"

"I never have," I admitted.

"I must be out of my mind, setting off with a man who can't even do that," she said disgustedly, cinching the bellyband. Then she became all woman. She turned and looked into my face. "You and Anne—she's very pretty . . . did you . . . I mean, is she—" Her sun-bronzed cheeks flushed again.

It never pays to laugh at a woman being a woman. I said seriously, "No, we get along together like a cat and a dog, or you might say brother and sister. We bicker a lot over her confounded second sight."

Leading the horse out of the stable, she nimbly mounted,

looked down at me and said, "I dreamed of her last night and she had your eyes instead of her own." Spurring her mount, she galloped away.

Later in the afternoon while I was assembling my baggage in preparation for early morning departure, she returned to her room and from the sounds I guessed that she was doing the same thing. Knocking on the wall, I said, "We ride in the morning?"

"At first light," she answered.

"Will you have supper with me?" I asked.

"Just because you're riding with me doesn't make you my beau!" she snapped. "Leave off pestering me now!"

So I supped alone in the public room, having refused several invitations to supper in order to get to bed early, and began to have misgivings about spending two and a half days on the road with that prickly lady. There was no doubt that if she weren't so defensively militant she would be a pleasurable tumble. Later, when I was going to sleep, my thoughts again strayed in that direction, causing Old Nick to stir alertly, but I forcibly thrust such thoughts out of my head, bearing in mind Cameron's warning about tampering with Georgia ladies who had vigilant menfolk.

Tondee had his man lash my packsaddle in the dark early morning, and with our saddlebags filled with food for daytime meals and fodder for the horses carried by the pack animals, we rode out of Savannah and onto the Post Road. I got no conversation from the girl. By the time the sun rose, hot and bright, we were well away from town on the narrow rutted track through the pine forest. She rode astride as Anne did, carrying herself erect and graceful. She had a lovely profile. "I like your upper lip," I observed.

"You best stop that talk right now," she said sharply, eyes ahead. "If I were a man you wouldn't say such foolishness. You want to get along with me, you treat me as if I was a man, hear?"

"I'll try," I answered, "but doubt if I can. I'm here with you because you're a woman and despite your sour temper, you're a damned attractive one."

"I'll show you a real sour temper," she retorted, "unless you quit going on about my female looks."

"That's like asking your brothers to stop talking about crops and livestock," I said. "People's looks are my bread and butter. I paint portraits for a living and faces are my stock-in-trade. You'd be surprised at how many muscles there are in the human face and how many of them have to work when you frown as compared to how few are needed for a smile. Look, I'll show you." When she turned to me I made a ferocious face. "Notice all that effort as compared to this." I smiled winsomely.

The corners of her mouth twitched and she suddenly laughed. "I declare, if you aren't the silliest man! But don't think I don't know all that fiddle-faddle was an excuse to get at that slick city talk about my femaleness, hear? I still think you could be a rebel spy sent among us to see who's conspiring, no matter about your knowing Anne and me having that funny dream."

An idea occurred to me. Digging down into a saddlebag through the boiled eggs, bread and so forth, I fished out my sketchbook, opened it to some drawings of Anne and Hector, and passed it over to her. "Oh, ye of little faith, behold my friends and one of yours."

"Oh, my glory," she breathed. " 'Tis Anne to the life! See her laugh! And this is her half brother Hector? She said he was in New York and she was going to him." She pointed to a drawing of Ira. "Who is that?"

"He's our friend, too," I told her. "His wife was killed and his shipyard burned by Liberty Boys. His name's Ira Tupper and he was the ship's captain who was present at Cameron's house when I killed the spy. Did anyone in Savannah mention to you that the ship's name is *Bonny Anne?*"

Hostility was gone. Her eyes were wide. "For . . . for our Anne?"

I grinned. "For our Anne. The ship belongs to Hector and me and is under contract to the British forces. When we launched her, Anne christened her and claims she and the schooner are twins. Now will you believe me, Marg?"

"I'm inclined to," she answered, "though 'twill be for my brothers to decide."

Although she was still somewhat reservedly cautious, the bristling suspicion was gone and we chatted a good deal more easily as we rode through the broiling heat, the horses black with sweat filmed over by red dust. At midday we paused to have lunch by a stream, where we watered the animals and fed them. Even with her face running with perspiration she was lovely. As we traveled on in the after-

169

noon she said suddenly, "What I don't understand is why the Crown would send a fellow like you into this country, a man who can't even pack a packsaddle, dressed like you're going to a ball at some fancy city house, a picture-maker by trade. Lord knows what'll happen if we come on a gang of rogues."

Smiling, I said, "I'll have you to protect me."

" 'Tisn't to joke about," she declared. "City ways aren't backcountry ways. There are men in this region who are mighty like animals, like wolves, ranging about to murder and ravish. Even with the militia out to guard the roads they sneak around through the brush."

"In other words," I said with irritation, "you doubt my ability to defend you."

"I can take care of myself against any man, even odds!" she flared. " 'Tis you defending yourself I was thinking on!"

"Stop worrying," I told her. "I can handle any clodhopper in this country. Tell me, what have you got against being a woman? A mannish female is a dreadful thing."

She was angry. "So's a prissy picture-drawer in fancy britches! Clodhopper! Mannish female! La-di-da English talk! You think I'm mannish because I won't let you have your way with me? Mister slick talk—"

"Oh, stop," I interrupted wearily. "The only way I want with you is peace. I'm sorry if I offended you and beg your pardon. Peace—for God's sake."

We had peace, silent peace. The heat and fatigue of riding all day was not conducive to jolly chitchat. I wondered what beautiful, feminine Anne MacDonald could have in common with this belligerent young woman who wished she were a man. As the sun sank in the west, the shadows lengthened and I broke the stillness. "Do we put up somewhere tonight or outcamp?"

"However you like," she answered distantly. "Foley's ordinary lies ahead. 'Tis no palace, with a pair of rooms thrown up in the loft. You might like to camp. It might be safer if Foley's in his usual style, drunk and roaring."

"But I'll have you to defend me," I said. "If there's a chance for a bed I'd rather sleep on that than on the ground among the ants and chiggers."

"Foley's a raving rebel and hates Loyalists," she said, giving me a withering look. "And he hates outlanders and he'll hate you for the English way you talk."

"My," I commented, "he sounds fearfully formidable. How is the food?"

"All right if he lets you have it," she replied, "and even if he serves you he's likely to make you wish he hadn't."

Annoyed, I lost patience. "See here, if the man's that offensive to you and you'd rather outcamp, say so and we shall. Otherwise, I prefer to sleep under a roof and off the ground."

"But you're the great strong *man* and my brave escort," she retorted. " 'Tis for you to decide where the weak female shall bide tonight. I only wished to do my duty as your guide, sir, by warning you."

"Oh, for God's sake," I muttered, and subsided into fuming silence, unwilling to pursue the nonsense into what promised to be a full-scale bicker.

We reached the ordinary at sunset, a ramshackle structure built of logs. After turning our animals over to a hungry-looking Negro, with sharp instructions about grooming and feeding them, I took our saddlebags and ushered Marg inside. The place was mainly a taproom, empty except for a serving counter and several tables with chairs. At one end was a loft, reached by a steep flight of steps, where in the twilight I saw a pair of roughly partitioned chambers. A back door opened onto a yard where a woman tended cooking food in a small cookhouse that was open on the side facing the main building. A fat, unkempt man stood behind her, waving his arms and delivering some kind of speech.

From the doorway, I called to him, "You, there!"

He turned, startled, and nearly fell down. He was quite drunk. Goggling at me, he said uncertainly, "Guests?" He wove his way to the door, peering at me.

I said, "There are two of us, with two riding horses and two packhorses. Fodder and oats for the animals and see they're curried. My companion is a lady and we shall stay the night in separate chambers. Give us warm water, soap and towels for washing, then supper. While our supper is being prepared, I will have a bottle of rum and two clean glasses with a pitcher of water. I shall also be obliged if you will strike a light in here."

"Aye, sir, yes, sir!" He bumbled into the taproom and as he managed to light a couple of candles he bellowed, "Welcome to the House of Foley, sir! Timothy Aloysius Foley, Esquire, at your humble service, sir! Welcome to the home of Liberty and Independence for all!" He stared at me. "Would you mind saying again, sir? My mind was taken up with instructing the help in the kitchen."

I repeated my orders, slowly and clearly, and he bobbed his head. "Aye, sir, and a supper fit for a king it shall be, sir! Though we don't hold with kings in this house— death to tyranny! Liberty or death!" His watery eyes fell on Marg and he smiled blearily. "No need for separate chambers. The front chamber up yonder has a fine big feather bed where you and your lady can frolic with plenty of room and sleep like lambs after your sport, sir."

Dirty, sweaty, tired and irritated by the man, I maintained my patience. "Two rooms, Mr. Foley. The lady and I are not wed, only traveling together. My name is Allston and the lady is Miss Ogilvie."

She had removed her man's hat and even in her travel-grimed condition her face was lovely in the candlelight. The man eyed her and scowled, "Oho, 'tis you, is it? Grown up into a woman. I'll serve no Tories in my house."

"If you value your license and wish to remain in trade," I said, "you'll comply with the law and do as you're bid. I have influential friends in government at Savannah. I'll thank you to show courtesy and look to your service."

Swaying a little, he sneered, "Likely you're a damned Tory, too, talking like a bloody Englishman, threatening me, telling me how to run my house." He leered at Marg. "There must be something missing from your man's gear, Miss Tory, not wanting a tumble in bed with a pretty piece of tail like you."

Catching the front of his shirt and hauling him close, I slapped his unshaven face so hard his head rocked, then flung him backward so that he went sprawling on the floor. "You," I told him as he scuttled around trying to get to his feet, "have a foul mouth, and so long as I'm in this pigsty of yours you'll open it only when you're spoken to and if you're not careful what you say with it you'll find it full of loose teeth. Get up, you filthy slob, and carry out my orders."

The woman came rushing in, helped her husband to his feet and said to him, "Go see to the horses, Tim. Go, now, and stay. I'll do here." Foley gave me a look of glazed hatred and staggered out the door. Mrs. Foley was thin and haggard, but she smiled and said, "Good-evening, sir. Marg, you've growed up real pretty and 'tis good to see you again. Foley won't be about anymore tonight. I heard what you wanted. I'll fetch the wash water."

With our faces and hands scrubbed, waiting for supper, I poured a couple of glasses of rum and handed one to Marg. She smelled it and said, "I've never drunk rum. Will this much make me tipsy?"

"Possibly," I answered. " 'Tis a man's drink."

I expected a show of indignation at the small barb, but instead she tasted the drink and made a face. "Medicine. I don't think I like it much and I don't like you when you say things like that."

Her face was pretty and composed, her tone mild. "Well," I said, "I don't like what was going on in your head before we got here. Was there any truth in what he said about you?"

"You know I'm a Loyalist," she replied.

Laughing, I said, "I meant about the tumble—" I didn't have time to duck as she flung the contents of her glass into my face, causing my eyes to burn like fury. Mopping my face with my kerchief I remembered the last time a woman had done that to me and reflected that Lady Beauvoir's wine had been kinder to the eyeballs.

"Your mouth is dirtier than his!" she exclaimed, and to my dismay she proceeded to weep, covering her face with her hands.

"Here, here!" I ordered, disturbed, "None of that, please, Marg! 'Twas but a clumsy joke and I'm sorry." I handed my kerchief to her.

Dabbing at her eyes, she gave me a shy smile. "The rum doesn't smell nearly so bad on your handkerchief. I'm sorry for what I did, too. May I have some more, please?" This time she drank some. " 'Tis better now, after the first taste. Will you also forgive me for being a silly wench for leading you on about Foley?"

"No harm done," I answered, seeing her as being remarkably feminine for the first time and thoroughly enjoying the charming sight. "He's been disposed of. But what did you expect to accomplish, see the city man quail and cower?"

She was hesitant. " 'Tis not a thing to tell to a stranger and especially a man."

"We're not strangers anymore," I told her. "If it has to do with that swine Foley, you'd best tell me, Marg."

She dropped her eyes and murmured nervously, "I

173

wanted to see if I could face him after all these years of . . .
of being afraid, Rob. The last time I stopped here was
when I was about twelve, with my papa. I was . . . doing
my business in the backhouse and—" She stopped, her face
flaming pinkly.

A pretty little girl alone in the outhouse and a man like
Foley watching. Anger surged. I growled, "Did he attack
you?"

She shook her head, then blurted, "He stood in the door
and shook his . . . his thing at me, rubbing it and it . . . it
spat at me!" The tears again, and the hand that held the
glass trembled. "I nearly died of fright!"

"I shouldn't wonder," I commented, fighting down the
urge to seek out Foley and kill him, and trying to retain
a calm appearance for her sake. "Then what happened?
Did he touch you?"

"No," she answered shakily. "He just . . . disappeared
and I ran out screaming. I was ashamed to tell Papa what
happened, so I told him there was a snake out there that
had frightened me. A long time later I was glad I didn't
tell Papa, because he would have killed Foley and might
have been hanged. Before we came here I kept saying those
things to you because . . . I was really afraid to come here
but I wanted to see if I was brave enough—oh, Rob, I'm
not making sense, am I?"

My heart went out to her. "You're making good sense,
honey. You'd been badly wounded in your mind a long
time ago and wanted to see if the scar had healed." I began
to see a foggy connection between the incident and her
desire to be treated like a man, though I couldn't quite put
my finger to it. "Is it healed?"

She nodded. "The sight of him makes me sick in my
stomach yet, but I'm not afraid of him anymore. If he
were to do anything like that now to me I'd kill him with
my knife."

"How many villains have you slain with that fearsome
weapon?" I smiled, glad to see the tense emotion gone
from her.

"None." She smiled back. "But just because I've told
you that disgusting story I've never told anyone before,
don't get any ideas or you might be first."

Mrs. Foley brought our supper, plain but tasty food.
"Tim's asleep in the barn. Don't pay him any mind. He's
naught but wind and bluster these days. I'll fix your beds."

174

It was a pleasant meal, surprisingly so considering the unpleasant introduction to it, and at the end I said to Marg, "Your eyes are like smoky gray stars and I still say your upper lip is sweetly formed."

There was no fiery leap to arms, only a sleepy smile. "Old slippery city-talking Rob. There's nothing wrong with your upper lip, either. That rum has put me to sleep, I declare. I'm sure I'll snore tonight. If I do, hammer on the wall and I'll turn over to stop it."

She did not snore. I lay as still as possible so as not to disturb her with the atrociously noisy rustling of the corn husks in my mattress and listened to the easy rhythm of her sleep breathing through the rough board partition that separated us. Thinking of how lovely her face must look in repose on the bed where Foley had invited us to frolic, my mind drifted on to logical fancies and Old Nick stirred. Forcing my mind to the more mundane problems of the forthcoming Loyalist head count, I went to sleep.

A sound awakened me. For a moment I thought it was Marg whispering and muttering in her sleep, then through the cracks I saw a moving light, a hand-held candle. Marg's voice suddenly cried, "Get out of here, you dirty pig! Get out, get out!" There was panic in it.

In one fast movement I seized my French pistol from under the pillow, rolled out of bed and plunged out the door, hearing her crying my name over and over. In her room Foley stood swaying, the candle in one hand and his limp pizzle in the other, mumbling incoherent obscenities. Marg was backed, crouching, into a corner, stark naked, her face a mask of terror as she called my name repeatedly in a strange, high and shrill voice.

I roared, "Foley, you son of a bitch!"

He turned his head to stare blankly at me, still fumbling with his pizzle, and mumbled something. Raising the pistol, I growled, certain that I was going to kill him, "You're not fit to live among human beings." There was a small nipple on the top of the pistol muzzle for sighting and due to his drunken swaying I had difficulty in lining it up with the center of his forehead. My finger slowly tightened on the trigger. I wanted a clean kill. Then my arm was suddenly knocked upward and the pistol fired with a deafening report in the small room, clouding it with acrid powder smoke. Mrs. Foley, weeping, clung to my arm and cried,

175

"Don't harm him, don't harm him! He could harm nobody with what he's got!"

I said to her, "Madam, I'm going to reload this pistol and if I lay my eyes on that pile of swill once more in this house while I'm in it, you'll surely be a widow."

"You won't see him again, sir!" she cried, pulling and tugging the sodden clot from the room. God knows how she managed to get him down the steep steps. I took out my own flint-and-steel from my breeches pocket and lighted the candle beside Marg's bed, catching no more than a last glimpse of the lovely nudity before she dropped the hunting shirt over it. "I didn't know—I went all to pieces," she sniffled. "I woke up and there he was and I was a little child again!" She gave me a wry smile. "I thought I was strong and brave, but I was nothing but a woman after all, wasn't I?"

"That's nothing to be ashamed of," I told her, sitting down on the edge of the bed as she skipped under the sheet again. "To be a woman like you is something to be damned proud of." She was calming, so I smiled, "And to be especially proud of what I saw unveiled. You're a wonderfully lovely lady, Marg."

There she went to blushing again. "That was horrible. I was going to sleep dressed like you did, but 'twas so hot and stuffy up here under the roof—Rob, even if I'd had my knife by me, I was too frightened to go at him. I was little Marg shrieking for Papa, then the pistol went off and there you were."

"Honeybun," I said, looking down into the lovely trusting face on the pillow and smiling, "you were shrieking for me, unless you called your papa Rob."

"I was?" Her gray eyes were enormous. "But I think I was thinking Papa. His name was Jamie. How awful to be naked like that in front of you!"

"The circumstances were awful," I said, feeling a wave of emotion I didn't quite understand, "but there was nothing awful about what I saw of you. Look, we'll leave this house before sunup, without breakfast. We'll have that on the road somewhere. I can't risk failing my task here by killing that creature and I shall if I see him again. Go to sleep and get a good night's rest." She smiled up at me, a little girl's tender faith in it, and something happened in my heart. Bending over, I kissed her lightly on the lips and murmured, "Good-night, honeybun."

Something like startled wonder came into the eyes. She whispered, "Good-night, Rob."

Back in my own cubicle the dry husks made a devilish din when I lay down, and from the other side of the partition she said, "I think I want to talk."

Another risk had presented itself, a powerful attraction toward her, now that I had seen her sweet feminine character and beautiful body. I said, "I'm playing the role of your papa tonight, puss, and Papa says go to sleep or I shall tan your backside, young lady."

There was an echo of a giggle in her voice. "You're a pretty good man, Rob Allston, but you're not good enough to do that."

"If I come into that room again," I said truthfully, "it won't be to spank your pretty behind, lovely lady, and how good a man I am remains for you to find out."

There was a silence, then a smothered voice said, "Damn you to hell, you're no better than Foley!"

But she went to sleep quickly, and as I listened to her regular breathing and snuggling movements I thought of how like being in the same bed it was and yet how damned foully different. Old Nick yearned, throbbing mindlessly and without conscience. He cared nothing for my problems. That I was going to have Marg was a foregone conclusion, and the only question in that regard was when. I needed her brothers and they would take a dim view of my tupping their sister. In New York I had been warned not to become personally involved. I would have to control myself until the work was done, that's all there was to it, I told myself. But that would take weeks, and Jamie Reid was not used to such enduring celibacy.

When I finally went to sleep I dreamed, and for once not about roads or Anne. Marg was in the dream—or dreams, for there were crazy overlapping ones of bewildering confusion. Only one I remembered: she and I, elegantly dressed, were dancing by ourselves in a vast and splendid ballroom, being applauded by a throng of handsomely costumed ladies and gentlemen. I looked down into her face and saw nothing but terrible, aching despair that reached out and touched me so that I felt it, too, and the dream disintegrated.

In the very early dark of the morning, sluggish with unslept sleep, I woke Marg with a knock on the partition, dressed and, finding Mrs. Foley lighting her kitchen fire,

177

paid our bill. From her I got a sack of food and fodder for the horses. The animals appeared to be still half asleep, too, as we rode through the pre-dawn forest hush. I was not yet shaved and that made me uncomfortable; my face never seemed to wake until after it had been scraped. Marg rode in silence, a dark figure in her man's clothing. I drowsed in the saddle and guessed she was doing likewise.

When the sun came up, I saw we were no longer in pine woods. The forest was of oak, hickory, beech, maple, sycamore and other hardwoods, tall, full ancient trees. The sun's rays slanted down in golden shafts and the trees were alive with birds, warbling, twittering and screaming. No longer sleepy, I was very much alive and exclaimed to Marg, "What a beautiful morning! I'm starved!"

Gone was yesterday's taciturn or belligerent hoyden. She smiled, "There's a pretty place ahead. Mrs. Foley gave us some bacon and some eggs, and coffee grounds, too. Would you like that?"

"Who is this marvelous stranger I find with me?" I laughed. "This adorable lady who speaks of heavenly manna in dulcet tones. Madam, you're ravishing this morning and even if you burn the food I'll eat it with reverent gusto."

"Oh, fish," she said, "you're giddy from no breakfast."

Under her instructions I built a cookfire from deadfalls and while she prepared the meal I shaved in the stream that burbled peacefully nearby. A curious deer paused to watch, then leaped away when our eyes met. Bacon and eggs and coffee were created by God to be consumed in the open air of a sunny morning while admiring a lovely young woman. "I hope you like this perfect day," I told her, "because I ordered it arranged especially for you."

"I do thank you, sir," she said primly. "I find it quite satisfactory in all respects. I fear 'twill be hot, though, later —or have you arranged otherwise?"

"If the weather today offends you in any way, honeybun," I smiled, "let me know instantly and I'll have a sharp word with Dame Nature."

She became serious. "Rob, tell me something. You've known a deal of ladies, good and bad in those cities you've lived in, haven't you?"

"A few," I answered cautiously.

She blushed and hesitated, then asked, "Is there anything

178

about me like . . . like a bad woman?" She watched me anxiously.

"Not a trace," I assured her. "You are sweet and good and pure. And you have the strength of character that will keep you that way. What in blazes brought that on?"

"I . . . I expected to be ashamed this morning." The blush again. "But I'm not even ashamed of not being ashamed. About you seeing me naked last night." She threw a stick at me and exclaimed, "Oh, don't look at me like that!"

I burst into laughter. "Marg, we're all naked under our clothes! There's no shame in what God has wrought! Foley, now, there's a great stinking mountain of shame because surely the Devil spawned him. But you? Marg, your body is beautiful, glorious! Celebrate it!"

"I think you're a heathen," she said, sipping her coffee, "and so must I be for having no shame. Have you seen many naked women? You sound like it."

"Honeybun," I told her, "I've seen 'em by the scores— young ones, old ones, plump ones, skinny ones. I'm an artist, you see. Sometimes it's necessary to have a nude woman—Greek goddess style or something of the kind— in a picture, so we hire a woman to come in and pose for us. And nothing racy goes on. She simply poses, puts on her clothes, gets paid and goes home."

"What a bold way to earn money," she said. "I'd never let a strange man see me bare naked for any amount of money."

"Well, I saw you last night," I said airily, "and it didn't cost a penny."

"That was different," she commented. "I mean, not counting Foley and all that, you're not a strange man. You're—well, you're Rob."

She could not have realized the implications. Clear signals had been hoisted. I felt slightly disturbed. The brittle person of yesterday would have been easier to get along with than this new one, this blushing, lovely and innocent young country girl who showed every sign of being compliant. If it had not been for the other considerations, I reflected, I could probably ease her down in the ferns and have her before the coffee dregs got cold, yet at the same time I sensed another, more profound and undefinable reason why that should not be done. But if we stayed there I could lose self-command. Just looking at her made my heart pound.

179

I got to my feet. "That's who I am indeed, for better or worse. Let's clear up these things and be on our way. Time flees and no man pursueth."

Dame Nature failed to cooperate with me and as we rode on through the day the weather was hotter, if anything, than the day before. It was more bearable, though, because of our new friendly relationship. She told me about her family and how they had hewn and hacked Elderbank out of the wilderness, and the deaths—several years apart—of her parents. Abruptly, she broke off and asked me, "Will you tell me what is the service you're to do here for the King? What is there in this backcountry that would interest him? We're but a scattering of common folk who struggle for a living."

She was loyal, strong-minded and intelligent, and I would shortly have to tell her brothers. It was clear that I had her trust now. I told her about the head count and the purpose of it. She hung on every word and when I finished she threw her head back and shouted to the sky, "Oh, thank you, God, thank you!" Then she brought her mount alongside mine and, laughing and crying, seized my hand and pressed it to her lips. "Oh, bless you, Rob! Oh, you dear angel! The King's army coming! Rob, 'tis our dream come true! How we've prayed—the burnings, murdering, seizings, trials and banishment! We'll have our land again our own!" Wiping the tears away, she said, "But 'tis so late—many have fled or joined the rebels in despair. Do those folks in New York know that?"

"They know it very well," I answered, shaken by her reaction, "and that's another reason why I was sent here from there, to tell you that and give you not only hope but promise."

"That was wise," she said soberly. "We can't believe the promises of Colonel Browne's Rangers anymore when they tell of the Crown coming back. Do you know of them?"

"I'm to work with them after a fashion," I answered. "I met one in New York—a Captain Hugh Wallbrook. Rather a nice chap, though I'm glad to be on his side."

She squealed. "I declare, Hugh in New York! There'll be no bearing him now! He's an old friend of ours." She blushed again, entrancing me, for it made her prettily maidenly. "He was sweet on me a little bit before he went off to St. Mary's to join the Rangers."

"Were you a little bit sweet on him?" I asked.

180

She was flustered. "Just a smidgen. He was an awfully nice boy. Rob?"

"Yes?" I said.

Looking at her mount's ears, she said slowly, "I'm sorry I was such a bitch to you yesterday. I didn't know . . . a lot of things."

Easy does it, old lad, I told myself. She's coming on all woman and you'll not be able to keep her off if she gets the bit between her teeth. Steering the conversation to a more impersonal plane, I said, "I understand why it was, Marg, and now 'tis all behind us. We're good friends now as we should be. Where do we put up tonight?"

"Well, there's Leavitt's inn," she answered. "Mr. Leavitt's a decent man who knew my father well. His place is clean and comfortable, but I don't know. There might be trouble there."

I said suspiciously, "Now, now, what are you about? More pranks like yesterday?"

"No, oh, no, Rob!" she exclaimed. " 'Tis just that Mr. Leavitt's gone Whig and his place is used by the militia who guard the roads as a kind of rallying place or whatever, and most of the boys know my family."

"I see," I murmured. "Dirty Tories and so forth, eh? I can handle that situation, I think."

"You probably can," she said, "but my brothers and I have to plow a straight and narrow furrow where rebels are concerned and we can't afford to get mixed up in squabbles with them. The militia boys blame Loyalists for having to give up the farm work to guard the roads. They drink a lot and when they drink they like to fight something terrible."

Nor could I afford squabbles. The affair with Foley had come close to disaster for my mission. I was in no position to flaunt swaggering gallantry. "They sound like the Quahaug Grenadiers back home in Massachusetts. Well, discretion is the better part, I suppose. We'll outcamp and entertain the snakes and ants tonight, eh? We'll need food and horse fodder."

"Mr. Leavitt will sell it to us," she said. "A peddler from Massachusetts stopped at Elderbank once. That's where all this awful trouble started. We don't blame those folks up there for getting riled up over things like the Port Act, but that had nothing to do with Georgia. Is Boston like Savannah, Rob?"

When I left Boston for London as a seventeen-year-old,

181

newly graduated from the Latin School, I had despised the city, yet now as I told her about it I felt nostalgia, remembering the familiar things, the Common, Hitchbourne's wharf where I learned to swim, the North End where I learned to fight, camping and fishing in Neponset and the Blue Hills of Milton, the good food at the Oyster House in Dock Square and how the bell of King's Chapel around the corner from my boyhood home would rattle the china with its ringing on Sundays. As I told Marg about it, it came to me that London was not my home despite the good things it had given me; I was a Massachusetts man. The thought did not linger. Memories awoke of "King" Hancock and his Liberty Boys rabble from the North End and how they had infected the city like a loathsome, disruptive disease, and so did distaste for my native city.

In the late afternoon we came to Leavitt's inn, a commodious house in good state of repair. I left Marg to mind the horses in the shade of a big tree and went inside. A dozen or so men were lounging and drinking in the public room and to a man they ceased conversation when I entered. Each man had a musket or fowling piece by him and while most of them wore the backcountry buckskin dress with linen hunting shirts, a few wore items of military uniform. A white-haired elderly man came from behind the serving counter and said, "Good-day to you, sir, and welcome. My name is Leavitt. How may I serve you?"

"How do you do, Mr. Leavitt?" I answered. "I'm Robert Allston, passing through from Savannah. My traveling companion and I are in some haste and wish to continue our journey northward without putting up for the night. I'll be obliged if you will sell us food and drink to take with us for supper and breakfast, and corn or oats for our four horses."

"Well, now, that's a pity," said Leavitt. "I have some comfortable rooms, sir, but if you're in haste to get on as far as possible in the daylight you will have to camp, of course. Tell me what you'd like and I'll see if I have it."

I rattled off the list that Marg had suggested and Leavitt nodded. "I have those. 'Twill take a few minutes to put together. Make yourself comfortable and help yourself to the drink and keep your score, sir." He went off to another room.

Going to the serving counter, watched by the silent militiamen, I poured myself a mug of rum and as I took a drink the conversations resumed. Several men peered out the window and one said, "Hey, looky there, 'tis the Ogilvie gal. Brothers left her at Savener, heard tell. Purty baggage, ain't she, for all them man's clothes."

Another commented, "By God, I'd admire to ride her through the melon patch."

There were guffaws. Somebody said, "I'd surely like to ride *her* melon patch. I got somethin' here that'd make her damn Tory eyes see good old Liberty stars and make her little royalist arse whistle 'Yankee Doodle'."

With my nose in the rum mug I wondered how long I could endure. Much more of that and I would be forced to dismantle a portion of the Georgia rebel militia. A darkly sun-browned young man wearing a single epaulet on a military coat stepped over to me and said, "How do. I'm Jess Ricks, cap'n of this company."

Shaking hands with him, I said, "Honored, captain. I'm Robert Allston."

"I know," he said. "Heard you speakin' with Mr. Leavitt. I'm not nosy, 'tis my duty. You talk like an Englishman. What's your business in this country?"

The interrogation didn't upset me. I had been surprised that we had traveled for nearly two days and a night without being challenged on the road. I answered, "For one thing, I happen to be escorting the lady outside from Savannah to her home at Elderbank plantation. Since you're an officer of the militia of this region and have a right to know—indeed, a duty to know—I expect to be a guest for some weeks at Goodowns plantation."

"I know that lady outside well enough," he remarked, looking out the window. "She's Tory." There was no hostility in his voice, merely a statement of fact. "There's nobody at Goodowns these days but the niggers. Who're you to be a guest of, Mr. Allston?"

Smiling, I took out my forged documents and said, "You're to be commended for your alertness, captain, but before you gaol me as an enemy Tory, read these. You'll find that I'm to be the guest of the Continental Congress."

The militiamen, who had been listening to the exchange, crowded around Ricks as he scanned the papers and reread them, his brows knitted with effort and his lips moving. "Well, damn my soul!" he exclaimed. "Great jumpin' goddamn bullfrogs! Benjamin Franklin *and* the Continental Congress!" He thrust the papers back to me, grinning. "I swear, and I thought you might of been a Tory outlander, travelin' with her and all!" He looked around at his men. "We got a real big one here, boys! This here gentleman's a personal friend of Dr. Franklin, comes from France to do a big job of work for the Congress! Got a letter there from Mr. Cameron, too, down to Savener! Yassir, we got ourselves a real honest-to-God big Patriot!"

Uproar ensued. The men, shouting and laughing, crowded in, shaking my hand and slapping my back, trying to force drinks on me. They had never seen any man connected with the rebellion other than their local leaders and here was one who knew near-legendary leaders. They excitedly pressed me to stay over, promising no harm to my Tory companion. That would never do, because some of them were already half drunk and the sun was far from setting.

Raising both arms, I pleaded for a chance to speak, and when the turmoil subsided, I said, "Friends, countrymen and fellow Patriots, thank you for your warm welcome. I shall remember you as one of the most soldierly groups of fighting men I've yet encountered in the great state of Georgia and you may be sure that the Continental Congress will hear of it from me. There's nothing I would like better than to remain here in the warm bosom of your comradely fellowship, but circumstances beyond my control militate otherwise."

The gaping mouths assured me I was making an impression even if most of them, unlettered, simple men, had only a dim notion of what the words meant. I warmed to my oratory. "Alas, gentlemen, stern duty calls. Regardless of her unfortunate political adherence, the lady who waits outside was placed in my charge for safe delivery to her home, to which I pledged my sacred word of honor. As the good soldiers and honorable gentlemen you are, you know I may not be delinquent in the discharge of such a sacred responsibility. I must be true to honor and trust in order that it redound to the greater glory of all patriotic Americans in the sacred name of liberty. Gentlemen, long live the United States of America! Death to tyranny!"

There was an openmouthed silence for a long moment and I was afraid I had overdone the nonsense, then a great shout went up and I was nearly buried under an avalanche of backslappers and handshakers. Leavitt appeared and I ordered a keg of whisky be given to the militiamen, which produced further noisy ovations. When Marg and I rode away the militiamen gathered in the dooryard of the inn and cheered, flinging their hats in the air, to which I responded with a wave of my own hat.

"Good glory," said Marg. "What happened in there? I was afraid for you when I saw them all looking out the window at me, the dirty Tory wench. Then all at once they were taking off the roof with their cheering."

"A writing gentleman in England," I answered, "a rather pompous ass named Johnson, said awhile ago that patriotism is the last refuge of a scoundrel. What you heard was a scoundrel taking refuge."

Her eyes flashed and she exclaimed indignantly, "Pompous ass he must be! My brothers and I are patriotic subjects of His Majesty, and it may be that you're a scoundrel, Rob Allston, but don't you dare call us scoundrels!"

"Keep your hair on, honeybun," I soothed. "What he meant was that patriotism is such a respected virtue that 'tis hard to attack a rogue who uses it as a cover for his misdoings, such as John Hancock. I simply delivered a most absurd speech when they pressed me to stay. I am supposed to be a flaming Patriot, you know."

"Old slippery-tongue," she commented. "I'm not sure you're not a scoundrel. You come on awfully slick and easy to everybody." She looked up at the sky, which was clouding over. " 'Twill be one of those hot close nights when the 'skeeters will be a curse and we might have a shower. We'd best get camped while a body can still see his hand in front of his face."

Several miles above Leavitt's she turned her horse off the road and led the way to a clearing, a small meadow with plenty of grass for grazing and bordered by a creek. "I've camped here with my brothers," she said. We fed and watered the horses, hobbled them and turned them loose, and she showed me how to make a bed of pine boughs. I placed mine on a hummock near our baggage and she arranged hers several yards away under a tree. While she got out the food for supper, I gathered wood for the fire, fascinated by the dreamlike quality of the light under the cloudy sky in the growing dusk. The scene in the clearing where Marg busied herself and the horses munched grass reminded me of old Italian paintings where colors are like brilliant jewels and nothing casts a shadow. There was not the faintest breath of wind and the sultry heat was oppressive. When I delivered my armload of wood she said, "Will you make the fire while I wash myself? I'm itchy, dirty and must smell like a blanket the old sow had her litter on."

"Go to it," I answered. She took a towel from her saddlebags and went off, while I laid and set the fire, glad to see that the smoke had a deterrent effect on the increasing mosquitoes. With a good little blaze going, I turned to see where she was, and was promptly filled with delight at the picture.

The gloaming had become an eerie twilight with colors grayed and brooding, and emerging from the dark waters of the creek, Marg, stark naked, was like a whitely glowing marble figure of Aphrodite. On the bank she stood drying herself with the towel. With her hair loosed and her unconsciously graceful pose, she was like a dryad. A strong movement started in my loins and I forced myself to turn back to the fire. I had not had a woman since Nassau and the needs of my body were becoming demanding.

Coming to the fire, dressed and smiling, she said, "Oh, I feel so good! You go take a bathe, Rob, while I cook. Mind the 'skeeters—they're coming on real thick."

Thick? They were solid at the creek, but the water was heaven, cool and refreshing. Submerged with only my eyes and nose out of water, I watched the girl at the fire. Under water, the mosquitoes didn't bother Old Nick, but Marg did; he stood out in defiant erection, waving in the creek current, and I desperately determined to ignore him this night, no matter what the provocation. It was going to be a difficult time.

The appetizing fragrance of frying pork chops and potatoes with onions filled the air when I joined her and had a drink of rum while I watched her lovely face intent on her work. When I asked her if she'd like a glass, she smiled over the fire, "No, thank you. I don't much like the taste. If 'tis supposed to make you feel good I don't need it at all." Serving out the food, she threw clumps of grass on the fire, which created clouds of acrid smoke to deter the insects, and we settled down to eat hungrily.

"Even-steven," she said.

"How is that?" I asked.

"Now I've seen you in your pelt, too," she explained, laughing. "I declare, you looked like a huge white ghost coming out of the water. I had but a quick look, you moved so fast. Kelpies on your tail?"

"The mosquitoes are so thick over the water you can walk on 'em," I said, hoping she had not seen my other, irrepressible tail flaunting himself in upright eagerness, and thought of *her* tail. It was an interesting, repeated and furtive play, watching her backside. The leggings she wore came to the top of her thighs and under the long hunting shirt she wore nothing. If I were on the ground, somewhat to her rear when she swung up into her saddle, I always caught a flashing glimpse of her nicely rounded white buttocks before she could deftly smooth the back of the hunting shirt under her seat. Such boylike peeping did nothing good for my reluctantly chaste condition. Old Nick, reading my thoughts, struggled. I led the conversation to safer ground. "Tell me about my other neighbor who lives on the north of Goodowns," I said. "You've mentioned him and Anne told me something about him—Jenks. Seems to be a bit of a pest."

"You'll get to know Abraham well," she said. "He tells everybody he has to keep watch on Goodowns for Angus MacDonald, and everybody knows he'll do anything to lay hands on it. He wanted his boy Jedediah to marry Anne, but she just laughed at Jed and that made him madder than a hornet. Not because he wanted to marry Anne, only because he hates to be laughed at. Jed's afraid of white girls. He's a nigger-girl chaser. Abraham's a justice of the peace and a big rebel, member of the County Safety Committee, though that's only because he thinks he can get Loyalist property by buying it cheap before it can be confiscated."

"A rather unpalatable fellow," I observed.

"He was a good neighbor before the troubles," she said, "and then he got land greedy—land crazy's more like it. He's got a big family and they all live on his place they call Jenks Town. He's very religious and is the minister of the church they built there. He does all the family marrying and christening, though he's not ordained in anything, really."

"With Anne out of the picture," I asked, "does he still covet Goodowns?"

"Oh, my goodness, yes," she replied. "He was friends with Angus in the old days. Angus loaned him money to get started with Jenks Town. My brother Peter says he wouldn't put it past Abraham to write to Angus offering

187

a false bill of sale to keep Goodowns from being confiscated, promising to give it back if the Crown wins. He wants Elderbank, too. We think he might try to get me to marry Jed."

"You!" I exclaimed, taken aback. "How the devil could that get him your brothers' property?"

"Abraham would make a good rebel lady out of me by clearing me with the Safety Committee," she answered bitterly. "Women aren't supposed to have any politics. 'Weak vessels,' he calls 'em. Then if my brothers were banished, they could make over title to Elderbank to me to keep it in the family and when I'd marry Jed, 'twould be the same as Jenks' property, you see? We know Abraham and how his head works and that's what we think he might try to do." .

"Ye gods," I commented, "what devious scheming. Would that really be possible?"

"Not as far as we're concerned," she said, "but you don't know Abraham. His committee's been down on us. We've taken the Test Oath abjuring the King but that doesn't mean much because everybody knows an oath taken under threat is so much wind. Peter and John have been arrested twice and fined once. If Abraham could catch 'em red-handed at playing Loyalists they'd be banished and Elderbank confiscated, but we know Abraham would step in and try to make an arrangement so he could get Elderbank before the state can."

"With you as his son's wife," I said. "What do you think of that?"

She made a face. "It makes me sick. I despise Jed and always have, since he was a little boy, doing dirty things with the nigger girls behind the barn. But if it came to protecting my brothers' lives—they could be hanged if things got worse—I'd agree to marry him."

My good feeling had gone. I had an impulse to argue with her that such a marriage would be not much more than prostitution. However, I didn't want to risk her anger; I was enjoying her company too much, if not the depressing subject of conversation. "What do your brothers think of all this?"

"They say they'll burn the place and sow the fields with salt," she declared, "then we'll all go to East Florida or the islands. But there must be a better way to work it out. Elderbank is our blood, our flesh."

"The better way is to hang on until the end of the year, Marg," I told her, "When the King's soldiers come to scatter the Abraham Jenkses of this country."

She beamed radiantly in the fire glow. "Oh, Rob, how happy my brothers will be when they know! Yes, oh yes, 'tis the better, only way!"

After cleaning up the supper utensils and checking the animals' hobbles we went to our separate pine branch beds, and I promptly found myself in mortal combat with a million mosquitoes who settled on every square inch of exposed skin. The air was windless, still and sticky with humidity. From Marg's direction I heard vigorous slaps and muttered imprecations. I rose and rummaged around among our baggage until I found one of the canvas horsepack covers and on my fragrant bed pulled it over me. It made for a hot and airless tent, but barred the voracious insects. As I drifted off to sleep I thought belatedly that I should have given the other cover to Marg while I was up.

Chapter XIII

A THUNDERING STEADY ROAR brought me wide awake. What seemed to be a full-blown cloudburst was drumming on my canvas shelter. My mind leaped to the girl, but before I could move she came violently bundling in with me. "Move over, move over!" she gasped. "I nearly drowned getting here! My bed's washed away!" As I gave her room, she ranged herself full length on her side against me, her body pressing against mine. "You were clever and I was stupid."

"Got enough room?" I inquired, sharply aware of her breasts and belly against me.

"Yes," she answered, her breath soft and sweet on my cheek, "but I don't know what to do with my arm. May I put it on your chest?"

"Of course," I answered, and the arm, light as a feather, slid over me.

She snuggled against me and her arm embraced more than she lay on me. She murmured in my ear, "This is nice."

Vastly disturbed, I muttered, "Go to sleep." I listened to her breathing and felt the rhythmic rise and fall of her breasts against my rib cage. This was the time. I had only to gently raise that hunting shirt, stroke and caress, kiss and soothe, and swollen, throbbing Old Nick would go to his delightful goal. Common sense wrestled with towering lust. It must not be. I put my mind to conjecturing up new methods of manipulating paint, made up schoolboy arithmetical problems, tried to remember old poems, speeches made on Declamation Day at the Latin School. Nothing brought Old Nick down. He surged and raged in the prison of my breeches. My blood raced and my heart thumped powerfully. The din of the rain on the canvas slackened, almost stopped, drummed to one more crescendo, then

191

stopped as though turned off with a spigot, leaving only the sound of spattering dripping from the trees. Carefully, so as not to awaken Marg, I pushed the canvas off. The night was cool and sweet with the scent of wet grass and woods. Somewhere in the dark one of the horses gave a satisfied low whicker. The fresh air calmed me and after a few minutes I went to sleep.

As far as I know, no dream accompanied it. My body awakened me, spouting and convulsing with the involuntary release of spunk retained too long. Marg had moved her head to my chest, and the spasming commotion half awakened her. "Wha—who—"

"Go back to sleep," I whispered, feeling blessedly relieved though damned wet below. After waiting for her sleep breathing to resume, I gently disengaged myself and got up. Sunrise was not far off. Going to the creek to wash, I found the water had risen a good two feet since the night before. The horses, though wet, were comfortably disposed. There was not enough firewood left for a decent breakfast fire, so I went scouting through the dripping woods to try to find some reasonably dry deadfalls. Grubbing about for the better part of an hour, during which I collected a good armload of wood, I walked back along the creek bank in the bright sunrise wondering if Marg was good at griddle-cakes. I had my mouth set for bacon and a noble stack of cakes drenched with molasses, all washed down with coffee of mighty strength, and my eyes were set for the sight of her lovely face and soft gray eyes smiling at me a cheery good-morning. Upon reaching the spot where we had bathed, I looked toward the camp and instantly slipped behind a tree.

Two shaggily bearded men, carrying rifles, stood over Marg, who had gotten a fire going with the fuel left from last night. Kneeling, she looked up at them. Their buckskins were black with age and grease. They grinned at her and one said, "Right purty thing, ain't she?"

"Ripe peach," agreed the other, "ripe and ready for pluckin'."

The first man guffawed. "What kind o' fancy talk is that? The way to say that word is fuckin', not pluckin'."

Still kneeling, Marg said calmly, "If you boys know what's good for you, you'll hightail it away from here before my menfolk come back with what they went to shoot for breakfast."

I quietly laid down my armload of wood. I was unarmed, for all the weapons were with the baggage piled behind her. While I was debating my chances to reach them without getting shot on the way, one of the men said to her, "Ma'am, you ain't never goin' to Heaven tellin' such lies tryin' to fool a pair o' poor boys. All the signs around here says you got one man with you. Henry, you piss around and find him and let some air through him whilst I see what we got in this here baggage. Then we'll have some plain and fancy fuckin' with this lady before she gits to cook breakfast for us. They allus cooks best after havin' a yard o' cock stuffed in 'em. Git along, Henry, my pecker ain't goin' to wait all day."

"You dip your wick afore I git back, Mose," warned Henry, "I swear I'm goin' to see how you like that for breakfast after I slice it off you. We draw straws for who gets the wet deck, like allus."

"Draw straws," nodded Mose. "Find that bastard and haste ye, goddamn it! I got me a hard-on like a bull!"

Henry came straight for the creek in a half crouch, cocked rifle at the ready, his eyes sharply searching. The other man remained standing over Marg. When Henry came abreast of the tree I stepped out in front of him and said, "Hello, Henry," and drove my knee into his groin. The rifle fired into the air and when he doubled over in agony I seized his head and gave it the Ira Tupper twist, feeling rather than hearing his neck snap. Without watching him drop I shot a quick look in the direction of the other man, ready to dodge, but saw only Marg standing by the breakfast fire looking down at the huddle on the ground. I ran to her and she looked at me with amazement on her face. "I killed him!" she exclaimed in wonder. "I really did! When the shot fired he looked and—good glory, Rob, I feel weak!"

Her knife was sticking out of Mose's back. I said to her, feeling weak myself, "Sit down. It's time for a little rum."

She sat down on a saddle and said shakily, " 'Tis not Christian to drink spirits before breakfast, but I feel heathen." She tossed back a good gulp, shivered and said, "How is the other one?"

"Dead," I answered, and smiled at her. "It isn't especially Christian to go around killing people before breakfast, either. Slaughter on an empty stomach is forbidden by the Prophet Jeremiah."

193

"Jeremiah was never in our fix," she said seriously, then saw me grinning. "You slick-talking villain! Jeremiah never said any such thing! You just made it up! Oh, the rum has made me light-headed! I'd better start breakfast."

As she got up and began, I went to haul the nearest corpse a distance away because flies were gathering. I pulled her knife out of him, wiped it clean and gave it to her, commenting, "Dirty talkers, they were. Should have had their mouths washed out with soap."

"Clarty," she answered, getting out material for mixing griddlecake batter, "Papa would have said they were clarty."

A new voice exclaimed, "Well, look a-here!" Jess Ricks walked into the clearing, followed by three of his warriors. "Mornin', Marg, Mr. Allston. We heard the shot before we found the rascals' horses." He stared at the bodies. "Won't do any more burnin' and murderin', they won't."

"They were very bad boys," I remarked, "and nasty-mouthed."

"Oh, they were, they were," he said. "Mighty bad. Dead set on gettin' theirselves hanged. Last week they set on the Thomson place up by the county seat. Killed Harry, ravished Becky, set the house afire and lit out with Harry's two riding horses. 'Twas them we found out yonder by the road hitched to a tree when we came runnin' over the shot."

"Well, I'm glad you happened along," I said. " 'Twill save me the time of going to make the report to somebody."

"No, you don't have to do that," he told me. "I'll handle it, haul the bodies in and all. Folks around here'll be glad enough to give you a medal for turnin' those two off. Henry Henderson and Moses Goodbody. Been in every gaol from Orangeburg to Darien."

One of the militiamen, examining Henry down by the creek, called, "Henry ain't got a mark on him, Jess!"

"I broke his neck," I explained. "And if medals are handed out, Miss Ogilvie deserves one. She killed this lad here."

He whistled, and smiled at Marg. "Gettin' pretty doughty in your old age, Marg. Good on you. Still got the knack with the knife, I see. I haven't forgotten how you shot, gutted, skinned and quartered the buck back when you

194

were about nine year old. How are those brothers of yours?"

She had the bacon frying and was mixing the batter. "Healthy and hearty, Jess. They miss you on the hunts. 'Tisn't like old times."

Looking down at his boots, he said, "I miss bein' there, too, but comes a time when a man has to stand up and take his side. You'd have been a sight drier and safer had you put up at Leavitt's last night. No matter what Mr. Allston said in his fine speech, I know why you didn't. No harm would've come to you, Marg, I swear."

Ladling out batter onto the hot griddle iron, her face was averted but I saw the blush. "I know, Jess, and thank you, but—will you and your boys stay and have breakfast with us? There's plenty for all if you're of a mind to share the table of a suspected Tory wench. Maybe Mr. Allston's presence, being a famous Patriot, will take the curse off my cooking."

He grinned at her. "There never was any curse on your cookin', Marg, and thank you kindly." He called to his men, "Boys, haul those skunks out by the road, then come rally around for some good hot lady-cooked grub."

"Marg," I asked, "how did you know I wanted this for breakfast?"

Neatly flipping the cakes on the iron, she answered demurely, "Don't we always have griddlecakes and bacon after disobeying Jeremiah?"

"Who's Jeremiah?" queried Ricks.

I explained and all the militiamen laughed, settling down to begin eating. Despite the grim prelude, breakfast was a jolly affair. The night's downpour had cooled the land and the morning was bright and sparkling. It took effort for me to realize that those laughing, appreciatively eating young men were enemy soldiers who would perhaps be killed in battle within a few months because of what I was doing in that country. Marg, laughing and bantering with the men, might have been serving a crowd of friends instead of enemies who would drive her family from their home if they could find an excuse.

When the men left, after a deal of handshaking and fond farewells, they took the bodies with them, and Marg and I resumed the journey.

The weather was comfortable and the horses spirited. We covered ground faster than before and, old comrades-

195

in-arms now, Marg and I talked to each other like two people who had known each other for years. She was now wholly feminine despite the rig she wore and watching her, listening to her animated voice, I wanted her more than any other woman I had ever met. Her eyes danced when she looked at me and there was a gladness in her smile that made me wonder if it was for me or pleasure over the good news I was bearing to her brothers. Early in the afternoon we emerged from the shade of the forest and rode through cultivated fields blanketed with burgeoning crops of corn, wheat and barley. "Oh," she cried in delight, "doesn't it look good! Isn't it beautiful?"

In sudden dismay, I realized what she meant. The journey was over and she would be taken from me. I was astonished at my emotion. "This is Elderbank land?"

"All six hundred acres of it!" she cried jubilantly. "Three hundred tilled and three hundred full of cattle and hogs! Oh, how good it is to be home! See! Here comes—ah, 'tis Peter! He could never ride around the barn except at a full gallop!"

Far ahead in a grove of trees set well back from the road I saw some buildings and from them a mounted man was galloping between the rows of what seemed to be a potato field, coming toward us. He reached the road and came at us headlong, reining in his horse abruptly so the animal reared. "I saw you from the house!" he cried. "What the devil are you doing away from Savannah? You might have been killed or worse! Henderson and Goodbody are murdering and raping and the militia's after 'em!" He was a rangy, broad-shouldered man some years older than his sister, with a rugged, sunburned face that was now scowling.

Marg laughed. "Mose and Henry have turned over a new leaf. They're dead, Peter. This gentleman is Mr. Robert Allston who was coming this way and consented to carry me home after Mr. MacGillivray told me you'd not be driving the second herd to Savannah. He killed Henderson and"—she giggled—"I made a good body out of Goodbody. 'Twas this morning before breakfast, no matter what Jeremiah said."

He stared at her. "*You* killed—you're touched by the sun! By God, Marg, you ought to be switched so hard you'd not be able to sit down for a week!"

"Gentlemen do not switch ladies," she told him, laughing,

"and you and John will be happy to know that I've brought a fine gown from Savannah and have decided to be a lady. Will you invite Mr. Allston to the house for a dram and a bite so I can show you how ladylike I've become?"

"I still say the sun's got you," he growled, and bringing his horse to mine, leaned over and shook hands. "How do, Mr. Allston. Come along to the house and have a drop."

The house was two-storied, of wooden frame construction, with a wide piazza extending the width of the front and painted with what appeared to be natural red ocher. The interior was light and airy, the rooms high-ceilinged, and, except for the whitewashed ceilings, was unpainted: floors, walls and sturdy home-constructed furniture were all stained and polished with oil or wax. A large Negro woman addressed as Hyacinth brought a huge platter laden with sliced meat, cheese, bread, butter, peach jam and pickles. Peter poured peach brandy into pewter mugs and said to me, "Will you explain, sir, how you come to be with my sister and what of the killing she was speaking about?"

A taller, lankier man about my age, midway between Peter and Marg, came in, smelling of sweat and cattle, and I was introduced to John. He got himself a drink of brandy and sat down, saying to his sister, "You look like you saw the Second Coming and you're going to be drawn straightaway up to your heavenly home."

Beaming, eyes sparkling, she exclaimed delightedly, "I have and I think I am! And so will you when you find out what I've brought home! Both of you! Rob, tell them, tell them!"

" 'Tis a rather long story," I told the brothers. "It begins in New York. You're bound to be startled, so I'll tell you this: I'm an agent of the Crown, here serving His Majesty."

Peter's face never moved a muscle. After giving me a long look, he turned to John, who was frowning at me, and asked, "Did you see them in the edge of the woods as you came by, John?"

Nodding and watching me, John answered, "They're watching."

Peter said to me in a level voice, "We'll give you a chance to tell your story, Mr. Allston, and it had best be

197

good. If it isn't, you're going to be delivered to the County Committee before the sun sets. Proceed."

"No, wait!" interrupted Marg, getting up. "Rob, 'twill be easier if I fetch your drawing book from your horse and let them see what's in it first." Without waiting for a reply, she flew out of the house, returning with the book, opened it and handed it to the brothers.

"By the eternal!" muttered Peter over the drawings. " 'Tis our Anne!"

Pointing, John said, "That one—he looks like old Angus the way I remember seeing him when we were boys." He looked at me. "How came you by these pictures?"

"I drew them," I answered. "I'm a painter of portraits by trade, and Angus is an old friend. His son Hector whom you see there is my closest friend. He and I came from London together and share the same house in New York. Anne arrived from here and joined us. She lives there with her half brother now. She reached New York unharmed after leaving here."

The brothers exchanged glances and Peter handed me the sketchbook. "Prove it. Draw a picture of my sister."

Taking out my pencil, I smiled at Marg. "I'll paint your portrait one of these days. Hold still for a minute or two." I rapidly sketched her head, neck and shoulders while she smiled radiantly at me.

Inspecting the drawing, the brothers grinned and John said, "Funny. I never figured her for being that pretty, but now I look at her I see it."

"Well, *thank* you," said Marg dryly.

Peter handed me back the book. "That settles that you know the MacDonalds and you take good likenesses. If your story's long, shorten it. This house and its callers are watched by small children posted in the edge of the woods who report what they see to their grandfather who's a member of the County Safety Committee but, as I told you, it had best be good."

I laid it out for them, talking swiftly, including the Noble affair and Cameron's role, and ended with our pre-breakfast massacre of the two bandits. They listened intently, frowning with concentration, and seeing no elation on their faces I added desperately, "Wallbrook. Marg says you know him. He was in New York representing Colonel Browne and met me at the British Army conference that got me into this. I understand he sometimes ranges through here. He'll confirm this."

Both men rose, grinning broadly, and advanced to shake my hand, Peter saying, "Welcome, welcome, sir. Hugh rode through here one night a fortnight ago and warned us you'd be coming. Even told us what you looked like. I'm sorry we had to put you through this, but everything you said had to check with what he said. We can never tell when the rebels are going to try something clever to trap us. I find it hard to believe that Cameron's not what he acts to be, though."

"Elderbank's been saved a couple of times by what we thought were miracles," pointed out John to his brother. "The county had it for fair and then the council at Savannah told 'em no, leave it alone for now. Now we know who that miracle was. Mr. Allston, Browne's Rangers took a count more than six months ago, through this backcountry and up yonder in the Carolinas."

Peter said, " 'Twas a poor count, from what I know of it. A deal of the men were afraid to talk with the Rangers, and so the Rangers puffed their figures to make it look better than it was because Colonel Browne was so hot to prove to Governor Wright the region will rise to support the Crown if the King's army comes back."

"Whitehall and the Army seem to have thought that such might be the case," I commented. "Will you help me then?"

They murmured agreement and Peter said, "With Abraham Jenks' little sprouts spying the house—he'll put 'em on Goodowns now with you there—we'll have to be wary. Abraham is dead set on catching us red-handed at conspiring treason."

"Marg told me about that," I informed him, and the idea came to me. "One of the reasons I was chosen was because as an artist I can move about freely with everybody knowing what I'm supposed to be doing. Let's say I'm doing a portrait study of Marg in preparation for the big picture I'm to do of Georgia. She's a fine figure of a lovely plantation lady. Would you like that, Marg? I can stretch it out for a long time so your brothers and I can work together."

She blushed and said, "Whatever you say, Rob."

"Well, dadburn the corncrib!" exclaimed John staring at her in disbelief. "Did you hear that, Peter? Is this our prickly female cowboy? Is this—"

199

"You stop that, you hear!" cried Marg, her face pinker than ever. "I'm only trying to do my share!"

Laughing, I told her, "I'll not paint you in that terrible rig you're wearing. You'll be supposed to be a plantation lady, not a bush-ranging cowboy, Marg."

"Likely she's forgotten how to wear a gown," remarked Peter.

"I'll show you!" she exclaimed indignantly. "I'll show you all, you . . . you *men!* I'll plantation-lady you all to death! And when you boys need another hand with the herding to the pens you can go whistle for one, because I'll be busy being a grand plantation lady, so put that in your pipe and smoke it!"

"From what you said," Peter asked me, "there's no time to be lost on this head count?"

"None at all," I replied. "We should get on it immediately, if you and John can spare the time from the regular work here."

"We'll make time," he declared. "We'll start tomorrow afternoon. Abraham'll have his big nose in the door at Goodowns before you take your hat off, likely, and you should tell him that picture-making of Marg will begin tomorrow—say, right after dinner each day. Give it to him heavy, because he's a suspicious man. And you've been here a suspicious long time now, so you'd best be getting along over to Goodowns. Come along and we'll point out the shortcut through the woods. No sense in going by the Post Road."

The ride through the woods, following the well-marked path, took about a half hour and as I emerged from the trees into a peach orchard I remembered Anne's story of her escape and death of her aunt. Once again the presence of Anne settled around me, a not disagreeable sensation. It was curiously like a homecoming.

Goodowns was the only stone house I had seen so far in Georgia, a large structure with crowstep gables and massive chimneys, definitely not of Georgia plantation style. Angus MacDonald, I reflected, had built for his beautiful second wife a Scottish manor house. When I rode around to the front I saw he had made one concession to regional architecture by building on a wide piazza whose roof was supported by square wooden pillars with Doric capitals. Beyond the sweeping lawns the Post Road went by, and on the other side were barns, stables, paddocks, storehouses, smokehouse and the like. Cultivated fields lush with crops, where I could see Negroes working, stretched to a distant line of woods.

I was no sooner out of the saddle when the front door opened and a Negro man stepped out onto the piazza. Middle-aged, he wore a decent suit of dark clothes. He regarded me with sharp eyes and said with only a faint echo of local Negro accent, "Good-day, sir."

"Good-day to you, too," I smiled. "You'd be Brutus MacDonald?" A former slave given his freedom by Angus, he had taken his benefactor's name.

"I am, sir," he replied. I noticed his eyes didn't miss anything in their inspection of me. "I regret that none of the family is at home, sir."

"Yes, I know," I remarked. "My name is Robert Allston and I have an authority from the Continental Congress to occupy the premises for a few weeks."

"Won't you come in then, sir?" he said with a slight bow. "I've been expecting you for some time."

The entrance hall was beautiful with parquet floor, lustrously polished paneled walls and a graceful stairway curving up to the second floor. I said, "How did you know I was coming?"

A pair of identical, very pretty Negro girls were lurking at the back of the hallway, their white teeth brilliant in their smiles. Brutus answered, "Captain Wallbrook of the East Florida Rangers apprised me, sir." He beckoned to the girls. "Hetty, Betty, go fetch Mr. Allston's baggage." As they rushed giggling past us to the door, he said to me, "Those girls will cook and housekeep for you, sir. They formerly served the ladies of the house, the misses Anne and Mary MacDonald. Have you any preferences concerning bed-chambers, Mr. Allston? We have several."

"I'd like one overlooking the front, facing east," I answered. "I like the sun in the morning."

"Miss Anne's is the best of that lot," he told me. "Judging from what Captain Wallbrook told me, I doubt she'll be returning soon."

The idea of occupying Anne's room amused me. "I'll take it. That'll jar her second sight if she turns it in this direction."

Brutus smiled. "Ah, she's been at that where she now is, has she? Many's the time she frightened the wits out of the

201

twins with that." The girls came in lugging my gear and he told them to take it to Miss Anne's room and air the place.

"Your daughters?" I asked, watching them bounce upstairs.

He shook his head. "No, and I'm thankful for it. They've only had their mother to raise them and they're rather a handful. You'll find them quite efficient at their work but inclined to frolic. Miss Anne is well? I've been concerned about her, so beautiful and alone in a strange country for the first time."

I told him about Hector and our house, and mentioned that I knew Angus well, and he smiled with pleasure. "Then 'twill be like having one of the family at home, sir."

It was a handsome house, a far cry from the spartan simplicity of Elderbank. Angus had lavished a mountain of money on this jewel box for his bride. Crystal chandeliers, deep-piled and brilliantly colored rugs, elegant French furniture, carved ceilings and gilt ornamentation delighted me, lover of luxury. The spacious library was solidly lined with books on every conceivable subject. It was where Anne had received her excellent education from Brutus and her Aunt Mary, often joined by Marg.

Anne's presence was quite strong in her former bedchamber and I could visualize how striking she would appear with her red-gold hair against the green and ivory decoration of the room. A silver-backed hairbrush lay on a dressing table and I picked it up. A single long red-gold hair lay among the white bristles. "Part of her is still here," I said to watching Brutus with a smile. "D'you know, sometimes I feel like a haunted house, haunted by her. I sailed here in a ship named for her, owned by her half brother and me, and I've just come from Savannah in the company of her close friend, Miss Marg. And here I am in her house, about to occupy her bedchamber, waited on by her servants."

"The twins claim they've seen her here since she departed," he said. "However, she was always one to make deep impressions on people who know her and I suspect the visions were no more than a habit of the mind, if you follow my meaning, sir. You'll want a room in which to paint and perform related works. After you're familiar with the house, please tell me which room you would like and I shall have it arranged for you."

"Thank you, I'll do that," I replied. "How do you prevent this house from being looted by bandits?"

"I maintain a patrol of one man at all times," he explained, "to keep watch for fire or armed strangers. Iron bars are hung at intervals over the grounds to be rung for alarm. We have a force of ninety-five hands and several guns. The people at Jenks Town and Elderbank stand ready to come if summoned by the alarm which can be heard a long distance and, incidentally, Mr. Jenks keeps close ward on this place. In fact, sir, I am sure you will meet Mr. Jenks soon."

"I know of that," I commented. "I'm curious to meet him."

When I was unpacked and settled in, I had the twins fetch me hot water for a bath and when the large portable tub was filled they stood smiling as I removed my coat and stock. "Haven't you got supper cooking? What are you standing here for?"

They looked surprised and one said, "We got to wash you, sir. We always help Miss Anne. Never washed a man." They burst into giggles.

"Vanish," I ordered. "Disappear. I bathe myself."

Clearly disappointed, they obeyed and I scrubbed the travel dirt from myself, thinking lascivious thoughts about the two vivacious and eager girls, and had to remind myself sternly about my rule which prohibited tupping maidservants under my roof.

Supper had been excellent and well served by my two ebony charmers, and I was in the library, browsing through the books and having a drink of peach brandy when the storied Mr. Abraham Jenks came calling.

He was a big one, nearly filling the doorway of the library when he came through it, a massive man whose bulk contained little fat. Hairy, too. A full, untrimmed beard fell like a pepper-and-salt apron over his chin and chest, and tufts of black hair sprouted from the nostrils of the big nose that jutted like a fleshy monument over a shaggy moustache that concealed his mouth. Small gimlety eyes glittered from under equally shaggy black eyebrows.

"Good-evening, Mr. Jenks," I said, extending my hand.

I nearly winced under his crushing grip, and in a deep, rumbling voice, he said, "Good-evening, sir. It is a surprise to find a guest at Goodowns." His diction was that of a man of little formal education who had gone to much effort in teaching himself to speak careful English.

"Will you sit and have a glass of brandy, sir?" I asked.

The chair into which he dropped himself squeaked in protest. "I would like that, Mr. Allston, and thank you, sir."

Handing him the glass, I said, "I had planned to call on you tomorrow. I was told at Savannah that you're a leading citizen in these parts and an influential member of the County Safety Committee, therefore will have an interest in my work here." I produced my forged papers and passed them to him, together with the letter from Cameron. "These documents are better than my explanations."

Taking a pair of spectacles from a shagreen case, he leaned toward the lamplight and slowly read the texts without comment. When the heavy brows frowned, I knew he was reading the nonsense about Franklin having an interest in the Goodowns property. He handed the papers back and put away his spectacles, then rumbled, "It seems to me the Congress would do better to fight and win the contest before planning monuments such as this picture-making. And we Georgians are thankful to Dr. Franklin for his extending the Post Road from Augusta to Savannah when he was postmaster general and for his work on our behalf in London when he was Georgia's agent, but he would do well to keep his hands off Georgia property. I shall write to Mr. MacDonald concerning that. Mr. Allston, we do not often have visitors from over the water in this remote country. You will find our ways much different than those to which you are used. I cannot say that I ever met an artist before. Is that your means of living?"

"It is," I answered, "and I do rather well at it. At least, I did in France."

He regarded me solemnly. "It does seem to be a strange way for an able-bodied man to earn his bread. Most do it as the Almighty Jehovah commanded Adam, with plough and sweat. I have heard that you carried the young Ogilvie woman home from Savannah."

"She was anxious to return to help with the work and I happened to be coming this way," I explained. "I needed a guide and she an escort."

"A good thing you did, sir," he said. "As county committeeman with duties connected with the militia, I received a report from Captain Jess Ricks this afternoon about the death of those two criminals near Leavitt's inn. All praise

204

to our Lord who gave your arm the strength to smite down those men of evil, and let us entreat His further aid in ridding our bounteous land of that other evil, the tyranny-loving Tories."

"Indeed yes," I agreed, getting into the spirit. "How can we fail with the power of the Lord on the side of right? His holy justice will prevail, even as great Jehovah smote the Philistines."

"Amen," he rumbled. "I must warn you that the young woman and her brothers at Elderbank are of that pernicious breed, though I shall place no blame on her, for she is but a woman, a weak vessel into whom poison may be poured, yet by the same token it may be easily tipped out."

Nodding gravely and feeling outrageously absurd, I said, "Was it not St. Augustine in his Confessions who wrote, 'What is more easily led than a compliant woman of good heart and weak will?' " I made that up on the spur of the moment and felt rather proud of it. "But regardless of her political affiliation, I have decided that I may use her face and figure among others in my large Georgia painting, so I shall be visiting Elderbank daily for that purpose for a while. I wished that you know the reason for my apparent fraternizing with those people."

The little eyes glinted. "She is most comely and will make a good wife for a Georgia planter. I am pleased that you will do the work there rather than here, for in this country we do not hold with young females visiting gentlemen living alone."

"A proper and sensible precaution," I agreed, feeling the strain of sustained hypocrisy. I intoned sanctimoniously, "How well we know that though action and intent be as pure as the fresh-fallen snow, ugly gossip can leave stains on reputations which years of God-fearing honor and integrity cannot remove."

"Well and truly said, Mr. Allston," he rumbled. "I've a mind to take that thought for my Sabbath message to my flock. It is difficult for me to understand how a sober and thoughtful Christian gentleman like yourself is led to such a calling as yours, making pictures of people that feed the vanity of them who dwell in Sodom and Gomorrah, as are all cities of the world in this age. But 'tis for the Lord to judge, not his humble servant." He lumbered to his feet. " 'Tis long past an honest laboring man's bedtime and I must go. You will be welcome at my house at any time, Mr.

Allston." My hand was once more crunched. "By the bye, sir, you will see my youngest son Jedediah on this plantation from time to time. He helps me keep ward on the place on behalf of Mr. Angus MacDonald who is an old friend of mine though we are now politically divided.

"The nigger Brutus is honest so long as he is under a white man's eye, but Mr. MacDonald's misdirected generosity in having the man educated gives rise to all manner of mischief. 'Tis a serious error to educate the sons of Ham to the level of the white man's learning and it goes against the Holy Writ.

"Also the extravagant appointments of this house of vanity is like unto a honeypot to the wandering thieves and eloping Tories. Earlier this year the sister of Mr. Mac-Donald and the superintendent were slain by marauders and the daughter was carried off by them, I fear. My sons and I pursued the villains but they evaded us."

He might know everything that transpired around there, but he had missed the spiriting away of Anne by Peter Ogilvie. I assumed a properly grim expression. "She must have suffered a brutal fate. Miss Ogilvie told me of the sad affair. I shall sleep sounder of night, Mr. Jenks, knowing you and your good family are on guard, and you have my sincere thanks, sir."

After he left I had another drink to wash away the taste of his visit. He and I would never be boon companions. One of the twins came in and asked, "You want anything else, Mister Rob? Hetty and me goin' to bed 'less you like somethin' else. You bed turned down." She was smiling shyly.

"Nothing else, Betty," I told her. "I've had a long day and I'm going to bed now myself."

"Mighty lonesome up there by your own self," she said, smiling less shyly. The offer could not have been much plainer. I was strongly tempted, but reluctantly invoked my self-imposed rule of no tupping the maidservants under my own rooftree in the interest of domestic tranquility and efficiency. I smiled at the pretty black girl. "I'll not be lonely. Miss Anne's spirit will keep me company."

She giggled. "We see that spirit sometimes, Hetty and me, but spirits ain't very lively company for a gentleman like you, sir."

"You'd be lively company?" I asked, fighting temptation.

"I'm willin'," she said hopefully with a wide smile.

"You're a sweet girl and I thank you," I told her, "but I'm very weary and must get to sleep. Good-night, Betty."

Crestfallen, she dipped a little curtsy and, murmuring a good-night, vanished with a flounce of her skirt. I turned out the lamp and went up to bed, ruefully meditating on my fatuous high principles. Anne's bed was marvelously comfortable. The light of a full moon flooded through the windows, bathing the floor with cool brightness. Crickets and frogs chorused, and a mockingbird loosed a torrent of liquid melody. It had been a long and rather eventful day, I thought, as sleep gently washed over me, and suddenly Anne MacDonald stood in the brilliant moonlight near the foot of the bed. "All your roads but one have woe, Jamie, and that one is bonny and blessed," said the crystal voice.

I sat up in bed and exclaimed, "The devil with your damned roads!" The sound of my voice awakened me and I found myself actually sitting up, but the moonlight had gone and I had obviously been asleep for hours. Crickets, frogs and mockingbird were silent. I went back to sleep.

Chapter XIV

DURING THE MORNING of my first full day at Goodowns I explored the buildings and grounds and was fascinated at the self-sufficiency of the plantation. The Negroes, who lived in cottages behind the barns, Brutus among them, operated a smithy where not only horseshoes were made but also all manner of ironwork for tools, harness and house fixtures. There was a skilled carpenter, a shoemaker and a tanner. Women spun wool, wove fabric and made clothes along with dyes to color them and soap to wash them. Some of the people were slaves, some free, but I could see no difference; Brutus treated them all alike with calm firmness and paternal good nature. He was, in effect, the lord mayor of a bustling little town.

After dinner I took my easel, a stretched canvas and my paints and rode over to Elderbank where I was greeted by a stunning new Marg, smiling and gracious in her new Savannah gown, a golden brocade creation with light yellow satin panniers and low-cut bodice which showed her superb figure off to delicious advantage. Slightly overcome by her remarkable fresh loveliness, I was shown to an upstairs spare chamber which they had designated as my painting room and head-count plotting room. "Marg," I said, "you are absolutely ravishing in that gown and my heart's broken that I can't start painting you right away. Your brothers and I must get to the other work this afternoon."

Smiling, she said, "Peter and John were flabbergasted when they saw me in it and they said nice things too. I know you'll not be painting me this afternoon, but I could hardly wait to show myself off to you. I never knew 'twas such fun to be a lady. Peter thinks I should wear a modesty piece, though; he said he hadn't seen a sight like this since he was weaned."

"I won't paint you at all if you cover up that splendid bosom with a silly modesty piece," I told her, wanting to bury my nose in the soft cleft between her white breasts. My self-control was going to be severely tested during the portrait painting, I could see.

"I do feel a little naked," she said, looking down, "but if you like it, then so it must be and I shan't be embarrassed."

While I was digesting the promising implicatons of that, her brothers came in, perspiring from their labor, and we sat down to work. At their direction I drew a small map of the region to which I had been assigned, from the mouth of Briar Creek to Augusta and from the Savannah River to the Ogeechee. Then they made a list of all residents in that area whom they knew to be Loyalist in varying degrees. After we gave each a number, we marked that number on the map at the approximate location of each man's home. Then we added to that number an alphabetical letter to indicate the degree of loyalty in the opinion of Peter and John as follows:

a. Those who would take up arms for the Crown upon arrival of British forces;
b. Those of firm loyalty, but for various good reasons could not take up arms;
c. Passive fence-sitters who preferred Crown rule, yet were willing to forsake the Crown if the rebellion succeeded;
d. The opportunists, side-changers, shiftless and untrustworthy.

Peter and John knew the people well, and thus we were able to classify almost half of the Loyalists without leaving the table. In a near moneyless society where men are dependent upon one another through barter and exchange of services, there is a knowledge of neighbors' characters unequaled in any other environment save, perhaps, in a prison. And it was that economic way of life which permitted the brothers, suspect as they were, to freely range the countryside without undue attention paid them by men like Abraham Jenks.

Peter laid down the law to me. He said, " 'Twas a harebrained piece of work, sending a stranger from foreign parts in here, no matter how well-intended it was. Even in good times the folk shy from foreigners, and in these times when a man's life can hang on his tongue they'd be witless to talk to you about loyalty to the King without knowing for sure you're who you say you are. News of your killing that spy at Cameron's house will spread like wildfire. Before they'd risk trusting you they'd report you to the committee, and you being who you really are, the end of that would see you hanged over at the county seat. You'll do no visiting until after we've cleared the way."

"You know best," I agreed, "but I'm concerned about you men taking so much time away from the plantation work. I'm no farmer, yet it seems to me the hard time of the year, harvest, will demand your time in a few weeks."

"Aye," acknowledged John, "so 'tis. On the other hand, if this work doesn't get done and the King's army doesn't come, we'll have no Elderbank."

"If need be," said Peter, "we'll rent slaves from planters, and pay with a percentage of the crops. A good many Georgia slaves have run off to East Florida to 'list in General Prevost's army, so hands are short here, but we've got friends in South Carolina over the river who will oblige us."

So it came to pass that in the early stages of the head count I had little to do with it. In the mornings I rode out to draw and watercolor landscapes and field workers, enjoying myself hugely and gradually becoming a familiar figure throughout the region. In the afternoons I went to Elderbank, conferred with the brothers and worked on the portrait of Marg, dawdling on it not only to keep it as an excuse for the visits but also because I slowly realised that time spent with her was the most enjoyable of my life. Her company became precious to me and when I was away from her she dominated my thoughts. I was constantly all of a sweat to make love to her and knew perfectly well she would welcome it; I knew the telltale signs of a woman receptive to advances and by word, gesture and expression Marg displayed them all, prettily, endearingly and temptingly. In her company Old Nick was more often than not eagerly risen, straining anxiously. Since arriving at manhood's estate my body had never been so long without the relief tenderly bestowed by a woman and that made our intimate association all the more difficult in the physical sense. The painting of Anne's portrait had purged me, to some extent, of sexual disquiet, but just the opposite was happening in the painting of Marg.

My nights became miserable with yearning for her and my bedclothes were often puddled by my involuntary discharges. Then one night I dreamed of the roads again. I trudged over a muddy road, bent nearly double with a heavy pack on my back, dripping wet as after being caught in a heavy rain. Ahead lay the triple fork, entering a grove of trees. The two roads to the right became dark tunnels under the trees, and the left-hand one showed light at the other end of its tunnel. A figure standing there in the light beckoned to me and I was filled with unreasoning fear. The pack on my back stirred, rolled off me and, embracing me, pulled me down to the ground, kissing me. It was Lord Beauvoir. I seized his neck to strangle him and the face became Marg's. Try as I might, I could not remove my hands from her neck as they crushed and I went to vigorously coupling with her, filled with horror as I strangled her. I spent, spouting great gouts of spunk, and felt her die. Then her face became that of Meg Barr-Pettit wearing the grimace of sexual ecstasy in death.

I woke up thrashing about, sick to my stomach, and the bed was drenched with my perspiration and the ejaculation from my loins. Dressing in the dawn, I went to the stables and went riding on Prince through the fields to rid myself of the revolting nightmare's effect. Another dream like that and I would be afraid to go to sleep of nights. Something was going to have to be done, even if it meant jeopardizing my mission and losing Marg's brothers as friends. I would simply have to take her and be done with it.

Having reluctantly made that decision, I returned to the house, shaved and had breakfast on the piazza. Hetty and Betty bustled about, serving me and watching me, exchanging mirthful glances and bursting out into frequent giggles. "I'd be obliged if you'd tell me," I said to them, "what you find so comical about me this morning."

They laughed hilariously and one said to the other, "You goin' tell him?"

"I dast you!" exclaimed the other, whooping. "I dast you, Betty?"

Betty said to me, "You promise you not get mad, Mister Rob?"

"I promise," I said, mystified.

"We doin' an awful lot of washin' sheets," she said. "Got more to wash today."

A light dawned. Embarrassed, I said, "I know you girls

212

have never served a gentleman before and I'm sorry it causes you extra work. There's no way I can prevent it, you know. It just happens."

They looked at me with wide eyes. "You don't go to do it, Mister Rob?"

"It happens in my sleep," I answered, "and this is a damned embarrassing thing to be discussing at my breakfast table."

"Lordy," said Hetty, "don't get a mad-on at us, Mister Rob. We was talkin' about it this mornin' when we strip your bed again. Betty and me are terrible sorry you got that trouble, not 'cause we got more work. You want we should help you, Mister Rob?" They both giggled, dark eyes sparkling. "Save the sheets?"

I leaned back in the chair and stared at them, astonished. "You mean, you both are willing to do that?"

"Willin' and ready, Mister Rob!" They were so excited they couldn't stand still, smiling almost from ear to ear, with one arm around the other's waist.

Watching them, I reflected that after all, they weren't my maidservants. I was only a guest in the house. My prohibitory rule was invalid. But—the pair of them? Brutus never made his inspection round of the house before late in the morning and it was only about seven. No callers could be expected. Despite the dream, I was ready too. Getting to my feet, I said, "Let's go have a look at that bed you've been complaining about."

"Want we should clear breakfast things and wash up first?" asked one of them, ever dutiful.

"After," I grinned. "Scoot upstairs, lively, now!"

They scooted, their dark faces merry, and were upstairs before I reached the bottom step. When I entered the bedroom they were both naked and lying side by side on the bed, their dark brown bodies sleek against the light green and gold quilt. They were not smiling now, watching me undress with intent interest. There was a curious silence in the proceedings that followed, an absence of speech only, for they were both far from being silent in their transports. My long-starved body took one after the other, and while I was engaged with one, the other did interesting things for us both. When I was capable of no more, after about an hour, I got up and began dressing, saying, "You girls are delightful, and thank you."

They were back to giggling again. "You delightful, too,

Mister Rob. Lordy, we ain't had no frolickin' since we come to the big house."

"What if you should have a baby or two?" I asked, enjoying the charming sight of them lying in close embrace.

"We got a special yarb medicine," said one. "Mama makes it. She don't want us to have babies till we're wedded. You want we should come here tonight, Mister Rob?"

"If you wish it," I answered. "I'd like it, but only if you really want to."

Betty—I could now tell them apart when they were naked because Betty had fuller breasts than Hetty—hugged her twin joyfully and said earnestly, "We want to. Tonight you ain't goin' to have to go nowhere and we ain't goin' to have to get up to clear the breakfast and things. Hetty, we best get to that work quick."

They came to my bed every night from then on, fornicating with abounding joy and in complete abandonment until I told them to go to their own beds in their quarters above the kitchen; unlike other Georgia houses, at Goodowns the kitchen was contained within the dwelling. The twins were light-hearted little savages, bubbling with high spirits and affection for me, which I returned, to their unrestrained delight.

They confided that Jedediah Jenks had been trying to have them for years, but they didn't like him and kept together when he came around, knowing he didn't dare make a move unless he had one of them alone. They were seventeen years old and despite their enthusiastic skills in bed I found they had experienced relations with males beginning whey they were small children, experimenting with boys in the bushes and barn lofts, though they confessed they had made love with each other ever since they could remember.

Sometimes, when my capabilities were suspended through diligent application, they demonstrated their mutual affection physically and I found it touching, rather beautiful and wholly stimulating. Outside the bedroom, they were hard-working and efficient, and refrained from taking personal liberties with me or in my presence, for which I was thankful.

However, while the arrangement had the effect of ending my wet dreams and I had no more nightmares, it had little effect on my desire for Marg other than to slightly diminish my raging sexuality toward her. One evening at supper I told myself that I must stop tupping the twins, that it was despicable infidelity toward Marg, and the thought startled me. Who was she to claim my fidelity? I resolutely thrust the thought from me and went to bed with the twins as usual.

One day just before noon I returned to Goodowns after a visit with some Loyalists who had accepted me on the word of Peter and John, went to the kitchen to see what my lovable handmaidens were preparing for dinner and found Jedediah Jenks sprawled in a chair drinking a cup of tea, smirking at the girls who were studiously ignoring him as they busied themselves. I had run across him on the plantation occasionally and liked him no better than his father, whose style of dress he affected. He never looked directly at me, and his nasal voice had an uncertain inflection in it as if he were not sure of his words' reception. Now he leaped to his feet guiltily as I entered, and I said, "Good-day, Mr. Jenks. Does your visit have a purpose or are you only passing time?"

"Good-day, sir," he said, looking at the hearth. "A purpose—yes, sir, there is a purpose. To Jenks Town. That is, my father wishes you to come. If you can spare the time, sir. Now. Before noon. Something to show you, he has, sir."

"Show me what?" I asked.

He inspected a bowl of potatoes on the worktable. "A meting-out. At noon, sir."

"What's that?" I pressed.

His gaze drifted to one of the girls' bosoms, then quickly darted to his own boot toes. "A family custom, sir. We cannot talk about it. We should start now, sir."

Intrigued, I said to the twins, "I may be a bit late for dinner." Their faces were frightened and I put it down to Jedediah's presence. To him I said, "I'll get my horse. Come along."

Jenks Town was a cluster of dwellings inhabited by the large family and their slaves, only one of which was allowed to be owned by each of his sons. All the land was Abraham's and it was worked hard by the tribe six days a week. No work, cooking or play was permitted on the Sabbath. The patriarch conducted three long worship services in the little church they had built, one in the morning, one in the afternoon and one after supper. It was a joyless

215

place, Jenks Town, filled with joyless people, but they were godly, by God.

Abraham welcomed me with his booming voice and sent Jedediah off to assemble his flock on the green in the center of the houses. In his severely furnished house he gave me a drink of peach brandy and launched into a rambling preachment about hard labor, discipline and the unending worship of Jehovah. With his fanatical eyes, vast unkempt beard and spittle flying from his mouth, he made me think of a Biblical prophet who had been out in the desert sun too long without a hat. Just when I thought I could no longer bear it, he glanced at the clock on the wall whose bawdy hands, as Shakespeare wrote, were on the prick of noon, and rumbled, "It is my meaning to show you, sir, as a stranger from Sodom and Gomorrah, how needful it is in this hard country to obey the commandments of the Almighty God if we are to transform it into a land of milk and honey. Laziness, disobedience and blasphemy are each one an abomination in His eyes, and joined together in one they are the Devil's delight. On the land He has given me to till and reap it is my humble duty to serve as his right hand in meting out loving punishment to erring sheep in the name of His greater glory. There is one who waits now for correction who is guilty of that Devil's delight. As a God-fearing man, come and behold the teaching."

There must have been at least forty Jenkses' men, women and children—with their slaves, gathered in a wide circle on the green. In the center was a post about six feet high, driven into the ground. I hadn't noticed him pick it up, but Abraham carried a long wagoneer's whip as he strode to the post. Now filled with apprehension, I remained on the outside edge of the crowd. Abraham boomed, "Obediah, fetch out your wife, our wayward sister!"

A bearded man with a set face drew out of the crowd an obviously very frightened young woman of about eighteen. He stepped back and she stood before her father-in-law with downcast face.

"Dearly beloved," bellowed Abraham, "on Sabbath last the foul fiend came to this unhappy woman, your sister Hannah, and led her into wickedness and blasphemy. Instead of coming with her husband to join our worship, she lay abed and tempted him with her flesh and, like Adam in the Garden, he fell. You will remember that when I saw

216

them not among you, I halted the worship and went unto their dwelling. And there what did I see? I beheld them naked and coupled, their flesh twisting and squirming, and she crying out with the Devil's passion for more as his flesh rammed in and out of her lusting body! Yea, I saw and heard even as did the Maker of their sinful flesh, high on His Heavenly throne!" He glared about fiercely. "For his part, I have ordered that my son Obediah live apart from his wife in another dwelling for the space of one month, neither speaking to her nor touching her if they should meet." He scowled at Hannah. "My daughter, do you confess in the sight of God and your brethren and sisters that you are guilty as charged?"

Her reply was barely audible. "Yes, Pa. But I—"

"Then," roared Abraham, "bare yourself unto the nakedness in which you were born, so God may look upon what he made!"

The crowd was utterly silent. The girl tugged her simple gown over her head and dropped it, her quite pretty body gleaming blinding white in the hot sun. Abraham poked her in the groin with the whip stock and shouted, "Behold the Devil's snare! The smelly hole between her legs! Let no man look upon it with lust lest God strike him dead!" He prodded harder and Hannah winced with pain. "See how she flinches from the righteous instrument of God! Was it the Devil's evil pizzle she would fling herself on her back and spread her legs to receive it into her feverish hole."

I was tempted to turn and flee, but was held by revolted fascination. The big man was clearly sexually aroused. "Ten strokes!" he shouted. "Ten strokes the Lord hath commanded me to lay on your sinful flesh! Embrace the stake and pray for His forgiveness!"

The whip whistled down on the slender white back and my guts heaved at the sound of it, and when I saw the red line appear on her skin I turned and ran for my horse, hurled myself into the saddle and departed Jenks Town at a furious gallop. I never said anything about the meting-out to anybody else, knowing I'd not be able to control my mad anger, and I never went back to Jenks Town except once, and that was a long time afterward.

Except for the omnipresent possibility of betrayal, I led a pleasant life at Goodowns. Being out-of-doors most of the time, riding about the countryside to draw, paint or visit, I took on the appearance of a planter, lean, sun-browned in sun-faded clothes. I was often a guest for dinner or supper at neighboring plantations and farms—except Elderbank and Jenks Town—and reciprocated at my own table, expediently inviting only known adherents to the rebel cause. At night my two Nubian charmers entertained me in bed.

But through it all, no matter where I was or what I was doing, Marg stood foremost in my thoughts. Each afternoon we spent at least two hours together alone in the painting room at Elderbank, mostly talking and enjoying each other's company because the portrait had long been essentially finished and I merely pottered around with it. She and her woman Hyacinth had made several gowns for her and I never saw her again dressed in the old cowboy costume of hunting shirt and buckskin leggings, for she had become the complete plantation lady, lovely, gracious and wholly desirable.

Then one day the head count was complete except for confirmation of the position of two fence-sitters. We three men went carefully over the map and coded list, tallied the figures and agreed that the British could count on at least one strong regiment of militia recruits. With the Creeks and Cherokees from upper Georgia who were to rise and rally to Augusta as arranged by the British superintendent of southern Indians, the recapture of Georgia was practically assured, we agreed. My problem was now how to send the report to General Prevost at St. Augustine; I had seen no East Florida Ranger yet and the time was well into September. When the brothers left the house to return to their plantation work that afternoon, I grinned at Marg.

Her soft gray eyes regarded me thoughtfully. "What's funny? Why do you laugh?"

"I'm not laughing," I answered. "I'm smiling. When I laugh I say 'ha-ha' and bare my fangs."

"Why, then," she persisted, "are you smiling that funny smile as though you'd been stealing cookies?"

With the job done and some time yet before I would depart Georgia, I could devote full time and attention to her seduction, which from the first overt move to consummation, I estimated, considering her obvious inclination, would take all of half an hour. "I'm happy that the spying mission is done, and so is your portrait. I think we've done well on both counts, don't you?"

218

"Yes," she answered gravely. "The portrait is beautiful and your skill makes me shiver. Now you'll make ready to return to New York?"

Nodding, I said, "I'll not enjoy leaving the friends I've made and especially you, Marg. But I'm not going today or tomorrow. Regardless of Jenks' watchers, you and I have plenty of time to socialize before I go."

"Socialize?" she repeated in a faint voice. Then she leaped to her feet and came in three swift strides to stand over me, her eyes blazing as she cried, "What right did God give you, Rob Allston, to come into people's lives and amuse yourself with them for a little time, then walk away as if nothing happened? There you sit, pleased with yourself and your all-fired generosity for giving us a small bit of yourself as if you'd done some great good thing! Damn you, damn you for a puffed-up heartless popinjay!" She spun about, back to me, her head held high.

Astonished and dismayed, I jumped up and turned her around to face me. Her eyes were closed and tears were seeping, her lower lip trembling. Something inside me gave way and an incredible delight swept me. An exhilaration more intense than ever before experienced sent my spirits soaring, my blood racing. With amazement it came to me that I was in love for the first time in my life. I held her cheeks with my palms and reverently touched my lips to hers. "Marg, my darling," I said gently, "I'll never walk out of your life, in this world or the next. I'm yours and you're mine."

Her eyes opened and she smiled tremulously, "Old slippery-talk Rob."

"No slippery talk," I said. "I love you. I never loved a woman before and I'm not sure what's happening to me. 'Tis the most strange feeling, as if I'm no longer me but part of you—" We flowed into each other in a curious way almost without volition, our mouths greedily kissing, arms grasping and bodies straining in an attempt to fuse into one. Passion, lust, desire and a frantic urge to give myself entirely to her soared to such a tempest that madness seemed imminent as our hips ground and squirmed together and our breathing became a wild snorting in the kiss. In another second or two control would be utterly lost and we would be down on the floor having at it, I realized dimly through the storm, so with great effort I broke the embrace to hold her off at arm's length.

Her face was flushed, eyes shining and half-closed and her smile was radiant. She was breathing hard, even as was I. "I knew 'twould be like this yet I didn't. I dreamed of it, hungered for it, sweated for it, prayed for it—and now 'tis more wonderful than ever I could fancy! I belong to you, Rob! My soul and body reach out for you—'tis a terrible storm of pleasure that I never want to end! Ah, darling Rob, if you but knew how much I love you!"

"I know," I said, "because that's how I love you, Marg." She moved in on me. "Kiss me again, quickly!"

Holding her off, I said, "Another kiss like that wouldn't stop at a kiss, honeybun. We'd be going at each other like rabbits."

"Oh, God," she breathed, reaching for me, " 'tis what I must have! To be one with you, to be part of you, don't you see?"

"Stop, darling," I said gently, and she desisted. "What if your brothers should come in, or Hyacinth? I love you to the point of insanity but there's no good point in being insane about it. I just now discovered I love you and 'twas like the most beautiful sunrise that ever was, beginning a new and marvelous day that will last forever for the two of us, when we shall have each other until the end of the world." It occurred to me that if I had not been tupping the twins, such admirable prudence would have never reared its tedious head, for I would never have been able to suppress my desire for her.

"It took you long enough to find out," she smiled, love beaming in the gray eyes. "I found out that night at Foley's after you went back to your bed. I felt so strange I thought I must be ill. 'Twas what I wanted to talk about and you told me to shush."

Full awareness dawned. "The next night—you plotted it all! Sly minx! You knew it was going to rain hard, and you placed your bed deliberately where it would wash away! You bathed before me to tempt me. . . ."

Her face was pink. "And I wanted you to . . . to take me when I got under the packsaddle cover with you. I had this great burning and aching and though I've never had a man, I wanted you to do it to me. I thought if you enjoyed me you might want to marry me." Her lovely face was serious. "Was there any sense in that, Rob?"

"Not much, I'm afraid," I smiled. "I didn't love you then, though I liked you and had a great desire for doing

220

just what you had in mind. But, you see, there's no sense in a man marrying simply because a lady is a pleasant toss in bed, which I'm sure you will be when we arrange for that."

"Will you want bairns, Rob?" she asked. "I do. I want to give you lots of 'em."

Wanting to kiss her and not daring to risk the fire, I took her hand and said, "A whole troop of boys and girls and the girls must look exactly like you. And one of the boys will be named Tom after a very brave boy I once knew who died in battle at my side."

"You never told me about that," she murmured, pressing my hand against her cheek. "For all you've told me, there's so much I don't know about how your life was before it became mine."

"You'll learn all there is to know in time," I told her. "I'm not the best, most noble man in the world and I've done some stupid things, Marg, but if one day I fail you, I swear I'll never stop loving you."

This time I couldn't hold her off. She flung herself at me and into my arms, and in seconds I knew it could not end in only the kissing. With our mouths locked, my one arm around her waist and the other pulling her soft buttocks toward me, pressing her hard against Old Nick, there was a deep whimpering in her throat. Then the voice of her brother John roared, "There, by God! I knew something was going on betwixt 'em!"

Though startled, I left off the kiss, continued to hold her in my arms, and grinned over her head at the brothers. "Aye, and you were right, brother John, and a pleasant something it is, isn't it, Marg?"

Nestling against my chest, she laughed and said, "Tell those rude gentlemen to go away so that something can go on. And on and on."

Peter's face was grim. "Unhand my sister, sir! Is this the way you repay this house? Unhand her, I say!"

Marg said, "He may unhand me but I'll not unhand him. And what better way could he repay this house than by doing what he's doing? Stop making fierce faces. You look funny."

"Brothers," I declared, holding fast to Marg, "upon my word of honor, I never until a few minutes ago put a hand on this lady."

221

She giggled. "And it took you overlong to get to it, old slow-wit."

Peter barked angrily, " 'Tis not funny, you silly wench! Mr. Allston, I'll give you one second to take your hands off my sister!"

The teasing had gone far enough. I let go of her, but she continued to embrace me and said to her brother, "I'm long past twenty-one, dear Peter, and you'll not order me now. Oh, not now, my good brothers! There's but one man in all the world whose bidding I'll do from now till the end of time."

Anger vanished from their faces, replaced by puzzlement. "What the devil does that mean?" demanded Peter.

Smiling at them, I answered, "It means that the roof has fallen in on me and it appears that you'll be my brothers, too."

"Well, I'm damned," muttered John, staring at us. "Does that mean—"

Peter, incredulous, broke in, "Are you saying—you both —what it sounds like?"

"We're saying that," I assured him.

Their sun-browned faces split with delighted grins and they rushed forward to shake my hand and kiss their sister, crying congratulations. John exclaimed, "So that's why she came back a lady from Savannah! Found out she was a female, by God!"

"And the blushes!" added Peter, laughing. "Every time the man was in the same room with her and sometimes not, there were the damnedest blushes for no reason I could see!" He became serious and said to me, "If you're to wed my sister we'll have to know how your living is, how well can a limner support a family."

"I'm not exactly a limner," I explained. "Actually, I make a rather good living from my portraits and a deal of money from investments in various mercantile enterprises. I'm afraid you'll have to take my word at the present, there being no way to prove my financial worth, but—"

"Not so fast," interrupted Marg, looking at me reflectively. "You're all taking a lot for granted. How can there be a marriage when no man has asked me for my hand? I've heard a deal of talk but no proposal."

Her face was softly lovely with tenderness. I said, "I just told you of the sunrise. Do I have to point it out to you

222

when the entire world is drenched in the magnificent colors of it?"

"That comes close to being slippery talk," she answered soberly. "I see the sunrise well enough and thank God for it, but there's a thing to be said, the most important saying that comes to a maid, to treasure and remember for the rest of her days. Will you say it now, Rob?"

The gray eyes pleaded. I stepped back away from her, made a formal bow, and said, "Miss Margaret Ogilvie, you have ensnared my heart beyond retrieving. I beg you do me the great honor of becoming my wife."

John said in a low, urgent voice, "Say the old thing, Marg, say it!"

"Aye," put in Peter, "the way it was, lass!"

Smiling and misty-eyed, she dropped a deep curtsy and said in a broad Scots accent, "Och, aye, wi' a' the pleasure o' the seven worlds, an' a fu' score o' bonny lads I'll gie ye, my own true love."

She flew into my arms and as we kissed, this time in more restrained, genteel style, Peter said fervently, "That will never again be used as a joke."

"Now we're betrothed," said Marg with a sigh of satisfaction, nestling once more against my chest. " 'Twas an old family saying, Rob, how Mama accepted Papa when he asked her to wed him and come away from Kirriemuir to the wild American country. After Mama was taken by the fever and when the work here was almost more than we could bear, Papa would say as a joke with some sadness in it, 'If the dear woman had kept her promise we'd have enough hands.' So I always tried to do the work of one of the boys he never had."

"I'll hold you to your promise, my girl," I smiled. "And here's an odd thought: I've often thought of having children someday, yet not until this moment had I thought of what it must be like to be somebody's father, and the idea strikes me as being as pleasurable as the process that will make me a father and you a mother."

Her blush was glorious. "Such talk in front of Peter and John!"

Peter cleared his throat and said, "We came back to the house just now, Rob, to tell you that after talking it over we've decided one of the two last men can be put under the 'D' as useless. The other, the miller Hodgkins, we'll have to talk with, but not today. Today is a holiday at Elderbank—betrothal day, and there'll be no more work, eh, John?"

"Aye," smiled his brother. "All sit and I'll fetch the jug and mugs." He beamed at Marg. "And you'll drink, too, if you can take it without getting giddier than you are now. Your intended may change his mind if he sees you falling drunk on your big behind."

We toasted the King and the bride, and they toasted me. We drank to defeat and disaster to France and the rebels. It was hard for me to realize what was happening. With heart-filled pleasure I basked in the caress of Marg's adoring gaze and told myself that at any minute I would awaken from this delightful dream to find myself in bed in my house in Portsmouth Square, that this entire American experience never really happened.

When Peter, businesslike, asked me my church, I answered, "Church of Scotland, though I haven't been in one for so many years that if I went now a lightning bolt would surely strike the steeple."

"We're Auld Kirkers, too," he said, "and since the one at Halifax district burned we've not been and minister's gone to Indian country. I'm told there's a new minister at Augusta, fresh come from over the water and he's no Whig. I doubt you know it, Rob, but in this backcountry where ministers are scarce as snowballs in July, more often than not a betrothed couple say their vows to each other before company and stand married. Later, a minister will journey through the countryside to bond them for the Church and christen the young that might have come along betwixt the one time and the other. If you're of a mind to do that, you and Marg can say your vows now, John and I will stand witness and you both can go about the business of making that score of bairns."

"Oh, yes!" exclaimed Marg delightedly. "Rob—"

"Hold on," I said. "I'd not object to that if it weren't for our position here. What if I were discovered to be a spy after Marg began carrying my child? And you two men were banished or worse? Do you think the rebels would accept your witnessing or Marg's word?"

John said dourly, "You're right. She'd be called the spy's whore and the child the spy's bastard, and they'd stone her if they didn't tar and feather her."

Peter nodded. "True. She might even be hanged with you, Rob. No, 'twill never do. It must be done by the minister and entered in the parish register. I'll send to Augusta by the post rider and ask Mr. MacLeod to make a visitation."

"It might be well," I pointed out, "to promise him he'll be paid for his trouble in the King's best coin, generously, and not in hens, geese or smoked hams. I have a fairly fat purse. When will it be, Marg? Name the day."

"Why," she said, surprised, "whenever you say, Rob."

She was an endearing innocent. "Honeybun," I explained, "behind the honor that goes to the bride in the naming of the wedding day there's a practical reason. The lady has a calendar of her own on which she marks her days, and some of those days are most unsuitable for that purpose. D'you see?"

The brothers looked uncomfortable and Marg flushed. "Oh, *that!* Oh, dear me glory, I never thought of it! Let me see—" She thought about it and I was glad to see she didn't count on her fingers. "Allowing for Mr. MacLeod's travel and all, will three weeks from today be good for you, Rob?"

"Any day is good for me," I grinned.

"Then so 'twill be," declared Peter. "But after the vows have been given, what then? If you were to set up housekeeping at Goodowns, the famous Whig from abroad and the Tory wench, Abraham Jenks and his ilk would come down on us all like wolves."

"Nothing could be proved," I said.

Peter was grim again. "The way we survive is to keep from giving them anything to prove, even the look of suspicion, and if suspicion came against you or us. Rob, the proof would be found sooner than I like to think, for yonder men are not stupid by a long shot."

"And what kind of a marriage is that?" said John in disgust. "With the picture of her done and so with the head count, how can they even see each other, let alone housekeep, with Abraham's big nose poking about everywhere?"

I commented, "I'll be leaving this country soon and Marg will come with me to London. I have a fine big house there, Marg, and it's past time I went back to work again." I smothered the thought of Beauvoir. "You'll love London and London will love you, Marg."

"But," she said, "we'll be here on our wedding day and I'll not give up my bridal night for the sake of Abraham

225

Jenks." She blushed but plunged on. " 'Tis in my mind that I'll live at Elderbank during the days and at Goodowns during the nights."

"Bless you," I smiled affectionately. "But it sounds a damned furtive thing."

"And have you a better, unfurtive thing?" she demanded. "We're a furtive lot who live a furtive life."

Peter nodded. "She's right, Rob. We must go on being furtive. The Jenks children don't haunt the woods between sundown and sunup, and there's nothing between here and Goodowns that would cause grown folk to prowl about in the dark. God save you, man, you've a right to have your bride in your bed."

"And I have a right to be there," announced Marg defiantly.

"Bless you again," I smiled, "and so you shall be. If I have to be but half-married, I'm glad 'tis on the right side."

So it was settled and we waited for the minister from Augusta.

I continued to visit Elderbank in the afternoons, dawdling a little over the completed portrait to keep some fresh paint on it just in case, and talking with Marg as lovers do everywhere, I suppose, saying extravagant things and making vast promises as we discussed our future together. We did much kissing and fondling which I struggled to keep under decorous control, which I only accomplished because the twins' rapacious appetite of nights drained off enough of my virility that I could manage it. However, as my love for Marg increased, constantly stimulated by her passionate words and actions and the nearing of our wedding day, I decided that it was time to end the pagan rompings in my bed. Marg now had a claim on me and guilt feelings grew.

In bed with my brace of little savages one night, I said, "Girls, I'm going to marry Miss Marg soon."

They flung themselves on me with squeals of delight. "We knew, we knew! Hyacinth, she told Mama! Oh, she goin' be one happy wife!"

Alarmed, I said, "Good God! It must be kept a secret!"

They consoled me. "No white man, no bad nigger ever goin' to know, Mister Rob, only you friends. You goin' live here, still sleep in this bed with her?"

"Of course," I answered, enjoying their naked bodies slithering over me. "But what's important is that I'm betrothed now and I belong to her. As much as I like you wonderful, sweet girls, we mustn't do this anymore."

"Why not?" asked Betty, gnawing on my earlobe with her lips. "You got aplenty for three of us. We ain't jealous. Miss Marg's a fine lady and we love her, love her ever since we can remember, just like Miss Anne."

"Shoo," said Hetty, straddling me and trying to fit herself upon temporarily exhausted Old Nick, and doing a lot of wriggling about it, "you got so much a body'd never know you and Miss Marg's been doin' it afternoons over to Elderbank."

"You might as well stop that," I said to her. "It isn't going to work. No, we haven't been doing it. I haven't touched Miss Marg except to kiss her."

They both made shocked sounds and stopped what they were doing. Betty asked, "Miss Marg don't let you? You got a right, betrothed and all."

Hetty said knowledgeably, "Miss Marg, she's a maid. Never had a man and don't know what she's missin'. Mister Rob, don't let her say no—lay her down and give her a good fuckin' and she cry for more. White ladies ain't no different than us under their legs."

Enough was enough. I said firmly, "No more of this, d'you hear? I happen to love that lady very deeply and I belong to her, and as fond as I am of you, I can't give away that which I don't own anymore. Toddle off to your own beds and good-night to you."

"One more time?" asked Hetty wistfully.

"She done had two and me only one tonight," said Betty. "Ain't fair."

I slapped their behinds and cried, "Go! I'm practically a married man!"

They kissed me and slid off the bed, and one said, "Not yet, you ain't. Ol' Nick, when he comes up all hard and ready, you call us quick and we fix that rascal good." They chorused a good-night and were gone.

Naturally, I missed them of nights after that and between my unrelieved condition and Marg's rising passion as the day neared I was in fairly desperate straits. As I fought temptation I thought of how Hector MacDonald would have roared with laughter if he had known of Jamie Reid's strange plight, resisting against his will the entreaties of, so to speak, three women, because while the

227

nightmares did not recur, the wet dreams did and the twins took to making pointed references to the condition of the sheets, often debating in front of me whose turn it was to do the washing of them, all the while casting roguish, inviting glances in my direction. I remained steadfast and ignored them.

I could not ignore Marg, however. One afternoon after I had diplomatically refused her permission to sit on my lap in the painting room, she said, "You tell me you belong to me as I do to you, yet you won't let me touch and explore your dear person, my dear person. And you won't do the same to me, though there is no part of me that isn't yours and you may do with me as you will. I have no more shame with you than I have with myself and that's mighty little. I've a powerful desire to see and touch the engine that you'll be putting inside me to make our children—I feel it nudging me when you kiss me good-bye each day and it makes me fearfully excited."

"Marg, darling," I told her, "if you were to see and touch, we'd run the whole course, hurdles, water ditches and all before we knew what we were doing. I'm a bombshell ready to go off for wanting to be a part of you, to hold you and love you with nothing between us. If we were not in our peculiar situation I assure you that by this time you would be completely familiar with every small wrinkle and dimple on Old Nick."

She giggled. "What a dear name for him! Does he show his dimples when he smiles?"

"You're making him weep at this moment," I said desperately. "Please desist. I wonder why no Ranger has been here since I arrived."

"Let me wipe his tears away," she said, laughing and coming for me, and I had another crisis to overcome, but failed. In the brief struggle her lithe body wriggled against mine and that triggered me off, strongly and wetly.

"Goddamn it," I muttered, working free of her arms.

"Oh," she exclaimed, drawing back, "did I hurt you, dear?"

"Just a minor bombshell," I answered wryly, and managed to depart the house before the spreading wetness stained the crotch of my light-colored breeches.

The next day when I was riding happily through the woods on my way to see her, Jedediah Jenks came riding from the opposite direction. After exchanging greetings, he reined in and I stopped to see what he had to say, which was, "Going to Elderbank, sir?"

"I am," I answered shortly.

"My father says you are drawing a picture of Marg," he announced, "and says it must be a marvel because you've been at it ever since you came to this country."

"By what marvel is that any of your affair?" I asked.

He studied a crow circling above the trees. "My father bids me tell you that I have commenced courting Marg, and as a nearly betrothed woman it is not fitting that you should be taking a picture of her."

Fury, dismay and revulsion seized me and I fought to control myself. There should have been no great surprise, for we had discussed such an attempt by Abraham, but since falling in love with Marg my mind had refused to accept the possibility. I was tempted to violence toward the fat fellow. Peter had cautioned against slips at this stage of the game. I didn't slip. "The lady's virtue is in no danger at my hands. You may inform your father that the portrait of her is nearly done and when it is, I shall go no more to that place." Touching spurs to Prince, I rode off down the path at a rocking gallop.

When I stamped into the house, Marg looked at my face and observed, "You met Jedediah."

"I met a pudgy-headed idiot," I growled, "who said he's going to court the young woman who lives here, by order of his father. I feel like a bloody buffoon. He actually warned me away from the woman I love and whom I'm to marry in a few days, and there was nothing I could say."

She said cheerfully, "Ah, darling, don't take on so. We knew it might happen. His heart's not in it and he's nearly as afraid of me as he is of his father. I can handle him so he won't interfere with us. I've just now sent for my brothers so we can resolve it."

I gestured impatiently. "No need for jawing about it! I'm ready to risk being thought over-friendly with Tories by it being known I'm marrying one. When that stomach-turning lump of tallow calls upon you next, you shall inform him how it is with us and send him to Goodowns for confirmation from me."

"But," she said slowly, "there's more to it now than just you and me, Rob. 'Tis Elderbank Abraham wants."

Peter and John, dirty-handed and perspiring, clumped

in, and Peter said, "It best be important, Marg. We're sweating new rims on the rick wagon."

" 'Tis important," she answered, "if our home is more so than repaired wheels." She related the details of Jedediah's visit.

John shrugged. " 'Twas foolish to think we could keep the marriage secret in the first place. Tell Jed you're spoken for and be done with it. We'll have to chance Abraham's nose being put out of joint."

"Correct," agreed Peter, putting his hat back on. "Tell the truth, trust in God and hope for the best."

"Stay," ordered Marg in a firm, strong voice I had not heard before. "You'll all three sit down and hear me out. Speak out, say you all. And what, pray tell, will Abraham do then? If there's no chance for him to get Elderbank the easy, painless and cheap way through me being his daughter-in-law, how long do you think it would be before you're banished and Elderbank confiscated to be sold at auction, and who do you think would arrange among his friends to get it? And how long do you think it will be before Abraham sets those friends of his sniffing out what Rob and you have been doing among the Loyalists? Peter, you yourself said we must give them nothing to be suspicious of. No slips, you said. Will you risk failure for the King's men, too?"

"Mr. Cameron down to Savannah," answered Peter, "will—"

"Papa always said not to depend on others," she told him.

I said, "Especially Cameron. He plays a different game and may not find it possible to intervene again in this matter."

Marg went on, "Abraham won't have to come out flat and say I must either marry Jedediah or there'll be banishment and confiscation. He knows we're clever enough to understand what is threatened." She looked thoughtful. "But I think he doesn't want to push too hard for fear of getting a straight-out refusal and that will make him go about the gaoling and banishment business. Let me handle Jedediah. I can keep him dangling until our soldiers come here."

I exclaimed, "D'you mean to say you'll endure that slimy slug's courtship even after you're my wife, let him make sheep's eyes at you?"

"Sheep's eyes never hurt anybody," she said calmly, "and he'd never dare touch me."

"But wait, now!" I cried. "The Army won't be here until December or January! For God's sake, you and I should be long-settled in London by then!"

She came to me, took my hand and said, pleading, " 'Twill be for but a short time, Rob, and then we'll have the rest of our lives together. If I flitted with you now t'would mean death or banishment for my brothers and the end of Elderbank! Please—"

I simmered, and Peter said angrily, "I'd sooner put the torch to Elderbank and join Browne's Rangers than hide behind my sister's skirts while she plays hussy to a man in front of her lawful husband!"

"There's dishonor here," glowered John, "for all of us."

"Dishonor!" Marg was fiery. "Where's the honor in giving up our home to flee like whipped curs to a foreign land? Where's the honor in running from your country because those rebel swine are grunting around? After the soldiers come, you men can take your guns and fight for your rights as I would if I were a man, but I'm a damned weak vessel of a female and I must fight for the right with a weak vessel's weapons! This is my home! This is my country! Run off to skulk in Florida if you like, you brave men! I'll stay here until my King's soldiers come to give us back our land, then I'll go freely and gladly with my beloved husband wherever he takes me!" She was magnificent in her pride and passion.

"That's all well and good," commented John, "but you're putting us between a man and his wife. When you marry Rob you'll take oath to cleave to him and forsake all others, and now you're saying you'll not do that."

The fire went out of her eyes and tears welled in its place. She looked at me and I could see the wrenching pain of her dilemma. "Oh, God," she whispered, "what must I do?"

I got up and went to her, took her in my arms and said to the brothers, "Count me out of the argument, gentlemen. I'll abide by what you decide, the three of you. If I were to insist that she come away with me and the worst came to pass for you here, it would be a blight on our married life together forever, no matter what Marg might say to the contrary. Though she's an angel, there's a good

231

bit of human nature in her, and that's human nature. I'll not want a wife with a bitter chip on her shoulder."

She gave a startled cry. "Rob, Rob, what are you saying? That you'll not have me now? Oh, dear God, I'd rather die! Don't—"

I hugged her. I said, "If you must stay, then I must stay. I'll never leave you."

"You're a good man, Rob," said Peter. "If you're willing to put up with that scheme of hers for our sakes, then there must be good in it. John?"

"It gripes my everlasting soul," said John, "but we'll endure it, I reckon. And Marg would do well to fall on her knees and thank God He's given her a man like Rob."

Marg smiled damply. "I do that every night. Thank you, Rob."

During that last week of my bachelorhood Jedediah presented his lumpish person twice at Elderbank and was entertained in the cookhouse by watching Marg and Hyacinth preparing and cooking food. Marg said he fidgeted a great deal as if anxious to be away and mostly stared at the floor. She kept him off balance by occasionally saying something innocuous to him in a cheerful but deliberately forceful way that was guaranteed to drive him back into his shell. Even in small childhood, she said, he had been afraid of her and Anne. I began to get used to the idea of the foul slob hanging about.

The Reverend Mr. MacLeod arrived on horseback with a Negro servant and a pack animal, and was bedded down in the best room at Elderbank in accordance with old custom. An intelligent, educated man, he had arrived in America sometime after I had departed New York and his story, as he related it, of how he reached his post at Augusta, passing through British and rebel lines, was a memorable saga in the annals of the Presbyterian ministry. The Elderbank painting room was chosen for the wedding chapel, being on the second floor and safe from prying eyes, and as the minister inspected it his glance fell on the portrait of Marg on the easel. "My word!" he muttered and went to it. He peered closely at the surface, backed off, stared, then went close again. "Extraordinary," he murmured, and gingerly touched the surface. "Why, 'tis still tacky!" Looking around at us, he asked, "May I ask who did this work?"

"You may, sir," I smiled. " 'Tis the bridegroom's gift to his bride. Your servant, sir."

He looked me up and down, then studied my face, and suddenly I saw recognition in his own, mixed with wonder. "The picture appears finished and 'tis truly magnificent, sir, yet I see no signature, Mr. . . . Mr. Allston."

All at once it hit me. I had become so used to the false name that I had overlooked telling Marg and her brothers my real one, and this parson so lately removed from Great Britain had somehow identified me through my painting style. I laughed and said to Marg, "Honeybun, I've been an imbecile. I nearly forgot my true name. The Army gave me Allston because my own is rather too well known. Mr. MacLeod, if you have identified me in that way you are a remarkable clergyman. Are you also an artist, by any chance?"

MacLeod appeared dazed. "Why, I hardly know what to say. This is nearly incredible! No, sir, I'm not an artist—or rather I'm a failed one. I studied for some years before being forced to admit I have utterly no talent, but my interest in art remains an obsession and I'm quite familiar with the techniques of the major British artists. I have long admired your work, sir. Just before departing London I attended an exhibition at the Royal Academy and had the pleasure of viewing some of your landscape and genre works. His Majesty opened the exhibition with some interesting remarks."

"Oho," I commented, "I left those pictures with my frame maker to sell on consignment. Smart chap. Did they sell, d'you know?"

"They were sold entirely before I left the premises, sir," answered the minister. "His Majesty said—"

"Excuse me, Mr. MacLeod," interrupted Marg, "if I inquire of this gentleman what my name will be when I wed him."

Laughing, I kissed her. "I must ask you again. Will you do me the honor of becoming Mistress Jamie Reid?"

Her eyes danced. "Ah, so that's it! Aye, I'll take you instead of Rob Allston, Jamie Reid. 'Tis odd how well it fits you."

"A good Scottish name to join with our family," remarked John.

"Aye," agreed Peter, "but he must use the other outside the house. Mr. MacLeod, you'll mind what I told you of our friend being on His Majesty's service."

"Yes, but I doubt His Majesty will be much pleased to hear of it," said the minister. "Mr. Reid, the King's little speech bore largely on you in an indirect way, though he might just as well have spoken your name because from the conversations I overheard among the guests all were aware of it. As an admirer of your work I share His Majesty's concern over your brave but reckless actions in the battle of the ship *Jason* and now to find you here—" He shook his head. "And I must say it was almost scandalous how the newspapers acclaimed you as a fighting hero rather than as one of our leading artists, particularly while your superb portrait of His Majesty was on view at the Academy. The public appears to have adopted you as some sort of dashing idol, even if the war here is not widely popular, and His Majesty publicly stated that you—"

The man was running on like an open ale tap. "I'm familiar with His Majesty's attitudes in that regard, sir. He made himself quite clear to me. However, I don't think he'll have me burned at the stake for serving him here in Georgia. And with regard to my presence here, I'll be obliged if you will hold off recording this marriage in your register until I'm away from Georgia which will be, I think, sometime in December."

"I shall do that, Mr. Reid," he replied, and smiled. "I doubt, too, the King will visit savage punishment on you."

"Rob—Jamie," said Marg, her eyes wide, "you know the King? You painted his picture just like mine? You're famous?"

"I did a portrait of him last March and we talked a bit," I explained. "As for being famous, 'tis mostly blathery gossip printed in the cheap newspapers. It doesn't take much to interest the people of London, whether it be a small child hanged at Tyburn or a duchess surprised in the wrong bed."

"Well, well," commented Peter, eyeing me, " 'twould seem our sister is moving up to high places. If all are ready, Mr. MacLeod, will you oblige us by now seeing she takes the first step to becoming Mrs. Reid?"

It should be evident from the detailed manner in which these recollections are written that I have a somewhat phenomenal memory, and so it is curious how certain

mind. The ceremony of my marriage to Marg is one of
highly emotional incidents are clouded and blurred in my
those. I can recall with extreme exactitude each word
spoken immediately before and after the vows, but the
memory of the actual rite is like what is seen through a
windowpane when a heavy rain is beating on it. Peter gave
the bride away and John produced the ring that had been
their mother's. Memory clarifies at the point when I kissed
Marg as my wife for the first time and Jamie Reid was a
married man.

Considerable confusion followed with much kissing of
the bride and a deal of handshaking, and though there
were only three other men in the room it seemed a large
crowd. A jug of peach brandy appeared and toasts were
drunk. There was beguiling wonderment in the soft gray
eyes that followed me constantly, and I could not take
my own off her, awed that the dear, lovely person was
my own wife who would bear my children and grow old
and bent with years beside me. There would not be much
wrinkling in her face and neck in time to come; I had
carefully studied her skin, flesh-padding and bone structure during the painting. Her physical charm would endure
into great age. I looked upon her without lust, surprisingly
enough, so overwhelmed was I by the enormous novelty of
my new status as a husband and potential father of the
small human beings whom we would create from our love.
The brothers and the minister drank and talked. Tongue-
tied for once in my life, I looked into Marg's serious face
and said, "Wife—"

I knew she felt the same way. I saw her swallow and
she answered, "Husband."

Then the booming voice of Abraham Jenks, apparently
speaking to Hyacinth at the front door, sounded from
below. Peter said to MacLeod, "This man is a rebel official
and a villain, though a neighbor. He above all must not
know what just took place here. Marge, you'd better slip
your ring off." Turning to his brother, he said, " 'Twould
be best to fetch him up. I think he's come to see the
picture."

Abraham came in, his black-clad bulk looming large
and his little sharp eyes darting from person to person.
He rumbled, "A social visiting is it, on a working day of
the week?"

Introducing him to the minister, Peter said, "Mr. Mac-

Leod is making visitation calls on Auld Kirkers in the district, down from Augusta because we have neither parson nor church of our own these days."

"I am a disciple of Mr. Wesley, sir," announced Abrabam, and launched into a sort of sermon about the value of missionary visiting as prescribed by St. Paul, citing the godless state of the folk in the backcountry and their need for salvation. Peter, John and Marg watched him without expression and the minister, faintly puzzled, tried to follow the rambling discourse. My dislike of the man must have shown on my face because Marg gave me a quick pleading look. Turning my back on him, I helped myself to the brandy.

The sermon trailed off when Abraham's gaze fell upon the portrait. He walked to the easel. "Ha, this is what I came to see. Mr. Allston has spent much time making it. Very pretty, Mr. Allston. 'Tis plain to see you might well make a living at such stuff."

"Thank you," I said dryly.

Standing back, he surveyed the picture. "A good likeness, though much prettified. A victory of vanity. 'All is vanity, sayeth the Preacher.' Is that not so, Mr. MacLeod?"

"In moderation, I think, sir," replied the parson mildly.

"I disagree, sir," rumbled Jenks. "There are no moderate degrees of sin, even as a female cannot be moderately with child. A sin is as complete at the beginning as it is at the end—aye, complete before the beginning of the act, for the very thought of sin is equal to the commission of it. The Almighty God admonishes us against creating graven images and here is one that is a monument to the sin of vanity harbored by the female whose image it is."

Anger surged. Controlling my voice with difficulty, I said, "An apology to that lady is in order, sir."

"I meant no offense," he said, making a slight bow toward Marg, "and beg pardon if such was taken. But in truth, Mr. Allston, you must admit that your means of making your living is a feeding of the vanity of the people who pay you money for such as this picture which has no value except for that."

Before I had first met him I disliked the man. After I met him I disliked him more. After witnessing him flogging his naked daughter-in-law I despised him. It was because of him my wife and I would not be able to begin our married life in the eyes of the world. Now he had

236

come uninvited to my wedding party and insulted my wife, my occupation and me. I hated the air he breathed. I set my drink down on the table and placed my hand on my smallsword hilt. "What I must admit is that you speak undiluted dung, Mr. Jenks. You may not understand it because of your limited and distant kinship with the human race, but that picture was painted solely because I wished to do it. The many other portraits I have painted and been paid for were commissioned out of love and respect or affection toward the subjects, human virtues you appear or lack. I do not cater to vanity, Mr. Jenks, nor do I tolerate boorish, insulting behavior. I find your remarks and manner such, sir."

There was absolute silence in the room and no movement. The man's eyes glittered at me. My mind held no thought except the desire to kill him, and forgotten was the fact that he was a powerful local rebel official and I an enemy spy, or that he was probably unarmed; he wore no sword and likely carried no pistol in his clothes. I suspect the events of the day had honed my emotions to a state where common sense was submerged. Loosening the sword in the scabbard by drawing it out an inch, I let it drop back with a loud click. Abraham sighed, smiling to reveal a stubble of brown teeth. "I gladly withdraw any remark you think not polite, Mr. Allston, and I regret the misunderstanding."

I said, "The misunderstanding was not mine, sir. 'Twas yours."

He made a bowing gesture. "As you wish, sir. Mine, no doubt. Will you tell me what you will do with this picture?"

"I can't conceive how that would concern you," I told him, sorry he had apologized.

"My concern," he rumbled, "is that I would like to buy it for a fair price."

"And what might be your idea of a fair price?" I asked.

He stroked his beard and my anger remained at the boiling point as I saw him looking from the picture to Marg and back again. "Two pound sterling, sir. What do you say to that?" He evidently thought it a princely sum.

"I'll say for that you might buy a fancy silver-mounted horsewhip to mete out God's loving mercy in high style," I answered, "but not this monument to vanity, sir. My going price for a picture of this size and content is the French equivalent of twenty British guineas."

"Ha!" he rumbled, frowning. "Who would pay such a fortune for such a thing? I find it hard to believe, sir."

I stared hard at him. "You call me a liar, sir?"

He raised a hamlike hand in a restraining gesture. "No indeed, sir. My meaning was that folk who pay such money for an item of no practical use must have more money than good sense. There are few men in Georgia who will see in their lifetime that much money all at once."

He had turned my wedding day from a merry and beautiful occasion into a pit of stinking slime. I snapped, "Then by God you've learned something today, haven't you? What in flaming hell do you want it for, anyway? The subject's no kin of yours, and that's a mercy of God considering some of your family customs!"

Now with pleasure I saw the anger behind the hairy smile, but he said in his normal sermonizing tone, "You are an impatient stranger within our gates, Mr. Allston, so I must explain to you that this female and my son Jedediah have grown up together and I have long intended that they mate and bear fruit. My son has commenced the courting, for 'tis time. I wish to get the picture for him because it is not fitting that any other man possess it, to look upon her image with lust and fleshly desire."

Nausea clutched my stomach. I growled, "If you come to me on the day they're married, with twenty guineas in your hand, I'll give your offer the consideration it deserves." Sour bile rose in my throat. In a moment I would vomit. Whirling, I managed to mutter farewells to the others and my bride, and fled from the house back to Goodowns.

Chapter XV

I HAD TO INFORM my household, of course, that Goodowns would have a new mistress for a while between
the dark and the daylight. Brutus, pleased, congratulated
me and assured me the patrolling watchman would toss
a handful of pebbles against the bedchamber window just
before sunrise so my wife could leave without being observed by the Jenks children. The twins were ecstatic and
immediately produced special sheets that had been stored
with dried honeysuckle and rose petals, then remade my
bed with them amid whoops of laughter that could be
heard all through the house. The afternoon seemed endless and my tension grew, for now full realization that I
was going to bed Marg gripped me and lust bloomed,
pulsed and throbbed. To no avail did I tell myself that
Jamie Reid had no business working up a fever over such
a simple matter as a romp in bed with another young
woman; this one was different, I was frantic with love for
her and the hope that she would be pleased and happy
with me.

I had little appetite at supper and the twins urged me
to eat, keep up my strength, solicitous as if I were ill.
"Mister Rob," pleaded one, "you got to store up milk on
your hips. Miss Marg, she's a strong lady, goin' to want
all you got to give oncet she ain't a maid no more."

"You want us to fetch her up to you bed when she
comes?" asked the other.

"I want you to clear away supper," I told them, "clean
up the kitchen as fast as you can, then retire. No more
advice, please."

"We women and this is your weddin' day," said large-
breasted Betty, "and we got duties to give advice. Don't
you go rammin' it into Miss Marg like 'twas us, 'cause we

239

stretched to fit and she ain't, bein' a maid. You love that lady, you be slow and kind, slip in easy—"

"Oh, for Christ's sake!" I cried. "Shut up!" I flung away from the table and went upstairs to shave for the second time that day and sponge critical body parts, even though I had bathed less than two hours previously. I wanted desperately to drink and was afraid to for fear I'd be half drunk on my wedding night and didn't want to miss a single sensation. In the wine cellar I brought out a special bottle of Amontillado I'd had my eye on for some time and took it with a corkscrew and a pair of goblets up to the bedchamber. The sun set and the clatter of kettles and gusting laughter from the kitchen ended. I undressed and slipped on my robe, then sat by the window to watch the fireflies over the lawn and worried about the difficulties of penetrating a virgin's hymen. Under no circumstances must I rush things, I warned myself. At the first sign of discomfort in her I must desist.

Stars began to blink on in the sky. Why was she so late? There were bears, poisonous snakes in the woods. Evil, soulless men were on the loose. Horrible foreboding seized me and just as I hastily reached for my breeches there was a small sound in the quiet house, the click of the latch on the kitchen door. Instead of relief, a wave of apprehension flooded me. I knew I should go downstairs, embrace her and triumphantly bear her up to our bower, but I could only stand, dry-mouthed with my heart pounding, waiting, watching the black rectangle of the doorway.

Her face was a pale spot suspended in dark space and it swam toward me into the moonlight where I stood. She was smiling and said, "Good-evening, sir. You must excuse this late visit. Have I a husband here?"

She was adorable. I said, "What a coincidence! I'm waiting for my good wife."

She flew into my arms and the fire of her passion shook me so that I had to break the embrace, for in another second I would have thrown her on the bed and ravished her, which was precisely what I must not do. "Whoa," I said. "Let's not start at a gallop. We've got all night."

"I want to gallop all night," she said, "and for all the rest of our life." She hoisted her gown over her head and instead of her glorious white nakedness there was revealed another gown, a white sleeveless affair that came to her ankles.

"What in God's name is that you're wearing?" I demanded, opening the wine.

" 'Tis my bridal gown for bedding," she giggled, whirling about. "I spent weeks embroidering on it before you ever asked me."

"What I can see of it is pretty," I told her, "but the only bed gown you'll wear will be the one you were born with, my love. Come, have a private bridal cup."

She raised her glass. "I give you my love and myself till the end of time, Jamie."

Touching my goblet to hers, I said, "And I give you mine and me, Marg." We drank, then I sat down in the chair by the window and pulled her into my lap, delighting in the soft weight of her body nestling in my arms.

"I thought we'd be popping straightway into bed," she murmured.

The hand on my encircling arm closed over a luscious breast beneath the dress. "No need for haste, honeybun."

"Are you shy, Jamie?" she asked.

I chuckled. "Good God, no. Why do you ask?"

"I've heard bridegrooms are sometimes bashful," she said. "You've been to bed with a woman before, though, haven't you?"

When we reached London she'd hear plenty about my past performances, no doubt. "I'll never lie to you. I've bedded a number of 'em. What difference does it make? I never loved any of them and I'm mad with love for you."

Her hand was inside my robe, feeling of my chest. "How hard your muscles are there where my chest is all soft squeezy breast. Well, it makes a difference because I shall have to give you more pleasure than all of them put together, and I don't know anything about it except that I lie on my back and you get on top of me. I want to do more than that for you."

"Sweet lady," I said, "don't worry, we'll give each other all manner of good things. There's an instinct that invites and guides us, you'll see. What's this opening for in the front of your dress, ventilation?" Exploring, I had found a hole in the garment low in the body and my fingertips roamed in there over silken thighs, then a thatch of hair. I felt her body quiver.

She gave a breathless laugh. "Hyacinth . . . oh, darling, what are you doing . . . helped me make this . . . oh, sweet . . . and said wives must not let their husbands see

241

them bare . . ." She almost groaned as my finger entered. "Ah, ah, Jamie . . . and the hole is for you to . . ." She tore the front of my robe open and laved my chest with kisses, her lips now moving restlessly. "Jamie, in God's name, take me, take me . . ."

Caution and prudence fled, and in a twinkling of an eye we were on the bed, stark, kissing and embracing in a violent storm which stopped the moment I began the entrance. With her arms around me, she quietly opened to me like a beautiful flower, her breath coming rapidly. There was no obstruction, and after I was in to the hilt in a smooth, perfect mating, she whispered, " 'Tis the glory of God. We were two and now are one. I feel your feelings. We're one flesh, one heart . . ."

It was true. It was not copulation, but rather a magic sacrament that blended us into a single entity. We disappeared as individuals of different sex, different minds. Her joy was mine. I was she. She became me. There was no division. We had given ourselves to each other, and in the giving had received each other. We ceased being human and became a constellation of fiery jewels wheeling through infinite space in incarnate splendor, then exploded into millions of diamond bits, showering in a rain of pure color through the universe.

We became flesh again, still joined, and when I kissed her I discovered her face was wet. "Have I hurt you?" I asked anxiously.

"Hurt me?" She pulled my face down and kissed my eyes and mouth. "You took me to Heaven! We were shooting stars and the beauty of it made me weep! Oh, my love, my true love, Jamie, I'm drunk with the wonder and holiness of it! Again, Jamie, again!" Her body came arching up and we went soaring beyond the moon again.

After that we rested, sipping wine. Marg chuckled. "I came here tonight all of a boil to be humped like a cow by a bull. Oh, I've had the dirty dreams about you, Jamie Reid, and 'twas all for naught because 'tis the most beautiful thing I'll ever know in my lifetime. And you being me and I being you there's no shame or dirtiness at all, is there?"

"You," I declared, "are an immaculate goddess before whom shame and dirtiness flee. There is no part of you that isn't pure. I thought I loved you before we came together here. It was absurd. Now I know what love is and I hope I'll prove worthy of it and of you."

"I wasn't pure at all," she laughed, "when I kept you stealing quick looks at my tail on the way from Savannah. I saw your eyes goggling one time when I mounted and when I realized what it was I thought to tease you more. It made me feel deliciously dirty."

"Oh, you devious jade!" I exclaimed, rolling her onto her belly and kissing her buttocks. "Had I known—had I but known!"

"I'm glad you made us wait until 'tis like this," she said, "with our vows taken and God blessing us. I was a silly, witless girl. Jamie, Hyacinth says decent ladies never enjoy what gentlemen do to them in bed, but I don't feel indecent at all. 'Tis all so *right,* so . . . so *beautiful!"*

"Hyacinth should stick to her pots and pans," I said, rolling my face on her sweet flesh and kissing, "and cut no more lascivious hole in nightdresses."

She wriggled in ecstasy from head to toe under my diligent caressing and whispered breathlessly, "I . . . I . . . darling, I want to . . . to do you . . . like that . . ."

Pausing, I said, "Obey your instincts, honeybun. There's nothing but love and goodness in this bed."

And she did. In all my womanizing experience there was never such a delightful, inventive and enthusiastic partner as she, as our love guided the giving of ourselves to each other, lavishing exquisite pleasure after pleasure in mutual joy. We slept in brief catnaps from time to time and during one of those intermissions I dreamed Anne MacDonald stood beside the bed looking down at us. She wore the green gown and her expression was unsmiling yet tender as she said clearly, "My love for you both is in this bed of mine."

"Is nothing safe from you?" I demanded angrily. "Keep your beautiful nose out of my marriage!"

Then it seemed that Marg sat up in bed, took Anne by the hand and said, "When the dancing is done there's a better road."

"You, too?" I cried at her. "Damn your roads, both of you!"

The sound of my voice awakened me and my wife was anxiously holding me, saying, "Jamie, Jamie, what were you dreaming?"

I laughed. "Promise me you'll never speak to me of roads, honeybun." I told her about it.

"Ah, Jamie," she murmured, "I've no wish to leave this road, for never in this world is there a better one, and this one will come better and better. And as for dancing, 'tis nearly dawn and our party's near ended for the night. Boost your big dear self on me and we'll dance again—"

We were hard at it when the watchman's shower of pebbles pattered, ordered us to return to the workaday world, and we reluctantly dressed in the pre-dawn darkness. When I escorted Marg to the kitchen door, the twins, building the cookfire for breakfast, sparkled wide smiles at us and Betty exclaimed, "Miss Marg, you some pretty this mornin'! Face all lighted up like the sun!"

"Mister Rob ain't no rain cloud, either," giggled Hetty. "He goin' to want a *big* breakfast, all that work last night!"

Laughing, I said to Marg, "And after that big breakfast I'm going to flog a pair of impertinent wenches."

"Why?" She was laughing, too. "I feel lighted up like the sun and you did work hard." The twins shouted with merriment. "You girls feed Mister Rob well today, you hear? Because he'll have a deal harder work when I come back tonight."

With their bubbling laughter behind us, we walked through the dark peach orchard to the edge of the woods, and Marg said to me, "That pair seem too wise about certain things, but they're sweet. Did I please you in the night, Jamie?"

"I'll never know greater pleasure, darling," I answered. "How do you feel?"

"Beautifully tired and sore," she said, "and I must look like something the cat dragged in and couldn't eat. I'll sleep today and rest up so I can teach your dear Old Nick a few manners tonight. My brothers will leer and poke each other in the ribs, and I don't care. Oh, wouldn't it be wonderful if we could have breakfast together and then go back to bed!"

"We'll do that every day after we live in a world without Abraham Jenks," I said. "God rot his goddamned vile bones. I was near to killing him yesterday."

"I saw it in your face," she commented, "and was so frightened I couldn't speak, and afterward my brothers said even while you said those things to him they were so sure you'd do it that they were thinking on how to hide Abraham's body." She gave a little cry and came into my arms. "Oh, Jamie Reid, will you have a care for yourself and all of us? Be patient and love me!"

"I was being thoughtless," I said, kissing her. "It won't happen again. Hurry home tonight, honeybun."

I went no more to Elderbank, of course, for the portrait could no longer be used as an excuse, and when Marg brought me the last of the head count, the report on the miller, my job was done. I folded the map and coded list small and tucked them into the cuff of one of my seldom-used coats in my bedchamber wardrobe, wondering when the devil a Ranger courier would come to take them to General Prevost in East Florida.

The courting of my wife continued, souring my life during the day and building my dislike of Jedediah into the hatred I felt for his father. Regardless of his fear of Marg and his silent lumpishness when he sat in the cookhouse at Elderbank a couple of times a week, I knew that in his stealthy mind he undressed her and perpetrated his peculiar vileness on her. He never stayed longer than a half hour, evidently complying with the bare minimum of his father's instructions. But Marg had declared she could hold the pig at arm's length and keep him off balance, and she did.

At night I taught my wife physical love and she was a phenomenal pupil. My love for her continued to grow. The hours we had to spend apart were interminable, aching deserts of loneliness, and our joy was matchless when we came together each evening. I had wanted a lusty wife, knowing nothing of love before having Marg, and the fantastic revelation of what love could bring when linked with lusty desire fulfilled my wildest fancies. In our bedchamber we took to keeping a lighted candle by the bed in order to see our bodies and what we did for each other, and one of my greatest delights was to observe the contorted grimace on her normally lovely face when she reached the zenith of excruciating ecstasy. We almost literally devoured each other, avidly, greedily seeking the receiving of pleasure through the giving of it.

Then Abraham applied pressure to Marg. Calling at Elderbank when her brothers were afield, he told her bluntly that unless she accepted his son and set a firm

245

date, he would move against Peter and John and see them tried for their lives as traitors in the justice court. Everybody knew they were Tories, he claimed, who refused to serve in the militia and who shunned the Patriot Party. Additional evidence could be presented. "I told him I would set the date, Jamie, and said nothing to my brothers about it."

"Jesus Christ," I groaned, "if this were a play on a London stage I'd leave in disgust! The plot is asinine, the heroine too noble to be believable and her husband a bloody fool for putting up with this foul nonsense!"

Stroking my hair, she said, " 'Tis but a little time compared to the rest of our lives together. I'll dillydally over setting the date. There'll be the autumn work when every plantation needs twice as many hands as it has for getting in the crops, herding the kine, slaughtering the pigs for sausage-making, smoking hams, tending the pitch and tar kilns and all that. And he knows I'm no farm wench, but a plantation lady who needs things from Savannah and Charles Town for her wedding and marriage chest. And females being weak vessels, I don't have to give reasons for being flighty stubborn."

"Nor do I have need for more reasons," I said, "for killing that bastard. I could bury him under the hog pen and his body'd never be found down there under his kin."

"Shush," she murmured, putting her lips on mine. "That's crazy talk and you know it. That's the first place his family would look, here and at Elderbank. They may look stupid, some of them, but they're sharp. Murder won't cure our fix and will put us in a worse one. Oh, I'm trollopy bawdy tonight! Old Nick, you dear rascal, take this, and this, and *this!*" Then she had to stop talking and it was lovely.

The next morning I rode over to the sawmill on the upper Beaverdam, where I painted a few watercolors and had a drink of whisky with the secretly Loyalist miller, trying to keep my mind off the despicable position in which Abraham Jenks had placed me, that of a sort of cuckhold in thought if not deed. Taking the back way home, I followed a turpentiner's path that brought me out on the fields behind the servants' quarters and I rode to Brutus's cottage for a chat. The Negroes hailed me with good nature, flashing white teeth as they paused in their work. Dismounting at the cottage, the first thing I heard was

Captain Wallbrook's voice declaiming inside, "If I had my druthers, Brutus, I'd've long ago opened up that Jenks son of a bitch to watch his guts slide out. Why, that Marg, I tell you—"

I walked in grinning and held out my hand. "If you're going to tell anything about my wife, my friend, tell it to me and be damned careful what it is. My God, am I glad to see you! The report's been ready for days!"

He was shaggily bearded and wore stained backcountry buckskins. Leaping up and seizing my hand, he shook it hard, exclaiming, "Well, by Joe, look a-here! An honest-to-God planter when I was expecting to see a New York fop! Brutus, you trained him well!"

Brutus smiled. "Good-day, Mr. Allston. I took the liberty of telling Captain Wallbrook about your marriage and the . . . ah . . . interference. Will you sit and have a glass?"

I did, and Wallbrook said, "I'll be leaving after dark so there's plenty of time. Too many folk in this region know me by sight. I was told to take you along to Fort Tonyn if your work was done."

"You may have the report," I told him, "but not me. My wife and I won't leave until after the Crown comes here."

He gave me a smile with no mirth in it. "That so? We'll have to see to that. You're a marvelous lucky fellow, by God. Anne MacDonald under your roof up there in New York and now you're married to the other prettiest girl in Georgia. See you treat her right or I'll strip your hide off in small skinny ribbons. I saw her first."

"Sour grapes," I laughed.

"Sour, hell," he said. "Sour rebel sons of bitches. I was set on that lady till one day I came home from seed-buying at Augusta and found my house in ashes, Ma and Pa dead and the stock run off. I went asking around, got a few answers and found two of those brave Liberty Boys hiding in their houses. Their womenfolk screamed pretty good when I scalped 'em and sliced off their balls before I cut their throats. Not being exactly in the frame of mind to go on courting, I lit out for St. Mary's, and that's how come she married you and not me, but I guess that makes us kind of related, so if you want, you can call me Hugh, brother."

"Jamie, here," I said, a little taken aback at the bloody recital.

Brutus remarked, "Their women still claim you ravished them, Captain."

He nodded and said grimly, "I know, and I might just correct that oversight one of these days when I'm back up there, though they're filthy sows."

"Well," I told Wallbrook, "you may be sure I'll cherish Marg. If it weren't for Jenks and this damned rebellion we'd be the happiest people in the world. I was worried when no Ranger showed up, afraid plans had been changed."

" 'Tis still on," he told me. "The general's chomping on the bit to get started soon as the reports are all in and hold up the idea. Man, Colonel Browne was that mad over the double head count that where he spat the grass'll never grow again, believe you me! Things betwixt him and the Regulars were never what you'd call sweet, us being paid by the Royal Council more than the Regulars and the Regulars not accepting Colonel Browne's rank except with and below Regular lieutenant colonels."

Draining my glass, I said, "I'll run up to the house and get that report and explain it to you. I want it off my hands as one less thing to worry about."

Mounting Prince, I rode to the big house, elated that it had turned out so well, and in the hallway at the foot of the stairs Hetty stood with a hand over her mouth, her face drawn with fear. Pointing up, she whispered hoarsely, "He got Betty, he got Betty!" I hurtled up the stairs and at the top heard muffled, whimpering sounds coming from my bedchamber, into which I plunged. Jedediah Jenks was busily raping Betty with one hand over her mouth, his fat, hairy buttocks rising and falling between her slender, dark and flailing legs.

"See how good it feels," he grunted, banging away, unaware of my presence.

Seizing the collar of his shirt and coat, I hauled him up and off with such force he went sailing backwards to land in a heap. I was astonished at the size of his erect pizzle: 'twas a veritable club. "You raping son of another son of a bitch," I said. "That's a free nigger and I think I'll see you hanged for that work."

He got to his feet and hauled up his breeches, glaring at me, and suddenly I saw a cocked pistol in his hand. There was no uncertainty in his voice as he cried, "I'll

248

see *you* hanged, mister picture drawer! I got your list of friends and the map where they live!"

I had my own pistol in my pocket and cursed myself for not having drawn it when I rushed upstairs. "You're a fool," I said coldly. "I'm an agent of the Continental Congress and all know it. You're a housebreaker, rapist and burglar, stealing my report of enemy Tories. Give up or 'twill be the worse for you."

"That's no list of enemies," he sneered, "not with the other stuff about loyalty to the King and rallying to support the King's army when they come here. Rapist, ha! How many times have you stuck your Tory prick into these little nigger cunts, eh? I'll wager you fuck 'em by day and that Great White Whore of Babylon by night." My face gave me away, I suppose. He exclaimed triumphantly, "I watched her sneaking over here at night, leaving in the morning, she who I was to wed." He grinned. "I told her before I came here I'd fuck her, wed or not, and gave her a taste of the tool I'll do it with before we hang you and her and her brothers!"

There were no two ways about it. Jedediah must be disposed of, quickly and neatly. The pistol muzzle was steady on me from five feet away. I said to teary, sobbing Betty, "Go fetch Brutus and the other menfolk, dear."

"I'm not finished fucking you!" exclaimed Jedediah. "Stay on the bed or I'll beat you when I finish this Tory bastard!"

"Go," I told her, smiling.

She edged toward Jedediah who stood between us and the door, then tried to dart past him. He reached out his free hand to grab her and in that second I launched myself at him. We went down in a heap and he was much stronger than I expected, but he had dropped the pistol and I slipped the Ira Tupper joo jitsoo head-twist on him. His neck broke with a sound like a wet stick snapping underfoot in the forest. When I stood up, Betty said, peering down at him fearfully, "He dead, Mister Rob?"

I went through the man's pockets and found my papers. "He'll never be deader."

"Never seen no man killed before," she quavered, sniffling. "He come on me here when I was dustin' and—ooh, 'twas dreadful, Mister Rob. 'Twas fun and nice when you and me and Hetty done it, but—"

"He always ties his horse outside the kitchen door," I

249

said, my mind working rapidly. A glance out the back window revealed the animal. The spying Jenks children in the woods watching Goodowns would be placed to watch the front of the house and the outbuildings, the road and the fields, and consequently not the back of the big house. It was unlikely they had seen their uncle arrive. Hetty came flying into the room and embraced her twin, and both wailed like banshees, Hetty worse than Betty when she noticed the corpse.

"Shut up!" I roared. "Be silent, damn it! Betty, did he hurt you, tear you or anything?"

"No, sir," she answered. "He just scare me and make me sick. You pull him out before he shoot, too."

"Well, take your herb medicine just in case," I ordered, "and what I want you both to do is take his horse right into the kitchen—"

They both shrieked in horror. "He shit and piss all over our clean kitchen! Please, Mister Rob—"

"Do as I say and do it fast!" I snapped. "The Jenks children must not see the beast, don't you understand! After dark we'll get rid of this swill and the horse. Scat. Scamper!"

In order not to excite the curiosity of young peepers from the woods, I kept Prince at a leisurely walk in returning to Brutus's house, where I handed my report to Wallbrook and briefly explained the coding, then said, "We have an unfortunate complication. I came on friend Jedediah Jenks just now raping one of the twins, Betty. He also had that report in his possession and knew what it meant. He was aware that Marg came to Goodowns each night."

Brutus asked quickly, "Did he otherwise injure the girl, sir?"

"She's unharmed except for emotional shock," I answered, "and with her sister, very angry about having Jedediah's horse in the kitchen so it won't be seen by his nephews if they're out there. Jedediah remains in my bedchamber."

"Alive?" asked Wallbrook, fingering the sheath knife in his belt.

"No," I answered. "His neck was broken. The question is, what do we do with the clot?"

Brutus said, "If I may make a suggestion, gentlemen— after dark we can remove the deceased and his horse to the path leading to Jenks Town and arrange the corpse to make it appear he was thrown or fell from the saddle. The animal will go home to his stable and the Jenks will come out searching for the rider."

"That's reasonable, I reckon," commented Wallbrook. "Seeing as I can't leave before dark I'll help you, Brutus. Jamie, how was his neck broken?"

"We had a short wrestling match," I replied, "and I applied an ancient Oriental touch."

He nodded. "I figured. That's twice you did that. Everybody's heard about you killing that scum down by Leavitt's. You'd make a tolerable good Ranger if you learned Indian forest-prowling ways."

Brutus said thoughtfully, "Perhaps twice is once too many. If there should be a slip in the matter of Mister Jedediah that would raise the suspicions of Mister Abraham—he is a sharp-minded man—there could be an unfortunate result. Broken necks are uncommon in this country. It is known that Mr. Allston inflicted one and now he will be known to have been in close proximity to the other. I am concerned, gentlemen, if you see my point."

"By God, you're right," agreed Wallbrook. "I've known old pus-gut Jenks all my life and hate him so bad I'd like nothing better than to dice him up for stew meat, but I'll tell you this: he's got a quick brain between his ugly ears. Jamie, if they were to take you, 'tis likely the Crown's plans wouldn't be much of a secret anymore."

"Nonsense," I said. "I'd tell them nothing. What kind of a man do you think I am?"

"A flesh and blood man like all of us," replied Wallbrook, "who hurts when hurt is given to you. You've got a lot to learn and 'twould be a pity if you had to learn the hard way what I know about prying secrets out of shy fellows. Both sides do it and there's nothing pleasant about doing it, watching it, hearing it or having it done to you. My friend, you'll come away with me to Fort Tonyn when I leave tonight."

"The hell I will," I snorted. "Nobody's going to take me, and I happen to have a wife here. I'll leave when she's ready to leave and no sooner."

Wallbrook sighed. "I'm a patient man. Look, you, even without this Jenks affair, you gave yourself away with that picture you took of Marg. Yes, I had a talk with that

251

parson up to Augusta; he comes in handy for our side. He asked me if I knew you, since you're a Crown agent in my region. I know you took another picture down to Savannah for Cameron. There's a sight of educated men of parts on the rebel side who know about pictures and famous artists just like MacLeod or better. 'Tis but a matter of time before it happens again. Hold, I'm not through. Now, take those false papers they gave you at New York. They were meant to protect you for only a short ride here, long enough to do your job, which is done. Sooner or later some bigwig from up north'll come this way and you'll be in a real kettle of soup. There's too much risk and 'tis getting heavier every day, not risk just for you, but for a lot of other people and the Crown. So pack your saddle-bags, my friend."

An idea struck me and I snapped my fingers, grinning jubilantly. "But of course! And my wife can pack hers! With Jedediah removed, Abraham's cute plan is shot to bits! There's no more reason for her to stay!"

"But, sir," said Brutus, "there are more unpleasant possibilities raised by that action. In Mister Abraham's mind you would be eloping with his late son's betrothed almost before the body is cooled. Think on it, sir."

"He'd have the militia out turning the country upside down looking for you and Marg, for one thing," pointed out Wallbrook, "and for another he'd holler conspiracy and clap her brothers into the gaol at the county seat. The only way is for you to come along with me, Jamie, and come back for Marg when the Army does."

They were both right. "Goddamn it!" I exclaimed. "That bastardly Abraham! He's the linchpin in all this! I'll send him after his foul son!"

The Ranger officer shook his head sadly. "Christ, you're a menace to yourself as well as everybody else. D'you think his safety committee's made up of a mob of numb-skulls? I doubt there's a soul in this part of Georgia that doesn't know what Abraham's trying to do to lay hands on Elderbank and—ah, what's the use? Enough of this horse-shit! Hark to me, Mr. Reid: you're a King's agent on His Majesty's service and I happen to know you were warned against getting mixed up in personal business. Your personal fix doesn't matter a pisshole in the snow so far as your orders go and how the Crown looks at you, you understand?"

252

Bristling at his harsh tone, I said, "Don't lecture me. I've done my job for King and country and I'm my own man now."

"No lecturing," he stated, his mouth grim. "Ordering. You're still under orders, and as the senior officer of British military forces present at this place, I'm now and hereby ordering you to haul your balky arse out of this country while 'tis yet in one piece. We'll ride as soon as your fat friend's fixed on the woods path."

"You know where you can stick your bloody orders, soldier boy," I scoffed. "If I'm still under mine, then I outrank you. I hold the civilian equivalent rank to major of the Regular Establishment, Captain."

He looked even grimmer. "For a smart man, you can be goddamn stupid sometimes. You're in a war. We're not playing children's games. You and I happen to be under orders from—if you want to go clear to the top—General Clinton. Right now we're in the face of the enemy. Disobedience of orders in the face of the enemy can be punished by death after a court-martial. The order I gave to you is not anything that just came across my mind, it comes from Major General Augustine Prevost of your goddamned Regular Establishment, mister civilian major, passed to me by Colonel Thomas Browne.

"The order tells you and all other Crown agents doing head counting in Georgia to get to hell out after the reports are turned over, and return to British military jurisdiction. Now you've got the order, witnessed by Brutus here. Leave off acting like a snot-nosed brat. You'll get your wife back in a little while, unless you'd like to make her a widow one way or the other."

Rebuttal was futile. Common sense told me all his arguments were valid. I surrendered, my heart sinking. "All right, I'll go from Georgia, but not tonight. I'll go within the next few days."

"I think that would be best, sir," commented Brutus. "After the burial of the deceased, with adequate reasons for departure made known to interested parties, to allay suspicions."

"I'll hold you to that," said Wallbrook, "and report it down south. How d'you figure on going?"

"I'm still a Whig in good standing." I told him. "I'll go to Savannah and then to Charles Town, then from there make my way back to New York somehow."

He frowned. "Risky. There's a power of rebels to pass through that way. Better you go south to East Florida."

"If that's an order, drum up your damned court-martial, Hugh," I said. "I live in New York, have friends there, including the officer who's supposed to command the Savannah expedition, which I intend to join by hook or crook. Anne MacDonald went there from here fairly easily, and she a young woman alone, so I rather think I shall do it easily enough."

"If I had the right to order you not to," he remarked, "I'd sure as hell do it, but all they told me was that you're to go back to British military jurisdiction. I'll tell you one thing, though: you being a Whig like you say in good standing, the rebel army runs a courier boat up to Charles Town, then one to Norfolk and so on—Alexandria to Baltimore or someplace up yonder. 'Twould be risky, like I said, but a good way to go if you keep your mouth quiet and stay sober. Down to Savannah the boat's dispatched by a fellow named Captain Roche of the Continentals, run by the garrison quartermaster."

Delighted, I exclaimed, "I know him! He's a friend of mine!"

"Who'd see you hanged higher than Haman if he knew who you are," said Wallbrook dryly. "Well, we've got some time to kill before dark. Brutus, you surely turn out a fine brandy. Is there any more?"

Rising, I said, "None for me, thank you, Brutus. I'll go up to the house and calm down the twins and look after things there. I'll see you after dark, Hugh. Marg will be there and she'll want to say hello, I'm sure."

The interior of Goodowns stank atrociously of horse. In the kitchen the mild-mannered beast demonstrated stupendous bowel and bladder capacity which kept the girls in a state of shrieking indignation and busy with shovels, mops and buckets, sluicing down the flagstone floor. The rape victim showed no trace of her experience as she shouted angry insults at the horse, who stood quietly inside the door as if a kitchen were his natural environment. I worried about the possibilty of casual callers and took up a tactical position on the piazza with a book and a drink. The afternoon was endless.

The twins served me a light supper, apologizing tearfully because of the horse's presence that required so much of their time and effort. They smelled of horse. When darkness fell, Wallbrook and Brutus slipped into the house and were carrying Jedediah down the stairs when Marg entered the kitchen, openmouthed at the appearance of the horse there. "What on earth? Hetty, Betty, why is—" The twins wailed louder than ever and I propelled Marg out of the kitchen into the hallway where at her appearance the two men halted their body-bearing, laid the corpse down on the rug, and Wallbrook, grinning at her, said, "How do, married lady. Prettier than ever, I see, even with your sweet mouth open."

"Hugh!" she exclaimed, staring at the body. "What in Heaven's name has been happening here? Jamie, my God—" She was pale and shaken.

"I think you'd better get rid of our guests, then come back to socialize, Hugh," I said, putting my arm around Marg. "This lady needs medicinal brandy."

I eased her into the library, closed the jalousies against vision from outside, and lighted a candle, then gave her a glass of peach brandy. Color came back to her face after she drank it. "Jed—that was Jedediah! You killed him when he told you!"

"Told me what?" I asked.

"That he knew I came here of nights," she said. "He told me today." Her face grew set. "Hyacinth had gone to the springhouse and he took out his pizzle—a great ugly thing—and tried to force me. I caught up a kitchen knife and went for him and he ran away."

Red anger surged. "I wish I had known that. I would have killed him more slowly. He brought his great ugly thing here and had it stuck into Betty when I came on him in our room. He also had found the head-count report, so you see there were a number of good reasons why he couldn't be allowed to go on contaminating the world. I've delivered the report to Wallbrook and he's leaving tonight after he and Brutus arrange your fat lover as if he had fallen from his mount."

"Fat lover!" She made a sick face. "I was shocked to see him dead but now I'm glad. He was a dirty little boy and he was a dirty man. Hugh has changed from a happy, giving little boy into a hard, cruel man. I'm very fond of him, though. Do you know what happened to his family?"

"He told me," I answered. "I can't fault him for coming to be the way he is. I'm thinking this is a hard, cruel country and I'm glad I'm not a part of it."

255

She looked at me. "Jamie, you are. You're no longer an outsider. Georgia is a part of you and you're a part of Georgia. Neither will ever again be the same because of what you've done here."

The constant awareness that I must shortly leave Georgia and her made me feel a little ill. Dreading to tell her, I put it off. Smiling, I said, "Be that as it may, you're one part of Georgia that will always be part of me, honeybun. But has it occurred to you that Abraham's nasty plan has fallen through, that he can no longer hope in your direction?"

Nodding, she said, "Of course, but he won't give up. He'll try something else, move directly against my brothers, maybe."

Hugh Wallbrook came in and announced, "Now I'm the one who needs a brandy. The smell of that pig." Helping himself to the drink, he said, " 'Twouldn't be so unpleasant killing folks if they only wouldn't let go front and rear in their breeches when they die. Well, here's to the bride and groom." He tossed off his brandy and refilled his glass.

"If you'd been in the neighborhood, Hugh," said Marg, "we'd have had you to the wedding."

He smiled at her. "I know you would, but 'twould have been a mistake. Brutus told me about it. Your man here came near killing the old hog for insulting you. I surely would have done it for that as well as for him seeing me there, which would've been right bad for you and your brothers, to say nothing of your hardheaded husband and the parson. Well, if I couldn't have you, I'm glad you got the next best man."

"Hear, hear," I said dryly.

Marg said, laughing, "I really married him because he's famous and rich and is going to take me to live in London. I know a good bargain when I see one. In case you don't know it, Hugh, I've become a real lady. Doesn't it show?"

"If you'd married me," he said, "there would have been an end to that tomboy-cowboy game of yours, girl. You'd have turned into what you are now, the damnedest, prettiest, most gracious lady that ever saw the light of day. I may be rough and gruff, but if I ever have a home of my own again that's what I want in it. Well, don't worry while he's gone from you, Marg. Us Rangers'll be passing through from time to time to look out for you."

256

I could have killed him. Marg's face blanched and shock was in her eyes. "Jamie—Oh, Jamie—"

"Oh, goddamn it," muttered Wallbrook. "Put my foot in it. Sorry, Jamie."

" 'Tis all right," I assured him. "I was trying to get up courage to do it."

I went to her and put my arm around her. "I was going to tell you later tonight, honeybun. Hugh brought me orders to leave here immediately on pain of court-martial. I'll tell you all about it later. I'll be coming back with the Army."

She was toughly resilient and, recovered from the blow, she said, "I might have known. There's too much risk now, especially after Jedediah. And because of him and his father I can't go with you now. Oh, Jamie, without you I'll die!" She smiled up at me ruefully. "No, I won't die. I'll only stop living for a while in my heart and soul."

Getting to his feet, Hugh said, "I've got a lot of miles to cover this night. I'll be riding along." He shook hands with me. "Good luck, Jamie. Give my regards to Anne when you reach New York." He turned to Marg, bent and kissed her outstretched hand. "I was joking about him being the next best man, Marg. That's me and he's the other. God bless you and keep you while you're absent one from another. Good-bye." He stepped back and simply vanished in the shadows.

"All the good young men," murmured Marg, "on both sides. He and Jess Ricks were like brothers, now they must kill each other one day. 'The flowers of the forest, all wede away.' And you—dear God, when will I ever see you again!"

"Let's go to bed and not think about that for a bit," I told her, and we did.

Breathless from our lovemaking, she nestled in my arms. "When will you go?"

"Within the week," I answered, holding her tight. "I'll go without you knowing when. Between then and now every second will be our farewell. 'Twill be like dying without knowing the moment, for when I go from you I'll die just as you said you will. I'll be only half a person until we're together again."

"Brutus gave Anne and me lessons on Shakespeare," she murmured. "I remember the play where the young lovers are saying good-bye and one of them said parting is such sweet sorrow. I thought it was such a beautiful, true sentiment, but now I know that to say my farewells to you would be wretched, unbearable sorrow. But then again, I'll bear it so long as I know we'll be together again.

"Jamie, I swear to you that if you should ever leave me forever, if you died, I will slowly go mad, then wither and die. And do you know why? Because you created me out of a silly girl, taught me to be a woman, taught me to love, taught me joy beyond belief. I'll not chance giving you any more of a puffed-up head than you have now, you dear rogue, by saying you're like a god to me, but in honesty I must say that 'tis close to that. I'm your creature and I adore you with every part of me."

It came close to unmanning me and I choked back the lump in my throat. "No puffed-up head. Humble. You make me feel humble. I adore you like that, as you said, and I'm your creature. I'll have Brutus send word to you that I've gone, and then you must put your mind to enjoying all the good things we'll share in London."

"I'll do that now," she said. "Will you have me presented to your royal friend?"

"I doubt it," I answered. "I said I wasn't really a friend of his, only a dauber who did his portrait and lots of artists have done that. My social circle is fairly far down. You'll have to content yourself with the society of plebeian sots and scoundrels like Hector MacDonald and myself as a general rule, though you'll go to parties, routs and suppers where belted earls and fat countesses are a shilling a dozen."

"I'm dying to meet Hector," she mumbled through a kiss on my chest. "And Anne! Oh, how I want to see her again! Won't she be fit to be tied when she learns we're married!"

"I have a peculiar feeling that she knows already," I said. "The dream I had on our wedding night. She might have been dreaming of us, her second sight working in her sleep. And the more I think about it, the more I think she knew from the beginning that we were going to be married. She told me a woman was waiting for me somewhere and it would be like this with us."

"Is that why she wouldn't have you, Jamie?" she whispered.

"I wasn't in love with her," I answered. "Mostly, she made me annoyed with her witchly prophecies and her

258

beauty raised hell with the artist in me until I finally painted her portrait and got it out of my system. Joking once, I suggested she marry me and that was when she told me—well, about you and me. Her second sight has arranged for a man for her somewhere, of course, and good luck to him if he can live with that confounded, unending foreseeing."

"You don't like her?" asked Marg. "That's strange. I never knew anyone who didn't like or love Anne."

In all honesty, I said, "I'm uneven about her. One moment I'd hate her and the next I'd want to fall prostrate and worship her. Then she'd irritate the devil out of me by saying something that rubbed me the wrong way. No, I can't say I don't like her. I'm looking forward to seeing her again."

She found my lips in the dark and kissed them. "When you do, remember you're all mine, darling husband. I don't care if you take other women to bed for what you told me was like a sneeze. I'll not be jealous or angry because I know you love me and only me, but I will be if the bedding is more than a sneeze. I know Anne as I know myself and like me she'll never be bedded except by the man she loves and will marry, and if you hadn't told me she told you she would meet and marry another man I'd always wonder why it wasn't you, because you and she would make such a wonderful couple."

"Hector was disappointed about that," I chuckled. "We've always been close and he wanted me for his brother-in-law. You'll love Hector."

She was zealously applying herself to me. "I happen to love you right now. Oh, Jamie, come over, come over, and love me!"

After breakfast the next morning I began preparations for leaving by sorting out the artwork I had done, astonished by the quantity. Some of the drawings and color studies would serve as bases for large paintings and some could be sold for a healthy sum in London. Brutus came in and admired the display, and said he'd have someone make a waterproof buckskin container for the works that afternoon so it would be ready for my departure in the morning.

"In the morning!" I repeated, surprised. "Come now, Brutus, I'm leaving soon, but not that soon."

"You must take a headstart on Mister Abraham's thinking, sir," said the black man. "He has a character that recovers quickly from hard blows. His son is now being buried at Jenks Town—they found him early this morning and bodies do not keep well in this climate—and you may be sure the father's thoughts are already on the future. And I am afraid Captain Wallbrook and I made a mistake we should not have. The dead man's head should have been bruised, since his neck was broken in the fall or throw from the horse. The father will think of that and then of other things in the same vein."

"Damn and goddamn!" I exclaimed. "I should have thought of that! It was my mistake, not yours! Oh, hell's fire, how stupid! Very well, I'll go—and go fast. Have Prince given a new set of shoes and have him saddled and the packhorse loaded about an hour before first light. I'll not stop to put up or camp, only to rest the animals. Give me a bag of food of some kind and oats for the horses. After I'm well away, send word to my wife, please. We've agreed it would be like this, with her not knowing till after."

"Don't tarry at Savannah, sir," cautioned Brutus.

"No fear," I assured him. "With a bit of luck I'll be away to Charles Town in no time."

My dinner was unusually light, which was all right with me because I wasn't particularly hungry in the light of my imminent departure from my wife. It turned out that the twins had been scrubbing and scouring the kitchen floor repeatedly all through the morning. "Still smell like stables," declared Hetty. "If Miss Anne come back, she goin' to be scandalized. Mister Rob, you goin' bring her back when you come for Miss Marg?"

Plantation servants knew everything that went on in the household. I said, "I doubt she'll be back until the rebellion's over. I'll give her your greetings. She'll like that. I'll miss you both."

Moving together, they put arms around each other's waists and looked at me with large eyes. Betty said, "We goin' to miss you, Mister Rob, somethin' terrible."

Hetty said, "You got as sad a face on you now as I ever see. You goin' make us cry, Mister Rob, 'less you stop."

"Well, damn it," I grumped, "I love the pair of you."

"We do you, too, sir," said Betty. "You want cheerin'

260

this afternoon, we do it." They smiled merrily. "All three frolickin' in bed like before. Miss Marg wants you happy."

Despite my melancholy, I burst out laughing. "You're incorrigible! Thank you, ladies, but while it would pleasure me, it wouldn't make me happy. Nothing can. I'm the saddest man this side of Hell and you know why." They both burst into tears, weeping on each other. I fled to the piazza with a book and a tumbler full of peach brandy. I told myself I must be careful with the drinking. It would never do to pass my last night with my wife and not be in command of myself.

The book, which I had snatched from the shelves at random, was a collection of ancient Scottish ballads set to music and it fell open to Thomas the Rhymer. The pages were discolored with handling, and as my mind followed the verse and simple melody I heard Anne singing it again. Then I reached the part where the Queen of Elfland shows Thomas the three roads and I slammed the book shut angrily just as Abraham Jenks rode up and dismounted. I forced myself to remember that I was supposed to be a rebel named Robert Allston, and said, standing up, "I can't wish you a good-day, sir, because Brutus has told me of your grievous loss. You have my sympathy, sir. Will you sit and have a glass?"

"Why, thank you, Mr. Allston," he rumbled, settling into a chair. "I must decline refreshment, sir. This is a day of mourning for my family and is a time of fasting and prayer."

Hatred for him seethed. I said gravely, "I was told it was a fall from his horse. The Lord giveth and the Lord taketh away. He works in mysterious ways."

"Aye," said Abraham, "His wonders to perform. And 'tis a mystery to be sure how the boy fell from his horse, that one having no more skittishness than a milk cow, and in all his life Jedediah was never thrown by a horse. His neck snapped, yet there was never a bruise on his head. A great mystery, eh, Mr. Allston?"

I had a prickle of dread and tried to appear thoughtful. "Brutus said it happened on the path to your place. The ground is mostly covered deep with pine needles. That could have cushioned his head without lessening the impact."

"No doubt, no doubt," he said, waggling his big shaggy head. " 'Tis hard, dreadful hard to see that fine boy taken

261

in the fullness of his youth to his eternal home just as he was about to take unto himself a wife. I spoke of that in my prayer this morning when we laid him to rest beside his mother, and asked Jehovah to reveal to me the meaning of that sacrifice." He leaned forward and peered sharply at me. "Mr. Allston, I know you have not been to Elderbank since the day of our awkward and unfortunate misunderstanding and I am obliged to you for respecting my son's suit in that direction. However, I am not blind. In the likeness you took of the young female and in her expressions toward you I think I saw something more than plain acquaintanceship. You are a gentleman of worldly style and experience and capable of turning the head of a simple country maid who is comely and ripe." His eyes glinted under frowning, beetling brows.

Jedediah had told him of Marg's nights at Goodowns and that was the purpose of this call—confrontation, accusation, denunciation to be followed by arrest. I was unarmed. I contemplated his massive body and wondered if I could shatter his thick skull with a stiff-handed chop to the bridge of his big nose where the skull is thinnest, as Ira had taught me. "You flatter me, Mr. Jenks." Yes, under the muck and dung of the hogpen would be a suitable tomb for Abraham, I decided, and shifted in my chair in preparation for sudden movement.

"I have never flattered any man," he rumbled. "I but speak my mind. Your visage and manner mark you as a bachelor with an attraction for the weaker sex, sir, and that young female at Elderbank is strong of hips and her breasts are rich with enticement. She is of an age when her body demands to be allowed to bear fruit and at such times Satan often seduces such a one into evil lusts that lead to fornication."

"Whatever the point of your remarks," I said, hating him passionately, "you mistake me, sir. I happen to be a happily married man, not a bachelor, and there is not a day that goes by that I do not yearn to have my dear wife at my side, nor do I have any interest in other women. What exactly is your point, Mr. Jenks?" I readied myself to wipe him from the face of the earth.

He leaned back in the chair and said with satisfaction, "Excellent, excellent, Mr. Allston. I am delighted to know that. My point is this, sir: this morning as I prayed for divine guidance beside the open grave of my son, the Almighty God answered me. Yea, even in a voice like a thousand thunders he spoke to me in my mind, saying, 'Go thou, my son Abraham, in thy son's place and take the woman to thyself and she will fruitfully multiply thy race!' "

Stunned and unbelieving, I stared at him. "You? *You* want to marry her now?"

"Sir," he intoned, " 'twas not of my wanting, 'twas the sacred command of my Lord to his obedient, worshipful servant."

"My Christ," I breathed, blind rage churning with revulsion.

"Praise His name," said Abraham, "from whom all blessings flow. I came to you, sir, because you would have been a formidable rival had you been harboring fleshly desires toward the woman, now the obstacle of my son has been removed, and I wished no further unpleasantness between us through misunderstandings. I am pleased, sir. With some training in proper female humility and godliness, she will become a good wife, though she is younger than my eldest sons. I have become long in the tooth but there is great power in my loins yet and those sons shall have new brothers to increase the name of Jenks, God willing."

My stomach heaved and raging hatred blinded me so that I could barely see him through the red veil. My mind's eye beheld the monster's vast body crushing down on the exquisite loveliness of Marg's, his vile pizzle tearing into it, his hairy face grunting and drooling as his filthy seed spurted into her purity, her sacredness. *Die, Abraham,* my mind shouted, *die, you great vicious, stinking mountain of pus and corruption!* The voice of the stableman, Rufus, penetrated the storm and I regained some command of myself; he was standing by the piazza telling me my horse had been fresh-shod and Brutus himself had selected a good pack animal for my journey on the morrow. I muttered thanks and the man went away.

"A journey, with a pack horse, Mr. Allston?" commented Abraham.

How could I leave Marg now? With the architect of most of our troubles now preparing the personal assault against her? Cool reason struggled with emotional distress and panic, and won. The situation had not changed in essence. As she had held Jedediah at bay, so she must with the master villain. The reasons for my departure were still preeminent and overruling. "My field work for the paintings is finished here in Georgia," I told him. "I'll be leaving for Charles Town in a day or two, possibly in the morning."

"Then my concern was for nothing." He climbed to his feet. "I am told you have made many friends in this region, Mr. Allston, and you will be missed. I doubt we shall meet again, so I bid you farewell and wish you success in your patriotic endeavors."

Taking his extended hand with repugnance, I withdrew my own before he could crush it and said, "I sincerely hope we shall meet again. Good-bye, sir." The next time we met, I would enforce payment for what he had done and would do before then. Watching him ride away, I mused grimly, there goes a dead son of a bitch. Brutus came walking over the lawn and when he came up on the piazza he said, "Good-day, sir." Looking at my face he inquired, "Are you ill, sir?"

I erupted. "That filthy tub of shit! That monstrous heap of stinking maggots! That goddamned rotten Scripture-spouting hypocritical walking obscenity!"

"Rufus told me Mister Abraham was here, sir," he remarked. "I gather he has upset you." He refilled my glass with brandy and gave it to me. "Please. It will help. Can you tell me what he said, sir?"

I tossed off the drink as if it were water. "You were right on all counts. His foul mind was planning even while he was saying prayers over his son's grave. He noticed the absence of a head bruise, and it appears that Jedediah had never fallen from a horse in his life, so we made two slips there. But, Brutus, the incredible scum came to tell me that he is going to replace his son, that he's going to marry my wife and make her fruitful with slimy Jenks spawn!"

Brutus was unperturbed. "We might have foreseen that, sir. In a sense it will be better than when Mister Jedediah was courting Miss Marg because he was slightly unpredictable in his mind, not being the master of it. The father has his mind set on the main chance and will not be overcome or diverted by bodily desires. He will accord Miss Marg courtesy and will not attempt to directly force her in any way, be it into marriage or otherwise, sir, and I am certain that Miss Marg will conduct herself with intelligent discretion without harm to herself or your marriage.

We have both known Mister Abraham for many years and are aware of his habits of mind. He is stern toward women but if they do not offend his religiosity he will show them proper respect in a paternal fashion."

"You've lived too long around him," I said, "and have gotten used to him. I see him differently and as a portraitist I know human character as a tool to my trade. I think the man is mad. Not yet as a hatter or March hare, but he's past sixty and might be coming down with softening of the brain. Brutus, watch him closely while I'm gone, I beg you, and help her brothers to guard her. She's brave and intelligent, but she's first and foremost a woman, very much a woman, and is apt to bite off more than she can chew in her desire to show herself capable of handling herself in a difficult situation."

"I understand, sir," he nodded. "I shall do my best. If you will excuse me, I shall go and inspect the progress being made on your picture packet."

I had a hell of a poor afternoon, between Abraham's latest gambit and my despondency over leaving, and made a manly effort to limit my nervous drinking. As might be expected, it was my success with that endeavor which was limited and when Marg showed up that night I had a mild edge on which made me anything but mild in my excoriation of Abraham Jenks. After she heard the story, she said calmly, "Brutus is right. 'Twill be better than Jedediah because I would surely have killed him myself the next time he tried to despoil me as he surely would. As Brutus said, the main chance is Elderbank, not me, and he'll want to take a wife to Jenks Town, not an enemy, so he'll treat me properly though the threats against my brothers will come hot and heavy, I expect."

"Don't fool yourself!" I exclaimed. "When the old bastard talked about your hips and breasts he practically drooled! I know he had a hard-on! I came damn close to killing him as he sat there telling me sanctimoniously how strong his loins are and how he was going to fuck you into bearing fruit!"

"Darling," she soothed, "I can cope with him, never fear. Have faith, Jamie."

I growled, "Faith! I'm sick! That heap of dog vomit lusting after you and you flaunting your body at him and being coy! You who were but a short time ago a wide-eyed virgin who had never so much as laid eyes on a man's

265

stiff rod, let alone understood the processes that made it so, and now you plan to manipulate that shrewd horny monster as if you were a veteran whore!"

"Tush, Jamie," she said. " 'Tis because your love has made me a veteran woman. I think when a virgin comes to end her state with the joy given her by her lover's stiff rod—what a terrible name for such a dear article!—a whole new kind of knowledge about men is born in her head and she suddenly rejoices in the new-found strength of her womanhood. There is no love in Abraham, only greed and, if you're right, an old man's lust which is mainly in his head and not his withered ballocks, I think. And speaking of those, come rest your handsome ones on me here and show me your own beautiful lust to match my own, darling, for time's wasting."

I didn't want to sleep that night. I wanted to do nothing but make love and talk, wallow and revel in her company, feeling and tasting her flesh, smelling her fragrance, hearing her breathing, her voice and gasps in ecstasy. But if I had thus behaved, her quick perception would have told her it was our night of parting and her sadness would be something I could not bear on top of my own, so after our passion had been eased for the time being I let her go to sleep in my arms. Remember this, remember this, I told myself, with her warm, soft nakedness nestled against mine, feeling the regular rise and fall of her breathing against my chest.

The road ahead of me ran straight as a die across the moorland under a darkly lowering sky. The mud sucked at my shoes as I trudged onward and then I found myself on a road that forked off to the left. A great sheet of lightning flashed and in the momentary illumination I saw, on the road I had been on, a group of people looking at me and laughing, their faces so clear I might have been but a few feet away. They were Abraham and Jedediah Jenks, Beauvoir, Hector MacDonald and my wife. They were jeering. Shocked and bewildered, I tried to go to her but was stuck fast in the mud and could not move from where I stood. Then with a great rattling roar, rain came down in solid torrents and I awakened to find the rattling was the watchman's shower of pebbles against the window.

Sick with the memory of Marg's laughing scorn, I buried my face in her hair and groaned, "Oh, my darling, my darling, why? Why?"

Stirring, still more asleep than awake, she came flowing against me, wrapping me in her arms and legs, murmuring, "Love . . . my own . . . Jamie . . ." We blended, merged into one and went soaring among the stars.

A few minutes later, behind the peach orchard at the edge of the woods in the pre-dawn darkness, I kissed her and prayed that the intensity of it would not betray me. "That was your special bridegroom kiss," she said, "and it makes me want to go back to bed again. Tonight let's make believe it's our wedding night again. We never had a wedding cake, so I'll bake one today and bring it over."

"There's a special bottle of wine in the cellar," I said, wanting to weep, "that will go with it like a flute to a violin."

"And after that we'll make more music in bed," she laughed, "and this time 'twill be you who will be sore and satisfied, for you've brought it on yourself by teaching me so well. Have a happy day, Jamie, and be ready for a happy night."

Forcing the words out of me, I said, "Good-bye, honey-bun. I love you." My heart shook as I saw her dark figure melt into the deeper darkness of the path through the woods.

About a half hour later dawn was lightening the eastern sky as I rode down the Post Road leading my packhorse. Passing Elderbank, I saw a lighted window and knew that Marg was having breakfast with her brothers. My other half, I thought, my heart and mind reaching out desperately to her. Once past and far enough away that galloping hooves could not be heard in the house, I spurred Prince and, with the packhorse reluctantly clumping behind, set off to cover distance as rapidly as possible with my mind now occupied by my immediate future.

Except for a couple of light rains, the weather stayed good and I made fast progress, pausing only long enough at intervals to rest and feed the horses and myself. I encountered few fellow travelers and two militia patrols before reaching Briar Creek bridge; the militiamen had heard of me and were delighted when I showed them some of my Georgia sketches and watercolors. Going through the town of Ebenezer I ran into a company of Continental foot and had a drink with the officers in a tavern. They told me they were on their way to Fort Sunbury where a

British attack was expected soon from East Florida. At this evidence that Cameron had done his work, I was pleased and expressed confidence that our brave lads would teach the dastardly British a lesson they'd not soon forget, and asked casually if this company was reinforcement sent from the north. No, I was told, Bob Howe's troops could handle anything Prevost could send against him; this company was a part of the Sunbury garrison that was being called in from outcamping guard at Hudson's Ferry on the Savannah. We rendered three cheers for General Washington, Bob Howe and Liberty, and I went on to Savannah.

Entering the town early in the afternoon, I rode directly to the riverfront where I hoped to find my enemy friend Roche. Leaving the horses tied above the bluff, I went down to the piers where a few small local craft were moored, and I had no difficulty finding the captain in front of a small office hut; he was shouting angrily at a slovenly, seedy-looking man, "No, a thousand times bloody no! Read your goddamned contract! If you don't like it, take your vessel off Army moorings and go back to hauling rotten fish and stolen niggers! And that'll be the blessing of the age because our good men won't have to suffer any more in that goddamned rat and flea-infested leaky shitbucket of yours!"

The man glowered at Roche, spat on the ground in front of him, and stumped away grumbling about jacks in uniform. Roche saw me, grinned with pleasure and shook hands. "By Jesus, look at you! A Georgia planter for sure!"

He appeared to have completely regained his health. Smiling, I said, "If I were free of my commitment to the country, I believe I'd really become one. I've had a splendid time here." I adopted a grave expression. "But I've received bad news from home in Boston—serious illness in the family. I'll not burden you with the details. The fact is, I was told you have something to do with the courier ship and that's the fastest and safest way to go north."

His face became concerned. "Why, that's a pity, just as you've gotten a start on that big piece of work. I do have something to do with it, and you shall have a space on the boat tonight. That officer messenger from General Greene's headquarters won't mind sleeping another night with Mrs. Hackett in the back room of her alehouse."

268

"Oh," I said, "I wouldn't think of displacing one of our soldiers on Army business just because I have a personal emergency."

Laughing, he said, "Every time that ensign comes to Savannah with dispatches he goes to Mrs. Hackett's for a glass and they both come down with personal emergencies. She's a mighty lusty widow, that one. Don't fret about it. The boat carries three passengers. There'll be you and a major from here and one to be picked up at Port Royal. 'Tis no luxury packet, I'll warn you, but t'will get you to Charles Town. You saw the master just now; the louse wanted me to displace a passenger so he could have aboard the mulatto whore he bought today, claims she's ship's cook."

"I hope there's no chance of running into a King's ship at sea," I said.

"Not likely," he told me. "These boats keep to the inshore waterways and only travel at night. This one will cast off right after sundown, so have your gear here by then. I'll log you aboard under the authorities of your letter from the Congress."

"I have my gear with me up on the bluff," I said. "I'll dump it here now and go get rid of my horses."

"Try Peter Tondee," he suggested. "He has a little horse-trading business for the benefit of his arriving and departing guests who need or want to unload animals."

Riding to Tondee's, I returned occasional greetings given me by townspeople and a few streets away from the tavern Alexander Cameron saluted me. He was walking alone and when we came close, without dismounting I said, "I'm leaving in the Army dispatch boat tonight. My job's done and the report's gone. You must know I had trouble up there."

Preserving his genial smile for the sake of passersby, he asked, "What trouble? Is your identity safe?"

"So far, it is," I replied. "I secretly married Margaret Ogilvie. Jedediah Jenks found my Loyalist report and I had to kill him. His family thinks it was a fall from his horse. Abraham Jenks thinks he's going to marry my wife so he can get possession of Elderbank plantation when and if the brothers are banished. I beg you to watch that situation."

"I wouldn't dare intervene again," he said, raising his hat to a man going by. "You were extremely foolish in becoming so involved at this time. You are not being foolish

269

in departing as quickly as possible. If you regain safety, inform your superiors that I have thus far accomplished my task regarding Howe at Sunbury."

"The minister who married us, MacLeod of Augusta," I told him, "is one of us and recognized me from the portrait I took of my wife."

"As sooner or later some visitor to my house will recognize that work," he commented. "I mustn't stand here longer. Go with God, Mr. Reid, and be careful." He bowed and strode away.

Peter Tondee obligingly purchased my horses and expressed sympathy over the cause of my departure. I had a good supper and walked back through the wide sandy streets to the riverfront.

Chapter XVI

THE DISPATCH PACKET was a pinky, a type of craft seldom seen in southern waters. A pinky is a sharp-sterned small schooner with a high poop, designed for riding the seas while fishing on the New England offshore banks. In her far-wandering travels this one had fallen on mournful days, her paint blistered and scabrous, rigging frayed, decks filthy and open-seamed. She stank abominably of ancient fish, foul bilges and excrement. Sleeping accommodations for passengers, master and mate were dirty hammocks slung from the overhead deck beams in the tiny fetid cabin under the poop deck, which was alive with fleas, roaches and flies. My eye caught the furtive scurrying of rats in dark corners.

The other passenger from Savannah was a silently morose Continental major who, upon coming aboard, climbed into his hammock with a bottle of rum. The master was even nastier seen and heard at close quarters than he had appeared when Roche dressed him down. The mate was a sodden wretch who spent most of his time cursing and kicking the four Negroes of the crew. Nobody said anything to me.

I remained on deck as the pinky slipped downriver in the early dark, breathing in the humid, swampy air of the Savannah. No longer diverted by physical activity, my mind became occupied completely for the first time with the bitter reality and sadness of my separation from Marg, and I had never felt so lost, alone and anguished. I wondered if she had started baking our delayed wedding cake before Brutus sent her the word and my heart ached in sympathy for the crushing shock of the unhappiness she must have experienced.

It was quite late when the vessel turned and bore off

northward into a wide channel through the marshes near the river mouth. Summoning up courage to face the ordeal of the odoriferous cabin, I went below and climbed into my hammock. It had been a long day and I went to sleep to the sound of the major's snores and that of rats pattering about on the deck below me. At some time during the night voices and walking on deck overhead awakened me briefly and, after surmising it was the stop at Port Royal, I went back to sleep.

At breakfast, a sorry affair of stale, wormy biscuit, rancid cheese and lukewarm water faintly flavored with coffee, the major and the Port Royal passenger agreed that the shipboard accommodations were something short of tolerable. The Port Royal gentleman, a Mr. Burns, was a portly, well-dressed fellow who introduced himself as a South Carolina delegate to the Continental Congress, returning to his duties there after a short holiday and political meetings at home. He declared that the Army should use more care in awarding contracts to these coastwise pirates and insure proper victualing for passengers. The gloomy major replied acidly that it might be better if the Congress insured proper victualing and clothing for Continental troops, and that led to a discourse by Mr. Burns on Congress's difficulties in funding the Army so long as states like Georgia refused to pay their share. Thereupon the major, a Georgian, angrily defended his state. Burns patiently soothed him by explaining the functioning and legal limitations of the Congress.

Despite my yearning for fresh air on deck, I had never known just what the rebel governing body did, so I lingered, listening and learning. I gathered that it operated under a standing base of laws called the Articles of Confederation which severely limited its powers to coerce the separate states lest it infringe on their sovereign authority, and in such matters of imposing taxes and placing levies for troops the lack of central authority would be fatal to rebel aspirations were it not for the generosity of the King of France in providing money, ships and troops. Though at times Burns's exposition verged upon oratory, it was clear and crisp and more or less silenced the dour major's arguments. Though I said nothing, it did not silence my privately held conviction that such a weak and undirected parliament could only lead the way to catastrophe. Burns

272

broke off his monologue then and politely inquired as to my reason for traveling in the dispatch packet.

It was not a demand, merely the sort of thing one says to a fellow traveler in the course of conversation, and if I had been fully alert I could have disarmingly passed it off with a casual half-truth, then changed the subject. Unfortunately, my proximity to danger for so long had made me carelessly over-familiar with it and when it neared me obliquely I ignored it. I told him of the drawing and painting in Georgia, explaining that it was the first step toward the thirteen great historical works envisioned by Dr. Franklin. He expressed warm interest and asked to see some of my work, so I obligingly opened my baggage to display it.

Inspecting the pictures, he said appreciatively, "Excellent, excellent, Mr. Allston. Splendid work. One can see you're no dilettante. The whole notion is grandly unique, a typical Franklin conception, and he made no mistake in selecting you to do the great work. These pictures are unmistakably of Georgia and Georgia alone. What marvelous characterization!"

Flattered into further foolishness, I said, "Why, thank you, sir. I hope you and your colleagues will be as pleased when the entire series is finished. For me 'tis a labor of love for my country, and when the thirteen pictures are painted it is my hope to spend the next years going on to paint the entire continent from one ocean to the other, for that, too, is destined to become part of the United States, don't you think, sir?"

He nodded, smiling. "There is some sentiment in the Congress to that effect, though I suspect the Indians out there may not share it, nor do the British, the French and Spanish. I'm afraid such expansion will not be seen in our lifetime, Mr. Allston, while our infant nation struggles to learn to walk in this uneasy world by itself. You mentioned having copies of correspondence in this matter. May I see them, sir?"

Alarm shrieked suddenly, sounded too late. I had no recourse but to hand him the documents, cursing myself for a goddamned witless fool. Scanning them closely, he murmured, "Remarkable. How came you by these, sir?"

I was a small boy again, testing with the weight of a tentative foot the first thin sheet of winter ice of the Frog

Pond on Boston Common. "From Dr. Franklin in France, Mr. Burns. I believe I told you that."

He said, "I shall say this, Mr. Allston: the language in the letter that bears his signature is close to his style, and the same thing applies to the authorization from the Congress. But, my dear sir, these papers are absolute forgeries."

The thin ice gave way and I went into the freezing water. "Forgery!" I exclaimed in not entirely feigned shock. "What are you saying, sir? How could that be?"

"I happen," he said, "to be a member of the Committee of the States and am also chairman of a certain key subcommittee of that body. Any such correspondence between Dr. Franklin and the Congress would pass through my hands and there would be a record of it. The same applies to any resolution passed by the Congress concerning this matter. I regret, sir, that I must say I have utterly no knowledge of it."

"That's incredible, Mr. Burns!" I sputtered, honestly aghast at this turn of events. "The doctor delivered those documents to me from his very own hands!"

"If that be true, Mr. Allston," he said gravely, "then either you or Dr. Franklin or both are engaged in some dishonest scheme which smacks of treachery. As for Dr. Franklin, I have been his personal colleague and friend for upward of twenty years, sir, and know his character well. Therefore I am left with the unhappy conclusion that you are either an unwitting dupe or you are consciously sailing under false colors for some nefarious purpose. Of one thing I am positive: you could not have received these papers from Dr, Franklin. I ask again, sir: how did you come by them?"

The rebel major at the end of the table scowled and produced a large pistol. He cocked it loudly. I said, "As I told you, Mr. Burns. If they're forgeries, he certainly didn't know it. He was very pleased over the Congress's approval of his idea."

Burns smiled grimly. "My dear sir, I doubt you have ever seen Dr. Franklin in your life." He tapped the papers with his finger, "I have examined a number of spurious documents as well done as these during the past year or so, all of them taken from captured British agents and spies. Through certain common characteristics in the handwriting, the origin of the papers has been found to be British Army headquarters. Well, sir?"

Leaping to my feet, I cried indignantly, "By God, sir, you're accusing me of being a damned enemy spy! Delegate or no, I demand you withdraw that charge, sir!"

The rebel major, waving the pistol at me, growled, "Sit down and answer up when you're told."

I sat, fuming with indignation, and Burns said, "I intend to enlarge on the charge, sir, not withdraw it. Since the beginning of your conversation I had a persistent nagging in the back of my mind. I was reminded of something. A few minutes ago the nagging stopped. Not long ago some British journals I've read carried some interesting notices of the doings of a famous London artist of American birth. Earlier this year he departed London, performed some heroics at sea against the piratical American rebels, turned up in New York with much acclaim. After two or three months he dropped from sight again."

I shrugged. "I know nothing of that, sir. I came to Savannah from Le Havre. I've never been in England."

He frowned with the effort of remembering, then said, "The timing of your movement parallels rather closely that of the distinguished gentleman from London, as does your appearance and excellent work." He said to the major, "I'll thank you to keep our friend under your gun, sir, while I have a look through his baggage." It did not take him long to find my drawing block but that did not worry me much, for I had not been fool enough to keep by me any drawings made before the cruise in the *Bonny Anne* except some of the MacDonalds, which I had used for my own purposes in Georgia.

He studied the drawings. "You are, I must say, possessed of skill and talent equal to the praises of them in the British papers, sir." He paused. "Bless me, after all these years!" He said to me, "The years have been kinder to Angus than to me. Evidently his flaming red hair has turned to white, though his face is young. I suppose, judging by the likeness, the younger gentleman he is talking to here must be the son by his first wife."

"I don't know their names," I said. "They were guests of Dr. Franklin and I happened to sketch them."

He shook his head. "Come, sir, that will never do. This is Mr. Angus MacDonald from whom I acquired my present plantation near Beaufort, eighteen years ago. His second

275

wife was my cousin and I was a guest at their wedding at Charles Town. He has not left London since he removed from the colonies. You, sir, took this likeness in London, and your name is James Reid. Save your denials for the court, Mr. Reid. I regret the necessity, sir, but I must cause you to be placed under close arrest until you shall be delivered to the authorities at Charles Town as a British spy."

Summoned from the deck, the captain listened to Burns and grinned nastily. "A spy, eh? So that Cap'n Roche put a spy aboard in place of my high yaller gal which I was rightful entitled to have for my cook. He put this here bastard aboard like they was lovin' brothers."

Burns said, "Then I think we shall later have a look into Captain Roche's affairs. Captain, pray secure him, and do it well. He's quite important." He smiled at me amiably. "We'll give the lion's tail a painful twist when the scaffold trap opens under you, Mr. Reid."

I was quickly locked in double irons, with shackles at wrists and ankles, separated by a foot of heavy chain to give me limited movement. The manacles were the best-conditioned gear I had seen in the ship and I wondered at it until I remembered Roche's suggestion to the captain that he 'go back to stealing niggers.' Then I was lowered into the hold, into such a pit of stink and heat it was almost impossible to breathe. Most certainly I would not have survived an hour had the hatch cover been in place as it would have been if the pinky were on the open sea. However, the latticed hatch grating allowed some small ventilation, though not much light. The pinky was carrying no cargo in the hold, and all that was in it was a heap of musty old fragments of sails and a tangle of rotted cordage, which I managed to haul, clinking and clanking my chains, to a spot directly under the hatch where the air was best, and I sat down on it to consider the situation. Small pattering noises came from the dark corners.

I could see nothing to be gained by brooding and re-chewing endless "if only's," so directed my thoughts to what lay ahead. There would be a trial, and Burns' reference to twisting the lion's tail indicated that it would be a highly publicized trial in order that it would be brought to the notice of the British public; in which case the proceedings would have to be scrupulously legal and the Whigs would go to great lengths to present to the world the appearance of civilized justice. In that event, I reasoned, the case against me would have to be proved by hard evidence, and that made me feel more cheerful, because the only possible incriminating evidence the rebels had were the forged documents, my drawings of the Mac-Donalds, and my use of a false name. The court would have to prove intent to commit the crime of spying, and there was virtually none, nor could it be proved that I had been caught in the act of spying.

The schooner's master shouted down through the grating, "Ahoy, you Tory son of a bitch! Have the rats et your balls off yet?" He went away without waiting for an answer, wheezing with laughter.

Resuming my cogitations, it occurred to me that I might just as well admit to being James Reid, artist, formerly of London, and what I was doing in Georgia was openly seen in my accumulated work from there. I was an American by birth, and as an artist desired to follow my calling without active involvement in politics and the rebellion. The false papers I had prepared in order to carry out, without impediment, the basic plan they described: the painting of thirteen great pictures for historical purposes, to celebrate the land of my birth, be the divisions of it called provinces or states, British or independent. As for my involvement in the sea fight between the *Jason* and *Sea Rover,* for all I had known, before it was over, the *Jason* was being attacked by pirates.

I argued my case with myself, knowing it to be flawed, full of holes big enough to drive a six-team dray through, but it was all I had to stand between me and the gallows. I hoped the court would appoint as my defender some clever lawyer whose ambitions to win a case would be greater than his devotion to the rebellion.

At the end of the day the hatch grating was lifted and a pot of mud-smelling fresh water and two ship's biscuits were handed down to me by one of the Negro crewmen. I drank the water slowly, relishing every bad-tasting drop of it. The hard biscuits I had to break by banging them on the floor of the hold, and that was a poor thing to do, I quickly discovered; the noise and smell of food alerted the rats to the glad tidings that supper was being served, thereby setting in motion something that I wish to God, after all these years, I could expunge from my memory.

Pitch darkness in the hold came while there was yet

twilight in the world above. I heard and sensed the gathering of the rats around me as I gnawed on my hard biscuits. They grew bolder, squeaking and twittering, and occasionally one would scurry forward in a brave rush to capture some crumbs fallen to the floor. I judged the location by the swift rustle of little feet and kicked as far as the chain on my ankles would permit. The single forays came more often, one rat after another. I gave up trying to eat the second biscuit, put it in my pocket, and concentrated on kicking away the animals who continued to come at me even though there were no more biscuit crumbs. Groping about in the cordage I found a rope's end about six feet long and tied a heavy knot in one end.

Above, there was a scraping and bumping. To my shock, it was the hatch cover being put on and battened down. My first thought was that it was a means of torturing me, but then reason told me the pinky was making ready to go out to sea; it had reached the end of possible inshore navigation for a space and was going to have to make a night passage outside.

But I had no time to contemplate that. The rats moved in on me, and the chill horror of what it meant nearly panicked me: they were after me, juicy, tasty Jamie Reid, to rend the flesh from my bones with tiny sharp teeth, thousands of teeth, in God knows how many voracious little mouths that would drink my blood. They could see me in the dark, but I could not see them. They ran over and around my feet, trying to climb my legs, nipping at my shoes and ankles. I stamped on them, kicked at them, feeling the floor grow slippery with their crushed bodies and nearly choking on the sickening stink of them. I lashed out with my rope's end, flailing the floor of the hold around me.

The schooner began pitching and rolling as she entered the open ocean, and that made my footing even more difficult. The crushed bodies of their comrades apparently drove the animals into a blood madness, for they were all over me, climbing up my body, tearing at my clothes, slashing at my flesh. I stripped the little squirming, snapping furry bodies from myself and flung them away, flogged at them with my rope, kicked and stamped at them. Time and again I lost my footing and fell, to be instantly swarmed over by a voracious blanket of living filth, squeaking and twittering, nipping and ripping, and each time when I managed to stand again I tore them off me. One got inside my shirt, and having no time to fish it out I crushed it to death in there with one hand, while peeling the others off my legs.

At sometime or other I began shouting at them, insulting them, challenging them, shrieking curses at them as I did my rat-killing dance in my chains, flailing the rope, flinging rats away with my hands. There was no rest, not for an instant, and eventually the fatigue that had been held in check by fear and revulsion began to work hallucinations in my mind. I suppose I became insane. I remember one of those terrible fantasies: I was running across an endless level plain under a sky of purple, pursued by a rippling carpet of rats that spread out to the horizon and then I was climbing the shrouds of the *Jason*, only to find the rats had gotten to the trestletrees before me and were waiting for me. I dove into the sea, which turned out to be not water, but roiling waves of rats.

I never heard or felt the jolting shudder and grinding crunch when the bigger vessel came alongside. I did not hear the shouts, the crackle of pistols and musketry. I was unaware of the hatch cover being dragged off, and I did not see the rays from the lanthorn that shone down on my dreadful arena, for I was berserk—a cursing, screaming, weeping madman in chains who ceaselessly stamped and kicked, constantly flailing with a rope's end, on a thick rug of bloody crushed rats.

I was wrapped from head to foot in a brilliant blue-white sheet of pain. I was motionless. The world was still and silent. I marveled at the pain; it was a thing separate from me, yet belonging to me, an interesting phenomenon which could be walked around, inspected from every side. It covered me tightly like a skin, almost affectionately, a brightly flaming agony spread over me evenly, with no points of greater or lesser intensity to mar its fiery uniformity. I contemplated it and wondered if it would go away thinking I was dead if I didn't move. Or was I already dead and in Hell, cooking? Who was I? I had no memory.

A man's voice spoke: "There's no square inch of him not nipped."

A vaguely familiar voice commented, "The spirits of ammonia you dowsed him with must sting like flaming hell—lucky he's not awake."

279

"It had to be done," said the first voice. "Those little buggers are filthy dirty things. Can't take a chance on the plague. I think he's asleep, not unconscious. Exhausted, you know. God knows how long he was at it, beating 'em off with the rope's end."

Hiding in my cocoon of encompassing pain, I wondered who they were talking about. The second voice said, "A long time, judging from the carcasses around him. By God, when we hauled off the hatch cover I never saw so many dead rats at one time in all my life."

Memory stirred, flickered, wavered, then focused: *rats!* I heard somebody screaming and as strong hands gripped me I discovered with amazement that it was my own voice. Opening my eyes, I looked up into the face of Lieutenant Lindsay of the *Jason*. Parched with thirst, I tried to ask for water but the words came out of my dry mouth as, "Wa . . . wa. Wa . . ."

Lindsay held a mug of cool sweet water to my lips. It was heavenly nectar from the springs of Paradise. I forgot the pain and when the mug was empty croaked, "More, more."

Obliging, he grinned down at me. "Got your hollow leg yet, eh, Jamie Reid?"

"Small world, shipmate," I replied weakly. "Could you lace that with rum? A lot."

The other man, evidently a Navy surgeon, produced a bottle. The rum started my insides living again. I was in a berth in a stateroom and by the size of the ship's timbers it was a much larger vessel than the *Jason*. I was naked and my body was completely covered with small gashes and punctures. Recollection swept over me in a wave of horror and I vomited, spewing water and rum while I wept. "Jesus, sweet Jesus!" It was devout prayer from the bottom of my heart.

" 'Tis naught but the water and rum," said the surgeon. "Best get some solid food into him, Mr. Lindsay, before he has more rum."

"I'll have some sent down from the wardroom," said Lindsay, and to me he said, smiling, "Whatever the hell you were doing in that damned little pot among those rebels is bound to be a curious tale. We had a devil of a time freeing you from those manacles until you simply went unconscious, out like a candle."

"Not a curious tale," I told him, "but one told by an idiot, full of sound and fury. What ship is this?"

"The frigate *Ariel*," he answered. "I'm her mother—ship's lieutenant. We laid alongside and took your great Yankee man-of-war last night. Trapped her cold as planned. You were a sight to behold when we lifted the hatch cover to have a peep at her cargo."

"I don't want to talk about it yet," I said queasily. I had a terrible thought. "My paintings! You didn't sink her, did you?"

His broad pink face smiled. "Not bloody likely. "We've got a hawser on her, towing her to St. Augustine. With a bit of refitting she'll make a fine little vessel for revenue patrol or dispatch work. Your baggage lies yonder in the corner and this is your quarters until we make port."

"Mr. Reid," said the surgeon, "I must take myself off. None of the bites are deep and with frequent exposure to sunlight and fresh air on deck they should be healed by the time we arrive. If any of them suppurate, show them to me. Good-day, gentlemen."

Lindsay said to me, "I'll go and find a messboy and get some food into you and then you must tell me how it is you're not in New York among the fashionable ladies, taking their likenesses and other things."

After the rat bites scabbed over a bit and I could wear clothes without discomfort, the cruise to St. Augustine turned out to be a pleasant holiday for me. The food was good, libations frequent. The officers were comradely and the weather remained excellent. Rolling over the blue sea under clear skies, the tall frigate was magnificent under its great cloud of canvas. On the whitely scoured weather deck, polished brightwork shone and the Navy officers' and Marine uniforms were brilliantly colorful. Astern, the little pinky splashed cheerily along at the end of the tow-line as if delighted to be freed from her filthy grub of a master, who had been the only man killed in her capture. I spent much time making drawings of gun crews exercising the batteries and the daily sudden rush to battle stations when the drummers beat practice quarters.

I ran into Mr. Burns in a passageway one day. Because of the report I had submitted to the ship's captain concerning the action, Burns had been forced to admit he was not a simple planter as he had first claimed and had confessed to his true position, and had been given the parole of the ship. He said to me, "Mr. Reid, upon my honor, if I had known what was in store for you in the hold I would never have permitted your being sent there. I beg you to accept my sincere apologies, sir."

"Taken, and thank you, sir," I answered. "Since you're related by marriage to the MacDonalds, sir, did you ever meet the daughter, Anne?"

His face became grim. "When she was a small child, before Angus went to London. At Beaufort last spring we were shocked to learn of Mary MacDonald's tragic death and even more over Anne's disappearance, taken by brigands. I suppose you know of that?"

I laughed. "I do, sir. You will be relieved to know that she now dwells in my New York house with her half brother and is the reigning belle of the British garrison there."

Genuinely delighted, he exclaimed, "Why, Mr. Reid, that's splendid news! If I had known that I would have allowed you parole until Charles Town! What a dreadful pity you and she are on the other side! By the bye, when I have a chance to write to Dr. Franklin I intend to tell him of your scheme concerning the series of pictures and I'm confident that he'll be only sorry the plan was false, as I am."

"It wasn't as false as you think," I said. "I was actually carrying it out with great pleasure and considerable passion. Bear in mind that I'm a born American, too, and love my country as much as any of you Whigs."

The amiable smile faded. "But you love the King and his misrule more, sir."

I bristled. "The worst kind of Crown government is better than the best that can be gotten from that goddamned stumbling, powerless debating society you belong to! When you've murdered all our young men and caused our country to be laid waste, disbanded and run down your ratholes to escape punishment, then let me hear your idiotic speeches about self-rule, liberty and freedom! I hope you drown in the blood you've made to be shed, you pompous carping rebel son of a bitch!"

He paled and then walked quickly away. We never spoke again. A long time later I heard he was exchanged for some important British prisoner. Looking back at the incident, I am a bit embarrassed by it. My abuse to a prisoner was decidedly ungentlemanly and the tenor of it was so violently political and unlike Jamie Reid that I was bewildered by my conduct, yet in considering an apology I rejected the idea and stood by my denunciation for reasons that were not clear to me.

However, the capture of such a high rebel official by the *Ariel* made her what sailors call a happy ship, when all hands are infected with good nature and go about ship's work with willing zeal, because of the effect on the captain, a rotund, extremely dedicated gentleman named Hornsby. It appeared that for some time the Royal Navy had been studying the rebel water-borne courier system with a view toward destroying it on the southern coasts. The Charles Town-Savannah packet routes and schedules were quietly watched and reported by pro-British Negro fishermen, and when Admiral Byron found that the craft had to leave the inshore waterway and run outside between the Edisto and Stono Inlet he ordered that it be intercepted. Ordinarily, such a task would have been given a smaller vessel such as the armed schooner *Jason*, but none such being available at the time needed, the job was given to the big frigate *Ariel*, much to Hornsby's unhappiness. It was his belief that *Ariel*'s proper employment was fighting it out gun for gun with an equal man-of-war; sending a King's frigate after a disreputable little bucket like the pinky was unsporting and much like using a sledgehammer to crush a gnat. Lying in wait was a problem for the tall ship, since she had to lie well out to sea so her royals could not be seen from shore, especially in the light of the setting sun. Fortunately for me in my rat arena the wind was right, the *Ariel* fast and the pinky was on time as scheduled. With the capture of Burns, Hornsby's disgruntlement vanished and the *Ariel*'s people basked in the sunshine of his nearly jovial amiability.

Nights were not a good time for me in the *Ariel*, because the night meant Marg, our married life having existed only in the dark hours. After spending the evening in the hearty companionship of the ship's officers, drinking and gaming in the wardroom, I would make my way to my stateroom and there lie in my berth immersed in memories of her and desperate loneliness, my body, heart and mind aching to be united with hers.

On one such night I lay conjecturing how quickly I might find passage from St. Augustine to New York, how

283

I could persuade the Army to let me accompany the Savannah expedition and how it would be to live again for a time in the same house with Anne. The beautiful face appeared in my imagination, the green eyes intent and unreadable. Hail, great oracle, I thought, you who know all. Make yourself useful. How may I best recover my wife?

It was probably the result of intense absorption in the problem and there was nothing supernatural about it. It should have already occurred to me. Nevertheless, the answer came with a suddenness that jolted me. I was a fool for thinking of going back to New York. At St. Augustine, General Prevost was even now making ready to invade Georgia from the south in order to link up with the expedition that would come from New York to take Savannah. Further, if the worst came to the worst and the Georgia campaign were canceled, I could somehow make my way up into Georgia from East Florida and carry Marg away, and to hell with Abraham Jenks, Elderbank, her brothers and the whole damned lot. With that decision made, I went to sleep in a more tranquil frame of mind than I had for days.

On the evening before arrival at St. Augustine I had supper with Captain Hornsby in his quarters, a comfortable apartment in the stern of the *Ariel*. It was a fine meal, prepared in his own galley from his personal stores, and the drink was excellent. Anticipating the effect on British authorities at St. Augustine of his delivery of Delegate Burns, Hornsby was in an amiable, expansive mood. He informed me that his clerk was even then preparing the final draft of his action report and the account of my vile imprisonment would be given a good part. "When the report is made public in London," he remarked, "I rather fancy the newspapers will fall upon it with some eagerness because not only is the collaring of a fellow like Burns an interesting event but your reappearance under such circumstances, Mr. Reid, will greatly excite the public. You are, after all, something of a popular figure at home."

"I'd much rather you made no mention of me," I told him. "If that isn't possible, then I'll ask you to merely refer to me as an American Loyalist named Robert Allston, which was my *nom de guerre*. As James Reid I must make a detailed report for the Army, confidential, I hope, and that should satisfy the needs of the Government."

"My dear sir," he said, "I have no choice but to submit a complete, exact and detailed account of the incident as reflected in my ship's log."

"Of course, sir," I agreed. "I only ask that my name be kept as far out of sight as possible and my part be minimized."

He smiled paternally. "Your modesty is commendable, Mr. Reid, but on the other hand you have just completed a gallant exploit for the Crown, showing high courage, ingenuity and fortitude. Not only is it my duty to report it, but the country needs heroic exploits to hold public support for His Majesty's position in this conflict. 'Tis no time for shrinking violets, sir, and from what I know of your reputation you've no call to be one, none at all."

"I'm no shrinking violet," I said. "I have two perfectly good reasons for wanting to be invisible for the time being. One is my wife in Georgia and the other is my King in London. You see, sir, my wife is a Loyalist of a Loyalist family. For several more good reasons our marriage had to be kept secret and those reasons will continue to be valid until Georgia is recovered by the Crown. She and her family risked their lives and fortunes to help me carry out my job for the Crown, and they deserve every consideration. The rebels have access to British journals and any public revelation of my actions and identity is liable to threaten the lives of my wife and her brothers. There is a politically powerful neighbor who watches them night and day, waiting to pounce at the slightest excuse."

Hornsby nodded. "I see. That does complicate the affair, I must say. And what of the King? Should my action report reach his eyes, your conduct will find favorable royal attention, I should think."

I told him of the King's comments made to me during the painting of his portrait, and what Mr. MacLeod had told me of the royal speech at the Academy exhibition. "To others it may seem a negligible thing in this day and age, the displeasure of the King, but my occupation feeds on high favor and acclaim. 'Tis my bread and butter. He's an honest, plain-spoken gentleman who means what he says, and I haven't any desire to further test his patience by having my antics flaunted before him, which were in direct disobedience of his personally expressed instructions."

"Your point is well taken," commented the captain, leaning back in his chair. "You have my sympathy. However, I serve the King more directly at his pleasure and if I were to submit a false, or distorted or incomplete report in the pursuance of my duty there'd be an end to his pleasure and I'd find myself on the beach seeking employment, probably, as a ship chandler's clerk, disgraced and ruined. I'll append a note to my report, covering your remarks to me concerning your wife and her family, with the request that your desire for anonymity be respected insofar as possible. I can do nothing more."

"But," I argued, "I know something of London journalists, sir. Once they get an inkling, they'll bribe an official and this business will be shouted from the rooftops." Another tack occurred to me. "And look here, Captain: having only just completed a difficult secret task for the Crown, I might be needed for another. My usefulness as a covert agent would be destroyed."

He chuckled. "Considering His Majesty's expressed opinions toward you, some made public, I doubt anyone in a position of Government responsibility will be rash enough to inveigle you into more of that dangerous sport. Who was it who got you into this game?"

"I volunteered," I replied. "It seemed a good chance to serve the Crown."

"Someone had to propose it to you," he observed. " 'Tis none of my affair, yet he might find himself boiled in royal oil one day, I fancy. About Mrs. Reid and her safety, there's actually not much chance of rebels there reading London newspapers' notices about you before our people seize the place. 'Twill take a time for my report to go to Admiral Byron, thence to General Clinton and from there over to Westminster, where it will be passed from office to office. Many things will have transpired before it reaches public view, if it ever does, and one of those, I sincerely trust, will be your reunion with your lady, sir."

It was sound reasoning and I felt better. "Thank you, anyway, for your kindness and consideration, sir. I hope it comes out that way."

"And so do I," he smiled. "As I said earlier, I know something of your reputation, Mr. Reid, as a distinguished artist as well as other aspects. Your actions in the *Jason* fight—Lindsay told me of it, apart from what I read of it in the papers—were wholly admirable and in keeping with the highest traditions of the naval service, even though you were a civilian passenger, and you well merit the public acclaim that has been given you, sir. It has been an honor for me and my ship to have you on board. I'll be pleased to have you go ashore with me tomorrow in my gig. St. Augustine's a wretched port. I must anchor outside in the open roadstead because even at high tide there's only a fathom of water over the channel bar. There's some satisfaction in that, though. Lying that far from the town keeps the damned fleas and ants from jumping aboard. You'll want lodgings, and they're in short supply. The Black Ox Inn is set apart for officers' quarters and I suggest you take up moorings there."

—

Chapter XVII

CAPTAIN HORNSBY'S low opinion of St. Augustine, I observed when I got ashore, was justified. Before East Florida fell into British hands, the place had been a drowsy little Spanish colonial town sleeping in the sun, dominated by the crumbling old fort that General Oglethorpe had tried to capture many years earlier. Now it was packed with Loyalist civilian refugees from the southern provinces, British and Provincial troops, and hordes of slaves, either runaway or brought by their masters. Shacks and tents were thrown up everywhere there was a vacant space except on the streets themselves, which were paved with a mixture of sand and crushed seashells, ground to a white powder by countless wheels, hooves and human feet. The stickily moist heat induced constant perspiration and the dust from the streets settled on exposed skin and clothing to give the people a strange ghostly appearance as they drifted aimlessly about in shabby groups.

Hornsby was good enough to delay his reporting to General Prevost long enough to go with me to the Black Ox and confirm my official status to the proprietor, who gave me a fine large room. The inn was a thick-walled stucco building dating from Spanish occupation, a spacious, cool and clean oasis in the dirty hot town. After settling in, I went down to the public room for a drink and to ponder what I should do first, and immediately ran into my fellow conferee in New York, Mark Prevost. He greeted me with great friendliness and stated he had seen my head count. "Top-notch bit of work, that. Precise and accurate. Just what we wanted. We're cracking on all sail now, recruiting every man jack we can find for our little Georgia picnic."

Elated, I grinned, "If I'm not a man jack, I'm a warm body who can shoulder a musket. Where do I go to take the King's shilling, friend?"

"You?" He stared at me in surprise. "You're joking, of course." Chuckling, he said, "You'll get no shilling from the King, old boy. You're going back to London on the double quick time."

"The bloody hell I am," I retorted. "I'm going back to Georgia on the double quick time, with your flaming army."

"The hell you are, sir," he smiled, summoning a waiter and ordering new drinks. "The King's given you rather more than a shilling. The general has a letter of instruction from Sir Henry about you. General Clinton in turn had one from Whitehall which he quoted in his to the general here. Generally, it directs that upon your return to Crown jurisdiction you're to be shipped off to London as soon as practicable."

My mind flew to Beauvoir. Aghast, I exclaimed, "My God! Am I to be sent in chains or some such goddamned thing?"

He laughed. "My dear fellow, His Majesty is evidently concerned for your safety and desires you removed from further possible danger so you may return to your cele-brated career. Sir Henry pointed out that the Whitehall letter was signed by Lord North and made it clear that the King's interest was behind it. I knew you were famous, but His Majesty's friendship for you came rather as a surprise. Next time you see him, put in a good word for me, old boy."

"Well," I said, calming down, "I doubt I'll be seeing him for some time, if ever. I'm not that friendly with him. I simply painted his portrait last spring. Since I'm evidently not under Royal arrest, I'll proceed with my own affairs. The fact is, I was married in Georgia and had to leave my wife there because of a damned rotten situation caused by this cursed rebellion and her Loyalist family. She's in con-stant peril. After I recover her I'll gladly go to London. You quoted from the letter: 'As soon as practicable.' It won't be that until I have my wife at my side, and you may tell your brother that. He ordered me out of Georgia and I was then an agent under his authority; I'm now a free British subject and subject to no man's orders."

Frowning, he said, "You married? Well, belated congratulations and all that sort of thing, but you were warned against such involvement, Jamie. That was in contravention of your instructions and the general cannot use that as an excuse for not complying with Whitehall's orders concerning you."

"Orders?" I cried. "Didn't you hear what I just said? Orders be damned! I want my wife!"

"I'm really only a spectator to the business," he said, "and happen to know of the correspondence unofficially. I'm no longer on the general's staff. I've got a regiment. You may not have noticed, by the way; I'm a lieutenant colonel now. In any case, you'd best have a bit of a talk with the general. Come along and we'll see if he's available. I daresay he'll drop what he's doing." It was a curious example of military punctilio, the way he referred to his brother as the general.

Shortly afterward, at Army headquarters, I learned that the general addressed him and referred to him as if they were not related, and not only that, the general's son John, a captain serving as adjutant, was treated as if he were not related. Nobody could accuse Augustine Prevost of nepotism; if anything, he leaned the other way and there were times later when I felt sorry for the general's kin. General Prevost was a serious, almost severe man, a little on the plump side. His English had a slight Teutonic accent, I thought at first, then shortly afterward I decided it was French. Subsequently my puzzlement was removed when I was told he was by origin a Swiss from Geneva. He welcomed me with an affable handshake and invited me to be seated, then fired a salvo of sharp questions about my mission. After listening to my answers, he said, "Capital, capital! If your man Cameron can keep Howe at Sunbury 'twill be a walk-in, very nearly. You'll have a mention in the dispatches, Mr. Reid, in addition to Captain Hornsby's. He was here a few minutes past. I daresay you'll be happy if you never see a rat again, eh?"

"You don't know how true that is, sir," I said fervently.

"Colonel Prevost said something about a Mrs. Reid in Georgia before he was called away just now," said the general, "and gave me the impression there's a serious problem concerning rebel actions against her, which makes you unwilling to comply with Lord North's instructions. Explain, Mr. Reid."

I related the entire tale, including the Jenks business, and he commented, "Awkward, devilish awkward for you, sir. The courage of your brothers-in-law gives me hope that all the Loyalists there are of a similar mold. Stout fellows. However, you need not fear—we'll extricate your good lady when we go there and deliver her safely to you in London, I promise you. I'll ask you to have faith in my ability to do that and go along to London in compliance with His Majesty's wishes. There will be a sailing to New York presently and your onward passage to London from there will be expedited by General Clinton."

"I'm sorry if I haven't made my position clear, sir," I said. "I have no intention of going to London except in the company of my wife, for only then will it be practicable in the terms of the letter from Whitehall. I request permission to accompany your army north into Georgia, sir, in whatever capacity open to me, as a private of foot or horse groom—anything."

He shook his head. "Not a particle of chance, Mr. Reid. The instructions clearly order that you not be exposed to further danger."

"Then I'll go by myself," I declared defiantly.

His face became flintly, something I was to see a number of times later to my discomfiture. "Mr. Reid, here in East Florida civil government rules under Governor Tonyn and his council and you have all the rights of a British subject. The lands north of the border, though contested, are legally under His Majesty's sovereignty and civil rule of the Crown does not exist. The Province of Georgia lies within my command. I am the lawful government there and my law is martial, not civil. I hereby forbid you to enter that territory on pain of being punished as the court-martial may direct after you are apprehended. Given the circumstances of war, sir, the punishment may be the extreme one."

Angered at the threat and the notion of being pushed. around by generals and King's ministers, I exclaimed, "You wouldn't dare, General! Not with what that letter from Whitehall indicates! If you were to try me by your court-martial, you'd—"

"Silence, sir!" He was angry now, too, but cold. "I'll thank you to conduct yourself with courtesy in my headquarters! I made no threat, I made a promise! I shall make no further attempt to persuade you to leave for London.

The substance of this conversation will be reported to General Clinton and I shall await instructions. I believe our business is concluded for the time being. Good-day, sir."

Back at the Black Ox, when I was cooled down from my dudgeon, I remembered his statement about a ship leaving for New York presently, so I wrote to Hector and Anne giving them a brief account of my adventures, including my marriage, and sent along a request to my New York banker for a sizable draft. In the next few weeks, however, I had no shortage of money after word got around among the wealthy Loyalist planters and refugees that the well-known James Reid was on deck with his paints and brushes. My room at the Black Ox became a painting room as well as bedchamber and I stayed as busy as possible turning out portraits at rather reduced fees, mostly to keep my mind occupied and off Marg.

Once again, however, no matter how drunk I got in the evenings—and I did that with grim determination, trying to attain oblivion—once in bed my nights were sheer howling woe. Separation from her and worry over her welfare became a dark malaise that began in my heart, spread to my bone marrow and permeated my mind and flesh. After several attempts to hire a guide who would take me up through Georgia, I gave up; they were all afraid of being caught and slain by the rebels. As a partial panacea and without enthusiasm I resumed my old custom of tupping some of my more attractive lady portrait sitters. It was an empty, animal exercise and provided no relief for my troubled mind. I began to fear for my sanity.

My emotional balance was not improved by a visit from Wallbrook, in town on a brief visit from Fort Tonyn, the Ranger camp at St. Mary's. He had recently been on a patrol that took him through Elderbank. Over a drink in the public room he growled, "If Colonel Browne hadn't told us all hands off Abraham Jenks, the law'll get him when we take the country back, I would have opened him up like a catfish whilst I was there. He's turned hard ticket now, coming on fair wicked with her, she told me, though he hasn't laid a hand on her. His ideas are sharpening up about what really went on with you, Jamie. And her. And Jedediah. Her brothers want her and themselves to flit while they can, but she won't budge. Wait till Jamie and the Army come, says she." He grinned at me. "She told

293

me that when you do come, she's going to make you eat every crumb of the stalest goddamn cake that ever was."

I nearly fell into pieces. Tears sprang into my eyes and I cried, "Oh, Jesus, Hugh, come with me! Show me the way! I'm dying by inches in this arsehole of creation!"

"Not me, old horse," he answered, looking sympathetic. "I know about your run-in with old Prevost, for one thing. He's right, but even if he weren't, I wouldn't risk being court-martialed out of the Rangers. Not now. I got a few scores to settle for myself when we go back up in there with drums and colors." And that was that.

A ship from New York brought the post. In his letter Hector was comical about me finally being trapped into matrimony, congratulated me and expressed great desire to meet the miracle woman who could do such a thing to James Reid. His Alice had jilted him to marry a wealthy fish merchant. "May her womb produce two-headed halibut and vampire haddock." He was toying with the idea of going as surgeon with a Highlander regiment because life was boring without me around to rescue from silly situations, et cetera, et cetera.

Enclosed with his letter was a note from Anne, expressing joy over my marriage to her dear friend Marg. She said she had dreamed of us both and of Goodowns several times, and asked how Brutus and the twins were. She closed with, " 'Tis a trite phrase and oversaid, but you must believe me when I say all my love to you both, dear Jamie and Marg, from your devoted Anne." I was relieved that she included no preachments about roads or news of second sightings, and the letters left me with a good feeling, as if I were surrounded by old and beloved friends. It wasn't until a bit later that I had the uneasy feeling that Anne's invisible presence may have come along to haunt me again.

A soldier from Prevost's headquarters delivered to me a letter which, he reported, had arrived with dispatches from General Sir Henry Clinton. The small spidery handwriting was unfamiliar to me, but when I opened it and saw the signature I came very close to tearing it up without reading it. Beauvoir had sent it to Clinton for forwarding to me. Carefully phrased in guarded language—the King was referred to as "our mutual acquaintance of some authority" —it made clear that Beauvoir's perverted passion in my direction was unchanged. My revulsion became fuming, helpless rage as I read that he had persuaded the King to have Lord North send those damned instructions about me to Clinton. "I suggest that the serious matter I last discussed with you in London may not be held forever in abeyance. I strongly urge and pray you, in the best interests of all concerned, write to me at your earliest convenience declaring your acceptance of the terms previously communicated to you by your humble servant." He ended by slyly once again offering me the use of his wife's body as well as his own.

Sick to my stomach, I went to the public room, where over a glass of rum I grimly resolved to fight the man. There had to be some chink in the armor of his spy system, some fatal oversight in his carefully contrived case against Hector, Ira and me. When Marg and I went to London I would declare war against the horrible little maniac and destroy him. Angus, with his assets, would help.

While I was thus brooding, Mark Prevost came in and joined me at my table. Greeting him grumpily, I ordered a drink for him and said, "Among the dispatches from Clinton your brother has received lately I wouldn't be surprised if there was one sending me to the Tower in chains."

"You're becoming a sour specimen these days, Jamie," he smiled. "Your face is so long you're liable to trip on your chin. Cheer up—I bring good tidings. By the way, there was a private letter for you in the box. Did you get it?"

"I did," I said sourly, "and that's why I just said what I did. There's foul business afoot in London and I suspect your tidings are foul, too."

"Not especially, at least so far as I can see," he remarked. "Sir Henry has advised the general that he has forwarded the general's letter concerning you to Whitehall, requesting instructions in the premises, and meantime your safety and welfare are General Prevost's personal responsibility which must not be delegated to any subordinate, since this is a matter of royal concern. The general is . . . ah . . . not happy."

"I can't fault him for that," I grumbled. "He may be happier if you tell him I'm goddamned unhappy about being singled out for such humiliating treatment as if I were some sort of royal favorite or pet. I'll thank you to tell him I regret being a carbuncle on his arse and 'twas none of my doing."

"When he told me to pass the news to you," said Mark, "he also instructed me to advise you that he is aware of your displeasure regarding this situation and it is somewhat more than mutual on his part. Nonetheless, since you are not legally bound to his authority in East Florida, he requests that you please cooperate to make his onerous charge from Sir Henry as less of a nuisance as possible by responding like the gentleman you are."

"I can well imagine his tone of voice when he said that," I commented bitterly. "A combination of rocks and icebergs grating together."

"Precisely," Mark grinned. "However, a bit of sympathy and understanding from you will go far, Jamie. Bear in mind that he has a war to get on with, a campaign to plan under most difficult conditions, not the least of which is insufficient troops. Sir Henry has directed him to recruit every available man in East Florida for the Georgia expedition and though we're trying to do it, most of our recruits for the militia are half-starved reluctant farmers and ploughboys."

"How am I supposed to cooperate?" I asked.

"By giving your word you will not attempt to go to Georgia alone or with a guide, as you recently tried to do," he answered. "That was reported to our intelligencers, incidentally. Also, you're requested to keep the general informed of your whereabouts. That is, if you leave town for any reason, first drop in at headquarters and tell the adjutant where you intend to be."

"Good Christ," I muttered, "I might as well be a prisoner on parole. All right, you have my word. I'll coopoerate." An idea popped into my head and I guffawed so loudly the other guests turned to stare, for it was afternoon and sobriety was the rule until evening. "Mark, my friend, it just dawned on me! Carbuncle on his arse indeed! Whither he goeth, so goeth I! Whatever those subsequent instructions from Whitehall might be, they'll arrive too late to keep me from going up into Georgia as the undelegated responsibility of your brother!"

"Being the excellent soldier that he is," said Mark, "the general's habit of mind is to carefully anticipate the future development of a given situation. He's already mentioned that turn of affairs and said with some emphasis that if it comes to that he'll hold you on a damned short rein. I rather fancy you'll be hearing from him shortly on that subject."

And I did. Four or five days later the adjutant, Captain John Prevost, called me away from my game of whist in the Black Ox public room. He was a serious officer slightly younger than I and by reputation a fine soldier. I rather liked him and had drunk with him on several occasions, but his conversation was tedious, tending to be entirely military. He said to me, "Sorry to interrupt your game, Jamie, but this matter is urgent. The general sent me here. Time is growing short and he wishes to dispose of a number of vexing details in order to put his full attention to the coming field operation. I'll speak frankly: he is resigned to having your company on the march north but is wary of what he believes to be your propensity for undisciplined, impulsive conduct where your lady is concerned."

"I'll speak frankly, too," I said irritably. "He might have such a propensity, too, if he were in my place and it was your mother who is in my wife's position. I've had the pleasure of talking with Mrs. Prevost several times lately and observed your father's pride and affection for her. And how would you yourself behave if that lady were a long distance away at the mercy of murdering, raping, traitorous villains?"

He answered severely, "I would carry out my orders and conduct myself like an officer and gentleman, sir, and so would the general in the course of recovering her, incident to executing the prime objective of the force under his command. And that, sir, is what will be expected of you if you accept this commission in the rank of captain in the East Florida Ranger regiment." He produced a document and handed it to me. "The general bids me warn you that if you do not accept, you shall go to Georgia chained to his baggage."

Delight swept me. Unbelieving, I scanned the commission. There was my name, sure enough, and the paper was signed by Governor Tonyn. "Accept it?" I cried, laughing. "Man, I'll wear it next to my heart! I could kiss you, John! And your crusty papa, too! Great balls of God, this is a miracle!"

"I'm glad you're pleased," he said politely. "It took a bit of doing, you know. The general wouldn't have you go as a private soldier and there was no way to rank you in the Regular Establishment, of course, and there were no vacancies in the Provincials we have here. Militia was out of the question." He went on to tell me the commission represented the final compromise in the extended squabble between General Prevost of the Regulars and Colonel Browne of the partisan Rangers.

As near as I could make out from the complex tale, Prevost was determined to have the Ranger regiment in his army and on an equal basis with the other troops in matters concerning rank and pay. Browne's rank, for one thing, was given him by the East Florida Governor's Council and Prevost demanded his rank be established with and below the Regular lieutenant colonels under his command. Ranger files were paid by the council at the generous rate of a shilling a day, much more than Regular files, and that was an extremely unsatisfactory condition, Prevost claimed, which would lead to morale problems among the Redcoats who were to be the strong core of his invasion force.

In any case, after much backing and filling, the issues were resolved and at some point in the mess Tonyn and Browne reluctantly agreed to accept me. I had met and knew both of them and we had gotten along in amiable style, but being a casual social acquaintance is rather different from accepting a comparatively unknown young man as an officer in the hard-fighting, hard-riding Rangers.

As it turned out, however, I was not completely accepted. John Prevost told me, "Colonel Browne will take you into his rolls only on the condition that you be schooled for three weeks at Fort Tonyn in fundamental training peculiar to his corps. After that, the general directs that you remain there until he arrives with his troops from here, at which time you will report to him for duties as aide de camp in temporary detachment from the Rangers. He bids me remind you of your word of honor and now of your place as an officer when you go to Fort Tonyn, because Georgia lies across the river."

I slapped him heartily on the shoulder and grinned, "I'll stand on my head to wait for him if he wishes, my boy! Convey my deepest thanks to your noble sire! I'll never give him cause to regret his trust and confidence!"

That evening I got merrily, uproariously drunk, my high spirits doubling the effect of the alcoholic ones, and I dimly recall entertaining a group of cheering officers by

singing a bawdy ballad Ira Tupper had once taught me
during an idle hour in the *Bonny Anne*, which began:

"In the Street of a Thousand Arseholes,
At the Sign of the Swinging Tit,
Lived a lovely Chinese maiden
Whose name was Hu Flung Shit. . . ."

Chapter XVIII

THE LONG RIDE north to Fort Tonyn in the wet, gray weather of October was physically wretched but I arrived with undampened ebullience, and the sight of the forested Georgia shore across the river made me happier. Colonel Browne gave me a cool welcome and turned me over to Hugh Wallbrook for my course of sprouts. Hugh greeted me with pleasure and congratulations, and promptly had me outfitted in the uniform of a captain of East Florida Rangers. Tilting my helmet, a pigskin bowl with a short visor and a strip of shaggy bearskin running over the top, fore-and-aft, and a thick chin strap, I felt myself to be a dashing picture and didn't resist my natural inclination to swagger outrageously.

The training was interesting. Very little of it consisted of orthodox European tactics. The emphasis was on forest skills—tracking, concealment, observing from cover, preparing traps for humans, ambushing and generally fighting Indian style. At times I felt a bit absurd, as if I were playing children's games, but I came off rather well, as was admitted by Colonel Browne at the end of the training period.

Not long after that, General Prevost with the main body of his army arrived from St. Augustine, a long, shuffling mix of Redcoats, Provincials and meagerly trained, recently recruited militia, followed by a longer train of ox-drawn supply carts, many of them carrying boats for all the river-crossings that lay ahead. When I eagerly sought out the general to report for duty, he eyed me with distaste and said, "Your purpose in my army is for your private satisfactions, Reid, while the rest of us are on His Majesty's service against his enemies. I won't tolerate whimpering complaints about your discomforts and there will be many of them. I have more to do than play wet nurse to London rakes or royal pets. As my A.D.C. you will maintain yourself within sound of my voice unless otherwise directed. To justify your presence among us you will be responsible for the command journal. Captain Prevost will advise you on it and supply you with the required orders and returns for it. That is all, sir. Good-day."

Simmering, with my spirits dashed, I ordered myself to keep my mouth shut. Getting back to Marg was the important thing, and if I were required to eat a steady diet of general officer's spiteful feces all the way it would be worth it. In his headquarters tent, John Prevost told me that at the end of each day's march and after any battle action, he would turn over to me the written material involved and I would write an account in narrative form with the orders and returns attached at the end as appendices.

"Christ," I said in disgust, "I'm an artist, not a writer. Are illustrations permitted?"

Excellent soldier of the King that he was, he looked puzzled. "That isn't covered in the regulations governing command journals." Frowning in concentration, he added, "But artists are often employed in the making of panoramic terrain drawings for tactical movement and artillery employment."

"If illustrations aren't forbidden, then," I told him, "they must be permitted, eh? I'll give your esteemed papa a manuscript which at my prices for drawings will be worth a nabob's ransom."

Several troop transports arrived and Lieutenant Colonel Fuser's light brigade was loaded aboard them. They were off to make a diversionary attack on the Yankee Howe at Fort Sunbury, thereby upholding Alexander Cameron's reputation among the rebels as an astute prophet, at least for a time. General Prevost, impatient and not knowing whether or not the expedition from New York had been blown clear across to Ireland by winter gales, gave the order for us to cross the river into Georgia.

It was a dreary time, that march up through southern Georgia—wet, cold, slow and thoroughly miserable. Prevost's orders from Lord Germain via Clinton were to "ravage" the countryside, but there was not much to ravage and he did little of it other than to send foragers out to bring in food for the troops. In my tent each night, by the light of a guttering candle as the almost constant rain pattered on the roof, I dutifully translated into plain English the quartermaster general's status of supplies reports, the surgeon's ever-swelling sick report, the state of discipline (the Negro drummers of the band carried out the floggings, which were frequent), miles covered and other stimulating, spicy stuff, leaving spaces for my drawings, which I did before going to bed. The artwork I savored like a good dessert after a dull meal and though he tried to hide it from me, General Prevost, when he inspected the journal, was obviously pleased. Bedtime was not too bad for me; every mile I recorded in the journal was bringing me closer and closer to my beloved Marg and I went to sleep contemplating her joy.

We were still many miles south of Sunbury when we received word that Fuser had been beaten off there and was licking his wounds, which meant that Howe's main force was still there and Savannah lay still undefended. The general sent word to him to remain in place and try to keep Howe occupied until we arrived. However, Christmas came and went with us still inching through the dripping forests, and then came a messenger with the marvelous news that Campbell had taken Savannah.

Howe had gotten the news of the British ships' arrival below the city too late. Leaving a rear guard in the fort to hold again Fuser, he ran his men to Savannah and had only time enough to hastily dispose his force along the road just south of the town. Approaching, Campbell found a friendly local Negro who showed him a path around to the rear of the rebels unknown to them, and he smashed into the rebel line front and rear, losing but three killed and ten wounded. The butcher's bill for Howe was ghastly: eighty-three killed and God knows how many wounded, while four hundred and thirty-three were captured. Howe himself fled to South Carolina and many years after the war I learned that he was court-martialed at Philadelphia for that defeat and discharged without guilt, poor soul, which was tantamount to saying, "We won't punish you for being stupidly trapped, but you don't get any bouquets."

On January 6, we finally arrived at Fort Sunbury and

took it after a brief token resistance which was an anti-climactic disappointment to me. After all the miseries of the dragging approach march I yearned for fireworks and all that happened was a puny little belch. Then it was on to Savannah and I was only about eighty miles from my other beloved half.

Chapter XIX

SAVANNAH was hard to recognize, swarming with the King's troops, horses and wagons, together with Loyalists who had rushed into town to escape the last minute vengeance of their rebel neighbors. All the Whig leaders had fled with Howe to South Carolina, even Alexander Cameron, discreetly preserving his spurious identification. Campbell had taken over the house on Bull Street for British headquarters and, upon arrival there, General Prevost told me to take myself off somewere to await his call if he should need my services. Campbell greeted me with warmth and congratulated me on my work that opened Savannah to him. I asked him when the expedition to Augusta would move, and was disappointed when he told me the general planned to consolidate Savannah's defenses and establish outlying bases to the north first.

The public room at Tondee's tavern was jam-packed with roistering officers of both the New York and East Florida expeditions. Fighting my way through the mob I located Peter Tondee and to my request he said, showing hardly a flicker of surprise at my appearance, particularly in Ranger officer uniform, "I'm dreadfully sorry, Captain Allston. My house is full, even the nigger quarters and the hayloft."

"My true name is Reid," I told him. "I'm willing to double up with one of your guests if he doesn't have the plague or leprosy."

Indicating a knot of noisily drinking officers of a Highlander regiment, he said, "The gentlemen who has your former room is there, sir. If he wills to share, I'll charge you only half price. The red-haired gentleman."

I hardly heard the last over the uproar, because I was driving through the crowd at the red-haired gentleman, shouting, "Hector! Hector MacDonald, you bloody monster!" Then we were embracing and babbling, shouting and punching each other in wild delight.

When the pummeling was over he drew back to survey me. "What in the name of God is this barbaric rig you're done up in, lad? The Household Cavalry of Prester John or Ghengiz Khan?"

"Have a care, you Caledonian lout," I grinned, "lest one of my barbaric colleagues in this crowd overhear your insults to Browne's East Florida Rangers and removes your tongue with a quick flip of his knife."

"Ho, ho," he snorted, "I've heard of that band of scalping brigands. At last Jamie Reid has found his proper level. Man, in heaven's name let's have a drink, forbye!"

With a bottle of rum and glasses we struggled to find a table with a couple of chairs and there was none. Hector went to where two young subalterns were sitting and, leaning over them with an expression of great solemnity said, "Och, lads, and there you are. I've looked everywhere for you. Have you reported to Colonel Campbell yet?"

They stared at him. "No, sir," said one, "does he—"

Hector frowned. "He's near exploding over at the headquarters. I'd not delay a second if I were you."

They scrambled to their feet and departed in bewilderment and anxiety, and we sat down in the chairs they had vacated. "A dirty MacDonald trick," I said.

"I didn't tell them Campbell wanted them, did I?" he returned. "Their own wee minds inferred it, the dear boys." We drank. "Ah, 'tis good to lift a glass with you, Jamie, once again. 'Twas on the chance of that I joined the Forty-first as sawbones."

"You lie in your teeth," I said. "You wanted to play soldier and wear a kilt, that's all. What did Anne have to say about this foolishness?"

He rolled his eyes and shook his head. "Jamie, you'd never believe the blistering language that issued from that beautiful mug, with great livid flames leaping from her bonny green eyes. She shouted and stormed and was magnificent beyond belief in her wonderful fury, blasting at me that 'twas bad enough to have Jamie Reid in mortal peril without Hector MacDonald going off to it, too. I told her for all her talk of Jamie's roads, didn't she think I had a road that I must follow, or didn't her second sight extend to half brothers. Jamie, as I live, she stopped dead away and those eyes grew as big as saucers and she whispered, 'When your roads have parted, have mercy, have mercy.' Then she burst into tears and ran up to her room. Wouldn't talk about it after. What d'you make of it, Jamie?"

"I refuse to make anything of it," I answered. "I want no part of her second sighting. Goddamn it, Hector, she's a perfect, flawless woman except for that, and it came near driving me mad. You know that. Talk about something else. What arrangements did you make about our house?"

"I made over a power of attorney to Anne," he replied, "so she can lease it during our absence to some responsible person. She and Quimby are off to London to visit our father for a time. She said something about wanting to see Rome."

"Best thing she could do, go to her father," I said. "She'll be out of harm's way there."

"You scurvy swine," he said sadly, "I hoped you'd be my brother-in-law, and now you've taken her girlhood friend to wife. Tell me about that lady, Jamie, and why she isn't with you now?"

I gave him the story and explained my apron-strings tie to General Prevost engineered by Beauvoir. "But when the Army goes to Augusta I'll be with it, by God, regardless of Prevost! To hell with his threats of court-martial!"

"Hapless wight," he commented, "it only serves to show what happens to you when kindly old Uncle Hector isn't around to instruct and guide you. While not a bloody-minded man, I've come to the conclusion that there are times when murder is morally justified. Your friend Abraham is a case in point and so is charming Vinny. Jamie, we committed a grievous error in not arranging a swim in the Thames for that nasty little chap and let the Devil take his itching hindmost. Aye, as you say, when we return to London, if we survive this arglebargle, we'll remedy that. I don't regret coming to this land and what has happened to us, but of one thing I'm sure: running from a problem is no cure for it, just as trying to flee from yourself is impossible, and I think we've both been guilty at times of that. I've already spoken to Campbell about the pilgrimage toward Augusta and he's promised me the post of brigade surgeon. I'm most anxious to have a look at

Goodowns, where Anne was born and brought up and where my poor dear Aunt Mary was killed last spring."

By the time Tondee called time in the public room and turned the taps to, there was no sober man in the house and Hector and I were drunker than a dozen tinkers. Sleeping double in the bed with him proved impossible with his snoring and thrashing about, so I wrapped up in a blanket and slept on the floor.

In the days that followed, General Prevost continued to concentrate on Savannah's defenses and established outposts at Port Royal to the north and Ebenezer to the northwest, and gave me no duties. With nothing but drinking and socializing to occupy my mind, so near and yet so far from Marg, I slipped back into a continuing despondency similar to what I had suffered at St. Augustine. Colonel Browne's Rangers were sent out in small detachments to observe enemy movements in the backcountry and South Carolina, often passing through the region of Elderbank, and I repeatedly asked Colonel Browne to assign me thus, but he refused on the grounds that I was still on temporary attachment to General Prevost's headquarters and not under Ranger command.

Then one day well into January it happened. John Prevost told me that there had been a running argument for days between the General and Archie Campbell. Campbell wanted to launch his expedition to Augusta to establish the base there and recruit the Loyalist militia my head count report had indicated was available for recruitment, while the general, cautious because of Ranger reports that rebel armies under General Lincoln were massing in South Carolina, was reluctant to possibly overextend his limited strength. By sheer persistence and cogent argument, Campbell finally won and was given command of a brigade made up of the Queen's Royalists, a regiment recruited at St. Augustine of South Carolina refugees, the East Florida Rangers plus a sprinkling of Regulars.

"I want to see the general," I declared.

"Impossible," said John. "His standing order is to the effect that if he wishes to see you he'll send for you."

"Oh, balls," I snorted, and forthwith marched past the adjutant and into the general's office.

Working at papers on his desk, Prevost glanced up, saw me and said flintily, "I did not send for you. Get out."

Standing at rigid attention, I saluted smartly and stated

briskly, "Sir, Captain Reid requests return to his regiment in order to take part in the expedition to Augusta."

"Denied!" he barked. "Dismissed!"

The military formalities having been dispensed with, I stood at ease and said, "I'm only too well aware of your disapproval of me and the disagreeable imposition placed upon you by higher authority, sir. Be that as it may, I have rankled for some time past about your accusation that I am a self-serving parasite and not in your army to serve His Majesty. While I most certainly desire to recover my wife, I also consider myself to be a soldier of the King in every sense and am capable of fighting for him as well or better than any soldier under your command." He glared at me, but I had his attention. "What can be so wrong with a desire to fight for His Majesty in the course of rescuing my wife? Is that dishonorable or cowardly self-serving?"

"You," he answered coldly, "are disobedient and insolent. You will return to your quarters and consider yourself under arrest."

I stood my ground. "Sir, you leave me no alternative. If you refuse me permission to go with the Augusta force and court-martial me for insubordination, I'll insure at the trial that the public will learn of my shame and humiliation caused by the toadying zeal of some of His Majesty's ministers and generals. I happen to know what you do not, sir: that those instructions from Whitehall stem from a situation so scandalous that when it is revealed it will shake the Government, perhaps bring it down. The King has been duped and I am a victim through no fault of my own, and heads will roll if I reveal the scandal in my court-martial testimony. If you ask why I have not come forward before this, to denounce the affair, I must inform you that my life is in peril at the hands of the powerful official who is behind it.

"Upon recovery of my wife, I intend to return to London and pursue my own war against that enemy of the Crown and destroy him. If I were to make his identity known through court-martial testimony, it is probable that he would have time to flee abroad; the situation in Government would be corrected, but the villain himself would go unpunished. I therefore beg you to approve my request, sir."

He was interested, yet still hostile. "Palace scandals have

309

nothing to do with me, a commander in the field. I have my orders, and I have given you one. Will you force me to summon an armed guard for you, sir?"

I hated myself for doing it, but there was too much at stake. "Very well, sir, call the guard and court-martial me. I am not without favor in the eyes of the London public and enjoy some friendship with His Majesty, to say nothing of influential members of Parliament. I respect and admire you, sir, yet I must remind you that your actions in this campaign will be placed under the closest scrutiny and your career may hang in the balance."

Leaning back in his chair, he surveyed me grimly, then said in measured tones, "You performed well on the march from Florida. Your command journal with its excellent illustrations is a model of perfection. Colonel Browne reported that your training conduct at Fort Tonyn was outstanding. Your appearance and behavior until now have been that of an officer and a gentleman. I was on the verge of mentioning you in the dispatches, which I suppose you will term toadying. Now you have shown yourself in your true colors. Your threat is contemptible, despicable and cowardly. I wish you had been utterly devoured by your brother rats in that rebel vessel. I shall show you my toadying, sir. You are no longer under arrest nor are you attached to my headquarters.

"I order you to go now and write a letter to me, stating that you have read and understand General Clinton's instructions to me concerning you, and you will carefully explain why you are flouting those directions. You will be as thorough as possible, bearing in mind that the document may be entered in evidence in official proceedings against you at some later date. Upon delivery of that letter to my adjutant, you will proceed and report to Colonel Browne for such disposition as he may choose. Now, get out of my sight, you damned whining political blackguard!"

It was a foul victory indeed. I had been sincere in my expression to him of respect and admiration. He was a good and honorable soldier, laboring under trying responsibilities and his contempt was a bitter pill, especially because I had never consciously encountered anybody who did not like me. This new experience left me with a sickening hollow in the pit of my stomach. I rode out to the Rangers' camp on the edge of town and reported to

Colonel Browne, explaining that General Prevost had released me for the Augusta expedition.

Browne's eyes flickered over me, inspecting. "I have no employment for royal favorites—"

He got no farther. On top of what had just happened it was too much to be borne. I blared, "I'm no such goddamned thing! I'm a Ranger officer even if I wasn't raised in this country as a shit-kicking cowbody or planter! If anybody—I don't give a good goddamn what his rank is— calls me that again he's going to be spitting teeth and wondering why his bloody nose is wrapped around his ears! I'll admit I came to your regiment in an unusual way, but that doesn't make me any less of a man, and if you think—"

He gave me a faint smile, raised a hand and said, "Hold on, Reid. I didn't refuse your report for duty. I started to say that friends in high places cut no ice in my regiment and that letter of instruction from General Clinton has nothing to do with me or my regiment. That's General Prevost's worry and if he's released you then I suppose he isn't worrying and to hell with it. We're all acquainted with your private troubles here. Many of us have known your wife's family for years, and Abraham Jenks's as well. If we can find that gentleman before he flits to South Carolina, we'll be arresting him on a number of charges. I expect your brothers-in-law will be joining the militia, though I hope to enlist 'em myself; they're excellent men. And we'll have some women's wagons along for those ladies who don't wish to remain at home without their menfolk. 'Twill be a pleasure to see Marg again and have her with us."

I was overwhelmed with joy. "Thank you, sir! Oh, thank you, thank you!"

"There's bound to be a bit of fighting," he said, "and you may not think so much of my kindness before 'tis done, so save your thanks till then. Take temporary command of Fourth Company. It has a present strength of only nineteen men, the captain and the rest being on scouting patrol in the back of North and South Carolina. Your sergeant is Bonnell, a good man. He's been with me since the start of the Rangers and you may depend on him."

"When do we go, sir?" I asked eagerly.

"There's plenty of time," he answered with a slight smile. "Will tomorrow morning at daybreak suit you? We're play-

311

ing dragoons in this show, all mounted. Another spot of unaccustomed luxury, rations and tents will be supplied by the Army. We'll live like the Grenadier Guards. I hope it doesn't spoil my ruffians. Report to me at five o'clock at the assembly point on the Post Road near the Mac-Gillivray plantation, just beyond the town. Now run along and have a look at your Fourth Company."

Riding through the Ranger camp, I found my first command hard at work repairing their kits, cleaning firearms and sharpening knives and sabers. They were a rough, rawboned group, typical of all the Rangers, and they had a way of watching me closely without directly looking at me. Bonnell was a heavy-shouldered, sun-browned man in his thirties who regarded me with faint reserve as I introduced myself. He was a plain, direct speaker. "Seen you trainin' down to Tonyn and on the march up here. Heard you was some kind of kin to the King and had to be careful cared for. Rangers is a poor place for that."

That had to be quickly damped. I said, "There's nothing to that. A stupid rumor. When I lived in London I had a small business transaction with His Majesty and somebody down at St. Augustine got wind of it. You know how those things can be blown out of proportion. Sheer horseshit, Sergeant. And you might as well know I'm not English—I'm an American from Massachusetts."

Some of his reserve vanished. "The boys'll be comforted to know that. They don't cotton much to the English. Well, I reckon you're close to bein' a cracker, bein' wed to Marg Ogilvie and all. My farm lies over beyond Jenks Town and I know them folks well." He spat on the ground. "Got a passel of trouble up thataway now, I hear tell just now."

Alarmed, I said, "Just now? What trouble? Where?"

"While you was comin' from Colonel Browne," he explained, "a patrol from Second Company come through here on the way to report to him. Said the rebels has moved about four hundred men in around the Burke County courthouse and gaol. 'Pears old Abe Jenks and his committee caught up about a dozen loyal men and gaoled 'em. Marg's brothers is among 'em."

"My God!" I exclaimed. "What of my wife? Does the patrol know how she is?"

Shaking his head, he said, "All they watched was the rebels at the courthouse. When they seen enough, they come away fast."

"Jenks has surely gone mad," I said, "to imprison Loyalists when all Georgia must know we're here."

Spitting again, the sergeant said laconically, "Mad or not, if we lay hands on the stinkin' horse's arse, he gets a fair trial before we hang him, Cap'n."

"I'll see you in the morning," I told him, and rode back to Tondee's, thinking. Marg alone at Elderbank, defenseless. Abraham had carried out his threat against Peter and John. By the time I entered our room I was quivering with anger and despair, and Hector, packing his baggage, paused to stare at me and exclaimed, "Man, you look like raging death! What's at you?"

"He's got her!" I roared. "The hideous hulking mad swine's gone and done it! Thrown her brothers into gaol and God knows what he's doing to her alone at Elderbank! They say he's to be tried in a court! *I'm* his goddamned court and I'm going to slash open his belly and make him eat his own intestines! I'll cut off his balls and make him eat those too!"

"Here, now, Jamie," he said, thrusting a drink at me, "steady down and tell kindly old Uncle Hector about it in slow cadence, eh?"

I told him, spluttering and weeping with tears of blind rage, and he said soothingly, "Och, laddie, there's naught to do till we reach there. 'Tis a poor fix, to be sure, for the brothers, but like as not your lady is comfortable in her own home. You told me she herself had no fear the man would try to force her. Like as not he's just using more leverage to bend her will and 'tis unlikely harm will come to her brothers because—" He broke off and slapped his thigh, crying, "That's it, my lad! That's it! Jamie, yon rogues know well how small our army is, spread thin, and the force going to Augusta will be no great host. If a part of it were split off to go for your friends in the gaol where the enemy is emplaced in considerable number—ah, Jamie, d'ye ken the noo? Bait, man, bait!"

My emotional disarray halted and I looked at him. "Oh, for Christ's sake, of course! It wasn't Jenks and his petty scheme! They'll have been told by their spies that we're readying to come that way for Augusta and they expect to wipe out the detachment we send to the gaol for rescue, then they can strike the weakened main body! They'll know that Campbell will only have a couple of Loyalist

313

regiments!" I laughed. "For a surgeon, you're a fair tactician."

"Ho," he said with dignity, drawing himself up, "for all I'm a sawbones, I descend from a race of warriors with the thinking of battle in my very blood." Throwing back his head, he bellowed, *"Fraoch Eilean!"* He grinned at me and said, "Let yon rebels and Jenks tremble at the sound of that, for 'tis the dreaded war cry of MacDonald of the Isles, 'The Heathery Isle!' "

I said, amused, "When you get to shouting in Gaelic you're sure to start singing in it, and that's a pity for we have to listen. I could bear the pipes better than that caterwauling."

"Then, by God, you shall!" he cried, throwing back his clothing that was piled on the bed and revealing a set of bagpipes. "I'm an honorary member of the regimental band of the Forty-first! Brace yourself for a wild fling and the sweetest music this side of Skye!"

The drones droned and then the room was filled with the skirling rant, making the air tremble and my blood race as it always did. One by one, officers of the 41st came up from the public room to stamp the beat and some went to dancing. Peter Tondee, fearful we'd shake his house down, came to ask us to move the party downstairs, so Hector led us down the stairs with his pipes howling bravely and there we spent the evening singing, dancing and drinking in which even the non-Scots merrily joined. After closing time, when we stumbled up to bed, Hector, long ago winded, exhausted and quite drunk, said, "A damned fine *ceilidh* that was, except your attempt at the sword dance was execrable and no doubt caused your Highland ancestors to whirl in their graves. Ye canna dance it wi'oot a kilt, ye domn colonial stirk, and this nicht ye'll kindly restrain yeresel' frae fashin' and fartin' aboot in yere drunken snorin'."

" 'Tis you who do that, you red-headed madman!" I shouted, grabbing a blanket and collapsing to the floor with it.

"I'll no undress this nicht on the eve o' battle," he said, falling across the bed. "God rest ye weel, who was to be my brother-in-law, ye turgid-witted lost man."

Drunk as I was, lying on the floor, I could not let that pass. "Lost? What the hell do you mean?"

"Not lost yet," came his mumble from the bed. "Nearly

314

but not all. Anne knows . . . knows . . ." Mighty snores gusted and before I could get angry at this echo of Anne's infuriating witchery I dropped into sleep, no doubt to snore as loud as Hector.

I was running on the old road again, headlong in great haste, for ahead on one of the forks stood Marg. As I neared her, I saw her face was horrified and she was signaling me to stop, but I could not. Then a vast dark pit opened before me and I went tumbling into it, end over end. Still falling, I awakened in a sweat to find the candles lighted and Hector shaving at the dresser. "I was just going to wake you, slugabed. 'Tis time to be off to the wars. Our host has breakfast for us downstairs."

The good breakfast, a dash of peach brandy and the lively ride to the assembly point erased my holdover from the night before, and I felt good when I reported to Colonel Browne who sat on his horse at the head of the column among Campbell and the staff. "Your company will have first turn at advance and flank outguard," he told me. "Bonnell has been told and knows what's needed."

"I've heard the County committee has my brothers-in-law in gaol," I said, "and my wife is alone at Elderbank."

"So have I," he answered without expression. "They'll keep. Mount out your patrols and be quick about it, Captain."

The sun was just peeping above the horizon and the army's drummers thundered into the long roll as I galloped back to my little company in the column. Bonnell gave me a casual salute and said outguards had been assigned. "We'll have to ride, too, you and me, Cap'n, Fourth Company bein' so shorthanded. Which is your pleasure, sir?"

Elderbank would come up on the left. I said, "Left flank. Order the patrols out, Sergeant."

I rode off with the five Rangers of the left flank guard and found it an enjoyable task, far removed from the choking dust thrown up by the long, trudging column. The flankers rode alertly through the fields and woodlands with calm ease, dispersed wide apart, carefully observing for signs of human presence. They were silent, intent, and even their horses moved with a minimum of sound. Later, between turns at such outguarding, I ate my lifelong expectancy of dirt as I rode in the middle of the slowly moving main body amid a thick, low-lying dust cloud. It

315

was the same road I had once traveled in company with a prickly tempered young woman who wore masculine garb and made me angry. And, oh, God, how I loved her! The army moved much slower than we had done, and the snaillike progress made me edgy, even at night when Hector and I got together for drinking and talking.

Arriving in familiar ground north of the Briar Creek bridge heightened nostalgia and my emotional state, which was a conflict between desire for Marg and bloodthirst for Abraham Jenks. For every hour of marching, the troops were given about a ten minute rest, and during one of those rest periods I noticed we had reached Foley's ordinary. I rode to it and from the saddle looked at it and mused how things had changed for me since that unpleasant night. Some officers of the Queen's Royalists went in and I heard Foley's voice bellowing about liberty and tyranny, offering free drinks. One of the officers came out laughing and said to me, "The loon is giving away his drink because he thinks we're Washington's men." It was a natural mistake, I thought; many rebel regiments wore similar uniforms to those of Loyal Provincials.

Then Foley came out, blinking drunken eyes in the full flood of sunlight, and in front of my horse he squinted up at me. Weaving a bit, he said, "I seen you before."

He was as vile as Abraham Jenks. Removing my helmet to give him a clearer view of my face, I said, "You have. I came close to killing you when you obscenely offended my lady, you nasty scum."

"You!" he howled. "You and that Tory whore!" He peered at the road where soldiers sat and sprawled, and then saw the color sergeant standing with the Union Jack limp in the quiet air. Foley emitted a sound that was between a scream and a bellow. "Redcoats and Tories! All of you!" Staggering about, he lurched back into the house shouting, "To arms! To arms!"

Orders against harming civilians being strict, I continued to sit on my mount. Then I'm damned if the South Carolinians didn't come backing out of the place with their hands raised, followed by Foley who held a fowling piece pointed at them. "Out of my house, you royal arse-sucking bastards!" he roared. "I'll not stain the boards of my house with your filthy blood!" It was spectacular, the drunken idiot taking up arms in the very heart of an enemy's army. Drink gave him a lion heart. Directly in front of my horse he swung his gun up to aim at me. "I'm goin' to blow your Tory fuckin' head off—"

My pistol was in the saddle scabbard with the cover buckled. Before he hardly more than started to say it I had divined his intention and my saber leaped to my hand, swept in a flashing arc down on him to parry the gun barrel and it bit into him to lay him open nearly a foot between neck and shoulder. A great gout of blood fountained out of the huge wound and I'm sure he must have been dead before he fell. The soldiers from the road came rushing, pursued by angrily shouting noncommissioned officers trying to restrain them. Mrs. Foley hastened out of the ordinary, looked at what was left of her husband and then up at me as I sat with the bloody saber in my hand. "For your sake, I'm sorry, Mrs. Foley," I said, pitying her worn face. "He was going to shoot me."

There were no tears, no wails. She said quietly, "He was a good man once. This was bound to happen. You know about him from when you were here with Marg Ogilvie, though I didn't know you were one of those Rangers."

"I wasn't at the time, ma'am," I answered.

Browne arrived at a gallop. "He fired at you, Reid?"

"Yes, sir," I answered. "My blow deflected his aim. He singled me out because I nearly killed him last summer after he tried to ravish my lady. Mrs. Foley witnessed it."

Removing his headgear, he said to her, "You've always had my sympathy, Mrs. Foley, and you have it now, but you're better off without him. He was never good enough for you."

Shading her eyes with her hand, she looked up at him. "So you say, Tom Browne, with all your money and plantations. Once on a time he was as good a man as you. 'Twas the bottle that done him this way. Well, you've killed him and you can bury him out back."

"I'll send a party to do it," said Browne, "and you may show them where. Captain Reid, I'll expect your written report of this for the record."

I wrote up the report that night when the army camped for the night near Leavitt's and when I delivered it to him in his tent, I said, "My company has outguard tomorrow morning, sir, and I'd like to take my left flankers to find

317

my wife and while I'm in the neighborhood I could arrest Abraham Jenks, I think, if he hasn't fled."

"I see no reason why not," he replied. "That was skilled sword work today. Those who saw it say it was perfect. I had no idea you were a trained swordsman, Reid."

I explained, "In London I took instruction from a French master as a means of exercise. He was quite a good teacher."

"Well, don't use Jenks for your exercise when you find him," he said. "We want him in one piece for a well-publicized fair trial as an example for his political colleagues. Apart from his treason, he's done nothing so far to merit execution in the eyes of the law, as much as I dislike admitting it. Simply arrest him and fetch him along to the provost guard in the rear."

When the column ground into forward movement the next morning, I dispatched my outguards and was just about to ride off with my left flankers when Hector, kilted and spurred, came riding hard to join me. "Ah, Captain Reid," he grinned, "this is the famous day of days when I have the pleasure of meeting the lady who took the place that was rightfully my sister's, and when I view the jewel box of my late stepmother! Lead on, my lad!"

In no mood for joking, my heart pounding with anticipation, I made no answer and led the others at a gallop in the bright, cool February morning. Flank security be hanged—I wanted my wife. We came out of the woods and onto the stubbled fields of Elderbank, and I rode furiously to the house, flung out of the saddle and rushed inside. The house was empty. The portrait of Marg was gone from over the sideboard where her brothers had reverently hung it. I found Hyacinth trying to hide in the cookhouse and when she recognized me she embraced me and blubbered, "Didn't know who you was! Them boys off in gaol and Miss Marg—oh, lordy, Miss Marg . . ." She whooped and slobbered.

"Where is she?" I shouted. "Where is she? Goddamn it, woman, answer!"

"Mister Abraham, he come and took her when the boys got to gaol!" she sobbed. "Say it ain't fitten for a lady to live alone in these times—"

But I was off, seeing the world through a red haze. Vaulting into the saddle, I raked my mount with my spurs

318

and went thundering into the woods and through the short-cut to Goodowns.

Hector yelled, coming along behind me and followed by the Rangers, "Man, what are you at? You'll kill the horses!"

" 'Tis a man I'm going to kill!" I shouted. "We're coming on Goodowns now! Stay and see the sights if you like —I've no time!"

"I'll not leave you now, you crazy loon!" he bellowed. "The sights can wait! Think before you act, you madman! Think!"

"There's been too much thinking!" We shot out of the woods into the Goodowns peach orchard. "There's your house!" We swept around the end of the house and as we galloped over the lawn toward the path to Jenks Town I caught a glimpse of Brutus and Rufus near the piazza, staring with open mouths.

"So help me God," cried Hector to me, " 'tis the house I was born in on the Isle of Skye except for the ghastly portico built on—"

The horses were laboring hard when we galloped out into Jenks Town, and there we beheld a remarkable sight. Abraham had not fled to South Carolina nor had his tribe. They were gathered there in a circle and they turned to look at us with frightened faces as we reined in. In the center, with his whip at the ready, Abraham took no notice of us and went on booming his "meting out" nonsense. There was a woman, naked, lashed to the post, and she raised her head and smiled directly at me. It was Marg.

My mind dissolved. Hector, recounting it later, said I hurled my mount into the crowd, scattering the people like tenpins, with my saber raised high. My horse reared in fright at the screaming Jenkses and when my helmet flew off Abraham looked at me and gave a wild roar of triumph, drew back his whip, but, Hector related, my saber flashed like lightning and Abraham's head soared through the air like a football. 'Twas a bit on the gruesome side, said Hector, when the decapitated body continued to stand for a moment with a thick geyser of blood shooting out of the neck stump.

Then it appears that I hurtled out of the saddle and before Hector could fall on me to restrain my insanity, I ripped open the corpse from breast to crotch so the gray, bloody intestines came oozing out. When my wits returned

319

I was holding Marg in my arms, weeping and trying to speak and doing a poor job of it, and she still stark naked was kissing me, hugging me and crying, "I knew you'd come! Oh, Jamie, I knew you'd come! I heard the horses and knew 'twas you!"

Hector appeared with her gown he had picked up from the ground, brushed me aside and dropped it over her head, pulling it down over her as he said to her, "Losh, lassie, you'll catch your death, running about like that."

Astonishingly serene, she accepted his aid in adjusting and buttoning the garment, saying to him, smiling, "A Scottish soldier—that means Jamie's fetched the King's army as he said he would. I thank you, sir."

On the ground beside us the bearded head of Abraham snarled up at us in a frozen grimace and his mutilated corpse was an obscene pile of garbage. His family huddled together, watching us and the Rangers with frightened faces. I said to Marg, "Your Scottish soldier is Anne's half brother Hector, Marg."

She gave a cry, stared for a second at his face and flung her arms around him. "Hector, Hector! Jamie told me so much—"

He kissed her and grinned at me. "This makes up for not being invited to the wedding."

"Marg," I said, "the portrait. Did he take it?"

" 'Tis in his house yonder," she answered, her face glowing.

I said to a Ranger, "In that house is a large picture of my wife. Bring it out, please."

The Ranger said somberly, eyeing the Jenks people, "Yes, sir. Then can we fire this varmin nest? He come at you and orders says we can. Old Jenks was pure pizen on loyal men."

"He's had his pay," I told him, "and his people here have suffered enough under his madness. No burning. Quickly, now."

When he brought out the painting, I took it and ordered the flankers to carry on with the patrol while I would deliver my wife to the army women's wagon. They mounted and rode off, and Hector said, "I'll carry the portrait, Jamie, while you carry your bonny bride."

With Marg riding pillion behind me, her dear arms around my waist, we left Jenks Town. I said to her over

320

my shoulder, "Did he mistreat you other than what we saw?"

"He never touched me, but 'twas not pleasant," she answered. "You were right, though; he'd been going mad for a long time. I'll tell you about it later. Let's just now enjoy being together again, Jamie."

We came upon the column as it was halted for a rest stop on the road where it passed through Goodowns. Brutus was talking and beaming with Campbell and Browne, while the other Goodowns Negroes grouped a distance away, smiling and laughing as they looked at the lounging soldiers. Marg's arrival set off cheers from them and I saw Hetty and Betty hopping up and down, clapping their hands in glee. Browne smiled to Marg, bowing over her hand, " 'Tis good to see you, Mistress Reid, looking so well. We'll have your brothers free shortly."

Archie Campbell, resplendent in his scarlet and gold regimentals, bowed, smiling. "Charmed, ma'am. Now I can understand why your husband made such a worrisome nuisance of himself, for you're surely the loveliest prize in Georgia." He said to me, "Where is that fellow Jenks? Fled?"

"Dead," I answered shortly. "He resisted, attacked me and I killed him."

Hector said grimly, "The truth is, he was about to publicly flog this lady with her lashed quite naked to a post and he objected vigorously to our interruption. By your leave, Colonel, I shall write up the report so Captain Reid may apply himself to aiding his lady recover."

"By all means do so," answered Campbell, frowning. "Flog her? Good God!"

"His whip he called the righteous instrument of Jehovah," said Marg. "He was a great one for serving God with it. He lashed poor Brutus here some days ago to make him tell what he knew of Jedediah's death."

"Brutus!" exclaimed Hector, wheeling to look at the Negro. "A few days ago? A MacDonald servant? I would have killed the monster myself, had I known!" He said to Brutus, "I am Hector MacDonald, son of Angus and half brother to Anne."

Brutus smiled at him and bowed. "I have been watching and listening to you, sir, and guessed. Welcome home to Goodowns, Mister Hector. As for the beating, the

321

marks are healing nicely. I assume Mister Jamie told you of the Jedediah affair? I told his father nothing, sir."

"I'll have a look at your back shortly," said Hector. "Colonel Campbell, I should like to spend a few hours here and rejoin the brigade at night camp, with your permission."

"I fancy we can struggle along without you, surgeon," answered the colonel. "At least until stepping off in the morning. Gentlemen, let us get on. Drum major," he called to the waiting leader of the drummers, "sound the long roll."

Browne said to me, "Stay by your lady for the rest of the day if you wish and let Bonnell handle the company. See the baggage sergeant for such additional furniture as you'll need for married housekeeping in your tent tonight."

So I rode with Marg in one of the women's wagons, with my horse tied behind, and told her about what had happened to me since I left her, disregarding the other women present, wives and daughters of planters and farmers who had joined the column along the line of march as volunteer militia, the fruit of my head count. We cuddled and kissed, adoring each other, and I told her also about General Prevost's instructions from Clinton without mentioning Beauvoir. "So you see, we'll be packed off to London just as quickly as he can find a ship for us, darling. There's no reason to stay now. The Crown is back here, your brothers will be delivered from gaol, Elderbank is safe, Abraham's soul is being singed in Hell, and our two halves are reunited. My God, I've been ill, honeybun, and now I'm well again!"

She giggled and whispered in my ear, "Not all united yet, Old Nick! Oh, you just wait!" Aloud, she asked, "Why does General Clinton want to send you to London, Jamie? What does it mean? Are you in trouble?"

I would never tell her about the shameful Beauvoir mess. I laughed. "No, no trouble. There's a high-and-mighty fellow over there who wants me to come back and go to work at my trade for a living and leave off playing soldiers. It's been a damned bother to everybody concerned."

"Who is the high-and-mighty fellow?" she asked. "Will I meet him?"

"Sooner or later, I suppose," I answered. "I painted his

322

portrait and he thinks I haven't any right to do anything but paint portraits."

She turned her lovely gray eyes on my grinning face, then smiled delightedly, exclaiming, "The *King!* Jamie, 'tis the King himself who wants you back! I remember what Mr. MacLeod said! Oh, you'll not wriggle out of it, Jamie Reid. 'Tis His Majesty himself who bids you return!"

The other women in the wagon were openmouthed and I guffawed. "Marg, he's not God, only a gentleman with a title and stubborn ideas about America and the duties of British artists. When I next see him I'll give him a piece of my mind on both counts."

Then the other women, awed at being in the company of a man who evidently knew the King well enough to promise him a tongue-lashing, eagerly bombarded me with questions about the royal scene in London, and so the afternoon went by, while Marg and I hungered for each other in totality. When the brigade went into camp just before sunset, I took Marg to the Ranger officers' tent area and sought out my tent which was marked with my name. To my surprise there was a Redcoat foot soldier standing at rigid attention in front of it and when we approached him he came to a stiffly quivering salute. He was short and scrawny, and he bawled, "Private Filkins reportin' h'as h'ordered, sir!"

Nearly speechless, I stared at him, the former sentry at Fraunce's tavern. "What in God's name are you doing here?" It struck me funny. "You're off your post, Filkins. That's back on Broadway in New York, in front of Fraunce's."

His face was startled, then he peered at me and the gap-toothed grin appeared. "Well, cor stone the crows, if it eyen't you, sir! Swelp me, wot a small bloody world! 'Ow do, ma'am, Oy've 'eard h'about yer rescue an' my Gord bless yer h'and the bryve cap'n 'ere, ma'am."

It developed that he was a sort of wedding gift from Archie Campbell, who felt we needed a servant. Filkins had come down with the Savannah expedition and was fobbed off on the Augusta brigade by his regiment as an assistant to the brigade armorer, in which position he was totally unsuitable by reason of having, apparently, all thumbs. With the man unemployable in a military capacity, my friend Archie, doing me a favor, had shunted the wight to me. Filkins confessed that he had never given service a try, but confided he had always had a "nurge" towards it.

"All right," I agreed, "we'll give you a trial. I'm glad to see you again and have you so assigned, but I'll tolerate no barracks language in the presence of my lady. I'll be obliged, now, if you'll fetch our supper from the Ranger officers' mess."

Saluting briskly, he cried, "Thank yer, sir! Done an' done, sir! Double quick, sir!" He plunged away at a run.

"I always thought Redcoats were big, broad-shouldered and strong," said Marg. "That one makes me want to take care of him like a frail child."

"He's a complete misfit in the army," I remarked, "and I shudder to think of what's in store for us with him as our servant."

We entered the tent. Filkins had been busy. On the folding tent table a pewter mug held a nosegay of cattails and ferns, the closest things to flowers he could find at that time of the year, and a pair of candles flickered in the growing dark. A second camp cot had been placed against mine, with the bedding arranged as if it were one bed. It was all quite cozy and wistfully charming. Marg looked about with shining eyes. "Jamie, 'tis our first together home! And *breakfast* together in the morning for the first, very first time!" Our embrace was so passionate that we nearly ended up on the cots then and there had not Filkins arrived with tureens of steaming food.

Nervously trying too hard as he set the table, his multi-thumbed awkwardness caused him to drop things. Marg, going to help him, said comfortingly, "Don't hasten so, Filkins. We'll not starve. Here—do it thus and thus, you see? Ah, now you've got it! Why, that's wonderful, exactly right. Perfect!"

There was worship in his eyes and voice. "Strike me, mum, nobody h'ever says that to me before. 'Tis h'always: 'Filkins, yer blood swat—' "

Impatient, I cut him off. "Never mind the rest of the service. We'll do for ourselves. Go twiddle your thumbs somewhere and I'll call you when we're done."

All my wishes, dreams, hopes and yearnings were fulfilled that night. Marg and I were one whole person again, merging and blending into each other as before. Devouring each other, we gave ourselves to be devoured, and there was little sleeping done. She told me about what had hap-

324

pened at Jenks Town just prior to my arrival. "After Abraham had Peter and John arrested—I knew 'twas the end of us all, you see, because he was mad as you had said, and I was wrong for thinking I could handle him—I told him straight out that I was your lawful wedded wife and he could go to hell. Then his sons carried me off to Jenks Town at his order and he told Hyacinth that I was to be under his protection. He kept me locked in a room and each day he came in to read from the Bible in a great shouting voice about the evils of fornication and such sins. This morning he told me God had commanded him to put me to death as the Devil's whore. Then I prayed hard, Jamie, that my God—the real God—would make me as brave as you would be in the same place."

Burying my face between her breasts, I said with effort, "I'd have prayed to be made as brave as you, my lovely Marg."

"After they tied me to the post," she murmured, caressing my back, "I put all my thoughts on you, sending my thinking out to you wherever you might be, trying to make you feel my love so you'd know my last thoughts were of you. And then suddenly a voice spoke in my ear. Jamie, 'twas Anne's voice! Abraham was ranting away about vile flesh and that lot, and the voice at my ear said, 'Hark to the horses, Marg, hark to the horses!' I think I felt the hoof-beats through the ground under my bare feet, Jamie, before I heard them. Abraham was making a fearful row in his preaching. I knew 'twas you and I prayed my thanks, then looked up and there you were! Oh, the glory of it! The sweetness of it! And your face was like the Avenging Angel's when you went at Abraham."

"I went out of my mind and I wish I hadn't," I said, "because the killing of Abraham is something I'd like to savor for the rest of my life. To hell with him. Hector told me Anne's off to London to live with their father. We'll see her there. You'll love Angus. A fine old gentleman with a Scots accent you can sharpen rocks with."

"I remember him when I was a little girl," mused Marg. "Hector looks much like him, I think. How fine it is, Jamie, that your best friend and my best friend are they and were before you came half a world away to find me."

I suppose we must have slept sometime, because when I woke to the rattling roar of the reveille drums I felt incredibly refreshed and vigorous. It was marvelously home-like in the tent. While I shaved, Marg used my hairbrushes to brush and put up her hair and we talked splendid casual nonsense. Filkins came in, cheerily beaming, bearing breakfast and looked embarrassed when I told him not to forget dumping the chamber pot which was under the bed; that had been another delicious bit of homeliness, listening to Marg tinkle into it during the night. The rising sun shone on her through the open tent flap as we ate breakfast and our hearts rejoiced at our first breakfast together as man and wife. I smiled—did I ever stop smiling?—and said, "Today I'll resign and you and I will ride for Savannah. And we can put up at Foley's; that dog is dead. We'll do in that feather bed what I thought of doing there a long time ago."

She giggled. "And I was angry because you said as much and angry that you didn't try. 'Twas the night I came to love you and it frightened me. There's a thing I must do at Savannah if we have time before the ship will sail."

"Of course," I said. "I want you to buy every decent gown you can find and everything to go with them—shoes, bonnets, small clothes. I have enough money to buy most of the town and 'tis all yours, honeybun."

"I didn't mean that," she said, making her face into what she may have thought was a terrible scowl but was enchanting to me. "I mean that I shall borrow a kitchen and bake you a damned great wedding cake, then sit and watch you eat every crumb of it, you absconding villain!" I exploded with laughter. "You'll laugh from the other side of your face. Why, I'd no sooner put our beautiful cake in the oven when here came Rufus from Goodowns"—her face crumpled and the dear gray eyes filled—"I . . . I wanted to die, Jamie! Never, never, never leave me again, for now I know I shall surely die if I lose you again."

"Then you'll live forever," I said gently, taking her in my arms, "because from henceforth we'll be together forever. Your lips taste of fried egg and sausage and I envy the egg and sausage because they're inside you where I belong."

The troops were forming in the road when I rode forward to where the command group was taking post, and Hector, also mounted, came riding to join me. He seemed rather pale and haggard, and was subdued in his greeting. "Don't tell me you got drunk with Brutus last night," I chuckled.

326

"You bastard, Jamie," he said. "Why didn't you warn me? You knew what would happen! My God, those twins —both of 'em at once and either one by herself is a god-damned volcano! I'm a dead man! All night it went on!"

I roared with surprised delight. "Hector, I give you my word I never expected that or gave it a thought! I should have known! Aren't they the pair, though? Pretty, sweet and gentle?"

"And man-eating sharks in bed," he said, shaking his head. He grinned then. "Such hospitality in my father's house. They served me a fine supper and themselves for dessert with gladsome cries and furious zeal, and dessert lasted until cockcrow. For shame, laddie. They told me all. You will be chagrined to learn that Hetty considers my tool to be superior to yours, and may be pleased to know that Betty strongly disputed that assertion. My God, man, there I was in New York worrying myself dizzy, and here you were living in that fine house and tumbling those dear maids every night! What unbearable hardship!"

"I hope they told you I never touched 'em after I be-came betrothed," I said.

"And if you had," he said, "now that I've met that gallant and magnificent wife of yours, I would have slapped your damned face when I met you just now, my friend. That lady deserves the best in return for the honor she's given you, and you'll bloody well live up to it."

"Idiot," I laughed, "don't you think I know that?"

We reached the command group and after an exchange of salutes and greetings, Campbell said to me, "If Mrs. Reid will be up to it tonight, I'd be honored to have you and her at my table for supper."

"Why, thank you, sir," I responded, my mind on Sav-annah and London, "but I don't think I shall be here tonight."

Colonel Browne, listening nearby, said, "Oh, then you've spoken with Sergeant Bonnell this morning."

"No, sir, I haven't," I answered. "Is there something I should know?"

He nodded. "I told the other officers last night and didn't wish to disturb you, under the circumstances. As soon as the brigade steps off, I'm taking four hundred Rangers, your company included, over to Burke County courthouse to spring that trap and free the bait. There'll be a few cuts and bruises. I'll not order you to come along, in view of

327

special conditions." He eyed me carefully and I could feel the other officers watching me. " 'Tis your decision, Captain Reid."

Peter and John were not only my wife's brothers, they were my great good friends. Marg and I could depart from Georgia knowing they were safe. My resignation could wait a day or two. But if I had possessed that cursed second sight I would have thanked him kindly, refused, and tendered my resignation. I said cheerfully, "I'm ready, sir. Mrs. Reid will be delighted to have her brothers freed."

"We'll ride fast, forced march," Browne said. "The supply wagons will follow as swiftly as possible, carrying only food, water, medical stores and munitions. 'Twill be a night attack and I'll be using the Creeks." The Creeks were the company of Indian scouts he had trained, a Yankee-hating crowd so savage on patrols that they were not allowed to work without Rangers along to prevent atrocities. "When 'tis over we'll rejoin the brigade by means of the road that runs east of the courthouse to the Post Road. Details of the action will be explained when we're on the ground. Very well, sir, get to your company and follow Third Company at close interval."

Four hundred mounted Rangers riding at the gallop was an exciting thing to see and, still more, of which to be a part. Filled with exhilaration, I rocked along in the saddle and thought of how happy the brothers would be to see me among their rescuers and how pleased Marg would be that I went. It was not steady galloping. At intervals we dismounted and led the animals, cooling and resting them, and at other times we walked or trotted them. The Rangers were like a crowd of boys going to a picnic, singing and joking. It was the first time for them to fight unified as a force against the rebels and they were eager to show their mettle. Bonnell told me that Browne was purposely holding back in order not to outreach the supply train too far because in the battle we would need what was in the wagons, yet he wanted to arrive as quickly as possible before the rebels could summon reinforcements after their scouts, who would surely warn of our approach, saw we were in greater strength than expected.

After a time, we left the Post Road and bore off to the left on the one that led to the courthouse, so narrow that we had to go from four riders abreast to two, and the stumps, boulders, bogs and creeks slowed our advance to a pace no faster than a walk. Consequently, it was nearly dusk by the time we reached the vicinity of the crossroads, moved off the road and dispersed to the right and left within the edge of the woods, concealed from the view of the rebel force around the courthouse.

I was fairly familiar with the area, having done some drawing and watercoloring there during the summer. The two-story wooden frame courthouse dominated the scene, and behind it stood the fieldstone gaol. Nearby was a general merchandise store and a couple of farm dwellings. The land around had been cleared for cultivation, and from the woods we could see the enemy hard at work digging trenches in a rough circle, with the courthouse and gaol in the center.

Summoning the officers and sergeants to his observation point, Browne said quietly, "Take a long look yonder. Fix it in your minds. The men are Georgia and Carolina hasty militia. Twiggs and the brothers Few, three colonels, head 'em up. We shall attack as soon as it's dark." One company would make a stealthy surprise attack on one quadrant of the circle and as soon as the enemy was thus engaged, two companies would strike into the opposite quadrant as the main attack and the Creeks would simultaneously send fire arrows to the courthouse roof. "When the roof is well alight," said Browne, "Fourth Company will advance from its reserve position and deliver the prisoners and withdraw to reserve again. I'll be with Third Company in the attack. Captain Reid, report to me when your job is done and the reserve is available again." He went over the signaling system and that was about all there was to say, though I felt like asking him, knowing the solid construction of the gaol from personal inspection, if my people were supposed to open the door with teeth and fingernails.

Back with my company, with the men sprawled about eating their spartan supper of cracked corn washed down with water, I told them the task we had been given and Bonnell said, "First thing I thought of, Cap'n, when he come out with that, was a batterin' ram."

"There's no tree big enough around here," I answered, "to burst down that door. I know that place. The door's made of oak planks three inches thick and strapped with iron bands. The lock is inside the wood of the door and has a dead bolt that lodges into the granite doorframe.

329

The walls are two feet thick. There's a window at each end about eight feet off the ground, about one foot square. What we need is a cannon, which we don't have, and if we did we'd probably kill the prisoners inside with it."

One of the Rangers said, "We could dig under thet wall, reckon."

"No time," commented Bonnell. "Any way you look at it we're goin' to have rebels crawlin' up our backsides before we're done. Got to be another way o' crackin' that corn."

Crackin' corn. These southern Loyalist troops had shown the British Regulars how to crack dried corn into meal by driving nails through the bottom of an Army tin water bottle to create a jagged surface for grinding. An idea formed. I said to Bonnell, "The hinges. I know the hinge bolts can't be knocked out, but the small bolts that fasten the straps to the door—that's the weakest part."

"Still need a cannon for them," he observed.

"We have our cannon," I stated. "I want a keg of powder, a keg of turpentine, about a dozen water bottles and as many nails." Nails were a sparse commodity. "If you can't find nails, we'll use knives. The supply wagons must have arrived. Lively, man, we haven't much time!"

A few minutes later Fourth Company sat about in the darkening woods, hurriedly fabricating bombs. The water bottles were three-quarters filled with powder, and turpentine-soaked rags provided fuses. Bonnell had collected the nails; no prudent Georgian would ever fail to pocket a loose, unattended nail. I outlined the plan and Bonnell told off the specific assignments by name. On arrival at the gaol, nails would be hammered into the door close to the strap bolts, the bottles then hung and the fuses set alight by torches. Men not engaged with that would form a defensive line for the gaol.

Complete darkness had fallen by the time we were finished, so I lost no time in leading the men at a run to a position opposite the shortest route to the gaol, and before we got there both the diversionary and main attacks were under way amid a great crackling of gunfire, shouts and whoops. Close to the courthouse a brilliant shower of flaming arrows arched into the air and landed on the building's roof. The dry shingles caught like tinder. Their first job done, the Indians' voices sounded in a wild ullula-

330

tion as they joined the bloody skirmish somewhere within the rebels' fortifications.

The roof was in flames, lighting up the night. I drew my saber with one hand and pistol with the other, and with my heart in my mouth I cried, "Forward—GO!" We plunged over the rough winter-plowed field, running hard. The battle raged on the opposite and right side of the circle from us, and all the rebels were there except some dashing in and out of the flaming courthouse, apparently trying to save supplies stored inside. I could see our Indians there, tomahawking and shooting. Trenches appeared underfoot and we hurdled them.

Then suddenly we were at the gaol and my Rangers went to work quickly and as surely as if they had rehearsed it. I shouted, "Ahoy, in the gaol!"

A muffled chorus of confused shouting answered, and I bellowed, "Stand against the wall on each side of the door! We're blowing it down with powder! Get away from the door!"

My torchmen lighted their torches quickly with flint-and-steel and when the oil-soaked fuses flared in the bottles I shouted, "Cover! Take cover!" The gaol door resembled a Christmas tree and those of us in front of it dove around the corner of the building to crouch, waiting. The rebels had become aware of our presence and musket balls began humming in our direction. My defensive line commenced return fire. I could feel the heat from the burning courthouse and the scene was as light as day. I worried about the fuses going out, their fire smothered for lack of air inside the bottles. I was too tensely excited to be frightened.

When the explosion came, it surprised and disappointed me. Foolishly enough, I had vaguely anticipated all the fuses burning at the same rate so all the bombs would detonate at once. Instead it was like the swivel guns of the *Jason* firing raggedly at will. My heart sank. I should have used the keg half full of powder for one mighty bomb. Cautiously when the explosions ceased I peered around the corner. All the bottles were gone but the damned door still stood. I pushed against it and it gave a little. The strap bolts were loosened. I yelled at my men, "Rally here! Rally! Shoulders to the door!"

A dozen men hurled themselves against the massive door. The hinges broke free and the door fell in with a crash, and the prisoners piled out, shouting cheers. I shrieked, "All hands fall back! Fall back! Haul arse! Run like hell!"

Prisoners and Rangers, we headed for the distant woods. The rebels were now giving us close attention with their musket fire, coming after us in running groups. Now fright and panic drove me, lent wings to my feet. I heard Bonnell call out, warning the freed men, " 'Ware the ditches, 'ware the ditches!"

It was when we were nearing the outer, last trench and I was contemplating with some joy the lessening distance to the woods line, that a giant hammer blow struck me under one shoulder blade. I lurched and staggered, then the hammer crashed on my head. I saw a bright shower of stars and went tumbling and cartwheeling down into a bottomless hole, just as I had recently dreamed. Unhappily for Jamie Reid, the poor light from the burning building and the disordered conditions of the moment prevented my comrades from observing the incident.

Consciousness returned in three successive stages. First, I was bitterly cold. Second, I had never been so thirsty in my life, and the third was the worst of all: pain. Inside my head it throbbed and pulsed, shaking my soul, and in my body it was a hurting that was almost majestic in its awesome immensity. Opening my eyes, I found I was lying on my back and could not move. The color of the sky was a dark purple, a sweet, rich and thick color so tangible that if I could touch it I knew it would run through my hands with velvety softness, warmly voluptuous. There was an amazing number of stars. Fighting the horror of the pain, I studied the stars and sought out familiar constellations. There was Orion with his club. I could just see him by rolling up my eyes to where he was in the westering sky. Astonished, I saw two Orions. God had mysteriously created a twin in the heavens. Pondering that, my gaze wandered across the sky and fell on Arcturus, but there were two of him, too. The pain racked and tore at me. Astronomy continued. Every star had a mate. The purple vault paled with the gentle flush of dawn and the stars began to fade. The flames of pain were charring my soul.

A man's voice came from nearby. "If them Tory bastards come at us again, 'twon't be in the dark this time."

"Third time'll finish us, sure," said another voice. "I

ain't goin' to wait for it if Twiggs don't get us out o' this fix fair soon. Fred, look yonder. See what I see?"

"Aye," said the first voice. "One o' Browne's murderin' sons o' bitches. Dead-lookin'. Maybe he ain't. I'll tackle him with an ounce o' lead." There was a metallic click and dimly I realized they were talking about me. I was about to be shot, coldly and carefully. I welcomed it. Death would erase my agony. I hoped the ball would drill into my skull and punish the pain there.

"Fred," said the other man, "put that musket by. You know the rules about wastin' shot. You're a hell of a soldier."

"Goddamn right I'm a hell of a soldier," said Fred. "That's the goddamn proud truth. What I really am is one hell of a good wheelwright and box maker from Orangeburg, and the reason I ain't workin' at it now is because o' dirty scuts like that'n lyin' yonder. I declare 'tis still breathin'. Watch it jump when old Betsy gives it a kiss."

There was a loud noise and a new sudden pain coming from my leg, a monstrous one that sprang up like a tree of fire and blended with the old agony. It was too much. I went tumbling down into the bottomless hole again.

The pain brought me back to life. I was in a cart, lying, for some reason, on my belly and it was jolting and bumping like the hammers of hell. The pain was incredible. I wished somebody would shoot me again. It was more than mortal flesh could bear. The dark hole received me again. There was a jumble of voices and the pain came back, mangling and chewing at me, mashing and smashing. Words reached me. A mumbling, grumbling voice very near me—why, it was Hector!—was saying, "Damn you bloody goddamned soldiers to everlasting hell, you've killed him if you can't get him to Savannah where he can lie— oh, you numb-witted, stone-headed imbecile—"

Archie Campbell's voice said, "Enough of that, surgeon. He's my friend, too. He wasn't ordered. He volunteered. His wife is waiting outside this charnel house. What are his injuries?"

I wanted to know that myself and was unable to speak. "Tell her his right shin was broken, a simple fracture that I've patched and splinted. A ball has been removed from his back." Hector's voice was trembling oddly. "His skull is cracked, I believe, and his brain concussed—I can't tell

333

about that until he comes to. I've finished sewing up his scalp. Wait! His eyes are opening!"

With vast effort I managed to open my eyes to narrow slits and saw a pair of Hectors' faces as through a haze. I croaked, "Heckor, why two?"

The faces became enormous and four eyes searched mine. "Thank God. Jamie, do you see two of me, lad?"

" 'es," I mumbled. "Two." The effort exhausted me.

"Ah," he sighed in a long hiss, "so. It is. Jamie, the ball that hit your head addled your brain to affect your vision so you see two images of everything. Your skull is a bit split. You've also got two great swollen black eyes. Don't worry, you'll be as good as new one of these days and . . . and you can try killing yourself again, you damned silly colonial gowk! You—hold on! D'you hear? Don't let go, Jamie!" His voice broke and he lapsed into Gaelic.

Campbell's voice interrupted. "You'd best see to Colonel Browne. He's in some pain. I'll have Mrs. Reid—" Down into the dark hole I tumbled again.

There ensued a period of confused impressions, tortured nightmares of pain and people fussing with me to inflict more pain. Somebody seemed to be forever feeding me soup, making me drink water through a straw. Faces passed before me like double shadows in a half-remembered dream: Marg, her brothers, Colonel Browne, Filkins, Bonnell, Wallbrook, Archie, Hector. I continued to yearn for merciful death to release me from my hellish existence.

Full consciousness returned. I was lying on my back in a bed that moved. The pain was a dull, total ache and my head pulsed in great slow throbs. All was dark around me and I heard the sound of plodding horse's hooves, the grind of wagon wheels. The horrible thought came to me that I was dead and was being taken in a hearse to where a hole in the ground awaited me. Panicked, I cried weakly, "No, no, I'm not dead! You can't do this to me!"

Marg's voice, somewhere nearby, exclaimed excitedly, "Filkins! He's come back! Come take the reins!" Beyond my head light appeared, and Marg came kneeling beside me, two of her, her faces marvelously lovely. Her cool lips touched mine and she said, "Of course you're not dead, darling, but you must lie still and not move your head. Hector's orders. How do you feel?"

"I hurt like merry blue-balled hell," I mumbled, "and I see two of you. What's happening?"

334

"We're going to Savannah with some other wagons with injured soldiers," she answered, gently caressing my brow, "and some women and children. Filkins is with us to help. Colonel Campbell said we may have him on loan as long as I need him to help care for you."

From the driver's seat beyond my head, Filkins' voice rang like Bow bells, "Cheer-o, Cap'n! 'Tis bloody foyne to 'ear yer voice agyne!"

I said to Marg, "If we have any spirits aboard, I'd appreciate a dram."

She gave me rum and water, holding the mug so I could suck the drink through a bent straw without raising my head and during that first experiment I learned to keep my head still, for the slightest attempt to move it caused such excruciating pain that I damned near fainted dead away. Nevertheless, the rum induced a soporific effect and reduced the awareness of pain and from then on I kept myself fairly numb with it.

No amount of rum, however, could modify the agony when Marg, assisted by Filkins, changed the dressings on my wounds, particularly the one in my back which necessitated my being rolled on my side. The double vision problem frightened me; if it were permanent I could no longer work as an artist, let alone a portraitist. I was so afraid of the answer I couldn't bring myself to speak to Marg of it, and was marvelously relieved when she volunteered the information that Hector had assured her that if I remained still and let my head heal properly the headaches and double vision would vanish gradually. Marg took care of the unpleasant details regarding my bodily functions and when, embarrassed, I suggested she leave that to Filkins, she simply said, "You're flesh of my flesh, my own person, and I'd no more let him do this to you than to myself. I have joy in it, serving you."

Hector and I had paid Tondee to keep our room reserved for us, so Marg and I moved into it. Marg, who had brought her portrait along in the cart, hung the picture at my request on the wall opposite the foot of the bed so I could bask in her presence during her physical absence from time to time. Filkins, under Marg's supervision, perceptibly blossomed into an efficient manservant and nursing helper. Friends called and kept me abreast of military events. The rebels were swarming all through South Carolina and when a strong army threatened Augusta, Campbell hastily withdrew toward Savannah, pursued by a General Ashe. Mark Prevost, with a force at Hudson's Ferry on the Savannah, circled around behind Asch in a fifty-mile night march and decimated the rebel army in a smashing attack from the rear at Briar Creek bridge, news which delighted me until the half dozen or so British wounded were brought into town and Hector MacDonald was borne, cursing and growling, into Tondee's, with an ankle smashed by a rebel ball. A bit of money and persuasion to the occupant of the next room—a major of the New York Volunteers—installed Hector there as my neighbor, and Marg and Filkins had another patient to care for.

Hector, though, could move about on crutches and spent most of his waking hours in our room, and the caring for his wound was done by Filkins, profanely instructed by Hector. It appeared that the other surgeons unanimously wished to amputate the foot as the best means of saving the patient's life under the threat of blood poisoning, but Hector, waving a loaded pistol, had refused to be taken to the Army hospital and ordered his bearers to take him to Tondee's. "If I can't heal myself then I'm no physician and unless I am, let the damned foot kill me," he told me. "Never fear, my lad. I'll heal myself and you too, into the bargain, with the blessed help of your good wife and that wee Cockney creature. It strikes me that the luster of British arms might be immeasurably improved by the loss of that individual from the ranks, while Britain's corps of serving men might be equally improved. You've always needed a man to do for you, Jamie, I've thought. I doubt you'd have much trouble buying him out of military bondage."

"I'd like that," commented Marg. " 'Twould be nice when we get to London to have a servant I know and who knows me. Have you noticed he no longer wipes his nose on his sleeve and his fingernails are clean?"

There existed a process by which a soldier could purchase his discharge by paying to the Crown an amount equal to that which he would have been paid in wages for the remainder of his term of service. John Prevost had told me about it once. I said to Marg, "No need to worry about my servants—they'll all love you at first sight, especially Kitty. All right, I'll have a talk with John when next he calls."

With a physician, and a good one, at my bedside much

of the time, I made rapid improvement. The headache lessened and the double vision vanished. At long last Marg and I experimented with making love in the night and managed a fairly successful union with her riding me like a Valkyrie, triumphant and glorious. After several weeks I was able to get out of bed to use the chamber pot and move about on a crutch. Hector and I drank a deal of rum and, when Marg wasn't present, plotted Beauvoir's downfall, for Hector knew his martial career was ended and he would go to London with us. Lack of shipping kept us at Savannah, however, well into June, and by that time I was not only moving around with hardly a limp, but was taking morning rides through the town for exercise accompanied by Hector and Marg. Hector could walk without a cane but his limp was permanent, and he complained bitterly that it would put him off in his stride when he played the pipes, which he was determined to do regardless of the law against a civilian doing so.

Eventually the day arrived and Filkins, whose discharge had been granted, came with us when we boarded the Royal Navy brig *Sprite* which would take us to New Providence where there would be a fleet of sail making up to be convoyed to England. We were in high spirits as the ship dropped down the Savannah River to the sea, watching our last view of Georgia slip past, and I said to Hector, "There goes our carefree youth and witless abandon, old son. We've been chewed up and spat out by the silly old Grim Reaper and while I don't know about you, I've taken the hint. From now on 'tis to be for Jamie Reid hard work, a seat by the chimney hearth, a sweet wife and a houseful of merry young Reids. Go ye forth and do likewise, for carousing days are done."

"I've a mind to do that," he answered, admiring Marg. "If Jamie Reid with all his calflike blunderings can capture the likes of this lady, there's hope for me, I fancy, though what there is about you that should merit her affection defeats me."

She said, smiling, "And despite your own calflike blusterings you know well what it is, Hector, and if you could bring yourself to speak the truth you'd admit you dearly love the man."

"Love? This jackanapes?" He was scornful. "God knows how I tolerate him! If it weren't for his absurdities I'd be a whole man today instead of having to clump about with

337

one leg shorter than the other! Let me give you the seasoned advice of kindly old Uncle Hector: never let the man out of your sight and guidance for an instant, lest he bumble into more Jamie Reid-like disasters. Now I'm freed of his responsibility I shall most certainly have the time to sift through the perfumed garden of British ladies and select the lucky one who will become my lady."

Chapter XX

THE *Sprite* was beating down the North West Providence Channel against the trades, beset by heavy rain squalls that didn't last long but dumped so much rain while they did that it was as if giant water buckets in the sky were being emptied on us every few minutes, momentarily blinding the watch on deck. Consequently, after supper we passengers remained below at the table, lighthearted and filled with pleasant anticipation over the prospect of changing to a London-bound packet at Nassau in a day or two. The time was just about sunset and I was in the middle of a description of the pleasures offered by Vauxhall Gardens, to which Marg was listening with happy attention, her lovely gray eyes sparkling.

"And I still owe you one," declared Hector, "for pushing me overboard and making me swim behind the boat all the way to Westminster that night, simply because I repeated a bit of folklore concerning left-handed people being in league with the Devil, after you getting so drunk at Vauxhall you couldn't find your behind with the help of a search party—"

At that moment all hell erupted on deck. Men shouted, "Quarters! Battle quarters! All hands, all hands!" Bare feet thudded, the carriages of the ship's twelve-pounders in the waist rumbled, and boatswains' pipes squealed. Leaping to my feet, I exclaimed to Marg, "Stay here below!" From somewhere close by there was a thunderous blast of cannon fire, followed immediately by a crashing, rending noise on deck. By the time I found my pistol the *Sprite*'s guns were in action, and rushing on deck I saw a large topsail schooner, her decks crowded with armed, uniformed sailors, coming alongside with men swinging grapnels. The *Sprite*'s gunners were firing into the enemy hull at point-blank range. In the fading light of day I saw the French fleur-de-lis ensign at the main peak.

Lieutenant Rolke, captain of the *Sprite,* his face oddly calm, shouted to the crew who were assembling in the waist, "Stand by to repel boarders!" He said to me, "The Devil appeared like magic out of a rain squall."

Swivel gun shot and musket fire were coming from the enemy, hot and heavy. The grapnels from her were hooking onto our bulwarks and as fast as our men hacked through the lines more were thrown and the two ships were less than six feet apart. My single-shot pistol would be of little use. The ship's armorer came running by with an armful of cutlasses and I seized one. "I'll bear a hand," I said to Rolke. "If I'm hurt, please look to my wife." The men of both ships, bristling with pikes and cutlasses, were roaring at each other across the narrowing space. The captain of the schooner was shouting something in our direction from his quarterdeck, waving a sword.

"The silly ass demands I strike," said Rolke. "Mr. Reid, you'll not be accused of cowardice if you stand clear and go below. I know your position well and General Prevost informed me of the matter before we sailed." He drew his sword, watching the enemy crewmen prepare to board his vessel.

A wave of anger swept me. "Goddamn Prevost and that goddamn position! A King's ship is—" The Frenchmen poured over the bulwarks, sending up a great shout, and I left the sentence unfinished as I ran to join the defenders. It was the *Jason* and *Sea Ranger* all over again, except that the boarders were no ignorant, untrained ploughboys, they were seasoned veterans of the French Navy. It was hot work. I quickly discovered I had not yet quite recovered my normal strength after having been laid up for so long, and huffed and puffed mightily as I slashed, parried, stabbed and cut, frequently switching the cutlass from one hand to the other. Perspiration dripped from my eyebrows and I gasped for breath in the milling, screaming mob.

From my own experience and what other survivors of such fights have told me, close boarding action is usually of fairly short duration due to the extreme expenditure of energy, emotional stress and sheer savage bloodshed in the encounter, yet to the participants it seems interminable. One loses his sense of orientation, blocking everything from his consciousness but the enemy in front of him. My weap-

340

on came to weigh about fifty pounds and my eyes were smarting so I could hardly see. In addition to the dusk there seemed to be a heavy fog; the men around me had a hazy appearance. Then I heard voices shouting for quarter in English with a French accent and became aware that there were no more enemies in front of me. Lowering the point of the cutlass, trying to catch my breath and blowing hard, I saw I was on the deck of the French vessel with a handful of British seamen around me. Wounded and dead men lay about. The fog was not fog; it was smoke billowing from the ship's main hatch and I saw tongues of flame in it. "Afire, she's afire!" shouted one of the men with me. "The bloody powder magazine! Abandon, abandon!"

We made for the bulwarks and through the haze I could just make out the *Sprite* lying about two hundred yards distant. During the fight the grapnel lines had been cut. I started to step up onto the rail to go overside and the world suddenly ended with a great noise and a brilliant light. I had a flying, birdlike sensation and knew no more.

I opened my eyes and beheld a barbarically exotic sunrise, and at that moment a deep male voice exclaimed in surprise, "Hoo-ee, you ain't dead, mon?"

I sat up. I was on a hatch cover, floating in a calm sea. A dead British seaman lay beside me, mouth and eyes open. Alongside was a wherry with little paint remaining on it, and in the stern sheets below a much-patched spritsail sat a large, broad-shouldered dark brown man wearing short canvas trousers and a woven palm frond hat. "Good-morning," I said.

He had a cheerful smile, showing brilliantly white teeth. "Plenty pretty mornin' for you and me, not for you shipmate, mon. Who win that fight? Last night I was fishin' over to Skillet Shoal, heard the shootin' then—hoo-ee! The light and boom was like Judgment Day!"

"We won, I suppose," I answered. "The French boat blew up after my friend here and I had boarded during the fight." The seaman must have pulled me onto the hatch cover and then died during the night. "If you'll be kind enough to take me ashore so I can reach Nassau, I'll be obliged."

"Long way to Nassau town, mon," said the man. "I'll take you ashore to Cibola—goin' home anyways—along of this ship you sailin'. Cibola folk be plenty happy for this

341

article, but you crew, he got to go drink at Fiddlers' Green, poor boy."

I rolled the body into the sea and said, "God's mercy on you and thank you, shipmate." The corpse floated, bumping against the hatch cover as if unwilling to desert me.

The man in the wherry, watching it, said, "Them as goes down to the sea in ships gets it for a 'ternal home. Lord take you and bless you, amen." He said to me, "Come aboard whilst I make her fast for towin'. Goin' be plenty slow pull. You want sweet water, have her from jug yonder under the thwart." Busying himself with the towline while I drank the brackish water with pleasure, he said, "You one plenty big fish to haul from the ocean. Speak like officer, got no uniform, fightin' battles. What kind fish you, mon?"

"I was a passenger in the Navy ship," I answered. "My name is James Reid and I'm on my way from Savannah to London. I must get to Nassau as soon as possible. There's a fleet of sail making up for the voyage to England."

With the hatch cover in tow, he hauled on the spritsail sheet and settled back to the tiller, chuckling. "James. Me, I'm Jimmy. You don' look like no James—nor like Jimmy nor Jim. Jamie sounds right, eh? Jamie and Jimmy. How do, Jamie!" His dark face was apologetic. "Cibola islan's a far piece from Nassau, mon, and trade boats stopped comin' a whiles past on account of them Yankee Whigs and Frenchies cruisin' these grounds."

"Nassau's only a few days sailing in this wherry," I said. "I'll pay you well to take me there, enough to buy a bigger and better boat than this."

His sudden calculating expression reminded me that pirates infested these waters in the not-too-distant past. "Eh, mon, you rich? Got plenty money?"

Warily, I said, "Not really. I've only managed to put some by for a rainy day, an occasion such as this. I'm far from being rich."

His brown eyes inspected me and a slow grin blossomed, then he threw back his head and shouted with laughter. "Hoo-ee! You think Big Jimmy's a pirate, eh! Take you to cave, hold for ransom! Pay up or walk Jimmy's plank, eh? Mon, my gran'pa on white side, he was one plenty bad pirate, so say my pa."

Liking him, I smiled, "No, you're not quite right for a buccaneer."

"Ho, what you know about pirates?" he scoffed. "How many pirates you ever see with your own two eyes, Jamie?"

"Hundreds," I assured him. "How can I forget how they killed me? They lashed me to the mast and pelted me to death with ladies' powder puffs. I carry the horrid bruises to this day."

He guffawed. "Mon, even should I be able to carry you to Nassau town, I'm not. Folks at Cibola need stories like that. No, sah, I'm plenty sorry, you got to wait for trade boat. This boat needed for fishin' every day." He gestured to the two baskets of fish near me. "Offshore, where big ones like them and you live, big fish Jamie. You stay to my house, best one on Cibola, plenty food and moko for drinkin', the wench keep house clean and neat, Bristol fashion. Bimeby one day a boat come by, take you to Nassau, eh?"

I could not complain. Except for a slight ringing in my ears from the explosion of the French powder magazine, I was unharmed. I reflected that the *Sprite* would have searched for survivors for a time, then darkness would have ended rescue efforts. Having encountered one enemy vessel, Rolke would have then pressed on with all sail for Nassau in any case. So I counted my blessings and among them was my new friend, Big Jimmy. News was scarce on isolated Cibola island, I learned, and Big Jimmy was anxious to know what was happening in the American rebellion, so as the wherry slowly towed the heavy, cumbersome hatch cover over the blue sea through the day, I told him what I knew of the war. The Cibolans were nominally British subjects, but from Big Jimmy's detachedly interested attitude I gathered they were rather like spectators at a cricket match cheering for their side to win.

Late in the afternoon, Cibola rose from the sea, first a dark, low-lying cloud, then a rather small island topped with several green forested hills and surrounded by aquamarine shallows from which coral heads and reefs sprouted, which I could see would serve to deter casual maritime visitors. The wherry entered a cove lined with white, sandy beach, and a crowd of some thirty or forty men, women and children, laughing and calling out, greeted us. Men ran out into the water to lay hold of the wherry and rush it to the water's edge, where they hauled it up to the high tide mark, all laughing and chattering. The skin colors of the people ranged from lighter than mine under the sun-

343

brown to a rich, wholly African blue-black; from tawny hair to crinkly black polls.

Big Jimmy and I got out of the boat and he announced, grinning around at them, "This here's Mister Jamie Reid, skipper of yonder hatch cover. He was cruisin' down channel under full sail goin' sixty knots when a pelican stole his mainmast and the sea horses ate the straw bottom out, so I salvaged him. Goin' to stay to my house. You gals keep you hands out'n his britches for a spell 'cause he's a mite peaked from bein' castaway." A laughing squeal went up from the women, some of whom were damned pretty. "I'll take this big fish and some o' what's in the baskets, and you folks help yourselfs." Looping a string through the gills of several fish, he said to me, "Le's go home, Jamie, see what that female woman got cooked for us in the pot. Mon, they best be plenty, two hungry mens to feed."

Leading the way through a grove of coconut palm trees, he strode to a neat, small, palm-thatched and white-washed house built of stone; I later found it was made of coral blocks, not stone. Near the house a woman, dressed in a knee-length sort of shift, was taking dried laundry down from a line. In a woven basket on the sand an infant slept peacefully. The mother, not hearing our footsteps in the loose sand, went on working as we approached from behind.

"Hey, female woman!" exclaimed Big Jimmy. "See the big fish Big Jimmy take from the sea this day!"

Startled, she whirled and hissed angrily, "Hush, you wake the pickanin, big baboon!" Then she saw me—and I saw Nancy Harris, my Nassau vision.

Her eyes became saucers and her lips moved without sound. I muttered weakly, "Good God."

The smile started tremulously, disbelieving, then became transfigured joy. "Rob! Oh, Rob! You real? You truly here? You ain't jumby?"

"I'm real," I said, slightly numb. "Are you?"

She dropped the clothes she was holding and flung herself at me, embracing me, kissing me. "God, he hear me!" Looking up at me with glad, starry eyes, she was just as pretty as ever, more so. "God was hearin' me all the whiles! Sittin' up yonder on his own cloud!"

Bewildered and taken aback, I could only think that my new friend had brought me to his home in good faith only

344

to have his guest turn out to be his wife's former lover and she was putting on a most indiscreet performance. Sure enough, he roared, "What the hell's at you, Nancy wench? You crazy? You stop before I bash you a good one on the stupid female head!"

Holding both my hands in hers, she laughed with delighted exuberance. "This big fish—he my own Mister Rob from Nassau that I don' tell you about, 'cause you don' believe things 'ceptin' what you see."

I said to the fiercely frowning Big Jimmy, "I must confess this is rather a surprise. The truth is, I met your wife when—"

Nancy's laughter pealed. "Wife! Hoo-ee, that big baboon, he my brother, Rob! He ain' got no wife, for all the gals call him Big Jimmy!"

"Come the day I get one," he said, looking her up and down, "she goin' have more meat on her bones than you, skinny wench."

She looked first rate to me, filled out beautifully. I said to her, "I'm afraid I'll be an imposition, what with your husband and Big Jimmy in the house. Perhaps I should stay elsewhere."

"Husban'!" snorted Big Jimmy. "Some sister I got!"

"My husban', he go away," she smiled. "Been gone plenty long time."

Jimmy slapped me on the back and beamed, "You know Nancy one time down to Nassau, I ain't askin' questions, she a big gal, ol' enough to make her own way." He scowled at her ferociously. "You don' get to feedin' us a big mess o' vittles, we goin' slice up you pickanin. Jamie, you like col' slice baby, tender small fellow?" He rubbed his belly and smiled fiendishly. "M-hm! Plenty good with hot pepper sauce, eh?"

Nancy squealed in horror. "Quit that talk, not even foolish jokes! Shame!" She smiled at me and said softly, "Heaven come to Cibola, make me want to cry and laugh, one same time. This you house now, Rob. You and Jimmy go in, have moko, be at home." She went back to gathering up her laundry, trying to watch me at the same time as though she were fearful I would disappear.

The house appeared much bigger on the inside, cool, immaculate and plainly furnished. The main room served as kitchen, sitting and dining room, with two bedchambers opening into it. A black iron pot simmered in the fireplace over a driftwood fire and the contents smelled delicious. Big Jimmy produced a pottery jug and poured a murky fluid into two cups made from coconut shell halves, explaining it was moko, made from the fermented cabbage-like bud of the coconut trees. At first it smelled and tasted awful, but after a drink or two I rather liked it. It had a powerful authority, especially on my utterly empty stomach.

Big Jimmy asked me, "Why she call you Rob, Jamie? You try to fool her?"

"When I met her before," I told him, "I was on His Majesty's service and had to use the false name of Robert Allston."

Nancy, entering at that moment with laundry and child, heard that and said, "I knew that time it ain' you name. What you true one?" I told her, watching her set the baby down and busy herself at the cooking pot, and she said musingly, "Jamie's plenty better. We got plenty James, Jimmies, good name, eh? Slumgullion, she ain' but almost done, maybe few minutes more." The baby woke and squalled. "You men ain't only ones hungry." Picking up the child she came to the table and sat down, pulled her garment down to expose a lovely brown breast, and gave the baby suck. It was a pretty picture.

"How old is your child?" I asked.

"Maybe four months," she answered. "I come home by las' tradin' schooner to birth him." She giggled. "You should hear what Big Jimmy say and how he look when I walk up the beach pushin' watermelon in my belly, hoo-ee!"

"You expect me to be happy, run and shout, you loose wench?" her brother demanded. "You and me, why ain' we either black or white, eh? 'Cause our grammas and their grammas listen to sweet words o' white sailormen, go into bushes and make jigajig."

"No white sailorman take me in bushes," she said, looking down at the infant whose tiny hands rhythmically kneaded the breast he greedily suckled. She raised her face and smiled at me, a secret, proud smile, and then abruptly held the child out to me. "Take him, see how han'some he is."

Taking the baby gingerly, I was surprised at his lightness. He was naked and plump, his skin a bronzy color. His little mouth continued to make sucking motions and a thread of milk ran off his chin. He blinked and goggled

346

up at me and I saw he had one brown eye and one green eye. I goose-pimpled and my neck hair bristled. I looked at Nancy and she reached over and took her son back, saying, glowing, "Han'some, ain' he?"

Stunned, wonderment and a sort of religious awe gripped me. I whispered, "My God, his eyes. Nancy, his eyes! D'you mean . . . this child . . ." Words failed me.

Her face was radiant, the baby sucking again contentedly. "Name o' Robert James Harris—firs' name for the papa, secon' for uncle. We call him Little Jimmy."

"There's no chance . . . somebody else . . ." I could hardly talk.

Laughing joyfully, she said, "Only one man I ever did jigajig with, and he my husban' in God's eyes, I his wife."

"Eh, wait now!" exclaimed Big Jimmy. "You don' tell me that! You don' say anything about that fellow."

"I tell you now, big baboon brother," she smiled at him. "That is the only man I ever love and when I see him now my heart, she rings like a bell."

I was filled with an incredible pride and happiness. "Nancy," I said, savoring the marvelous picture of her with my son at her breast, "you are wonderful, unbelievable and magnificent! He's absolutely perfect! How good you are!"

Her eyes were full of love. "Our baby, he's perfect 'cause you are, Jamie."

Big Jimmy emitted a bull-like roar and leaped to his feet. "Woman! You sittin' there sayin' this fellow I haul from the sea, this one, he the papa of Little Jimmy?"

She looked at me, twinkling, and I said to her brother, " 'Tis true, Jimmy. If you'll look closely, you'll see we have the same eyes, and the time is right. I'm very proud. Nancy is a good, sweet and wonderful girl, and I feel humble at what she's done. Nancy, I'm sorry, I can't marry you legally. I was married some time after I saw you, in Georgia, and I was on my way to London with my wife when I went overside."

"Bless all," muttered Big Jimmy, sitting down again and staring at me, "so 'tis, green and brown. I got a sister with a bastard. I go fishin', haul in the bastard's papa. Take him home, she say they man and wife—"

Putting the baby into his basket, Nancy said as she ladled out bowls of the slumgullion, "Legal married's one thing Cibola ain' got, Jamie. Love and God-married we got."

The stew was superb. The world was superb. Nancy, eating across the rude plank table from me and also devouring me with her sparkling eyes, was superb. Big Jimmy, tucking the food away with gusto, said, "Mighty tasty, wench, mighty tasty. Near as good as col' slice pickanin, which I'm plenty glad we don' eat now on account o' it might give his papa a bellyache." He grinned at me. "Ho, so it ain't a fish I fetch home, 'tis a brother in the law, 'ceptin' no law. Time you was wed, Nancy."

She looked at me, suddenly anxious. "Will you take me, Jamie?"

Puzzled, I said, "I don't understand."

"We ain' got parsons," explained Big Jimmy. "Oldest person in you family, they make the weddin'. You live on Cibola, you got a God-wife here and a God-baby from God-marriage, you make Cibola weddin' to make you man and wife for Cibola folk. You got one more wife someplace, it don' matter. You here. You take this female woman for Miz Reid, mon?"

Her eyes were pleading. I said, "But there already is a Mrs. Reid and I love her very much."

"She ain' on Cibola, Jamie," said Big Jimmy, "and Nancy is, so's our pickanin. We got one Cibola family." She pointed to one of the bedchambers. "Yonder we sleep man and wife and baby."

It trickled through to my understanding. For all the lack of formalities and casualness of it, the Cibolans insisted on some degree of solemnizing the union of a man and woman. I smiled at Nancy and said, "You do me great honor. I'll be delighted to take you as my Cibola wife, Nancy."

Big Jimmy laid down his wooden spoon and leaned back, beaming. "Then you Mister and Miz Reid from now on, God bless you, by the word o' Big Jimmy Harris. Now I got a rich brother by Cibola law and Little Jimmy ain' no bastard no more, got his real papa and mama by him."

"I'll tell you this, Jimmy," I told him, "regardless of my real wife or anything else, I know I'm very much a part of this family and I'll see you have enough money for a fine boat. And I'll see that Nancy and Little Jimmy never want for anything. I want my son"—I paused, celebrating the grand sound of that word—"to have all the things that will make him a gentleman, and that means that he shall have a decent education at proper schools."

"*Our* son, Jamie!" Nancy was ecstatic. "We build him like a ship, you and me. You laid the keel, and me, I launched him!"

Big Jimmy had consumed three bowls of stew and belched with satisfaction. Getting to his feet, he announced, "I'm goin' by the beach, gam with folks. Tell about married family in my house." He strode out.

Looking after him, Nancy said, "That Big Jimmy, he one plenty good fellow. He ain' comin' home till late, late, so' you and me can be married, talkin' by ourselfs and makin' jigajig. You talk to me, Jamie, whilst I wash dishes, clean up. You voice makes me shiver from my heart down to you know where, and you-know-where been plenty ready since I set my eyes on you."

"I want to kiss my bride," I grinned, going to her and taking her in my arms. There was no gradual warming up; she exploded with unbridled passion and I had forgotten her barbaric carnality. She was a roaring fire out of control and in seconds we were in the bedchamber and on the bed, still clothed, and our coupling was furiously mindless, primitive almost to savagery. I lost track of the number of times she climaxed, her lithe, supple body arching, shuddering and straining, writhing and thrusting, even though we had been only a few minutes on the bed. When I had to stop, she pulled my head down and kissed me long and deeply, then smiled up at me, "I know you don' love me, Jamie, but I got enough love for you for two of us. I give you all o' me, wish there was more to give. I don' mean about jigajig, I mean all. I love with all I got. You say to me, 'Nancy, die for me,' I do that, Jamie. Now I got to clean up after supper, feed Little Jimmy again, then we come back to bed, eh, and shake the house down."

Thus began the most tranquil, simple chapter in my life. The Cibolans accepted me as Nancy's husband and Little Jimmy's father, restored to her through a pleasant little miracle. The men worked hard at fishing, building and repairing houses and sometimes hunting the wild goats and pigs that roamed the hills, using spears, while the women tended garden plots, cared for the children, cooked, made cloth from tree bark and watched over the fermenting pots from which was made the potent moko drink. Young children ran about naked, and nudity was the rule for all when bathing in the ocean or in the streams. There were frequent impromptu parties in the coconut grove near our house, begun quite by accident and developing into a community rout, with moko flowing like water and much choral singing to music supplied by wooden flutes and goatskin drums. They were all good singers, and the women sang one part while the men another, and the enchanting sweet sound of it was something I always in later years remembered with pleasure.

Nancy made me a pair of canvas trousers and palm frond hat, Cibola style, and I was soon dark brown from working in the sun with the men. I picked up the dialect easily enough and was soon regarded as a fellow Cibolan in good standing. After initially falling into deep depression through thinking about Marg, I learned to suppress thoughts of her; there was no ship to take me from Cibola and the only way I could make my second separation from her at all bearable was to take advantage of and be happy with what fortune had sent me, or placed me in.

I became an artist again quite suddenly. Nancy and I were swimming and playing well out from the beach in water up to my armpits and we were both overtaken by physical desire at the same time, so being conveniently naked we came together like a couple of fish. At the height of my transports I became all at once poignantly aware of the beauty of what we were doing, the sea, sky, beach, Nancy—the entire little world of Cibola, where all hues, tints and values were perfectly keyed as well as relationships between the charming Cibolans. When we went back to the beach I told Nancy about it, going on at great length about the striving of the artist to duplicate in pigment what God did with light. Surprisingly, though she had never seen a painted picture, she understood and asked many perceptive questions. "You want this paint, them brushes," she said, "go see Ol' Diggory at his house."

Her "lookman," or obeahman as he was sometimes called, lived back in the hills and I had never seen him. When a Cibolan had a difficult problem, he would make a pilgrimage to Old Diggory with a gift of food or some small thing of value such as a plank washed in from the sea. The witch doctor was the island magistrate, physician, prophet, magician, skilled in the lore of earth, fire, water and light, and he had always lived there, unchanged within the memory of the oldest inhabitant among the people.

Following Nancy's directions, I walked up into the hills—consultations had to be accomplished in strict privacy—and on a hilltop, under an ancient tree, I found Old Diggory sitting on a low three-legged stool in front of his house, a wattle hut. He wore a sheetlike immaculate white robe, and was a tiny, frail man with skin the color of lampblack. His wizened face was a marvel of seams and wrinkles and I could hardly see his sharp, alert eyes that were nearly lost in the wrinkled folds of his eyelids. Motionless, he watched me approach.

"Good-day to you, Diggory," I said. "I am Jamie Reid, husband to Nancy Harris." I sat down on the earth before him.

"I see you." The voice was a crackling rustle. "Before, now, then."

"Yes," I commented, "Nancy told me about the before. You are a wise man and I have come to ask for your help."

"I see you," he murmured.

"You know I am an artist," I said. "Making pictures is like breathing to me. It is my life and reason for living, and on Cibola I have nothing to paint with. How may I get paints and brushes?"

"I see you," he said, unmoving. "What colors?"

"If I have what we call primary colors," I answered, "I can mix all others. The primary colors are red, yellow and blue. A white would be helpful, though I can do without it."

He was silent for a long minute, then: "I see you. Water or oil for mix?"

I began to understand his reputation and felt a bit awed. "Oil." There was no paper on the island, so watercolors were precluded.

"I see you," he rustled. "Brushes. Sticks, got pig hair tied to end. Paint like water or thick like coconut butter?"

"Pasty like coconut butter," I replied.

"I see you," he acknowledged. "How much? How many brush?"

Other than simply to paint, I had no specific intention in mind. Thinking about it, my Cibola family leaped to mind. The picture formed. I said, "Enough to paint a picture all over one side of the Harris house."

"I see that and it will be plenty good," he said in a remarkable burst of loquacity. "Soon."

351

Nodding, I said, "As soon as possible. It will not only make me happy, but will make others so."

Again there was a silence, longer this time. "I see you, Jamie Reid," he said finally. "When picture finish I make smokes for you to see. I make paint for you, brushes. In you own country you make paint, no magic. No magic here. Berry, root, bugs, squid ink, dirt from groun'—all color there. Ol' Diggory know. Go now, come back two day. I see you." The audience was over.

I spent the next two days mainly studying the blank house wall, composing the mural in my mind, full of delighted anticipation. With a stick I experimented with compositions in the loose sand in front of the wall. Nancy and Big Jimmy spoke in hushed tones in my presence, for to them I was about to perform some great magic with the help of Old Diggory. When the two days were up I practically ran all the way up the winding paths to the lookman's house and was utterly delighted with what he had done. Set in a frame of boards, the colors were contained in goatskin bags, with flaps to keep out dirt. The red, yellow and blue pigments were absolutely pure, so sweet that tears welled in my eyes, and in addition he had come up with a brilliant, sparkling white made out of what only God and Old Diggory knew. There was a pot of oil that smelled rather like a mixture of cotton seed and varnish, and bless his prescient old heart, he had included a pot of turpentine, raw and cloudy, but nevertheless turps. The brushes were straight, smoothly carved slender sticks with thick, neatly trimmed hog hair bound to the ends in various sizes from fine to very broad. I was more awed than ever; it was as if he had read my mind when we had talked. I asked fervently, "How can I ever thank you? This is beyond belief!"

"I see you," the whisper rustled. "Go work."

I fled down to the coconut grove, clutching my precious paints and brushes, and immediately went to work. Posing bewildered Nancy sitting on the sand with my son in her lap, I quickly roughed in their figures on the wall with a few directional lines made with a charred stick, then myself standing, and Big Jimmy approaching, holding a string of fish. The marks were unrecognizable to any but me, and curious Cibolans came to sit and watch my mystifying activities at the wall of the house. The whitewashed coral surface would, I reflected, soak up paint like a sponge and

352

I had no idea of the drying time of the pigment. I decided the entire composition would have to be done as quickly as possible, all at once.

I had acquired a sizable, smoothly polished piece of hardwood board for a palette, and went to work, painting faster than I ever had before, fairly flinging the paint on the wall and using both hands, constantly running back and forth from a viewing point near Nancy to see how the work was progressing. The figures took shape, grew in depth. Once, I became aware that the entire population was sitting and squatting silently among the palm trees, watching.

Painting Nancy's likeness, I saw her pretty face illumined with a radiant glory as she saw what was happening. It is impossible to adequately describe in words the transcendent beauty of her expression, but it was not impossible to paint, and paint it I did, my heart overflowing in the warmth of her selfless love for me. I had done enough self-portraits for practice exercises that my likeness was no difficult thing done from memory. Big Jimmy's face, figure and aura were distinctively marked in my mind and he was easily brushed in. Little Jimmy, being a baby, required thoughtful analysis for a recognizable likeness, but he went in quickly once I had the key.

With the coconut grove's sun-splotched trunks and sand for a background, I hastily daubed in the mass of spectators, giving likenesses to the nearest ones. The entire mural, close up, resembled nothing but a jumble of color; from ten or more feet away it all fell together and I was proud of it when I walked back to Nancy, grinning triumphantly. She and the crowd were still, their eyes wide, entranced, as they gazed at the house wall. Kneeling, I kissed Nancy and Little Jimmy, and laughed, "Eh, female woman, not bad for four hour work, you think?"

The sound of my voice broke the spell. The Cibolans leaped to their feet, cheering and exclaiming, pointing and gesticulating, but Nancy continued to stare at the wall. "Jamie," she said, her face suddenly showing fear, "you take our souls and put them on wall! You take my love, give it to that Nancy! Please, don' give my love . . ." She was nearly in tears.

With an arm around her, I said gently, " 'Tis but a picture of you and your love as I see and feel it. Whenever you look at the picture you'll know that I knew your love

353

and this is my thanks, my humble gratitude for gifting me with it."

Big Jimmy came striding through the grove carrying a string of fish exactly as I had painted him. "Hoo-ee!" he boomed. "Why all you lazy folk here? Why you ain'—" He stopped short and stared at the house. "God in Heaven," he muttered, eyes wide, "see that thing on my house. A lookin' glass! We here, still we there!" Then he roared with delighted laughter, dropped his fish and embraced me, shouting, "You bigger obeahman than Ol' Diggory! Magic! No wonder you rich, mon, makin' pictures like that! Ho, all han's! We got to have one plenty big party, this day, now!"

The mural on Big Jimmy's house was probably the greatest event in Cibola's history. Nobody wanted to leave off looking at it, as if they were afraid it would disappear if they turned their backs for a moment. Families built cookfires in the grove and the party was launched early. Jugs of moko circulated. Flutes and drums appeared and singing began. Little Jimmy slept peacefully in his basket amid the uproar and his mother clung to me as if I might vanish along with the magic painting at any second. Big Jimmy, drinking lustily, kept coming to me, shaking my hand and slapping my back. When dark fell, the flickering light from the cookfires, which had become festive bonfires, made the figures of the mural seem to move, much to the awe and delight of the crowd.

The evening and party were well advanced and I was suffering no pain from countless libations of moko when Old Diggory himself came slowly through the dancers, singers and drinkers to me, the crowd falling back respectfully. He leaned on two canes and moved slowly, with great care. In front of me he halted and peered up at me. "I see you," he rustled, faintly heard above the party din. "Good picture. Now you come, see smokes." He turned away and headed through the grove away from the people.

Big Jimmy said solemnly, "Firs' time he tell mon to come his house. He got plenty big magic for you, Jamie. You go now, don' wait."

"Me, I'm scared for you, Jamie," said Nancy, holding me, her head on my chest, "but you got to go. Ol' Diggory, he don' say come 'ceptin' 'tis powerful conjure. I wait for you to home, Jamie."

The full moon lighted the island almost like daylight

354

and I quickly caught up with the slow-moving old man as he mounted the slopes. The journey down from his house and back again was obviously a tremendous effort for him and I was deeply touched. "I'm honored and pleased that you came to see my picture," I said to him.

"Don' talk," he sighed.

The hill path was quite steep, his progress slow. I doubt he weighed more than fifty pounds. I said, "You must be weary. Let me carry you, Diggory."

Surprisingly, he stopped moving and said, "Carry. You don' tell. You, me, we two make conjure magic. You picture great magic. Carry me."

Pleased at being admitted as a fellow sorcerer to his intimacy, I scooped him up and decided he weighed no more than thirty pounds, robe, canes and all. The effort of climbing and carrying dissipated the effects of the moko I had consumed, and I was sober when we reached his hut. He said, "Come inside, sit."

I sat on the earth floor in the dark while he moved about, and then a small fire in the center of the floor under a roof hole lighted the place. The fire was burning in the center of a large six-pointed star outlined in white powder. Old Diggory sat on his three-legged stool opposite me and behind him, hung from a string stretched across the 'hut, were a number of cloths inscribed with cabalistic designs. Passing a hand over the fire he muttered something and the flames turned blue. He had shed the white robe and wore only a breechclout on his tiny shriveled body. "I see you," he murmured. "Now you see you. I speak no more to you, finish, after speakin' this: you go by bad paths, plenty bad paths, to fin' good one. One thing you got to fin' before. Maybe you die before, don' ever fin'." It was those damned roads again. I felt a quiver of irritation and he rustled, "You don' like, don' matter, don' change paths. Look in smokes. See. Think. I tell you nothin' more." Moving his clawed old hands over the fire, he set up a mumbling chant in some language unknown to me, and the flames eerily ceased flickering and became a steady glow. The blue became purple, then violet and that changed to red, and at the same time the light became a cylinder mounting upward. I felt dizzy, staring at the slender, red-glowing column, and it became a pulsing, rosy shaft, the pulse duplicating my heartbeats that had become fast, drumming in my chest. Everything faded away but the

355

shaft of light, and from that point on I have only fragmentary impressions of what I saw, but I recall well the emotional storm I suffered.

The light slowly changed to an icy cold green. I was disembodied and alone in empty space. The loneliness of absolute infinity filled me with fear and horror, then despair so immense that I hungered for death. I looked down a long, long corridor and saw Marg, called to her, and when she turned her face to me there was no recognition in it. She walked away down the corridor and vanished. I stood on the road, facing the triple fork, and all the people I had ever known walked past me, ignoring my pleas, though what I was pleading for I do not know other than some sign of recognition. Hector and Anne, hand in hand, walked by, Hector's face red with anger and Anne's beautiful and thoughtful. I screamed at them, raged and wept, and they went on without looking at me. The interior of Westminster Abbey flashed and I had a wrench of grief that would have surely killed me if it had lasted more than a part of a second. A horribly ugly man's face loomed, hung by itself in endless space, a goblin with an enormous hooked nose, prognathous chin, unmatching-sized eyes and a twisted mouth. His eyes were alive with wisdom and when the wry mouth curved in a smile I was enveloped in a kind of holy warmth and comfort. Gratefully, I asked timorously, "Are you God?"

"Are you, Jamie?" he smiled. "That is the mystery."

I couldn't bear to think of him leaving me. I cried, "Don't go, don't go!"

The smile was incredibly tender, the ugly face a miracle of beauty. "Seek me, Jamie, seek me." He faded and a soul-chilling wave of grief drowned me.

Suddenly, though I could see nothing, there was a Presence. It was around me, inside of me, making me a part of it, soothing, loving, comforting. I wanted nothing else, it fulfilled all my chaotic needs, hopes and desires. Adoring it, I whispered, "Never leave me. All have left me but you."

The Presence answered, not in words but in feeling, "You must leave."

"But you," I wept, "you must stay with me!"

This time I heard the words in a far off, faintly heard voice: "So it must be, Jamie. Your road is waiting and so am I."

356

Then I was cold, shaken by despair and came to myself lying full length on the floor of Diggory's hut, weeping and sobbing. The fire had gone out and all was dark. There was no sign of Old Diggory and I did not look around for him, for I was drained and trembling, heartsick. I stumbled out of the hut and down the hills to the coconut grove where all was still, the party gone. Nancy stirred sensuously against me when I got into bed, half-awake, but I was in no mood for lovemaking, so I rolled over and went to sleep, exhausted.

In the morning while I was shaving with Big Jimmy's sharp knife, Nancy said dolefully, "Ol' Diggory make you smokes. Make you sad, Jamie, makes me sad. You don' jigajig las' night nor this mornin'. You got a heavy heart."

She was dear and sweet, and I was going to break hers. "Nancy, darling, trust me. I'll send for you and Little Jimmy. My wife will understand."

She flung herself into my arms, clinging to me. She didn't weep and carry on. "My Jamie, my Jamie, my husban', Ol' Diggory say you got to go, you got to go. I trust you till I die, no fear. When, Jamie?"

I kissed her gently. "As soon as I can be given a pitpan and stores. I'm going to paddle to Nassau. Nancy, you've made me very happy, but I have duties and responsibilities back in my world. As soon as I arrive there I'll send for my sweet Nancy and our handsome Little Jimmy, along with a pile of money for Big Jimmy to buy his new boat for Cibola."

The island men, gathered together by Jimmy, accepted Old Diggory's message to me as immutable, but told me in no uncertain terms that I was crazy to venture on the open sea in a pitpan, a shallow canoe carved from a tree trunk. Even if it could be spared, the wherry was so old and crumbling that a stiff blow would disintegrate it; it was never taken to sea in threatening weather and now the harrycane season was nearing. Remembering the vision of Marg walking away from me without recognizing me, I remained firm and the men reluctantly gave in. They warned me that if the sharks didn't get me first, the British, French or Americans, sailing upon me in the Channel, might take me for other than an islander with my sun-bleached hair. The British might press me into the navy, and I told them that was no problem. The point was, they informed me, that the French or Americans were the

357

danger. I saw the point and so my hair was dyed jet black. To be on the safe side, Nancy gave my body a coat of dark brown dye that the women used in making cloth, and I took on the appearance of a genuine Cibolan in my wide, knee-length canvas trousers and wide-brimmed palm frond hat.

Chapter XXI

DISASTER was preordained, of course. To attempt paddling a skittish pitpan more than one hundred and fifty miles over open ocean, against prevailing trade winds in the Caribbean autumn, was a challenge that must have made Neptune roar with laughter. For one thing, I had over-looked the problem of sleep; the light, shallow canoe required constant vigilance with the double-ended paddle to keep it headed into the seas and on course, and after a day and a night of that sort of thing I went to sleep quite involuntarily, sitting up. I awakened almost immediately, but had dropped the paddle and the wind and sea had taken fiendish control of my vessel and brought it broadside on to the choppy seas. Frantic paddling with hands was an absurd exposition of futility, and then I capsized. My food and fresh water supplies went down to Davy Jones. Fear of sharks seized me and in panic I scrambled onto the upturned bottom of the pitpan to lie there on my belly, drifting with the sea and wind. I went to sleep again.

A grating and bumping aroused me. I discovered the pit-pan was aground in gentle surf washing against a rocky ledge, so wading ashore, hauling the canoe out of the water, I took possession of that tiny, sun-baked realm. So small that I could almost spit from one shore to the other, it was nothing but bare rock encrusted with seabird droppings, though during my tenure as lord of the land I saw no birds.

It was a rather grim time. Fortunately, frequent rain squalls delivered abundant drinking water which I caught by using the pitpan as a reservoir. Most of my waking hours were spent in combing the shallows for food, nibbling on periwinkles, sea urchins, mussels and small crabs, vowing that if I lived through the experience to regain civilization I would never, never eat another sea food meal. With the full blaze of the sun reflecting from rocks and sea, my skin was quickly cooked blacker than the dye of Cibola. After five days and nights of that existence, with the supply of edible shellfish decreasing perceptibly, I concluded that within measured time I would be a sun-bleached skeleton with the gentle trade wind blowing through my ribs.

I was trying to catch a nimble little fish caught in a tidal pool one morning when I happened to glance up, and beheld a splendid sight. Four large ships were bearing down on me from the southeast, all canvas set including studding sails as they raced before the fair wind. Running to the highest point on the rock, I leaped up and down, waving arms and shouting, and to my intense delight the nearest one came about and hove to, lowered a boat, and I was saved, but not before I spied the French fleur-de-lis flying at the peak.

She was His Most Christian Majesty's frigate *Chimere*, fifty-four guns, and a very smart ship. Even before her boat nosed against my ledge, I became a very Cibolan fellow named Jimmy Harris who had been driven out to sea by a storm. My rescuers were sympathetically under-standing in broken English and apologized for not being able to put me ashore at a place convenient to my home island, for they were under orders to proceed with all speed to join Admiral General Comte d'Estaing's fleet. Accordingly, I was put to work as a scullery boy in the officers' galley. After a square meal and a shave, for my light brown whiskers were at suspicious variance from my dark skin, the razor borrowed from one of the affable *cuisiniers*, I resumed normal optimism and put my thoughts to the problem of getting away from the French. Unfortunately, none of the galley crew, with whom I lived and worked, could tell me where d'Estaing's fleet was, so I philosophically bided my time.

I was squatting in the corner of the galley one day, peeling potatoes into a pan of water, when a highly polished black shoe lifted the rim of the pan and turned it over, and a harsh voice growled, "Filthy black careless animal, observe what your stupidity has done!"

An impeccably uniformed sergeant of the Marine guard glowered down at me and I realized that this was the feared and hated Le Chaton, The Kitten, as the cooks furtively called the man. I got to my feet and saw a swarthy, be-moustached fellow with glittering black eyes full of contempt. He was rather short, with broad shoulders and narrow waist and held himself with arrogant superciliousness. My quick professional inspection of his face indicated he was of Mediterranean ancestry, the nose high-bridged with flaring nostrils, the lips full. Humbly, I said in my lame French, learned from the Haitian whore and British Army interpreter in New York, "A hundred pardons, my sergeant. To avoid such an accident was why I placed myself obscurely, sir."

"You contradict me to say you were not in the gangway, black pig?" he demanded.

"It was but what I thought, my sergeant," I said, "and I thank you for correcting my error, sir."

The black eyes darted from one of my eyes to the other. "But what is this? A nigger beast with the eyes of a white man, at least one eye." He scrutinized my face, scowling. "Under that unspeakable color you resemble a human being. Why do you have the audacious insolence to imitate a white man, vile negritude shit?"

Resolved to keep the peace, I wrestled with my rising temper and said politely, "Your pardon again, my sergeant. It was my mother's thoughtlessness in enjoying the affection of a white gentleman."

The effect was arresting. His face darkened under the onrush of blood to it and his eyes fairly burned with fury. I had struck a sensitive nerve and it occurred to me that his Mediterranean strain was probably Negro, which explained much of his attitude. He exclaimed angrily, "And did she also enjoy yours, animal? The black whore with the diseased cunt, did she cry out with joy when her son fucked her?"

"Alas, my sergeant," I answered, "she was denied that experience because she died at my birth, I am told."

The galley crew worked busily all around us, casting apprehensive glances at Le Chaton. He grated through his teeth, "Like mother, like son, is it not so? Do you not sometimes follow her example by enjoying impalement on the pricks of white gentlemen?"

It was obvious that he was determined to goad me into rash action. I replied, "My sergeant, I do not share that taste which is said to be popular with some white men." It was the wrong thing to say, but I couldn't stop myself.

361

Though the eyes remained angry, the full-lipped mouth smiled. He said in a velvety voice, "So, the black scum accuses white men of perverted lust, is it not? I am a white man, therefore it follows that I am so accused of degeneracy."

"But, my sergeant," I said hastily, feeling trapped, "I merely said some white men, sir, and my meaning, though poorly expressed, was that among men of all colors that habit may be found to some small degree, or so I am told, sir."

"Scrapings from a black whore's womb," he declared, "you are insolent, mutinous, insulting and lascivious." He glared around at the crew. "You all heard this depraved pig of pigs accuse me and all white men of perversion." Eyeing me, he said, "Is it not true that by opening this revolting subject of conversation you thought to entice me into an unnatural act to satisfy your animal lust, no?"

Self-command slipped. I said, "These men listening heard you open the subject, my sergeant, not me. I did not accuse you of anything, nor did I accuse all white men."

His smile was nastily triumphant. "Additionally I am now charged with lying. The captain will find this of much interest." He faced about and marched briskly out of the galley.

The *cuisiniers* expressed sympathy and explained that if any of them testified against Le Chaton the captain would not believe them, for the captain had complete faith in the sergeant. They would be punished for lying, perhaps for conspiracy to mutiny, and Le Chaton would persecute them to the point of desertion or suicide. It had happened before in the *Chimere*.

In less than an hour I was taken on deck under guard and at the foot of the mizzenmast the captain, a brilliantly uniformed officer, listened to the sergeant's charges with careful attention, then asked me what I had to say. I haltingly explained the truth of the affair, but with no witnesses to support me the captain pronounced me guilty as charged. He then reproached me for thus repaying his kindness in rescuing me and stated that under the law I might be hanged from the yardarm for mutinous conduct and behavior contrary to nature. However, there was a need for my brutish strong back at the end of the voyage, so therefore he sentenced me to twenty-five lashes and hard labor of indeterminate duration upon arrival at port. In the interim I was to be confined in the ship's brig.

The drummers beat all hands to witness punishment and the crew stopped work to assemble. The Marine guard formed in ranks and Le Chaton stood stiffly with them, staring straight ahead. As the French seamen triced me to the hatch grating against the bulwarks, spread-eagled, I sentenced Le Chaton to death.

It was worse than I expected. Each stroke was laid on at a single drum beat, the drummer counting, and the waiting for that damned thump made the lash hurt more. The drum would thud, the cat-o'-nine-tails would whistle, and the claws would rip into my skin. As I had done before with pain, I tried to disassociate myself from it, but long before it was over I was unconscious, mercifully enough, even though they brought me around briefly by pouring a bucket of cold seawater on me.

When I came to I was in the brig, a dark compartment deep in the ship. A lanthorn gave a feeble light and a man was gently rubbing a soothing oil into my lacerated back as I lay on my belly on the planks. I dimly recognized him as one of the surgeon's mates, an elderly, silent man. I murmured, "Thank you, friend."

"It is not too bad, this back," he said. "Scars will always remain, but you will live, which is more than I could say for those who were given fifty to one hundred scratches from the paws of Le Chaton. In two days time we make port, then you will be exposed to God's healing sun." Stoppering his oil bottle, he got to his feet and picked up the lanthorn. "My friend, I do not know why you have come among us with dyed skin, nor do I care. I am a man of peace and a lamb of God. But this road you have chosen is an ill one. If God in his infinite mercy preserves you through your future trials on this way, in His name I implore you to seek the road to goodness, mercy and salvation, for that is the road you must travel to attain a full and tranquil spirit with love for all, and remember this, my friend, unless you love all, you cannot love yourself. Peace to you, brother, in the name of the Father, the Son and of the Holy Ghost, amen." The heavy door shut behind him and I heard the bolt clank home.

My back was excruciating agony. I lay in the dark and resentfully thought there must be a mysterious worldwide conspiracy to harass Jamie Reid with reminders of the goddamned roads he must travel, though there was evidently some disagreement among the plotters as to which highway would be best for me. Anne MacDonald was in favor of a blessed, bonny road. Old Diggory had launched me onto this entirely disagreeable one, and here was a frustrated old French Gospel-shouter urging me to be a monk or something like it. Ah, well, once in port, wherever the hell that was to be, I would find a road to take me away from my Gallic masters.

Sometime later—it may have been a couple of days or a fortnight for all I knew—I was taken up on deck. It was night, and the ship was at anchor in calm water. The fresh air was like wine after the stinking lower decks of the *Chimere,* and I could smell vegetation and mud. The weather deck was crowded and there was much activity. Somebody came to me, one of the galley cooks, and murmured a farewell as he pressed my old palm frond hat into my hands. As my eyes adjusted to the darkness, I saw that some of the ship's eighteen-pounder guns were being hoisted and lowered into a bargelike craft alongside. Marines' boots clumped and I heard Le Chaton's hated voice barking commands, then the men climbed over the bulwarks and down to the barge. A loop of rope dropped around my neck and at my side Le Chaton said, "Negro scum, we go ashore and I do not wish to be deprived of your company. Quickly, into the boat!"

In the barge, with Le Chaton standing near, holding my tether, I was shoved to an oar, an enormous sweep, and ordered to row. From the stern a man's voice barked, "Give way together—*stroke!*" It took all my weight and strength, and the effort opened up the lacerations on my back again, causing me to gasp in agony, at which Le Chaton chuckled and said, "Exercise is good for you, black beast. After your holiday in the brig you have become soft. Do not shirk or you shall taste my claws again, vile pervert."

The world condensed into nothing but me, the great oar, my pain and the voice of the man in the stern calling the rowing cadence until early dawn light brought me some awareness of my surroundings. The gun-laden barge was being steered up a narrow, muddy river and about thirty black or brown islander laborers with me were rowing the barge, grunting and sweating, though the air was chilly. I wondered where in the hell we were.

The barge slid alongside the riverbank below a steep

bluff where a number of soldiers stood waiting. Le Chaton ordered his Marines ashore, removed the tether from my neck and said, "I shall be near and watching, so work well, whoreson."

The *Chimere*'s guns were hauled ashore over a ramp, then secured to a tackle that was anchored on the top of the bluff. Soldiers and laborers tailed onto the tackle and strained, inching the iron monsters with their massive timbered carriages up the nearly perpendicular slope while noncommissioned officers shouted curses and encouragement. With my heels dug into the clay and streaming sweat nearly blinding me, I felt a frightful explosion of new agony on my back and through the shock I saw Le Chaton swinging a whip at me. He was laughing. The pain came close to paralyzing me as the whip struck again. "It is not just!" he cried. "You do not do your share! Pull, animal, pull!" The whip whistled and I became an animal indeed, a straining, grunting, bleeding lump of flesh without conscious thought.

A cold shock brought me back to humanity. I was lying on the ground, drenched from a bucket of water someone had flung on me. A French officer, leaning over me, his face concerned, said in English with a brogue that came straight out of Dublin, "Holy Jesus, boy, 'tis a sorry lump of meat you have for a back! What mischief have you been at to bring you that?" The guns were up on the bluff and the Marines were gone, Le Chaton with them.

Shakily getting to my feet, I answered, "No mischief, sah. Don' know why I got beat. Maybe 'cause I don' speak Frenchy talk, sah." I noticed other men in non-French uniforms standing about watching and suddenly realized the uniforms were rebel Continental. Whatever I was into, it was a joint French-American enterprise.

The Irishman nodded. "That often happens. Understanding breaks down in the face of ignorance." My legs felt like paper and I swayed a bit from weakness. The officer produced a flask, unscrewed the cap and poured it full, handed it to me, and said, "Knock this back, lad, before you fall down again."

It was brandy and good. "Thank you, sah," I said gratefully, returning the cap.

"Are you a paid hand or punishment?" he asked, inspecting my torn back.

"Paid, sah," I lied, the *Chimere* men having departed

the scene, "but no pay take the sting out o' whips. Me, I'm feelin' plenty poor."

"No doubt," said the officer. "You'll be no good on the gun teams or in the ditches with that damned back. I'm Captain O'Dunne of Dillon's regiment and I'm in charge of labor gangs here. I'll take your word that you're not a criminal—you don't look like one, though I may be wrong. I'm short a man in the regimental officers' camp gang. What's your name?"

"Jimmy Harris, sah," I answered.

He beckoned to a French soldier, who trotted over and saluted. "Murphy, I want you to go to camp and tell Major Burton the eighteen-pounders will be on the line by midnight if these bloody Yankees' goddamned wheels hold up. The shot will be there by sundown. Take this man along and deliver him to the officers' camp gang; he's on the light-duty list. Get along with you, now."

Murphy and I trudged along a rough, potholed road, he with his musket carelessly sloped on his shoulder. We overtook and passed a group of Negroes pulling what appeared to be a twelve-pounder on crazy, wobbling wheels. He said to me in English that was intriguingly accented with both Irish and French, " 'Tis a sorry back you have there, lad. Sure, it hurts to look at it."

"Hurts plenty to wear it, sah," I answered. "Don' know why they do it, them Frenchies. Where we at, sah?"

"A couple of miles from the camp," he responded. "Ah, faith, and I hate the place, with them damn Highlander pipes laughin' at us all the day. 'Tis no good, this gambol, and well we know it without them pipes remindin' us. The chance is gone, like the dew under a summer sun, for when we came on that first day we could have swept the town and Prevost would be now a guest of France, but no, Comte d'Estaing had to—"

Startled, I interrupted, "Who that Prevost, mon? Where he livin'?"

Murphy, glancing at me, said, "Sure, you've just come ashore and maybe wouldn't be knowin'. Prevost is the Redcoat general and he lives in Savannah and that lies dead ahead on the Bieulieu Road past our camp."

If the sky had fallen on me I couldn't have been more staggered. I had made a full circle and was back at the starting point. "Oh, mon," I said faintly, "that surely is some plenty hard nut to crack, them Britishers."

"If it wasn't for them foul bagpipes," he commented, "I'd say hard but not that hard. I was at Grenada and the nut cracked well enough there for us. You'd be knowin' of Grenada a while back? 'Twas this way." He embarked on a private soldier's highly colored account of battle, to which I listened absently, nodding and making appropriate sounds, my heart going like a horse race. I was back in Georgia. My excitement was nearly uncontrollable.

And I had a devil of a time concealing the excitement when Savannah hove into view beyond the French camp and the American camp over on the left. On the far side of the town were many ships' masts and yards where the vessels lay in the Savannah River. On this side, well out from the town proper, were the British fortifications of sandbagged walls, redoubts and abatis—sharpened stakes driven into the ground at an angle to delay attackers. On the largest redoubt, opposite the French, the Union Jack rippled in the wind and then to my ears came the most beautiful music I had ever heard, the challenging skirl of the Highland bagpipes. "Come drink our blood!" they invited, gloating. "Come feast on our flesh! The widow and orphan makers wait for you!" My spine tingled and my blood raced, and I knew how right had been the judge who had sentenced my piper uncle to hang, for here was the proof that the pipes were an instrument of war. The sound of them had already cowed Murphy and his fellows. If the Highlander regiment was the same one that was there when I left Savannah, it was the Seventy-First, and I gave them a quiet blessing.

And the work I was put to in d'Estaing's officers' camp was a blessing. The other laborers and much of both armies, French and American, toiled at digging trenches and parallels, back-breaking pick-and-shovel work in the night. About all I had to do was work with hoe and shovel, improving tent drainage ditches, filling old and digging new sanitary holes, sweeping and cleaning. The trench diggers, however, were driven hard and constantly fired on by British batteries. A lightning British sortie, darting out and back quickly, created havoc by setting the French and Americans to shooting at each other in the night, the frightened men killing many of both allied armies. The French Navy ships below the town poured cannon fire into it in concert with the artillery on the camp side. Nights in Savannah were turned into hell by the savage mortar-

367

fire bombs called carcasses which set fire to houses. At every opportunity I studied the ground between the French camp and the British lines, watching the slow progress of the night-dug ditches moving through the half mile or so of cleared and swept land in front of the abatis-bristling first British trench. I was beside myself, so near and yet so far. Each night just after sundown the French ditches were filled with troops to guard against surprise sorties to destroy the French works. I worried over the problem of escape like a dog with a favorite old bone.

The camp gang supervisor, a fat, middle-aged corporal named Dwyer who despite his name spoke no English, approved my diligence and rewarded me by assigning me to the maintenance of the headquarters group of tents, and there I learned what was going on from the highest authorities by simply listening to the discussions that went on inside. General Lincoln, the American commander, rode over every day for consultations which usually became debating wrangles and acrimonious bickering. The Americans wanted to sit the British out through accepted siege practice; d'Estaing was worried about his fleet, lying at the mouth of the Savannah, being caught in a harrycane, so he wished to storm the town and have done with it, then get to hell away to sea. The storming would be difficult, d'Estaing said, only because Lincoln had permitted Colonel Maitland to return to Savannah with his Highlanders from Port Royal. Lincoln said it had not been agreed that that was his job at the outset, and further, if d'Estaing had immediately stormed the town on arrival instead of demanding a surrender from Prevost, there would have been no truce period given Prevost to consider terms, during which Maitland had brought his reinforcements into the town. In addition, the Americans were furious at d'Estaing for demanding the surrender only in the name of his French King. It was an uneasy alliance indeed. When no Americans were present, the French contempt for the Americans was quite vocal. I nearly laughed aloud one day when I heard Admiral General Comte d'Estaing say to an aide, "I reconnoitered the enemy trenches yesterday. General Lincoln, you will notice, was braver. He reconnoitered the Augusta road." Another time I almost shouted with joy when I heard him say when the pipes of the Seventy-First Highlanders ranted from the Spring Hill redoubt, "Monsieur de Sane would be quite helpful if he could place a mortar shell on top of those infernal bagpipers. Surely, that mournful harmony is not to be borne. On the other hand, however, they tell us where Prevost has placed his best troops."

It was well into October, and clad only in my Cibola trousers and palm hat I might have been cold if I had not gotten used to the weather. My dye and sunburn were holding up not too badly. For cold weather insurance I had stolen, as all the laborers did, breeches and shirt from an officer's tent. A newly landed party of officers and officials arrived in camp late one night and the next day I heard new voices in the headquarters. Scratching with my hoe outside, I learned that some had come from France and others from Haiti to observe the capture of Savannah. The admiral general was rather testy.

That afternoon the American general and his staff plus field commanders rode up in a great troop and went inside. Listening carefully, I heard the storming orders being distributed. Point by point, everything was gone over in detail; order of battle, artillery preparation, diversionary attacks, the main assault straddling the Augusta road, signals, disposition of wounded and prisoners. There was a vast amount of argument. The storming would take place very early the next morning, beginning at half past two.

From what I could see, the allies had about ten thousand men, and my guess, coupled with what I had overheard, put British strength at less than four thousand. Blockaded and besieged, Prevost had his back to the wall. I thought despairingly how strange it would be to see Savannah again with streets thronged with French soldiery. The conference broke up and the Americans galloped away. I pottered about with my hoe, making a show of industry. Someone emerged from the headquarters behind me and halted near me, evidently looking at me. "I say," said a whispery, silky voice that made my blood run cold, "what ghastly vandalism, marring such a magnificent back. You must have been an extremely naughty boy."

It could not be, yet it was. The director of His Majesty's secret service was in the French camp! Wondering if my experiences had affected my mind, I went on scraping with the hoe, my head down. "No, sah. Bad man do that. Jimmy Harris plenty good boy, work hard."

"Whoever he was, he was no admirer of beauty," said Beauvoir. "D'you work after hours, Jimmy? There might be some silver in it for you."

369

I needed no map drawn. The work would be decidedly odd. My mind worked swiftly. "Yes, sah, I surely would like silver. Ain't been paid for seems like two months."

"Splendid," murmured the unpleasant little man. "My tent is the last one in the last row behind here. Come there after I have supped, which will be shortly after sunset. I shall give you a whole shilling if you give me satisfaction, dear boy." He strolled away.

After I had my own supper of rice and cracked corn in the laborers' camp, I donned my stolen breeches and shirt and without a clear idea of what I was going to do, walked through the gathering darkness back to the officers' camp. There was a great deal of cannonading and musket fire going on, promising a brisk night. The morning would be even brisker, I mused gloomily. Most of the French-Irish officers were absent from the camp. Readying their troops for baptism in the morning, I reflected. Coming to the last tent in the last row, I knocked on the tent pole and said, "Jimmy Harris here, sah, for that work, sah."

"Come in, dear boy, come in," called Beauvoir.

Lifting the tent flap, I stepped inside. There he was, seated at a campaign desk at the other end of the tent, wearing the identical orange robe he had worn—a century ago?—when I had delivered Emily's portrait to him. His smiling face in the soft glow of the lamp which hung from the ridgepole looked surprisingly young. I stood in the shadows near the door and hated him. There was a camp bed to one side, and on it, asleep, lay a man. My heart nearly stopped when I saw it was Le Chaton. He was snoring and his uniform was in disarray, unbuttoned. At his desk, Beauvoir poured drink from a bottle into two glasses and said, "Come, dear boy, no need to lurk there. Draw near, be seated and have a drink of good brandy with me before the work, eh?"

I was too far into it to retreat. Stepping forward into the light, I said, "Thank you, my lord. I believe I will."

He froze and for once I saw uncontrolled emotion on his antique-cameo face: shock, amazement, then unreserved delight. "Jamie! My dear, sweet, marvelous Jamie! Why—I can hardly speak! Oh, my dear, dear boy, if you only knew—come, come, sit, sit, oh, I nearly swooned dead away!"

Sitting down in the camp chair and accepting the glass,

I said, "You already have a guest. I hope I'm not interrupting another bit of work."

He giggled grotesquely. "I do hope you're not jealous, dear boy, for you know you will always be first in my heart. The fellow drank nearly a full bottle of my good brandy and became quite useless. After a bit we shall rouse him and send him home. Passionate chap, really, before he got drunk, but playing the gentleman in such matters is hardly my greatest pleasure."

So much for Le Chaton. It explained everything. The brandy was not peach, it was delicious distilled essence of sunny European vineyards. "I know what you mean, my lord," I nodded, forcing a smile. "Or should I address you as my lady?"

"Oh, you are utterly adorable!" exclaimed Beauvoir. "What entrancing magic has wrought this change in my dear stubborn beloved? Ah, look at you, sweet boy—barefooted, unkempt, dark-skinned, with your poor lovely back vilely desecrated! Tell me, love, are you here by reason of some new mad scheme the Army devised, as a spy perhaps?"

"No, Vinny," I answered, feeling my way along for the role to play. " 'Twas simply a devilish run of bad luck. I was lost at sea and rescued by the French after a time on a southern island. They took me for a native islander and brought me here as a laborer. Can you tell me what you do here?"

He reached out, took my hand and pressed it to his lips, and the naked love in his eyes was horrible, but I let him caress my dirty hand and watched Sleeping Beauty from the corner of my eye. Le Chaton snored on. Beauvoir said, "I am faint with emotion and hardly dare ask it, but —Jamie, dare I believe that tonight we shall at last attain my dreams and delicious fancies?"

I said with some truth, "Why not, my lord? I've learned my lesson and tonight my dreams and fancies will be attained, too. Will you tell me how you come to be here, you wilful jade, or must I paddle your pretty little bottom?" That was the stuff to feed the troops.

"Gorgeous, lovely, Jamie," he sighed, coquettishly batting his eyelids. "Afterward I shall demand you do that and I fairly tingle at the prospect. I am here, dear boy, in the course of my official duties as director of the British branch of His Most Christian Majesty's intelligence bureau.

I am making a personal inspection of the French spy system, in short, throughout the New World and thus far have found it to be shockingly inept."

That rocked me. "You? In the French service? Good God."

The glacial smile was one of amusement. "The game's the same, regardless of sides, my sweet, as you will see when you go home with me to Paris. He reached over and laid a hand on my thigh, giving it a squeeze. "You will come, of course, eh?" The hand stroked my thigh.

My repugnance was close to making me sick, but the role had to be played so I endured the touch and smiled winsomely. "I look forward to it, dear Vinny. May I ask how the change happened?"

" 'Tis a tedious tale, to be sure," he murmured, "and when 'tis done I'll thank you to send that fellow on his way, for we'll have need of my bed. Tomorrow I shall have another bed fetched in and my tent will be love's Paradise. Why, the fact is, Jamie, after all my kindnesses, taking her from her disgusting Irish bogs and elevating her social position, that treacherous bitch of a wife of mine quite suddenly and without warning brought a suit of divorcement against me, conspiring with that wanton boy, Fergus. You will remember that dimpled young rogue?"

"Your footman," I nodded. "Handsomely turned legs and a beguiling eye."

"But a fickle, heartless strumpet," said Beauvoir. "I saved him from transportation for life when my gamekeeper at my Sussex seat nabbed him at poaching and all I asked in return was his affection. He was most talented, really, in amorous exercise and marvelously indefatigable with Emily and me."

"All three together at once?" I asked.

"But of course, my dear," he smiled. "Emily was a bit reluctant at first but after I coaxed her a little, she performed in an astonishingly diligent fashion. You would have been delighted, Jamie. The triad romping was what I had in mind when I proposed to you in London, you stubborn Adonis, and often in the lists of love with Fergus I closed my eyes in ecstasy, fancying 'twas you who embraced me."

The roving hand was nearly to my crotch. Dropping my eyes to it, I said, "First things first, dear Vinny, I pray you.

I must hear your tale before we go on to more pleasurable matters."

"Cruel Jamie," he said, practically pouting, but he withdrew his hand, to my enormous relief. He poured more brandy, then went on with his narration. Having forced Emily and Fergus to cooperate in his vileness, he was caught completely by surprise by their action in enlisting the court authorities against him. Aware of his powerful spy system, the court quietly investigated the plaintiff's charges as supported by Fergus, a thoroughly nasty package involving multiple sodomy, adultery, forced fornication and brutalization. Names were furnished and the roll of witnesses was long. Criminal action against Beauvoir arose from the civil proceedings, and the Government was stirred to investigate his official conduct of office. That resulted in a charge of high treason.

He said, aggrieved, "The perfidious Irish slut broke into my locked private correspondence. I had been having a bit of a fling—a charming little romance, really—with a gorgeous young gentleman of the French embassy before the declaration of war, and of course he was withdrawn with his embassy. How he wept! You must not be jealous, darling Jamie; 'twas but a pastime for me. We naturally continued to correspond affectionately, and as he was in a rather privileged position in his government he often passed me interesting tidbits of information. In order to encourage that, in return I supplied him with a few morsels from our government. 'Tis an old intelligence custom, this give-and-take, much the same as between lovers. This is a dreadfully drawn-out tale and I must shorten it.

"The jury returned the expected verdict and I felt most uncomfortable when the lord justice donned his absurd little black cap, you may be sure, love. I was not enamored of the scaffold, so a golden key opened all my prison doors one night. I was foully seasick in the filthy lugger that carried me across the Channel."

He took my hand again and kissed the palm, a horrible sensation, for I felt his wet tongue. "Precious hand. How I love you, my own! Do you know, in New York I was nearly out of my senses with jealousy toward that redhaired, green-eyed doxy of yours. Her expression when she looked at you made me furious. 'Twas she who caused me to teach you another lesson by sending you to Georgia, you know. Can you ever forgive me, pet?"

"On the contrary," I answered, "I'll ever be grateful to you for that. I learned a great deal and gained much satisfaction."

"Then I am happy indeed," he murmured. "I was quite naughty, actually. I arranged to have you live in her house as a means of forcing you to think of her and of me, her superficial beauty as opposed to my extraordinary powers, knowing that your good sense would compel you to admit that my protection and affection were infinitely more desirable than access to her body, though I imagine she provided you with fairly vigorous . . . ah . . . fucking, eh, love?"

Discussion of Anne coming from his filthy mouth enraged me, but I held on to control. "That was naughty of you, Vinny, but clever—most clever. Then you entered the French service on reaching Paris?"

"Quite," he nodded. "But, alas, when I sought for my pleasant Gallic playmate to resume our delicious liaison, I discovered that his government, pursuant to the notoriety my affairs had received in London, had looked into his affairs and subsequently hanged the poor dear. Notwithstanding that, I was welcomed most cordially with my interesting bundle of Crown papers I had fetched along with me, and—lo—here we are."

When not watching him or Le Chaton while he talked, I had been covertly inspecting the material spread on his desk. I noted diagrams, time schedules, regimental designations, the signatures of Lincoln and d'Estaing. There was no doubt of it; this was a complete set of the storming orders that were issued that afternoon. I smiled at him. "You land on your feet like a cat, Vinny. I've always thought there was a deal of cat about you, sleek, silent and surefooted. When I come to caress you, I'm sure you'll purr."

The finely sculptured face lighted with cold joy and he sprang to his feet, holding out his arms, exclaiming, "Oh, my darling, how I shall purr!" He came at me, hurling himself against my chest to embrace me, and I am sure he never felt it when I wrung his head to break his slender neck. Pushing his body aside with my foot, I gathered up the storming order documents and thrust them under my shirt, then turned to attend to Le Chaton.

He was standing by the bed, swaying a bit and goggling at me with bleary eyes. "What . . . who . . ." he mumbled.

His tunic was unbuttoned and his breeches were down. His sword belt, with the sergeant's short sword, lay on the floor beside the bed. I walked to it and picked it up, drew the sword and handed him the belt and scabbard which he automatically took, staring at me. "You . . . you are the nigger of the *Chimere*," he said vaguely.

"I am," I agreed, "and you are the lady sergeant of the *Chimere* who protested too much. I trust you had an enjoyable impalement on the cock of the white man who lives in this tent, black beast."

He gave a confused bellow and charged awkwardly, his legs hampered by the half-masted breeches, and I drove the sword into his chest. He was still alive when I knelt over him and cut his throat from ear to ear, flung the bloody weapon down, and said, "One good cat deserves another, you son of a bitch."

As I started out of the tent I suddenly remembered something and went back, rummaged around in Beauvoir's trunk until I found his purse. It was fat and full. Carefully I counted out twenty guineas and put them in my pocket, paid at last for Emily's portrait. Then I walked out and headed for the French trenches.

Chapter XXII

THE FRENCH-AMERICAN ARTILLERY was banging away at a good clip, firing into the town, the muzzle blasts lighting the night with bright flashes. Near the Spring Hill redoubt a British battery responded about every fifteen minutes with a brief cannonading directed toward the enemy ditches, the foremost of which, I had observed before sunset, was within about three hundred feet of the first line of British fortifications, a wide ditch protected by abatis.

I had no definite plan in mind other than to proceed by the most direct route to the British lines, which meant passing through the parallels, big trenches dug parallel to the British works, each dug successively closer under cover of night in order to place troops and cannon ever nearer the enemy. A system of zigzag connecting trenches ran between them. Forward of the advance parallel more connecting trenches extended out to holes where sentries were posted to guard against surprise sorties.

The trenches were heavily populated with soldiers under arms and men working with picks and shovels to improve the system, and there were so many people that I passed through unchallenged in the dark and confusion. British cannon balls soughed overhead and some, short-ranged, thudded into the ground among the ditches. I hoped to God I would not be killed by my friends. Passing through a connecting trench I came upon a soldier urinating in the latrine recess dug in the wall of the trench and, acting on impulse, I seized his neck and applied pressure to certain points as taught by Ira Tupper. He collapsed, unconscious. I donned his tunic and hat—oddly, they fitted me—heaved him up out of the ditch, shouldered his musket and continued on my way. I worried about passwords and countersigns; they were changed daily and I had no way of knowing what they were this day.

There was an amazing lack of conversation going on in the trenches, especially as I knew many of the troops were Irish, members of a people who surely invented human speech. I concluded they were nerved up by both British cannonading and what they would be required to do at half past two in the morning. The advance parallel was a bit dreadful. A British ball had just landed in it, creating an untidy mess among the thickly packed soldiers and the injured survivors were doing much groaning and crying out in their agony. However, it was lucky for me, because with the attention of the troops thus diverted it was easy for me to find the entrance to the ditch leading to the outlying sentry post. Crouching, with the musket held in the bayonet attack position, I groped my way forward as noiselessly as possible in my bare feet. From the direction of the American line there was the sound of some spirited musket fire. Three times since I had been in the French camp the nervous and frightened allies had accidentally fired on each other in the night and killed a number of friends, and I hoped the sentry's apprehensive attention was occupied by the American shooting, for if he challenged me with the password it was into the soup for me. Failing to receive the countersign, he would cry an alarm before I could kill him, and his mates in the parallel would pour deathly fire onto the swept glacis in front of the British works.

But the poor lad was squatting in his hole, and from the dim shape of his hat I could see his head was turned toward the Americans. I didn't have to get close, the bayonetted musket was long. Taking careful aim, his bent torso half-seen half-guessed, I drove the needlelike bayonet into his chest, dropped the musket, and scrambled out on the ground in front, where I got on my belly and crawled.

Dark as the night was, I knew there were men on both sides skilled at night vision and men with extra acute hearing. Though the artillery boomed and muskets crackled, such vigilance would be maintained. Inching along, propelled by elbows and knees, I fretted about the rustling of the papers in my shirt, the scraping of my body against the earth, and worried that the sentry's body would be discovered before I had covered the gap between the opposing forces. As I worked closer to the British abatis I also worried about the British sentries, who were certainly as nervous as their opposite numbers. "Please, God," I whispered, "I've done enough dying. Don't let it happen again, please."

The Spring Hill redoubt was directly ahead; its protecting battery spouted flame and iron, the balls moaned overhead. I began to sweat, wondering about my reception when my presence was detected. From overheard discussions in d'Estaing's headquarters I knew Prevost, according to deserters, had placed militia in the first line of defense and his trained troops in the second. Militia were notably quick—too quick—on the trigger.

Then suddenly I was at the abatis, a solid bristling oak wall. Taking my life in my hands, I got up and boosted myself over, slid down the tops of the stakes—and kept on going down into the ditch behind, setting up a miserable din of sliding down the loose earth to the bottom, a noisy ten-foot drop. From somewhere on the other side, a musket barked, then another and another, and I heard the balls strike the earth near me. Frantically, I shouted, "Leave off, you silly bastards! I'm coming in! Captain Reid of Browne's Rangers! Cease fire, you stupid shits!"

The shooting and my shouting touched off the French and their lines erupted with musketry, immediately followed by the Americans, all firing wildly in the night. Ahead, I heard a confusion of men bellowing something, and I flung myself at the opposite wall of the ditch, scrambling up with fingers and toes digging in, and near the top somebody's hands gripped me under the armpits and hauled me the rest of the way. Several men were there, kneeling and crouching; somebody got me by the throat and threw me down, knelt on me, and hissed, "Who the hell are you, you goddamned spy?"

Another man muttered, "Don't kill him, don't kill him. Orders, John, orders!"

I said, "I'm no spy. I'm Captain Reid and I've just escaped from the French."

The man holding me banged my head viciously on the ground. "He's dead, goddamn you, he's dead!"

"If the Rangers are still in the garrison," I gurgled, for the man had a stranglehold on my neck, "they'll recognize me. Let me up, blast you!"

The grip loosened. "Jamie? 'Tis you? Jamie Reid? Alive?"

Now I recognized his voice and was filled with towering

happiness. "John, I'm alive and right now I've never felt better. Where you are, there's bound to be Peter. Peter?"

The brothers fell on me, embracing me, and literally bore me off to the rear, through a ditch lined with troops to some earthworks built behind the ruins of a building under the sandbagged wall of the redoubt. Peter said, pumping my hand, "God in Heaven, what a miracle! I can't believe it!"

"I don't even believe it now!" exclaimed John.

"We can talk later," I said. "Right now I must find General Prevost. The enemy will attack at half-past two. I have the orders with me."

"Half-past two!" ejaculated my brother-in-law. "Then— John, I can't leave the line. Show him where my horse is tied behind the redoubt. Jamie, the general's headquarters are still in the house on Bull Street. If we live through tomorrow we'll have the grandest party as ever was in Georgia!"

On the way through the fortification, John said, "Marg's in London, if you don't know it. She's been too poorly to write, I reckon, all cut up over you, the newspapers say. She'll be a joyful woman now, by God!"

"No more than I'll be a joyful man when I reach her," I laughed.

Galloping Peter's horse through the sandy streets, I smelled charred wood. A cannonball came soughing and thudded into the street behind me. There were no lights anywhere. The big house on Bull Street was dark and there was no sentry in front. Prevost could not spare able-bodied men from the lines, I decided as I dismounted and tethered the horse to the hitching post. I heard voices coming from under the house and recognized that of Captain John Prevost, so I felt my way to the cellar door and went down the flight of steps, opened the door at the bottom. In the candle-lighted cellar the general was at a desk studying a map and his son was talking with a clerk. They looked at me, frowning at the intrusion. I must have been a peculiar sight, barefooted, dark-skinned and wearing a French soldier's coat; I had lost the hat when I killed the sentry. "I beg your pardon, General, Captain," I said, advancing and taking the orders from my shirt. "I have a matter of some urgency, sir." Prevost stared with incredulous eyes, his mouth ajar. Placing the documents on his desk, I told him, "These consist of the storming order, sir, issued this

380

afternoon by General Lincoln and Admiral General Comte d'Estaing. The time is for half-past two tomorrow morning. I hastened here as fast as possible, sir."

"Reid, Jamie Reid," whispered John.

The general said, "Well, well." He dropped his eyes to the orders, gave them a quick scan and then brought his fist down on his desk with a mighty blow, and leaped to his feet crying, "Just what I thought! Exactly! Reid!" He came around the desk and seized my hand, "Man, I withdraw all the poor things I ever said about you! I want you to give me a written account of how you acquired this order and how you made your way here! Captain Prevost, I'll be obliged if you will summon the staff and regimental commanders immediately, and warn the Seventy-First to prepare for a move to the Augusta Road redoubt, within the hour, sir! Here, Reid—sit down, man, sit down! Whose set of orders is this? If 'tis found a set is stolen they may change the date and time."

"I killed the man," I explained, "and he was no French officer. I doubt the body will be found until his servant goes to the tent in the morning. He was but an official visitor, an observer. An English traitor, Vincent Lord Beauvoir."

"Holy Mother." Prevost shook his head. "Beauvoir. Unbelievable. And you killed him into the bargain, on top of all else. You know you're supposed to be dead, don't you, lost at sea in a naval action?"

"So my brother-in-law in the militia of the line indicated," I replied. "By the bye, 'tis his horse—Peter Ogilvie's—tied outside and I'd be sorry if the poor beast were hit by one of these balls that are flying about."

"I'll have the animal put under cover," he said. He turned to the gaping clerk and ordered, "Move this gentleman's horse under cover in my stables, Tibbs, and then rally the rest of the clerks here. We've a long night of work ahead." As the clerk ran out of the cellar, the general poured a glass of whisky and handed it to me. "You can use this, I expect. Now hear me: this is the second time you have emerged from enemy lines and fallen into my hands. This time I shall not let you escape, my dear man, nor will I delay your return to Great Britain. Further, I will not permit you to risk your neck during the battle tomorrow morning by remaining here in Savannah. I have a courier ship lurking in hiding near Hilton Head.

381

As soon as you have finished writing the report I have asked for, you will be transported to that ship with orders to the master to proceed with all speed to London. I'll have a dispatch box for you to carry along, if it will not inconvenience you."

"It won't, sir," I smiled. "I've had enough of Georgia and this war. I'll appreciate a bath and some clothing—and a full meal. I've been living on rice and cracked corn for a long time."

"Sorry," he said, "that won't be possible here. I want you gone and on the way to London with all possible speed. Please use the table yonder and hasten that report."

A horrid thought struck me. "Hold on, General," I said. "Am I under arrest? Do you think me a returned traitor? By Christ, sir, I'll not have that, no sir! I've had my face rubbed in shit, lived like an animal and—"

"Gently, gently, I pray you, Mr. Reid," he smiled. " 'Twill help if you do as I've requested—pick up a quill and write, quickly, for in minutes this cellar will be extremely noisy and full of gentlemen."

Annoyed, nevertheless I complied, scratching out a highly abbreviated account of my sojourn at Cibola, ship (pitpan) wreck, rescue by the *Chimere* and so on. I covered less than a sheet of paper and was finished in a few minutes. Prevost was busily jotting notes, glancing from time to time at his map of Savannah's defenses, and when I handed him the report he read it quickly, got to his feet and said solemnly, "Mr. Reid, as a soldier of the King, permit me to extend to you on behalf of my little army my most profound expression of gratitude for the service you have rendered us and His Majesty." The clerk returned with several others. The general handed him my report. "Make a copy of this instantly, then fetch me a dispatch box." Returning to me, he went on, "Far from being under arrest, sir, you have my deepest respect and I am honored to have your acquaintance." He rattled on in that strain for several minutes and it puzzled me because it was so unlike him, the hardheaded old matter-of-fact Genevan warrior.

Then off again I went from Savannah in the company of a red leather dispatch box, being rowed swiftly by six powerful Negro oarsmen through the swampy channels north of the town in South Carolina. Fatigue, the whisky and the rhythmic click of oarlocks lulled me, so I lay down on a thwart in the stern sheets and went to sleep.

A jarring thump and scraping jolted me awake, and somewhere above me a Down East voice said with some emphasis, "Damn your eyes, Cox'n, what kind of stump-jumpin' ploughboy are ye, takin' my paint off like that!"

Exceeding joy fairly lifted me out of the boat, dispatch box in arm, onto the ship's deck. Laughing, I said, "Charge off the damage to the owners, you miserly Abenaki! Let's get this peapod to sea!"

There was a hiss of indrawn breath in the dark. "Who . . . who . . ."

"You sound like a goddamned owl, Ira," I chuckled, and flung my arms around him. "Jesus, man, you'll never know how sweet that ugly voice of yours sounds to me!"

"*Jamie!*" he exclaimed, giving me a bear hug. "You bastard! You terrible bastard, 'tis you! Oh, my sacred lovin' Jesus!"

"Easy, easy," I cautioned. "I've got a damned sore back. I've just come from General Prevost and you're ordered to haul arse for London, old son, with me and dispatches for Lord Germain." The *Bonny Anne*. I was home again, standing on her blessed deck, and suddeny felt like weeping with happiness.

Ira said, "I swan to Godfrey if you ain't the livest dead man who ever was! Great Jehosaphat, the biggest miracle since the loaves and fishes! London, ye say? Aye, quickly and gladly—the sooner we take *Bonny Anne* away from this hole the better. The damn rebel patrols have been a sight overdue to find her. Go below and have a drink, but light no lights; the ocean hereabouts is full of unfriendly folk. By God, Jamie. Jamie Reid! Comin' out of the night to me and *Bonny Anne!*" He turned to somebody nearby. "Roust 'em out, Mr. Starr. All hands. We'll set a course for The Lizard."

In the dark cabin I groped about, found the spirits locker, and helped myself to the rum. I sat down to the table, took a long drink, savored the moment and felt the warm friendliness of the *Bonny Anne*'s cabin around me like a comforting cloak. The rum was ambrosia. Then without warning I burst into tears, not knowing why, and stifled the sound of my sobbing by burying my face in my arms. It did not last long, and left me wondering if I had lost my mind. I was suddenly horribly weary. Nothing mattered but sleep. The schooner was under way, heeling easily in the light breeze. I went to my former stateroom and to sleep like the dead man I had been supposed to be, but later, after many hours of slumber when my exhausted body had been refreshed, the dream of the roads came back.

It was amusing in a sense. I saw Marg ahead, standing on one of the branching roads watching me approach, and hurrying toward her with joy, I was abruptly halted by the appearance of Anne MacDonald directly in front of me. She was smiling radiantly, almost jubilantly, at me and I said, moved by her dazzling beauty and smile, "So now you smile on me at last, bonny Anne."

"I'm not that bonny Anne at all," she said in bubbling merriment. "I'm *Bonny Anne* who's wedded to the sea. Do you not feel me holding you safe, dear bonny Jamie?"

I wanted to take her in my arms and kiss that gloriously happy face, for her beauty was a wonder and her happiness infectious. Beyond, Marg stood, watching. "I must get to my wife, *Bonny Anne*. Why are you here?"

"You made me a promise and I'll not let you forget it," she smiled, "which you may when you get to your wife again after I take you to her."

"The figurehead," I said. "You want your figurehead."

" 'Tis not my figurehead, 'tis me you will make, bonny Jamie," she laughed. Then she sang from the real Anne's song:

"And if ye dare to kiss my lips,
　　Sure of your bodie I will be."

"For shame," I grinned, "a married lady carrying on like that, though God knows I'd like to kiss you now."

Crystal laughter rang. "My husband is wide and deep and great and there's no jealous drop in him for you, bonny Jamie. When you've made me and kissed me, there's another road you must go, and this is how you will make me." She held out her arms to me and raised her face, on which shone inexpressible delight and joy. She was *Bonny Anne* welcoming her bridegroom, the sea. The lovely green gown, blown by the sea wind, pressed against her body, the plumes of the bonnet pushed back and her red-gold hair, partially uncaught, rippled like a glorious banner. "And so you will kiss me, bonny Jamie."

Then I was kissing her and kissing her, and she eagerly

384

responding with great passionate fire. My juices surged, gathered and spouted, and the convulsion awakened me, wetly. It was past midday, and the *Bonny Anne* was racing over the great Atlantic swells, faithful to her declaration in the dream that she would bear me to my wife. But that road business—my God, now the bloody ship was babbling about it! There would be no more roads for Jamie Reid but the one of a happy married life among his children.

Going up to the poop where Ira was talking with the mate, I was amazed at the way the schooner, under all sail, was flinging herself over the sea at a fantastic rate of speed and I had the distinct impression of joyous frolic. Ira, grinning, said, "By Godfrey, Jamie, ye look like a Trinidad boatman." He introduced me to Starr, a quiet, capable-looking man.

I said, "At this speed we'll be in the Thames next week if all this sail doesn't tear the sticks out of her."

Ira, smiling, pleased, said, "She'll not let that happen, the dear lass. Ye'll not believe it, but we just now measured it and she's loggin' sixteen knots. Until about an hour ago she was lallygaggin' along at eight, then the breeze freshened and she let go like a racing horse."

I laughed, and to the startled looks of Starr and the helmsman I shouted forward, "Good-morning, *Bonny Anne!* I love you!" An extra big wave smashed against the counter and the spray saucily drenched me.

"There ye go," chuckled Ira. "Ye got your answer. She never did that before. 'Twas like she said, 'Don't say that to me, Jamie Reid, unless ye mean it.'"

"I meant it and she knows I mean it," I said. "We just had a conversation in a dream before I woke. It seems I'm committed to that figurehead you and I discussed a long time ago. Ira, if you have any decent clothes I could borrow or buy—I have twenty guineas in my pocket—and enough fresh water aboard for me to have a bathe today I'll be your servant forever, but first I demand a breakfast of staggering size."

Ira said to Starr, "I leave the deck to ye so's I can take care of this poor starvin' half-nekkid stowaway. Come along below, wanderin' Boanerges, and whilst I tend to ye, ye can spin me a yarn that I expect might be hard for some folk to believe, but bein' acquainted with ye I'm willin' to listen."

He had an excellent cook on board and a good cabin boy to serve the afterguard. The breakfast was a vast one of ham and eggs, fried potatoes, bread and butter, jam and strong coffee. While I devoured it, Ira produced a spare seaman's outfit of wide trousers, seaboots, woolen shirt and short, warm coat, topped with a snug stocking cap. " 'Tain't Macaroni, but 'twill keep ye from freezin' up come November, though I calc'late ye should be home before December if the weather holds good. Four weeks, mebbe. *Bonny Anne*'s done it before."

The cabin boy fetched hot water for bathing and shaving, and when I stripped Ira exclaimed, "Jesus Chirst, Jamie, what did they do to ye, man? Your back . . ."

" 'Twas done by a playful kitten's claws," I said, "and he'll play no more."

What I had thought was the remains of Cibola dye proved to be mostly ingrained dirt, and diligent scouring with a patch of canvas and strong soap brought out natural skin color as I related my adventures to Ira. I was clean and feeling splendid when, dressed in my nautical rig, I sat down to another mug of the good coffee with a stick of rum in it.

Ira rubbed his long chin reflectively. "Waaal, ye been fair busy, ain't ye, Jamie? Not countin' what else ye been up to, seems like ye got yourself two wives and a boy by one of 'em. Ye'll have a mite of sortin' out to do one o' these days. As for the other work ye done, things around London'll turn some hectic and ye got some surprises due, Jamie. Ye was quite a hero before ye died and twicet the hero after. Nope, I was wrong. What ye got is a wife, child *and* widder. Ye been gone to the other shore in the sweet by-and-by for a spell, Jamie."

"Ho," I grinned, "I'll show that lovely widow of mine how alive I am! You've never met her, Ira .While the *Bonny Anne*'s at London I order you to live in my house and bask in the sunshine of her joy. I'll even permit you to adore her. Oh, *Bonny Anne,* drive faster, drive faster!"

He said gravely, "*Bonny Anne*'s doin' her best for ye. Trust her. But there's somethin' ye should know, Jamie. Ye'll be lookin' for a happy quiet time with your wife and I misdoubt ye'll have it. There was quite a stew over your passin'. The newspapers and people come on mighty strong. Heroes is fair scarce and I reckon one was needed amongst all the bad news of the wars, so you was elected—

famous handsome young artist, dashin' about fightin' on sea and land, spyin' for the King among the enemy, then bein' killed in another sea battle. There was a memorial service over to Westminster Abbey. Power of folks was there, they say, weepin' like babies. The King and his kin was there."

"Why, that's insane!" I exclaimed. "They're all crazy! My God, there are thousands of real heroes in the King's service! Like General Prevost at Savannah!"

He shrugged. "Seems like they picked you, Jamie. When ye come riz from the dead like Lazarus, after killin' Beauvoir like that and all, I reckon there'll be a kind of celebration for ye. And for your wife. Ye see, Jamie, seems like folks was some took with her, the papers says. Beautiful, faithful, grievin' widder of the noble hero."

"Well, I'll soon put that to rights," I declared. "Anyway, if what you say is true, the hurrahs will blow over in a day or so and to hell with it. What do you know of the Mac-Donalds?"

"Angus is healthy and we got plans worked out for after the rebellion," he answered, "with me directin' our shippin' for American ports. Hector's set up as a stylish doctor in London, gettin' fair rich, I hear tell. I been sendin' him his *Bonny Anne* profit shares, and your shares I been sendin' to your estate, care of that lawyer of yours. Angus told me Anne's livin' in Rome now, along of Mrs. Quimby; didn't stay long in London."

"She once told me she might do that," I commented. "She thought the climate there might be more like Georgia's. As for me, I've had a bellyful of that climate and there's none better than cold—damp, foggy, stinking dirty London's, so far as I'm concerned. And I'm all of a fever to get back to work at portraits." An idea hit me. "And I'll work up some great pictures out of all that Georgia work I did. Marg will have taken it home to Portsmouth Square." I laughed with pleasure. "Remember the Benjamin Franklin idea for thirteen historical paintings? Ira, I'm going to do them before I die! As soon as I'm settled in and back on schedule, I'm going to get busy on the first, the Georgia one. Goddamn it, Ira, you're looking at a happy man!"

"Ye deserve what ye get, Jamie, after what ye been through," he said, "and you're owed a lot, I figger." He smiled, his Indian face amused. "I'll not go home with ye directly, Jamie, on tyin' up at the Admiralty quay. Ye'll be wantin' a private time with your lady, I'll wager, before ye so much as take off your hat. Besides, I'll have to carry the general's dispatches over to Lord Germain at Whitehall first thing."

Laughing, I said, "I'll take no more than a couple of hours at that first private time, Ira, for we have years ahead of us for making babies, and one of the score of them we'll have will be named after you, along with one named for Hector. Oh, the marvelous times Hector and I are going to have again! Speed on, *Bonny Anne,* speed on! The best time of my life is coming!"

Chapter XXIII

THE NOVEMBER DUSK was coming on, damp and raw, when the *Bonny Anne* was at last tied up at the Admiralty quay on the crowded, noisome Thames in London. The smoky mist promised a night of pea soup fog. Mistaking me for a jolly jack tar in my seaman's garb, the hackney driver was insolent, but I loved him. I loved his wretched swaybacked nag that was long overdue at the knackers, and the vehicle, which was disintegrating with age and stank of encrusted vomit, was a golden chariot bearing me to Portsmouth Square and my wife.

The graystone front of my house beamed on me. In the entrance hall the grandfather's clock in its lustrous case ticked with slow, sonorous dignity in contrast to my heart, which thumped like a kettledrum. No perfume of Araby was better than the homely, familiar scents of furniture polish and wax, and the fine faint fragrance of appetizing supper cooking in the kitchen at the back of the house. In the darkening drawing room I saw the Elderbank portrait hanging over the mantel and my excitement became nearly intolerable. There was a lighted lamp in the library, my favorite room, and a sea-coal fire glowed cheerily in the grate. A drinking glass with a bit of port wine remaining in it stood on a table; she would have had it before going upstairs to arrange herself for supper.

Hurrying up the staircase, I looked in my old bedchamber and found it empty, so I peered into the others and saw nobody. Walking down the hall, I entered my painting room and in the gathering gloom saw my painting gear from America laid against the wall. A sound caught my attention, so walking to the tiring room I opened the door—and instantly turned to stone.

By the light of a candle, stark naked on the couch,

Hector and Marg were vigorously coupling, lost in climactic transport. With his face down between her neck and shoulder, Hector was plunging into her with swift, powerful drives and her upturned face, eyes closed, wore the contorted grimace of peaking ecstasy that I knew so well, whimpering, straining grunts coming from her parted lips. Even as once upon a time Beauvoir had stood unmoving in that same doorway, so stood I. All my mental and physical processes had halted. I might as well have been a visitor to this planet from some distant world, viewing the strange mating practice of the human race for the first time. Marg's intensity of passion lessened and she opened her eyes, still clasping Hector to her with arms and legs as he continued bobbing his posterior between her thighs. Her eyes looked directly at me, widened, and then she screamed. And went on screaming.

My invisible chains fell away. Stepping back, I closed the door and walked out of the painting room, unfeeling, unthinking. Going downstairs I saw the faces of Kitty Bumpus and Filkins looking up at me with something akin to horror on them. They had been drawn by the din set up by Marg, I reflected hazily. I said to them, "I've just now arrived home. Mrs. Reid was overcome. Dr. MacDonald is attending her. Go back to your work, please."

Filkins' snaggle-toothed grin was amazed delight. "Blimey, sir, 'tis you! The master 'isself! 'Ow did yer—"

"Get to your work," I said, walking past them to the library. Rum had no taste. I tossed off a full tumbler of it and refilled the tumbler, sat down by the fire and stared into space. I was dead, an intruding ghost, a Cibola jumby, feeling nothing and thinking nothing. I became aware of Hector, now dressed, standing in the room looking at me. His face was drawn and chalky.

"Jamie," he said in a low, choked voice. "Jamie." His lips were quivering and his eyes were wet. "Thank God." I stared at him, a stranger. He whispered, "You were dead, Jamie. Marg . . . we're . . . we were betrothed, to be wed after her period of mourning was done, Jamie. As God is my witness . . ."

A bitter worm stirred inside. "You had better luck with this widow than the last."

"We love each other," he said. "That's a rotten thing to say, Jamie."

390

" 'Tis a rotten world filled with rotten people," I murmured, looking into the fire.

"I know how you must feel, Jamie," he said, pleading, "and you may think me rotten at the moment, but not her, Jamie. Never her!"

The worm thrashed into full life and emotion revived. I had the urge to kill him. Eyeing him carefully, I said, "Be glad I was not armed a moment ago. But not too glad. I may yet kill you both."

"Kill me if you will," he said, face tense, "but I'll not let you harm her. I know you must have been through some hard times and what happened upstairs was a frightful shock to you as well as to us, but you'd do well to give some thought to what Marg has been through because of you, Jamie."

I drank off my rum and took more. "I've put nobody through anything. I'm the one who has been put through, especially coming home to a loving wife and finding her fucking with my former best friend before my eyes."

"I'll forgive that, Jamie," he said in a stifled voice, "but I warn you, do not insult her again."

"How may a trollop be insulted by being called a trollop?" I asked.

Clasping his smallsword hilt, he exclaimed, "I warned you, sir!"

"You're a sorry champion of honor," I told him, "even if there were honor to defend. If you attempt to draw that sword, your goddamned neck will be broken before it clears the scabbard."

His hand came away. "Aye, I see it in your eyes. You want to do it. Jamie, in God's name, for her sake we must not fight! You don't know, man! Christ, you don't know!"

"I know more than I ever wanted to know," I said.

"Before this goes further, will you let me explain the thing that happened to her, Jamie?" he asked. "Please? Now you're back, the storm will strike again and there's terrible danger to her reason."

I said, "Don't come at me with some garbled physician's horseshit in a try to excuse yourselves. That woman is no Meg Barr-Pettit."

"Will you at least let me try to explain?" he begged.

" 'Tis immaterial to me," I said dully.

"May I have a drink?" he asked. "I need one badly."

I shrugged. "Why not? Help yourself, as you have to other things in my house."

Filling a glass, he growled, "If the need of it weren't so great, I'd be damned if I'd touch your bloody drink. Damned and gone to hell! Listen, she loved you with every breath of her body, every pore in her skin! She was your invention, your creature, and you were her life! From the moment you disappeared in that explosion she began to die—wither, fade and shrivel inside. We had to restrain her from flinging herself overboard when the captain declared you lost. Her will to live was gone."

Mine was gone but I didn't have to be concerned about it, for I was already dead. "That's a pity."

"By the time she came to the house," he went on, "she had stopped talking entirely and it was nearly impossible to get her attention. She cared nothing for her appearance and had to be bathed and cared for like a child. My father and I called in the best men in the field of nervous disorders, not only British doctors but from the Continent, and they could do nothing but, like me, watch her reason fail and death approach. Dressed and bathed, she moved about like a mechanical doll and had to be accompanied every moment by a capable nurse. And what made her condition worse, constantly reminding her of you, was that the public attention centered on her. Each day, for weeks after the news went out that you were dead, there were hordes of women in the square outside, dressed in black and kneeling, praying and weeping in sympathy for her. Britain had lost her golden hero and mourned beside the grieving widow. If she went out, tearful crowds followed her. Westminster—Jesus, I had to escort her to the service for you, and she fainted dead away twice but wouldn't let me take her home. All she could say was, 'Jamie's here. Let me stay with Jamie.'"

"But she recovered quickly, I suppose," I commented, "when afterwards you took her home and introduced her to your soothing prick."

His face was contemptuous. "If there's any decency left in you, you'll give some thought to the hell that will be repeated—indeed, 'tis started now—with you come home from the dead. What I did was talk to her, care for her, encourage her to live, persuade her to realize that you were gone forever and life goes on. One day she got up in the morning and it was as if her grief had been turned off

392

by a spigot. She was not the same woman as before, more serious and mature. By that time I was uncontrollably in love with her, and little by little she came to return my love. You were officially dead. We became betrothed. That is what happened."

"And butter won't melt in your mouth," I sneered. "From the moment you first laid eyes on her when she was tied naked to the post at Jenks Town you had a hard-on for her and then worked it off for a bit on the twins at Goodowns. You were always greedy for my leavings."

His face was ashen. "I always thought you were basically a decent man, but you're despicable. Here you've come swaggering back from some sort of adventure that I know damned well included a number of other women's beds, and you expect to find the entire world had stopped during your absence, to resume moving again now that glorious Apollo is resurrected, without a thought to your wife's—"

"Balls," I interrupted. "Counter accusations won't wash. I saw you a few minutes ago with your pizzle sloshing in my wife's cunt, and there's an end to it."

Marg's voice trembled, "Jamie. Don't. Don't."

Unnoticed by either of us, she had entered the library and was standing staring at me, her face white and drawn, dark circles under her eyes. "Good-day, madam," I said, rising and bowing. "Please be seated." Her lips were quivering and her hands were shaking. "Hector, give your friend a dram of spirits. She appears in need of it."

He gave me a black look, eased her into a chair and solicitously handed her a small glass of brandy. Taking it blindly, gazing at me, she whispered, "I want to die."

The gray eyes were wet, anguished. I said, "You wouldn't enjoy it at all. 'Tis a poor, uncomfortable thing." Under her eyes my interior began to melt. My love for her surged and collided in a great smash with memory of how I had just seen her. I fell apart and shouted at her, "Come die with me, be dead with me! The cat's claws rip your back, you starve and live in mud, the blood is a river. The damned iron monsters try to pull you down—nigger, nigger, comes The Kitten, but now he'll never drink your blood again—" Everything ran together in a blur and I could hear myself bawling incoherent nonsense.

Hector was doing something to me, and as control returned I saw he was trying to put my shirt back on, for I was standing naked to the waist, weeping. "Jamie, Jamie!" Hector exclaimed, forcing my arms into the sleeves of my shirt. "Who did that horror to your back, man!"

Marg's eyes had gone oddly blank and she was saying in a plaintive voice, "Who has been hurting Jamie? Why have we all hurt Jamie? Jamie's dead and we hurt him. I want to be dead, too."

"Oh, my God!" Hector gasped and went quickly to her. "There, now, Marg, 'tis all right. Jamie's home and the hurting is all over."

Watching the pair with curious detachment, I was relieved to see her eyes resume normality. In her nearly usual voice she said, "Jamie, I'm sorry you saw . . . upstairs. Hector and I are . . . we—"

"I've told him about our betrothal, Marg," said Hector.

"We were in your painting room looking at your pictures from Georgia," Marg told me, "admiring and remembering you, Jamie. 'Twas like being in church and we were both filled with love for you and each other, praising God for His having let us share you, know you and love you, and 'twas my idea to do that in the little room that once was yours." Her eyes filled again. "I wanted your spirit to know and share the joy I found once again, with the man you loved as a dear brother. There was nothing wrong in it, in the why of it, 'twas only—"

" 'Twas only my unfortunate resurrection that spoiled it," I cut in harshly. "A lofty excuse indeed for an impromptu little fuck. Forgive me for intruding on such a holy moment." The sound of my voice shocked me and the voice revolted me. A devil had gotten to me.

She looked as though I had slapped her face and Hector barked, "Marg, go and pack a valise. You'll stay in my father's house until this matter is disposed of. You'll not remain in this house."

I snapped, "Shut your goddamned treacherous mouth! I'll do the disposing of this matter, and be assured I haven't yet ruled out disposing of you into your grave! This woman is still my wife!"

"The blame is mine, Jamie," said Marg, staring down at her hands. "If someone must be killed, let it be me, I pray you, not Hector."

"Bah," I snorted, "he played on your weakness, your frailty, which I doubt was as frail as he'd have me to believe. He was jealous of me from the first time he saw you and certainly thanked God when I was lost at sea in the fight." My mind was beginning to function rationally. "All this gabble is useless. Common sense is in order. And so is a divorce."

"On what grounds?" bristled Hector. "Adultery based on what you saw? Not a bit of it, sir! You are legally and officially dead and she is your widow. We are publicly known to be betrothed. I agree that a divorce should be got, but under no circumstances shall I permit any blame to be attached to her. While I suppose you have become an efficient butcher and may kill me when I try it, if you attempt to besmirch Marg in a court action I shall make every effort to kill you, sir."

Marg screamed, "Stop, stop! God in Heaven, where did friends go, where did love go? You talk of killing each other over me, and I'm the one who should be killed! You were dear friends until I came into your lives and because of me you're enemies! I'm a destroyer!" Tears were streaming down her face. "An hour ago upstairs we talked of our threefold love and now 'tis hate! I'm shamed to death and want to die!"

Watching her sob into her handkerchief, I said, "As I was saying, a divorce must be had. She may use my lawyer, Bartram, who is a clever fellow, and since I'm interested only in being shut of the situation, she may use any grounds against me Bartram believes to be practical. Abandonment, perhaps, or cruelty. 'Tis nothing to me. However, it occurs to me that the action should be delayed for a bit until the public interest in my return subsides.

"Contrary to your revealed opinion of me, MacDonald, I have no desire to expose this woman to distressing notoriety. Judging from what I've heard from you and other sources, she occupies a certain position in the public eye, and a separation or divorce first off might place her in an awkward light."

Hector regarded me suspiciously. "You mean for the time being she'll continue to live here and you'll present the public appearance of man and wife until the furor dies?" He scowled fiercely. "From what you've shown me here, she'd not be safe from your tormenting."

"I have not asked for your agreement or advice, sir," I told him. "I have merely declared what will be done. During that period, for the sake of servants and general observers, you will continue to visit this house as before

395

and you will refrain from conducting yourself as my wife's paramour during those visits and keep your lechery toward her invisible. I will occupy my own bedchamber and she may have the choice of the others. We shall go out socially together. I doubt the hue and cry over my return will last more than a few days, and after that you may have her, and welcome. I shall pay all costs connected with the divorce as my gift in celebration of your pure, sweet passion."

Hector said, "A moment ago I had an impulse to shake your hand, but after that caddish slur—oh, Jesus, Jamie, not only shake your hand, but embrace you. This is a terrible, horrible fix, yet all through it I've wanted to shout for joy that you're alive and well, man!"

"I've no desire to touch the hand that rested where it did not long ago," I remarked sourly.

"Let be, Jamie, let be!" cried Marg pleadingly.

"But, madam," I said sardonically, "why do you object to the mention of it? Such ecstasy as I observed should be long treasured, cherished in your charming bosom. Was it your first coming or were there more before I rudely appeared?"

She covered her face with her hands and Hector grated, "I'm seeing you for the first time, Jamie, you vile blackguard."

"And I, you," I returned. "This is a day we must establish as a household anniversary, 'Recognition of Old Friends and Lonely Itching Wives Day.'"

Leaping to his feet, he exclaimed, "If I dare leave her alone with you, I must leave this house before something worse happens!"

"Like hell you will!" I snapped. "Do you think yourself a dog who can shit in my garden and walk away because you don't like the smell? You will remain, sir! Ira Tupper brought me over from Savannah and after he's delivered dispatches to Whitehall I expect him here for supper. You two will behave in the expected manner as my beloved wife and dear friend, and pretend not to be the pair that made me cuckold."

He sat down slowly. "So this is the man I called my brother, my friend. This is the man I wanted to marry my sister. I see him for what he is and it makes me sick. One day you'll come face to face with him and may God help you, for you'll be sick, too." He turned and looked at

Marg and in their exchange of silent communion there was something that made me think of watching my own funeral pass by. There was no doubt of their love.

Marg said to me gravely, " 'Tis kind of you to arrange it so for me, Jamie, for my sake, and I thank you. I think it will be hard, yet best. I'm afraid 'twill be worse for you."

She remembered that much, at least. I answered, "I'll not suffer. There must be five or six women in London I haven't yet bedded."

Hector said acidly, "And what of the gossip about the famous hero having to find his sport in other than his wife's bed? What then of his wife's public image? What—"

"Ah, shut up," I growled. He was right. It would reflect on Marg. "Well, pretty Kitty's long been hot for it. I'll break an old silly rule and let her warm my bed."

"She's Mrs. Filkins now," said Marg, "and three months gone."

"Oh, well," I shrugged. "MacDonald, is Lady Beauvoir yet in town?"

"No," he replied, "gone home to Ireland and you'll not have to be concerned about Beauvoir anymore. There was a great scandal and he fled to France."

Nodding, I said, "He told me about it just before I killed him at Savannah. Pity. Emily would have been a pleasant diversion. Marg, thank you for thinking of my comfort. That was most wifely."

"Damn it!" she blurted, her eyes filling again.

"You . . . killed Beauvoir?" asked Hector. "At Savannah?"

Ignoring him, I said to Marg, "Ira Tupper told me Anne's in Rome. Do you hear from her?"

"No," she answered, wistfulness in her voice. "She's written to none but her father. She was at . . . at Westminster and left right after for Rome. She wept when she said good-bye to me. We all wept at Westminster." Her eyes became wide gray saucers. "The choir sang and you were there and I wanted to be a part of you again and there were all those strangers who had no right to be a part of you because 'twas I who loved you not them and they had no right, no right, and when the ship blew up there was nothing but smoke on the sea and I was going to jump into it to find you and be with you forever and the men pulled at me and made me lie down and they tied me into the berth and—"

"Marg!" said Hector sharply. "Marg! 'Tis all done and gone! 'Tis long over!"

Her eyes lost the glassiness. I said, unnerved by the exhibition, "I'm sorry you went through that, Marg. I wasn't hurt and here I am, unchanged."

Her face was vaguely puzzled. "You look like Jamie and your voice is like his. I don't know . . . I don't know you, I think." She smiled wanly. "I seem to be light-headed. 'Twill pass."

Concerned, I said to Hector, "It might be best for everybody if I went into seclusion somewhere in the country— an old wound or swamp fever or something—and that would lessen the strain on Marg."

"They'd smoke you out," he said. "You'll recall that I was a journalist here once upon a time. Your first plan is the best for Marg's sake. You said you killed Beauvoir in Georgia and came here in the *Bonny Anne*. She's under Army charter. Why were you traveling in her, Jamie? How did you get back to Georgia? What was Beauvoir doing there?"

"I was taken by the French as a nigger slave," I said carefully, "and there is an experience I wish on you. I also wish on you the labor, the starvation, the degradation and most of all the cat. Ah, the cat would love you, you bloody wife-stealer." Careful as I started, I was losing control again. "The French and rebels were set to make their omelet and I wrung Beauvoir's neck and cut The Kitten's throat." I shouted, "D'you hear? I killed the pair of 'em and neither was my wife and best friend—and gave the orders over to Prevost!

"Ah, you can bet your miserable cuckolding rotten life, you red-headed treacherous turd, that I'm a skilled murderer and the day after I left the French and rebels' corpses were stacked in windrows in front of Savannah because of me! I'm a dead man and Death walks with me, by God! I walk through rivers of blood clear to my knees just as Anne sang that I would and I've traveled her goddamned roads one after the other and this is what they brought me to!" I was laughing uncontrollably and weeping, too.

"Jamie, stop, please stop!" I heard her but couldn't obey, then Hector thrust a drink at me and exclaimed, "Drink, man, drink!" The rum brought me around. Hector said dully, "I did this to you both. I'm ashamed."

398

Marg, surprisingly, got to her feet and said in a brittle voice, "I must see the kitchen about more places at supper."

When she had gone, Hector said, "Regardless of the blame for all this, you've seen how close she is to the edge. I speak only as her physician now. She hasn't had time to completely recover from the last experience. I beg you to be kind and gentle with her, Jamie, for she cannot stand much more of being torn in two directions."

"Physician or no," I said, "don't you dare instruct me on my conduct toward my wife. The only reason I suffer you under my roof is out of deference to her. The sight and sound of you makes me want to vomit. I shall now go and see if among other things you may have overlooked I still have some decent clothes in my wardrobe. Feel free, as usual, to help yourself to my drink, sir."

In my room, Filkins came in answer to my ring and eagerly brought me hot water for my bath, laid out clean linen and a suit of clothes, helped me dress and pelted me with questions, but here again the devil of perversity in me asserted itself; I liked the man and enjoyed his concern, yet could only brusquely, harshly, bid him be still. However, when I went down to supper all my senses were functioning again and I greeted Ira, who had arrived meanwhile, with some degree of normality. On the other hand it became quickly evident at the table that my plan of a pretense to happy relationships was a failure, because Marg was silent and subdued and Hector was stiffly, scrupulously polite, an utter stranger.

It was immediatcly apparent, too, that Ira felt the tensions, for he kept shooting alert glances from person to person though he projected good cheer and pleasure. "By Godfrey, Jamie, when we was last in London together they wouldn't let me closer'n a country mile to Lord Germain, but this afternoon when they sighted them dispatches from General Prevost I got pretty near an hour with him. Got a lot of talkin' done. I honed my own ax some, but most of the talk was about the General's fix and all. Whilst I was there he fired off a note to Lord North for the King. Some pleased, he was, as was all present. I'd say all hell's goin' to come adrift when the news gets out about you, Jamie. She's goin' to be a spar-snappin', lee shore blow. You folks'd do well to double up moorin' lines and let go all anchors, batten down your hatches and hold on tight."

"A tempest in a chamber pot," I decried. "It won't

amount to much. Ira, while we're all together, would you like to buy my share of the *Bonny Anne?*"

Glancing at Marg, to whom he had just been introduced, he answered, "I would, Jamie, if your lady would sell."

It knocked the wind out of me. I had not thought of that. As a dead man I owned nothing. My widow, now regarding me with soft gray eyes that had a trace of pity in them, had inherited my entire estate. This was not my house, my table, my food and drink. I was a phantom guest without legal rights or identity. Hector's face was stony. The food in my mouth turned to sawdust and my stomach went hollow. All I needed was a grave to lie down in. It was unbearable. "Excuse me," I mumbled, left the table and went to the library where I had a big drink of brandy, staring into the fire and trying to think. Bartram—I would send for him in the morning and have him commence my officially legal resurrection and regain my possessions. I felt as though I were once again on the hatch cover, floating on an empty sea.

Ira came in, helped himself to a drink and sat down to regard me with sharp eyes. "Hector's gone and your lady's retired with a headache. She's some pretty, Jamie. D'ye mind if I was to say it ain't the same here as I figgered 'twould be?"

"Welcome aboard," I muttered.

He sipped the drink. "Hector acts like he's got a chicken bone caught thwartships in his arsehole. Your wife's all tore up, stove-in some bad. You're actin' like doomsday was overdue. Jamie, I got a thought in my head that don't bear lookin' too close at."

I needed a friend. "You might as well look close at it."

" 'Tis some bad, Jamie," he said slowly.

"Aye," I agreed, " 'tis that bad, Ira."

He drank in silence. "Things ain't always what they look."

"I came to surprise and was surprised," I told him.

"Ah," he nodded, "so that's the way 'twas. Maybe you was mistook, Jamie. A friendly hug. Hector's always been one for bussin' gals."

"He couldn't have been more friendly," I said. "They were stark and in the short strokes when I walked in."

His eyes narrowed to slits and his face was very Indian. "That was the idee I had. 'Tis some bad, and a wonder ye didn't kill Hector. Calc'late I would have."

I explained what had happened and how I had devised a solution. "I'm in hell, Ira."

"Ay-yeh, I s'pose so," he said. "But not long ago ye would have killed him. Ye'd be in worse hell then. I hope you and her can carry it off; there's a wild look in them gray eyes, to say nothin' of what I see smokin' in yours."

"Smoking in mine?" I said. "Ira, right now I don't feel much of anything unless 'tis like being a rag doll being thrown about by a crowd of children. Back in America I began to think I was being used like that by people and events, and here it is again. What in hell have I done to deserve it? What's happening to me? I was always a fairly happy man, liking people and people liked me. I worked hard and made my own way. Life was good to me. Now I'm dead and my closest friend is my wife's lover—everything's gone up in a puff of smoke. 'Tis as if some evil genius has set out to destroy me."

He stroked his chin reflectively. "Don't let it frizzle ye, Jamie. Ye was luckier than most till ye ran onto Beauvoir. I ain't sayin' your luck's run out—mebbe somethin' catchin' up with ye. Don't get jizzicked; keep steady as ye go. Likely, 'tis still comin' on."

"Whatever it is," I said bitterly, "what else can it do to me? After what I've been through, now this. Ira, I feel dead, lost, as though I don't belong here. Maybe this is a dream I'm dreaming and I'm dying somewhere back there on the other side of the ocean."

"You're not dreamin', Jamie. 'Tis real enough." He got to his feet. "What's done can't be undid and ye got to go on livin'. I'm as fond of ye as if ye was my own son or brother, Jamie, and respect ye for what ye done over yonder, but I ain't takin' sides in this row. I like all three of ye too much. I'll be berthin' aboard *Bonny Anne* so's to stay clear. Good-night, Jamie, and God bless ye—and that sad lady with the headache upstairs."

I remained in the library, drinking slowly and steadily to no purpose, for the alcohol had no effect on me other than to make me more morose and dull. The only conclusion I reached was that I would lose myself in my work, take on all the portraits I could humanly handle. At length I went up to bed where I composed myself by lying on my back, hands folded on my chest. Now, I mused wryly, I am an ancient Celtic warrior king supine atop my sarcophagus, mourned by my faithful, beloved queen during the

401

intervals when she is not frolicking in bed with my noble and loyal chief knight. Soon the legions of the worms will invade the fortress of my flesh, and the battering squadrons of the grass will send down roots to separate my bones. How many times must Jamie Reid die? Cowards, wrote Shakespeare, die a thousand deaths, heroes but once. But when was I ever a coward, Will?

Marg's voice, through the door, said, "Jamie, I must talk."

"In the morning," I replied.

"It cannot wait and I can't sleep," she said, opening the door and coming to my bedside in the dark.

"To all intent you're now another man's wife," I told her, "and if such enters my room in the night it can only be that she has a burning quim."

Her voice, though low, was strong and firm. " 'Tis your right to be angry and hurt, Jamie, but 'tis wrong to lash out to try to hurt others, wrong to yourself because it only makes your own hurt worse. I came here to make you know I love you and suffer with you, but 'tis a different kind of love than I had. You will always be my dear friend, a beloved brother. I beg you not be cruel to Hector. 'Tis not your nature to do it, and going against your nature will do you terrible harm, Jamie."

"What the hell do you know about my nature?" Reaching, I found her arm and pulled her toward me. "So I'm a dear friend, am I? You're fond of fucking old friends. Come to bed, honeybun—Old Nick's up and ready to tickle your kidneys."

Pulling away, she exclaimed, "You're doing it *now*, don't you see? You're trying to hurt me, but 'tis you who are being hurt, don't you understand?"

"Get out of here!" I snarled. "I wouldn't have you in my bed, with your cunt still stinking and oozing with his filthy spunk, you goddamned treacherous trollop!"

The door closed softly and the latch fell with a tiny click. My anger cooled, then all at once what I had said to her struck me with awful impact. Shame and horror washed over me. Another man had said those words, not Jamie Reid. Defenseless, vulnerable and tender, she had pleaded with me for mercy and I had flogged her just as sure as Le Chaton had done it to me. She had said before supper that while I bore the face and voice of Jamie Reid, she didn't know me. Neither did I.

Chapter XXIV

WAKING TO a dull gray morning that matched my mood, I heard a curious sound, a muttering of many voices and an occasional shout outside the house. I got up and went to the window overlooking the square and saw a great mass of people. Men, women and children from all walks of life, judging by their clothes, were standing there gaping at my house. Then suddenly scores of hands were raised, pointing at me in the window and a thunderous shout went up. The upturned faces were laughing and grinning. Men raised children up in their arms. Women waved kerchiefs. A chant began that fairly shook the windows and it took me a moment to realize it was my name. "Mad," I said. "You're all crazy." Feeling impelled out of courtesy to do something, I waved, and a mighty roar went up. "Good God," I muttered and turned away to get dressed.

Thus the public insanity began. Bartram, journalists and tradesmen had to literally battle their way through the mob to come inside. The newspapers came and I found the Government had let out the news of my resurrection late the previous evening. They needed a hero, it appeared, to offset reverses in the French war and the American rebellion thus far, and I was elected to the pantheon of British gods. Everything was grist to the journalistic mill, madly distorted and blown out of all proportion. I was crowned with every superlative in the English language and called dashing, handsome, sublime artist, lionhearted, heart of oak, gallant reincarnation of St. George, Britannia's golden treasure, et cetera.

Invitations to social affairs of high degree flooded in and I felt bound to accept as many as time would permit, so Marg, serene and gracious in public, was plunged into the London high life she had been so curious about so long ago. We were feted like royalty, the subjects of endless toasts, and at home we never spoke to each other. She took her meals in her room, explaining to the servants that she was unused to the excitement and constantly exhausted.

Just when I thought the hysteria was slackening, General Prevost's aide de camp arrived with the report of the defeat of the French-American armies at Savannah. My part in it was well-covered without elaboration, for Augustine Prevost was a cool, matter-of-fact officer, but there I was in the eye of the harrycane again. The journalists would have had it that I was personally responsible for the victory, so before that got too far out of hand I sent for some of them and informed them in no uncertain terms that General Prevost and his brave troops, English, Scottish, German and American Loyalists, were the heroes. However, I was the one who had slain the arch-traitor and unnatural monster Beauvoir and by doing so had captured the key to victory, so the worship of Jamie Reid continued unabated.

With a shouting, cheering tail behind our coach, Marg and I were obliged to attend the thanksgiving nonsense offered in my honor at Westminster Abbey and I damned near died of embarrassment, emotion and concern for Marg. The music wrenched my soul when the great choir's triumphant hymning soared to fill the nave with glorious sound. My chest hurt and I found it hard to breathe. Remembering what I had been told about the other service, I took Marg's hand and through it I felt her entire person trembling. Her face was chalk white. The royal family was present and when I looked at the King he nodded slightly, gravely, and those around me began whispering.

After about three weeks of playing our false role of devoted couple the strain began to tell. Marg was losing weight, constantly trembling and there was a lost look in her eyes when we were alone in the coach going or coming from our public appearances. I summoned Hector and told him as her physician to attend to her and that I didn't give a damn what went on behind closed doors so long as Marg's condition was bettered. On my part, I was nervous, irritable and sick in heart and soul. Somewhere inside me there was a rotten festering. A foul disease had taken root. Nothing mattered much and the world, once so beautiful and entrancing, was a dung heap of hypocrites, sycophants and empty people going through ridiculous motions. I neither had the time nor the inclination to begin portraiture again. At home I drank a great deal and talked absurdities with Filkins, mostly about "the old days"; he was surprisingly good company and it was not until the whole affair was ended and done with that I learned he knew precisely what was going on in the household and why, but had said nothing to the other servants out of dogged loyalty to both mistress and master. The little Cockney sparrow was a splendid man.

Came the King's birthday and I learned what the whispers at the Abbey had meant. I was created Sir James Reid, K.B.E. The entire day was seen through a brandy fog, for I had given up rum as being too weak to numb me properly. There were blank spaces in my drinking days by then, and that evening I came to myself to see I was with Marg, both of us wearing our best clothes and smiles, at the birthday ball of His Majesty. The company was gorgeously turned out and a band of musicians were tweedling and noodling gay music for dancing.

His Majesty appeared in front of me, bowed to Marg and said jovially, "Jolly party, eh, Sir James? And Lady Margaret loveliest of them all. I daresay I'd not have forgiven you at all for your rashness if you hadn't fetched home from Georgia such a gracious ornament to pleasure my eyes and ears. Ah, there's a minuet. Will you not do us the kindness of dancing with your dear lady for all to admire, sir?"

There could be no refusal. I bowed and Marg dropped a curtsy, and the King displayed his handkerchief to the musicians and guests to indicate we would dance alone. No sooner had we started than I was dead sober, for this was the dream, identical to the last detail, I had had while traveling with her on the Post Road. The shocking grief was in her eyes, her face drawn and colorless. She moved with grace, yet made me think of a spring-wound doll. Her hand in mine was icy. The music was endless, the magnificently garbed company smiling admiringly, and she gasped to me, "Jamie . . . help. I'm losing my mind. Help . . ."

Fortunately, the music stopped and when I escorted her from the floor I made hasty excuses about my wife's delicate health and the excitement of the day, then we went home. All the way, she wept in great shuddering sobs. I wanted to take her in my arms and comfort her but instead,

405

outraging myself, said irritably, "Oh, stop it. You're making a spectacle of yourself."

Upon reaching the house, I sent for Hector and had Marg packed off to bed, and when Hector arrived I told him to look after his woman and be quick about it. Then I went to my painting room to sit among my ghosts of the past and get properly drunk. After drinking a full tumbler of brandy at my drawing table, I idly began sketching at random. With the memory of the King's face fresh in my mind, I set about drawing his likeness—and to my unspeakable horror I found I could not draw. In panic I got out a canvas, put it on the easel and tried to paint, but I might just as well have been a two-year-old with a bit of chalk. It was the end. My last reason for existence was gone. The devils that controlled me had taken it away and now I was truly a Cibola jumby, the walking dead. There was a loaded pistol in my room. First, I thought numbly, I would write a note to Marg, begging forgiveness for my cruelty.

With paper and pencil, I struggled for coherent thought and desperately tried to write, but it was an illegible scribble. I stared at the mess, my mind teeming like a mass of worms, and then saw something in it. I tentatively touched it up. A fish? A bird? A dab of shadow here, a stronger line here. A woman. Flying through the air with hair streaming and arms outstretched. Recognition came like a cold shock. "By God!" I exclaimed. "There you are, *Bonny Anne!*" Memory of the dream of the ship drenched me. "Just as you said, you bonny minx!" My despair lifted. I was not yet defeated. If brush and pencil failed me, then hammer and chisels must be tried. I pushed the brandy aside and fell to work improving the *Bonny Anne*'s figurehead drawing and before daylight had the thing worked out to scale from each elevation—front, sides, top and bottom.

From then on, all my free time was spent in the painting room or on errands relating to the figurehead. With the ship still in port, I got from Ira the locations of the bolt-holes and the thickness of the cutwater to which she would be fixed. I bought lumber for scaffolding in which she would be carved, spent hours at lumberyards selecting the wood for her, bought tools—mallets, chisels, gouges, augers, rasps, a drawknife. From Angus MacDonald I borrowed the New York portrait of Anne and, when I leaned it against the painting room wall to serve as model, her beauty nearly felled me. Her perfection was too great for human memory to hold. I said to her, "You'd never smile on me, you solemn witch, but I'll carve a smile on your sister that will be the wonder of the world!"

And so I went to work making the chips and shavings fly, day after day and night after night. I dared not drink, working with those razor-edged tools and the hard exercise made me feel better. Creative enthusiasm buoyed me and I paid only scant attention to what went on outside the painting room. The social carousel was slowing down gradually and, thankfully, Marg and I saw less and less of each other. She never came to the painting room and knew nothing of what I was doing there, and if she had intruded I believe I would have forcibly ejected her because with each succeeding day I was more crazily in love with the figurehead, caressing and talking to it as I worked.

Done with the carving that entailed the use of sharp tools, I was drinking heavily again as I smoothed and polished the voluptuous contours with sand and pumice. The imaginary wind pressed her carved gown against her figure and I lovingly rubbed the swelling breasts, belly and thighs, often kissing them and babbling drunken lover's sillinesses to her. The wooden face smiled radiantly and joyously and I could hardly wait to commence the painting. From the canvas leaning against the wall, Anne Mac-Donald's beautiful face glowed, dreaming green eyes looking through and beyond the figurehead, ignoring us, and I often taunted her as I embraced and kissed the sculpture.

In the meantime, at my direction Bartram had begun efforts to bring Nancy Harris and Little Jimmy to England with the aid of a colleague at Nassau. I had told him I owed her family a heavy debt for sheltering me when I was a castaway on Cibola, and among other methods of repaying I was going to insure the boy had a decent education. My estate had been returned to me, of course, and Ira had bought Hector's and my shares in the *Bonny Anne* before he sailed again for America. I was showered constantly with requests for portraits and turned them down with the explanation that I would be unable to work until after I had a holiday. I tried not to brood on the possibility that the holiday might be permanent.

I bolted the outstretched arms onto the torso of the

figurehead and started the painting. At that time, ships' figureheads were painted in simple colors, skin areas plain white, for ease of repainting by seamen. but my work was a sculptured portrait, a three-dimensional likeness, and to it I applied my notable skill with paints and brushes. It was madly exciting, for I was not only excited, I was also I think, quite mad at that time—to say nothing of being drunk. The grain of the wood disappeared under the priming coat of gesso over varnish, then the windblown gown became green. Red-gold hair glistened and rippled in the sea wind, the soft green-blue plumes of the bonnet bent back. The creamy richness of her skin on face, neck, bosom and arms seemed to pulse with life. The jubilantly smiling lips reddened. A bit of red in the black of the pupils of the eyes lent extraordinary depth to the viridian tint of the green eyes.

It was an insane night. My long unrelieved sexuality boiled and steamed as I made love to the figurehead with my brushes and drank brandy from the bottle. At some point I stripped naked and worked, Old Nick standing up stiff and swollen. Laying in the light flush of color of her cheeks, I crooned, "Sweetheart darling, you're mine and the sea will never have you, my dear happy love. I made your body and gave you your joy—"

With her outstretched arms on each side of me, I was Pygmalion, deliriously expecting that at any moment those arms would fold around me and draw me to her suddenly soft, warm bosom, my Galatea alive and burning with passion. Then the painting was done except for the last, final touch. With my finest, smallest rigger I applied a tiny spot of pure white to the exactly right place on each convex eyeball. Her face instantly blazed with life, the green eyes dancing with exuberant joy close to mine. Excruciating pleasure gripped me, overwhelming desire surged. I flung my arms around her shoulders and kissed the painted lips, oblivious to the still-wet pigments, and my body shuddered and convulsed in powerful sexual climax as Old Nick spouted, spattering the carved body.

I backed off, laughing, and cried, "Now you're mine, all mine, and the sea will never have you with my mark of love on you!" She smiled ecstatically at me, delighted, and drinking from the bottle I capered around the room singing senselessly. I sneered at the canvas portrait, "Witchly bitch, did you see it? Did you see it? See how your sister

408

loved it! See her smile the smile you'd never give me! And I made her, I gave her birth—I, Sir Jamie Pompous Arse, leader of all the other jumbies of the seven worlds! 'Kiss my lips,' says she, the real Queen of Elfland, not you, bitchly witch, 'and sure of your bodie I'll be!' Aye, and now she's had my bodie and the juice of my passion is wet and sweet on hers! My new bride, my love, my lusty *Bonny Anne!*"

Drinking and lurching, I defiantly sang her song, the Ballad of Thomas Rhymer, my naked body smeared with paint from the figurehead, sometimes going in between the arms and kissing the lips again, relishing the taste of the paint. Lust rose again and there was no spontaneous ejaculation; I used my hand, embracing my wooden beloved with one arm and kissing her. I recall sprawling in a chair in front of the canvas portrait, clutching a fresh bottle of brandy and shouting angrily, "I went my roads, you unsmiling twit! I went to the end like you told me to do and see where it got me! Let's see you laugh! Laugh, goddamn you, laugh! I'm a joke, look at me, curse you, not out there! Look at my back that's scored like a cheese grater! You can't see the wound of the musket ball there anymore! You and your stinking roads!" I picked up the nearest object, my shoe, and flung it at the canvas. "They took my wife, my best friend and now my living! You did this to me, you damned beautiful witch! God rot your bones! But your sister loves me and to hell with you!"

I have a dim recollection of kissing the carved lips again, then I went tumbling down the old familiar dark hole to the tinkling sound of silver bells worn by the horse of the Queen of Elfland.

I stood, indecisive, on the road, staring at the dark figure that beckoned from the left-hand branching road. I took a halting, fearful step toward it and a curtain of writhing, snakelike vines sprang up in front of me. A man carrying a glowing sword emerged and came toward me. His face was familiar. "Who are you?" I asked.

He laughed and I saw it was Jamie Reid. "I'm who you think you are, and yet not that at all. I'm more than you are and less than you are, but now I'll be forever more than you are because I'm going to kill you, Jamie Reid, once and for all. You don't deserve to live." He drew back the weapon for the thrust.

"But what have I done so wrong?" I protested

"If you don't now know, never will you know," he grinned, and stabbed.

Pain lanced my belly and I awoke to find myself lying naked and paint-smeared on the shards of a broken brandy bottle, a jagged piece pressing against my stomach. It was broad daylight. Dizzy and sick, I got to my feet, then saw Marg standing in the doorway staring openmouthed at the figurehead. "What the hell do you want here?" I demanded harshly.

" 'Tis Anne!" she exclaimed, her wide eyes on the sculpture. "What joy! What beauty! Jamie, I can almost hear her laugh!"

" 'Tis the other one you hear laughing at stupid, sorry Jamie Reid," I mumbled. "This one is my new bride. I was going to give her to the *Bonny Anne* for the figurehead, but not now. We've had a jolly, loving night together and we'll have many more. The sea will never have her for she's no longer virgin. I asked you, what in the goddamn hell do you do here in my privacy?"

Without looking at me, she whispered, "I can bear no more, Jamie. I . . . I'm leaving today. I've found a house in the country." Then her eyes turned to me, taking in my paint-smeared nakedness. "Oh, my God, Jamie, what have we done to you, what have we done? Forgive us . . ."

Affection for her bubbled up but my perverse devil shouted, "Forgive, shit! Get you gone! Get out of my house, out of my life! Gallant, devoted and faithful wife, go to your lover and fuck happily forever after! Goddamn you for a treacherous whore, to hell with all of you and if I ever see that filthy son of a bitch again I'll kill him on sight! Tell him—"

But she was gone.

While I bathed, shaved, dressed, brandied again and breakfasted, I mulled over the situation and reached a conclusion. Ordering the brougham brought around, I went to Bartram's offices in the City. The good man was shocked when I told him to represent Marg in a suit of divorcement against me on grounds of repeated adultery with one Nancy Harris. Upon her arrival in London, I said, Nancy would be instructed to testify as to our relationship. The simultaneous petition for my adoption of Little Jimmy, declaring him to be my natural son, could be entered as self-admitted guilt in the matter. I said, "I'll ask you to supervise my affairs in my absence, for I'm going away for an indefinite period. Miss Harris is to occupy my house with our son and will be given anything she needs or desires. I shall probably marry her on my return and I wish you to so inform her. But nobody is to know where I've gone. I'll be obliged if you'll keep me informed of the progress of these legal matters and forward letters, if there are any, to me. I'll inform my butler, Filkins, that all inquiries are to be referred to you, if that is acceptable, sir."

"Of course, Sir James," he nodded. "And where do you plan to go? The Continent?"

"Too many traveling Britons to recognize me there," I said. "I must be alone and unknown. I've had a bad shaking, as you can imagine from all this, and need a chance to pull myself together. 'Tis in my mind to have a painting holiday in the Scottish Highlands."

"Ah," he frowned, "you'll be unknown there, to be sure, but that's a cold, uncomfortable place, wild and cheerless at this time of the year. Perhaps in six weeks or so, well into the spring, you'd find it more to your liking, Sir James."

"I'm a cold, uncomfortable, wild and cheerless man, Mr. Bartram," I told him, "and intend to go tomorrow or as soon as I can hire a properly equipped coach for the journey."

He was thoughtful. "Beyond Perth there's no road for such a coach. From that town you'll go by horseback and with a guide, the latter especially, for otherwise you'll be hopelessly lost."

"I think I am that now," I remarked. "How may you forward the post to me there?"

"I have a cousin at Inverness who is a Writer to The Signet," he replied. "That is a fairly central town for the Highlands. I shall forward your letters to him for delivery to you or your agent."

"Thank you," I said. "Please advise my wife of the divorce action and help her as necessary."

That afternoon, after some searching with the aid of my own coachman, I hired a large, commodious and heated coach-and-six, driven by a decent middle-aged man assisted by his grown son. The following morning I gave worried Filkins instructions regarding the house and the arrival of Nancy, then departed London for the wilderness where I would exorcise my demons.

411

Chapter XXV

ONCE CLEAR OF LONDON and rolling over the countryside under gray, weeping skies, all my defenses began to topple and molder away. Alone in the big coach, despair mounted swiftly. With an over-ample supply of brandy, I drank and brooded. Somewhere far behind me the real Jamie Reid had died and his place was taken by an impostor named Sir James Reid, a wealthy and famous ass, from one point of view, who had no ability to paint portraits, no wife and no friends. From another viewpoint he was a whimpering, wounded animal going off to seek a hidden cave where he could lick his wounds, sodden with drink and self-pity. Dead Jamie wept for his lost love and lost Hector, lost talent and lost life. Sir James ranted and raved, pissing and vomiting on himself, calling down curses on the heads of the guilty pair, proclaiming himself a knight of the British Empire, faultless and pure, victim of base treachery, hero of many battles and friend of the King. Dead Jamie argued, sobbing, that Sir James was a fake, a living lie, a dummy stuffed with straw and not a Briton at all, but an American who had lost his country along with wife and best friend while traveling a foolish blind road. Dead Jamie accused Sir James of destroying his God-sent gift of painting portraits and Sir James reviled Jamie as a gutless wonder who could only crouch in a corner of the coach and weep. And both of them drank and drank.

At night stops the coachman and his son carried me into the inns. They tried to keep me clean, washed me and fed me, shaved me and combed my hair. I have only a dim recollection of it. Several times the coach was invaded by the rats from the rebel pinky and my shrieking brought the men from the box to calm me and pretend to drive away the horde of small monsters. Le Chaton sometimes

413

rode with me, whispering vile promises while I chased him around the interior, trying to kill him again.

There came a time of slow, straining progress up steep grades, snow flurries and driving sleet, and the small stove in the coach did little warming. Wrapped in a cocoon of blankets I drank my brandy, sang and wept, and was pleased at the warmth of my urine when I voided my bladder. I don't remember any more of that dreadful journey, and that's a mercy.

I came to myself one day in a clean bed, bearded like a Turk and feeling as weak as paper. A bald-headed man with a red face sat beside the bed watching me with a critical eye. "Decided to come back to us, have you?" He had a gentle Scots accent that reminded me of my father's. "Will you stay a while the noo?"

"Hello," I said. "Where have I come back to?"

I was in Perth, in the house of the man who was a physician named Crieff, delivered there by the coachman, who then had gone back south. I had been there for more than three weeks, hovering on the well-known brink with pneumonia, delirium tremens, exhaustion and near starvation. Crieff told me that there were times in my delirium when I argued so persuasively about wanting to die he was tempted to let me have my way, but concluded that my desperate frame of mind might be simply the result of having stayed overlong in England, a common symptom for a good Scot. "And that I must assume you are, Sir James," he said, "despite your birth far over the water, else you'd not be here in your time of trouble."

"Then you know me," I said. "I'd hoped to be anonymous in this country."

"I'll honor that hope and say nothing in the town about your name," he told me. "As for knowing you, I've sat and listened to you recite your autobiography again and again, so I know to whom I shall send my bill for services which I'm pleased to inform you will not now include a sum for burial. My wife and I will have you up and about soon enough."

They did, and during the fortnight or so he and I became good friends. He evinced no curiosity about the troubles that had brought me there, and I supposed he had heard enough in my ravings to put a few things together. I merely told him I needed solitude for a while. He arranged for me to buy a pair of garrons, wiry Highland

414

ponies, one for riding and one for packing, made a tracing of an old Highland map he possessed and urged me to hire a ghillie to act as servant, guard and guide. When I declined the servant, he said with some feeling, "Losh, man, without a man you can be lost forever up yonder!"

Remembering Bartram's similar comment, I answered, "I'm lost now." Dimly now, I also recalled Hector's drunken declaration at Savannah on that subject. "I've been lost for some time, following poor roads."

Cocking a sharp eye at me, he said, "I had in mind terrestrial geography only. Lad, you're not lost now. You know well what's troubling you and you're fighting with yourself to keep it hid. You're on the right road. You're not the first troubled man in the history of the world to go into the wilderness to fight with your devils. 'Tis a hard road, Jamie, but blessed by those who have taken it before, and you must not turn back." Was *this* the blessed road? I must have made a face, for he said, "From what I've seen of you in that bed I daresay you've run out of roads, my friend, so heed me—unless you want to return to the one I just took you from, and there's a dirty way to go, like a foul beast. Well, if you'll not take a man with you, follow the sun to the west and you'll come out of the Highlands on the edge of the sea."

I rode out of Perth on a bright May morning, wearing a Scots broad blue bonnet and plaidie slung from my shoulder, towing the other pony loaded with my food, clothing and painting equipment. People I met called friendly greetings to which I replied almost absently, because having left Crieff's good company I was ominously alone again with nothing to divert my attention from Jamie Reid. A stranger in a strange land, stranger to myself, I followed the River Tay to the Tummel, using Crieff's map tracing, rode through the Pass of Killiecrankie and into Glen Garry. At night I hobbled the garrons, rolled up in the thick plaidie and slept on the ground after my mind became exhausted with chasing itself like a squirrel in a wheel, trying to find the answer to why, why, why. My loneliness, physically and emotionally, was complete. I wandered for days on end without seeing another living person. The rocky, barren mountains still ribboned with snow, and the sky heavy with clouds looked down on me with haughty contempt, a stricken insect wandering blindly

415

below. My drawing and painting things remained untouched although landscapes cried out at me; I was afraid to confirm what I already knew. My soul felt withered, shrunken. False Sir James stood on a crag a thousand feet above the floor of a glen, shook his fist at the sky and bellowed, "Damn you, God, leave me my soul! You've taken everything else!" Real Jamie, tempted to jump from the crag, wept and cried, "God, help me! Help me find the way! Show me the way!"

I meandered westward, crossed the Great Glen, occasionally buying food from suspicious crofters who spoke no English and offered me no hospitality, and I wanted none. One day I came to the shores of a lovely loch nestled among hills and an unusual warming peace touched my spirit. The secret beauty of the place, hidden away in the Highland fastnesses, spoke to me softly, gently, and the next thing I knew I was busily engaged in painting watercolors with all my old skill. In no time I finished three separate views and they were so good that tears sprang to my eyes. I was a painter again. In my horse pack there was a bottle of Perth malt whisky, untouched all this while, so in celebration, confident that I had whipped my demons, I opened it and drank from it, sitting on a boulder. Peace and well-being swathed me. Some birds dove for fish. A light breeze rustled the tree leaves and my garrons munched in the gorse nearby.

Behind me in the low brush a twig snapped, and my Ranger training brought me full alert. The twig had snapped under a foot, but the shrubbery was hardly three feet high. A child? "Hello," I said. "Come out. I'll not bite, I promise."

A man's strong voice, educated and with a musical lilt, said, "I'll come out, sir, if you'll take my word that neither do I bite."

"I'll chance that," I said, "if you'll share the bite of my whisky with me."

He stepped out into the open and I came close to dropping the bottle, for he was less than three feet tall, with a large head set atop a child's body and very short bandy legs. It was his face that stunned me though, for it was the goblin face I had seen in Old Diggory's magic smokes on Cibola island. I relived the moment and heard myself asking humbly, "Are you God?"

His smile transformed grotesque ugliness into extraordinary beauty. "No more nor less than you are, sir. That's one of my favorite mysteries. I'm Ian Kilronan and was watching you paint. You have superb command of the brush, sir."

I bent down and shook his tiny extended hand. "My name is James Reid. Jamie for short—excuse me, sir—Jamie to my friends."

He chuckled. "I'm a bit short in body, but there's nothing short about my drinks." Taking the bottle in both his small hands, he gulped a hearty drink. "Aye, that would be Dewar's malt from Perth, and full-bodied it is."

Fascinated, I said, "I've met you before, sir, and you answered my question then almost in the same words as now."

"I don't know how that could be," said the little man. "I haven't been away from this country since my university days and that was many years before you were born, Sir James."

Taken aback, I exclaimed, "How do you know me, sir?"

"I stay abreast of the times," he answered. "London newspapers and such." He grinned delightfully. "Haven't I the right to know you when I see you? You claim to recognize me from before. Where did you meet me?"

"In a wizard's hut on an island on the other side of the world," I replied.

The goblin face was interested. "Astonishing! We must have a talk about that." He looked about. "You are camping on my land, sir, and I forbid it. We can't have gypsy artists lurking about. You must accept the hospitality of my house, I'm afraid." Keen eyes studied my face. "Before you decline on the grounds that you must be on your way, let me say you have time for a decent visit. Your next appointment is probably some time off and in this remote place guests from afar are rare indeed, so I command you to give me the pleasure of your company."

I liked the odd little fellow tremendously, but the reference to an appointment made me uneasy. "I'll be delighted, sir. Appointment?"

The smile was warm and wise. "All of us have appointments as we go our destined ways. You've had one with me since your wizard introduced us. Leave your things here—I'll send a ghillie for them. Put me on your garron; my speed of walking will hardly match yours." I lifted him to the saddle, surprised at his lightness, for despite his

417

smallness he gave the impression of being massive. Crossing a field as I walked beside the pony, we entered a long tree-lined and grass-grown drive. "I was not hiding from you, you know. My peculiar appearance puts strangers off rather badly when they come on me without warning. If I were not who I am, I'm afraid the children of my people would stone me on sight. I should explain that I'm the lord of these lands of Glasdhour, twelfth earl of it. You will address me as Ian, however, and I demand to be numbered among your friends and shall call you Jamie."

"Thank you," I said, pleased. "That number now is increased to exactly one."

"So that's the way of it, eh?" he commented. "I find that hard to believe. We shall talk of that, too, I think."

Glasdhour Castle loomed, a great ancient fortress with curtain walls, tower keep, corbeled turrets and crenelated ramparts. Where the moat had once been in front, there was a formal garden of hedges and flower beds. On the cobbled forecourt a flock of white doves strutted. I said, "It looks very old."

"Parts of it are fairly venerable," he answered as a servant appeared, a tall fair-haired and bearded man who wore a law-forbidden kilt. He said something in Gaelic to the man and pack animal who lifted him down, nodded to me and led the pony away. Ian said to me, "Few of my people have English, but if you speak slowly and simply, with gestures, they'll catch your meaning." Toddling beside me on his tiny legs as we entered the inner courtyard, he said, "The oldest sections of Glasdhour date from not long after 598, which was when the first Kilronan came over from Dalriada in Ulster to marry the daughter of the Pictish king who ruled what is now the earldom. The princess inherited on her father's death, you see, and here I am. And so are my people, too, for that matter; they're all Kilronans, though from time to time broken men from lost clans have come to us and taken the name. 'Tis not like a Saxon fief, Glasdhour; 'tis a Celtic family and all Kilronans are the children of kings and my blood is no more noble than theirs, and don't think they don't know it, the prideful fellows."

Inside the castle, he gave me a brief tour of the main living rooms and I was astonished at how his diminutive size no longer obtruded on me. His voice and demeanor were quietly authoritative and unless I were looking directly at him I had the impression of a tall, broad-shouldered man of great strength, such as those of his ancestors who looked down from the old portraits that lined the walls. He pointed to a door. "That opens on the turnpike of the tower keep and your bedchamber is up there on the first landing. Forgive me for not showing it to you; the shortness of my legs makes climbing the stairs a tedious affair, so I rarely attempt it. 'Tis a comfortable room and kept in readiness for distinguished guests. It has ghosts in residence, of course—*tannasghan* in our native tongue, but so does every room here; they're for the most part Kilronans and enjoy having mortal guests in the house, so please don't be alarmed at any spectral phenomena you might observe. The tower dates from about 700, built on an older one. Your room was constructed and furnished as it now is the year before that Italian chap discovered your homeland for the Spanish Crown; until my father's day it was continuously occupied, so you see the spirits have had time to settle in."

"I'll not be alarmed," I assured him. "Your ghosts could never be as alarming as my own." I felt a strange intimacy with him, similar to the golden cord in portrait painting, as if he had been a close friend as long as I could remember.

"I hope you will introduce me to them, Jamie," he commented, leading me into his library, a huge room walled with filled bookshelves. Stacks of more books and periodicals were on the floor. "Sit you down, lad, and we'll have a dram or two of Glasdhour maiden milk." He produced a jug of malt whisky and poured drinks, his short arms and tiny hands displaying steady strength. "Tell me about that vision of me."

After a hesitating start, I told him the story of my Cibola sojourn, omitting nothing. "I've sent for Nancy Harris and my son. Though she's colored, I'm going to marry her."

"Ah," he murmured, "I see a faint ghost of one of your ghosts, Jamie. Your Old Diggory is interesting. Narcotic herbs, flammable colored powders, mind-focusing chants and second sight. A powerful combination."

"But how did he make me see you?" I asked. "I saw others, but they were all people I had previously known."

Smiling gently, he said, "Your own second sight. 'Tis very common here in the Highlands and the Western Isles. We

419

all have it to a greater or lesser degree, I think. I've often thought of it as an atavistic heritage, a primitive instinct of which most modern folk have lost awareness."

"My mother, who was from the Hebrides, had it," I admitted, "but I never thought I inherited any of it. If it brought me here I'm glad I did."

"But far from glad of the circumstances," he remarked. "As I told you, I keep up with the times in my reading. I have followed your notices in the London journals with considerable interest as have most readers. You would not be roving alone in these remote glens at this time of your life if you were not suffering through a grave personal crisis, Jamie."

"I'm roving these remote glens because a man in Perth told me if I would save my life I must stay on this road to the end," I said, "and I seem to be badly lost."

His big ugly head nodded. "Not lost in the physical sense, of course. Why did he tell you that?"

"I had just tried to kill myself," I answered.

"If you expect sympathy from me, Jamie, you're knocking on the wrong door," he said, "though I'll not call your suicide attempt stupid." A kilted manservant appeared and said something to him, then withdrew. "Come, my boy, and have supper and you must tell me about this American war our German monarch is pursuing against your countrymen."

It was an excellent meal. He knew more about the causes of the American rebellion than I did. Recounting some of his family lore, he told me that until his grandfather's time the steward was sent, after the earl had eaten supper, to the top of the tower where he shouted to the four winds, "Hear this, ye kings and princes of the world! The mighty lord of Glasdhour has dined and ye may now sit down to your suppers!"

Afterward we went back to the library and he said, "I think you have an interesting experience coming your way, Jamie. See here." Opening a chest, he took out a small, wonderfully carved and gilded harp. "Do you know the clarsach?"

"I've never seen anything like that before," I answered. "That's a beautiful thing."

Ian smiled. "He'll love you for that. He loves compliments, but only if they're true and that happens to be true. His name in our antique tongue means Voice of

420

Truth. Ireland was his birthplace and he sang at the first Kilronan wedding feast at Glasdhour."

"Why, 'tis more than a thousand years old!" I exclaimed.

"Aye," said Ian, "all of that. You'll notice the royal guarding Lyon of Dalriada carved on him. He came over the Irish Channel with Angus, Lorne and Eric who made Alba into the land of the Scots. Adamnan wrote that St. Columba himself listened intently to my dear friend on occasion, for the Voice was wise then and as the centuries have flitted past he's gathered a bit more wisdom." Sitting on a low footstool, Ian placed the harp between his little feet and trailed his fingers over the strings, filling the room with great harmonious chords. "Ah, my darling," he murmured to it, "you're in fine tune and eager to sing a lay for Jamie Reid, are you? Then sing away." His hands moved rapidly and a golden torrent of sound burst forth.

Something incredible was happening. Ian's face was intent and his hands and fingers moved swiftly over the strings, but the clarsach was in command. Man and instrument had exchanged places. I had just time enough to register that impression before I was swept away on the flood of music. The harp was singing directly to me almost as if it had called my name, and it was singing about me, telling the story of my life. Lilting, merry and carefree was London, sinister discords were Beauvoir. The gray, rolling majesty of the Atlantic, torn by bitterly cold gales, made me shiver. Lascivious madness clashed with death and Meg Barr-Pettit came alive. I quailed, wanted to run, flee from it, but could not move. There was pain and love, sweetness and bittterness. I lived it all over again. Then there was a mounting, soaring exultation of great love that lifted me on glorious wings—and abruptly I was thrown into a cold dark valley of aching despair where anguish and loneliness crushed my soul. I could not bear it. I was crumbling into foul, decaying fragments. I shouted, "Stop! No more, no more!"

The harp paused for a fraction of a second, then sounded a harsh discord as if displeased with the interruption. Ian's sharp eyes watched me. A great melodious ripple of music danced in the air, followed by the most beautiful melody I had ever heard, bathing me in marvelous happiness. Then quite suddenly the music stopped, leaving me on a high pinnacle of delight. "Oh, go on!" I begged. "Go on, Ian! Please!"

He smiled. "He'll not go on, Jamie. He's rather a tease sometimes. 'Tis an ancient Celtic trick of story-telling, quitting before the end. You must find that for yourself. 'Tis more satisfying when you've earned it that way."

"Then it was the harp and not you," I said. "That's an eerie thing."

"It may seem so to you, having just met him," he commented, putting the clarsach back in the chest. "To me 'tis a perfectly natural thing. In every Kilronan generation the eldest son is keeper of the Voice of Truth from time of birth." He chuckled. "If we ever speak a lie, 'tis said, he'll never sing again for us, so you see I'm an honest man despite myself. Pour us our whisky, lad. 'Tis time you filled in the gaps left in the song that was just now sung."

Filling the glasses, I said, "I don't want to burden anybody else with my private woes."

"I am not anybody," he stated. "I have been a part of your life since Old Diggory joined me to it. I have a right to know of what I am a part."

"You saw me blubbering and crying out during the music," I protested. "That was bad enough. I've no wish to unman myself again before another man."

"Since when has sorrow or grief become unmanly?" he asked. "Or is it that you're simply afraid to openly reveal, admit even to yourself, that Jamie Reid is not what he appears to be?"

That struck too close to home and I said angrily, "You're a prying busybody, nosing about where you have no right! Is this the treatment you accord all your guests?"

"As I said, I have the right," he smiled, "and you are not all my guests. 'Tis high time some prying was done in order to learn what has brought you this far on this road you travel."

"You too!" I exclaimed. "Roads, roads, roads! Those everlasting goddamned roads! Everyone I meet lectures me on them! I dream about them! My mother spoke of 'em with her dying breath! Damn those bloody roads!"

His homely face wreathed with pleasure. "There, you see, Jamie? It didn't hurt a bit, did it? You've already told much in those few words. 'Tis a beginning, and among our people the teaching is that every good story has three parts, a beginning, a middle and an end."

I wanted to unburden myself, but I knew once started

422

it would be a frightful display. " 'Twill embarrass both of us."

The smile vanished and he regarded me seriously. "Jamie Reid, I am eighty-four years old and there is nothing in this world or the next that will embarrass or surprise me, particularly the torment of a friend, his passing sillinesses or his failures. Embarrassment usually feeds on private shame, which must not be secretly cherished as if it were a private treasure. These alarming ghosts that haunt you have to be brought out into the light of day where they'll fade and vanish unless you'd prefer to keep them around to spice your existence."

I sat staring at him. I was a man drowning in the pus from my festering spirit and this bizarre little man was throwing me a lifeline. Twice I had asked him, spontaneously, if he was God, and twice he had answered that God lived in both of us, but I was convinced God had deserted me and dwelled in him alone. I was heavy laden, therefore I must go to Him for rest. Ian sat silently watching me, waiting. The tide in me surged, flooded and the words spewed out of me, tumbling almost incoherently from my mouth. I began with boyhood and my discovery that I was an artist, and once started no power on earth could have stemmed the torrent of self-revelation. I took no drink except to moisten my dry tongue. By the time I reached the Beauvoir episode I was reliving, as during the clarsach's song, all the old emotions. It was all there, the women, battles, pain, love, hate and despair. When for the second time I reached the shore of Loch Glasdhour I was wholly wrung out and the night far advanced.

"You'll be weary, Jamie, and I shouldn't wonder," said Ian, getting to his feet. "Thank you for telling me. Get you off to bed, my lad, and have a good night's sleep."

I did, falling directly into the deep sleep of a spent man. I wouldn't have noticed it if the castle ghosts had gotten into bed with me.

Ian spent most of the next day riding over the estates with his baillie, conducting the business of Glasdhour among the farms and hamlets. I was in better spirits than I had been for a long time, so I occupied myself by dashing off watercolors of the castle and gardens. After supper I presented Ian with the pictures and he was delighted. "I'll have them framed and hung in here in the library where I can see them most often. Please don't be tempted to paint a portrait of me for I'll not have it. 'Twould be ill company among my full-bodied forebears."

I said, "You concern yourself with my interior. Why do you concern yourself with your exterior?" Grinning, I pointed out, "At your age you should be rid of vanity. But I pride myself on painting more than a superficial likeness; the interior of the subject shines through, and I know what yours would show."

He was amused. "And what would it show, Jamie?"

"At first glance," I replied, "it would show your exterior as it is. The second glance and succeeding study would show a tall, handsome gentleman with a keen intellect and stout, warm heart. That is not empty flattery, Ian. 'Tis what my trained eye perceives."

"Why, thank you, my boy," he smiled. "There are times when I feel myself quite tall and forget my unfortunate features. However, you employed that gift, of course, in painting your wife's portrait in Georgia. You knew her better than most other, less perceptive men know their wives. Loving you, innocent and naive, she told you truths about herself. Did you listen, Jamie?"

She had told me, I suddenly now remembered, that if she lost me she would go mad, wither and die. It was the truth. Only Hector had saved her from madness and death. At dear cost to me, but the cost to her would have been a terrible and ultimate one. And all the while she had declined into that horror because of me, I was living in pagan pleasure with Nancy on Cibola. All my rage and brutality toward Marg and Hector, my contemptuous disbelief of his story about her, now nauseated me and I tasted the bile as my gorge rose. Stammering, I confessed what had happened, and that led into a hellish jungle of my thoughtlessness and callous arrogance. I was a sorry spectacle at the end of the evening, distraught and bleary-eyed with tears, but I felt better.

That was the pattern of our evenings together for the next several nights. I talked and he listened. He never made a judging comment or critical remark except as contained in a question that unlocked the door in my mind to free the close-guarded thought. There were times when I hated him and would have fled the castle if I had not been dimly aware that a great cleansing was going on inside my head.

One day he said to me, "You're finding a friend again

424

in Jamie Reid. You should. He's worth having as a friend. I'd not mind having him for a son. The Kilronans always had troops of sons until I came calling. I was the first and last. 'Twas said that when I was born my father took one look at what had come out of his wife's body and turned away, never to touch her again. As for sons of my own, what woman would have the courage to bed with me? I could have planted my seed deep enough; God saw to it that I had that much of a proper man's body. But the only woman who ever smiled on me with love was my mother, and she was blind to my uncommon style of beauty." He glanced sharply at my face and what he saw there made him say gruffly, "Damme, sir, I want your sympathy no more than you want mine! 'Twas God's will. Excuse me, I have accounts to tally."

The tower ghosts had by that time lost their shyness. There were no glowing wraiths, clanking chains or hideous screams. The room rustled with sibilant whisperings whose words I could not catch, and I gained the impression of a crowd of people watching and discussing me; friendly, curious folk. I bade them a cheery good-night after I snuffed the candle and curled up in bed each evening and they would thoughtfully fall silent. "Aye," said Ian when I laughingly told him that, "always be courteous to them. They're all Highland lords and ladies of dignity, pride and understanding hearts."

He said to me one night in the library, "The supplies party I sent to Inverness should return tomorrow. I hope there will be letters for you in the post, bearing the news you expect. With that and your improved spirits, no doubt you'll be wanting to be following your road to its end and then be off to London."

"The road has ended here at Glasdhour, Ian," I told him. "I've no reason to wander on. I'm eager to get back to work, so if Bartram's done his work I'll be off to Perth, thence to London."

The goblin face was concerned. "I mentioned your improved spirits, not *healed* spirits, Jamie. I doubt you've cast out all your devils, and this surely is not your road's end. You've yet a distance to go."

Laughing, I said, "And distance to go lies between here and London, for there lies the end of my road. Thanks to you my head is straight on my shoulders and I can live with Jamie Reid, with all his warts and cankers. I'm an artist again and have no hatred for any man or woman, only friendship."

He said gravely, "I'm pleased to hear you say that, my son. I shall miss you more than you know, and I pray that I shall see you again before you go off to America, when the war is ended, to establish your art academy."

"If you may not come to London," I assured him, "then this Mohamet will come to the mountain of Glasdhour with all dispatch and eagerness. But I don't think my American academy will ever come to pass if the rebels win; I've spied and fought against them."

"Old hatreds die," he commented, "and a new nation will need men like you. Young countries must have young men who see visions, not old men who dream dreams, as they do in the old countries on this side of the water. Your America will be *Tir nan Og* come to life, the Land of the Living, where all who dwell there are forever young in heart and spirit."

"*Tir nan Og?*" I repeated.

His smile had a twinkle. "We of the Celtic race, of which you're a member Jamie, have had since long before the recorded history of man a belief that somewhere over the Western Sea lies a marvelous land where no man grows old and there is no hunger, sickness or hurt. Fountains never go dry, nor do fruit trees stop bearing. The women are staggeringly beautiful, willing and bursting with love. All is true and right and there is no evil."

I guffawed. "Some of the rebels believe that about America. The miracle will happen when they've kicked out His Majesty."

"Keep an open mind, Jamie," said Ian. "There's an old magic in the West. Have you ever contemplated the steady movement of mankind westward? We follow the sun. Adam and Eve went westward from the Garden, and their descendants moved successive civilizations ever in that direction along the Mediterranean, through Europe, and now they reach out across the sea, chasing their vision of *Tir nan Og,* though other peoples than the Celtic have different names for it. Plato called it Atlantis. Aye, there's magic in the west, Jamie. Even a lonely anguished man who goes a-wandering to seek peace with himself will turn his face in the direction of the setting sun."

"Oho," I laughed, "I might have known all that philosophizing had me as the target! No, sir, I'll go no farther

426

west. Beyond these hills there's only land's end and the water's edge, and I've sailed over the Atlantic Ocean enough not to be curious about it."

He shrugged small shoulders. " 'Tis your decision. Think long and hard about it, Jamie."

Sure enough, the Inverness party brought me two letters from Bartram, and the fattest one I quickly opened. The divorce had been granted and Bartram had managed to have it done quietly so it did not reach the press, which, so far as I was concerned, reported me on an extended holiday in Switzerland. Nancy and Little Jimmy were living in my house, happy and healthy. Nancy's honest testimony had quickly decided the judge. Marg had refused a property settlement and alimony. With Nancy's wholehearted consent, the adoption petition was granted and my son was now my legal heir. With a bit of polishing in language and social graces, Nancy would be a sensational wife, I reflected with satisfaction, and would become the rage of London with her dark warm skin and sparkling personality.

I began reading the second letter and a thunderbolt exploded in my head. In clear and precise script Bartram conveyed his sorrow and deepest sympathy, regretting that it was his sad duty to report the untimely death of Miss Harris. In the tragic manner of so many visitors from sunnier climate, she had been taken ill with an inflammation of the lungs and had passed away six days after the divorce hearing. My hands shook so violently I could hardly read. Marg had sent along a note:

Dear Jamie wherever you are—I was with Nancy through her illness to the end. In the short time I knew her I came to love her. A sweeter, dearer girl never lived. She told me to tell you that she'll wait for you on the other side and you must not grieve for her because she lives on in Little Jimmy for you. Hector and I pray for your happiness and beg you to forgive us if you can for our part in the awful thing that happened to Nancy. We love you so. Hurry back to us, dear Jamie.

I went mad with fury. How dared they take upon themselves any blame for Nancy's murder? It was I, Jamie Reid of the foul, defiling touch who had struck down that loving girl, the mother of my child! I had brought her to London for my own selfish purposes, forced her to degrade herself by confessing to fornication while I fled like a coward. I had used her love for me as a weapon. I had taken her child from her. Everywhere I went I left a trail of death and grief caused by my self-aggrandizement, lust and arrogance. Nancy would wait forever where she was— I would never arrive, for the bells of Hell were ringing for me: murderer, adulterer, betrayer of innocent trust, self-centered clot of human scum. My mind became frothing jelly. A long way off, Ian's voice shouted, "Jamie, sit down, man, sit down!"

I struggled to speak, but instead of words there came out of me the agonized howl of a mortally injured dog. Then I was stumbling up the turnpike steps of the tower keep to my chamber. Kneeling beside the bed, I buried my face in my arms and cried, "Strike me down, God! Strike! Damn you, God, kill me!" I could not pray for forgiveness because what I had done was unforgivable. I hungered for the punishment I deserved, eternal damnation. Then, although it was daylight, the sun streaming in the windows, the ghosts of Glasdhour surrounded me, whispering. I could not see them, but my confused mind did. Some of them were identical with the portraits in the great hall, splendid Kilronans of centuries past who ruled as kings with power of pit and gallows, made war, and considered themselves equal in rank with the monarchs who had reigned over all the Scots. The ladies were gracious, educated and pious, fluent in English, Gaelic, French and Latin. Somehow I knew them all and they were my dear friends. I listened. They were not talking among themselves about me; they were talking to me, instructing me. The words I could not distinguish, but the sense was clear. Kneeling by the bed with my head in my hands, I opened my mind like a cup and let the wisdom pour in, though at the moment I did not know just what was happening; it was only much later that I understood. It went on for some time and then the whispering ceased.

I became aware that my knees were sore, my position cramped and rather absurd, so I stood up, stretched, feeling remarkably well. My past performance struck me as pitiful, and it was difficult to believe that it was I who had thus raved, wept and carried on like an hysterical woman. Going to the window I looked out at the hills and mountains beyond Loch Glasdhour and thought of that dear man, Ian Kilronan, who so wanted me for a son. I had a son, and in my childish petulance I had forgotten him. Little Jimmy needed me. I would raise him to be a decent, honorable gentleman; strong and kind.

Portrait painting would no longer be for me an end in itself, I reflected; I would employ it to build a base for my American academy and would put my God-given talent to work for my country, paint those great national, purely American pictures, no matter who won the cursed bobble. I had friends in London who knew Benjamin Franklin well and he would work for me, open the way for me to return to my native land, that beautiful *Tir nan Og* beyond the Western Sea, and London could go hang. I was no longer interested in those childish pursuits of empty pleasures.

The hills and mountains beckoned beyond the loch, blue-hazed in the light of the westering sun. Ian had urged me to go that way and he was a wise old gentleman. I owed him much. It would not take me more than a week at the most to travel westward to the end of land and that would please him; meantime I would make the most of it, enjoying a real painting holiday before returning to London, to Little Jimmy and my plans for the future. I looked around the room and said, "Thank you, ladies and gentlemen. I shall be forever in your debt." Then I went down to the library.

Ian put aside the book he had been reading and looked at me as I sat down. The beautiful smile lighted his ugly face. "How do you do, sir? Have we met before?"

I laughed. "You're joking, but in all honesty I don't think so. I have the odd feeling that the old Jamie Reid has vanished into thin air. Ian, please don't be embarrassed if I say I love you and all the Kilronans, and I respect and admire you enormously. I'll be honored if you'll regard me as a sort of son."

"Ah." He got out of the chair and poured two glasses of whisky, handed me one and raised his. "To us, Jamie, my son." We drank, and he said, "I must confess I loved the old Jamie Reid too, though he was often younger in his outlook than he should have been."

"He was a spoiled brat," I commented.

"Not exactly," said Ian. "Merely a bit late in reaching maturity, a fairly common circumstance among singularly gifted individuals, I think. The moment you walked in it

429

was evident that a significant change had occurred and I must say that it becomes you quite well, Jamie. You'll be getting along now, I suppose."

I told him of my plans. "I'm eager to be with my son. I'll take ship at the first port I come to, but I promise you I'll not leave the United Kingdom without first coming here for a visit, Ian, and I'll bring your little brown grandson along. You'll love him."

Ian took out his handkerchief and blew his great nose. "Damme, I must have caught a chill. A grandson. Well, well. I must remember to rewrite my will. God bless you, Jamie Reid."

"God bless you, Ian Lord Glasdhour," I smiled. "In the morning I'll go to the west and follow the road to the end in humble obedience to my noble Highland father, sir, and if beyond the Atlantic surf I see no golden land of *Tir nan Og* I shall proclaim in London that Ian Kilronan is a sham and a false prophet."

"It may be that there will be nothing but surf there," said Ian, "yet somewhere waiting for you is the end of the song that was sung to you by my good friend, for that is as sure as the bright sunrise on a clear morning, Jamie. Come, pour us another dram and tell me of your plans for my wee brown grandson."

My departure from Glasdhour was wrenching and thankfully brief. With my saddled and packed garrons waiting on the forecourt, I squatted and shook Ian's hand, and he said in his strong, resonant voice, goblin face gentle with its beautiful smile, *"Am fear nach seall roimhe seallaidh a 'na dheigh, Seumas,* which means the one who does not look forward will look back, Jamie. You've looked back enough. Your bonny road lies ahead, and great joy waits there for you. Go with God and remember your promise to me." He leaned forward and kissed me on each cheek.

"When I first saw you in the vision and again when I met you in person," I said, deeply moved, "I asked if you were God. Now I know that God lives in your heart and has blessed me. Little Jimmy and I shall visit you next spring, that I swear, so stay out of drafts and catch no more chills, Father Ian. Farewell until then, great friend."

I mounted and did not look back, and after an hour or so of riding the anguish of parting subsided somewhat. Going into the hills beyond the loch I discovered that in the emotion of leaving I had forgotten Dr. Crieff's map tracing. I shrugged it off; all I had to do was follow the sun. In the western Highlands there would be a watershed and I would follow the burns and streams to the sea. Early summer had come and the weather was bright and warm, the rugged landscape beautiful. I sang bawdy, merry ballads to my garrons, my voice echoing in the glens. In no haste and in high spirits, I paused occasionally to sketch or watercolor anything that caught my fancy.

I saw more red deer than people, more eagles than houses. I camped the second night with a shepherd and his flock, sharing my whisky with him. He had no English and my Gaelic was sparse, but we had a fine companionable time laughing at our mutual inability to sensibly converse. He was a white bearded old man with a wonderful sense of humor, and offered me the use of a pretty little ewe—there was no mistaking his meaning—if I desired a wife for the night. Full of whisky and laughing, I rolled up in my plaidie and went to sleep. In the morning I awakened to find myself alone on the hillside with only my saddle garron and baggage; the old rascal had gone off with his sheep and my pack pony, honest enough—in his way—to leave me the rest.

Loading my gear on the remaining animal, I struck out on foot, leading the beast, and it wasn't long before the hard walking made me curse my idiocy for agreeing to make the senseless march to the sea instead of going back to London the direct way through Perth. However, once I got used to the trudging my good spirits returned. Rounding the flank of a mountain not long after that I stopped, spellbound, for there, in the far distance, I saw the shining broad Atlantic. I would never have believed that the sight of that familiar ocean could have filled me with such violent excitement. The sun-glimmering vastness was stunning, filled with magic and mystery, and I was a Celtic child of my ancestors, thrilled by the promise of *Tir nan Og* that lay out there beyond the horizon. Gone now was my resentment; reaching the sea was all that mattered, my only goal. I paused no longer to draw or paint, walking as fast as the rough ground would permit.

Now the hills became lower and all streams flowed westward. For the first time since leaving Glasdhour I came upon a road and followed it, passing occasional farm cottages and passing through villages where the people greeted me pleasantly in Gaelic. In my weathered broad

431

bonnet and dirty plaidie I looked like any of the Highlandmen except for my well-made breeches and shoes. The narrow road wound through a glen along a broad stream and when I came to where it ended, the stream flowing into a great loch, I smelled the sea and was filled with delight. The road followed the northern shore and I saw the loch was salt water, tidal, and seabirds circled over it. There was no stopping for me then, not even for food.

The shore of the loch swung around northerly and I came on a fishing village there. To the west, across the narrowed loch, was a range of steep hills that rose from sweeping fields and moors. There were a number of fishing boats drawn up on the rocky shingle with men working about them and, going to the nearest man, a busy, gray-haired old chap with great shaggy eyebrows, I asked how I might reach the opposite shore.

He was mending a net, and the odd-shaped instrument continued to flash in and out without pause, nor did he look up at me as he said with a broad accent, "Three ways there are—you can fly, swim or wait for the southrons to build a bridge."

I laughed. "I have no wings, the water is cold and even if the bridge was built in the next five minutes I wouldn't want to wait for it. You've got a fine boat here. I'll pay whatever is asked, to be taken across."

The knitting stopped and he looked at me with bright blue eyes. "Will you, now?" Eyeing my pony, he said, "There's no boat here big enough to ferry yon beastie."

I could carry my baggage over the hill range. All told, it weighed no more than thirty pounds. "You can have him with saddle, blanket and bridle if you'll take me over right now."

He inspected the pony. "You must have more money than wit. He's a good animal."

"If you won't take him because your honest conscience stands in the way," I said, grinning, "then in addition to the ride across, you may buy him for one shilling Scots."

"'Tis a bargain," he said hastily. "Taken and done. I'll be wanting a bill of sale so no man may say I lifted the laddie from a daft stranger."

I scribbled the bill on a page from my sketchbook and he paid me the coin. He gravely shook my hand and said, "I'll call my sons and put the boat in the water."

432

Three brawny young bearded men rolled the boat on logs down to the water, stepped the stubby mast and we were away, borne westward by a brisk southwest wind with the father at the tiller. The distance was less than half a mile and during the voyage one of the sons helped me fashion a rope pack for my baggage to sling on my back. The young man cocked an eye at the southwest sky where clouds were low, dark and heavy, and said to me, "You'll have a wet and windy walk at you."

"I've been wet and windblown before," I laughed. "The Western Ocean lies directly beyond the hills, doesn't it?"

"Aye, every drop of it," he answered, "give or take a few drops of it under the keel now."

"Likely there's a road to it through the hills," I suggested.

The boat's bow grated on the graveled shore. "Aye," replied the man, pointing. "There's a bit road in yonder field. She runs north. Walk her till you reach the path bearin' away to larboard. That's the road to the *beinns*."

They called good-bye and shoved off, and I shouldered my pack, walked through the heather and thistles to the road, a rough and stony narrow track. The landscape was one of wild grandeur, almost treeless, with no house in sight, the steep, high-peaked hills stabbing against the onrushing dark clouds from the southwest. There was no doubt of it. I was going to be very wet shortly unless I found shelter along the way.

After a few minutes of walking, the pack gained weight and the rope suspenders dug into my shoulders. The small rocks and pebbles underfoot made walking difficult. The afternoon light darkened and raindrops spattered, the wind steadily increased, fortunately on my back, and once again I told myself I was a damned fool for undertaking this pilgrimage to satisfy Ian. Thunder rolled, reverberating among the hills, and lightning flashes became more frequent and brighter. The rain became a downpour. Drenched, my shoes full of water, I trudged along, bent under the pack, and said aloud, "Jamie Reid, what in God's name are you doing here at the end of the world?" Then the heavens really opened. The rain came roaring down solidly like a waterfall and the lightning poured in jagged rivers of flame in the daytime darkness. I wondered if God was about to grant my mad plea of not so long ago and strike me down. And I worried about missing the "lar-

433

board" turn in the dark and rain, for it was hard enough to stay on the road. There was almost no visibility.

About the time I thought I might drown while walking, the rain slackened and the wind dropped, the thunder and lightning moved on to the northeast. The darkness gradually lightened to something approximating late afternoon in the shadow of the high, steep benns to my left. Ahead, I saw a grove of trees, an unusual sight thus far on the sweeping bare moorlands, and the extent and form of the woods gave me the impression they must have been deliberately planted, which meant they were likely on an estate of some sort. That indicated there might be shelter for the night. Feeling better, I trudged a little faster through the puddles and mud, anxiously looking for some sign of habitation.

I had gotten fairly close to the trees before the horror commenced. My mental awareness was sluggish due to weariness and soaking discomfort. Between the trees and me was a triple fork in the road, the right branch bearing sharply away to wind over the fields to the east, the main track continuing north and the left road led into the grove, mounting upward toward the hills. The latter, I reflected with brief satisfaction, was the road to the benns the fisherman had told me about. Then as I stood at the fork, hesitating, I looked at the murky dark tunnel that led through the dripping trees and the full cold shock of recognition struck me like a blow. My blood froze, flesh crawled and neck hair bristled. In how many ghastly nightmares had I stood in that place, wondering which of those three roads was the right one for Jamie Reid?

I had walked into the damned dream and it was real.

Here was the darkling green, eerie light, the weight on my back, the mud and wet. This was the plain under a sunless, moonless sky. The wind had ceased, and in the still air there was no sound but that of dripping leaves. In a moment hordes of faceless men would spring from the ground and rush at me with swords; the pack on my back would turn into vile, lascivious Beauvoir. Under the trees ahead the rotting, stinking corpse of Meg Barr-Pettit lay in wait to couple with me. The other Jamie Reid would come, laughing, to finally kill me. One part of my mind shrieked in panic, "Go back, turn and run, run!" The other part said grimly, "Go you now to the end of your miserable roads and be done with it."

434

The dreaming terror of the years had to be confronted and vanquished. With immense effort I advanced one foot, then the other, going slowly forward in complete fearful revulsion that was the cumulation of every one of the road dreams I had ever experienced. With my heart pounding, water-filled shoes sloshing in the soupy mud, I entered the dark green tunnel of trees. Then, peering apprehensively ahead, I smothered the scream of horror that rose in my throat, and stopped dead in my tracks, for where the road emerged from the far side of the woods I saw the motionless dream figure, dim in the half-light of fading day. The scream nearly burst again when the figure, as I knew it surely would, raised an arm and beckoned to me once, then twice.

In the seething state of my mind a coherent thought took shape. Ian had foretold of an appointment I must keep, and this must be it. If this, I told myself, is Death and the end of my foolish roads, then I must go to meet it like a man. With that decision, fear fell away. Stepping out briskly, I strode to the waiting figure. Details appeared, sharpened, and I saw the lovely green gown, the bright glow of red-gold hair, and the beautiful grave face of Anne MacDonald.

All of God's wonderful world came marvelously into place and I wanted to shout with joy and delight, where a moment ago I had nearly screamed my horror. Before me stood all the sweet answers. Halting in front of her, I looked down into her intent green eyes, reveling in them, and asked, "Am I now a different enough man for you, bonny Anne?"

The eyes searched mine for a fraction of a second, then the perfect face blazed with a brilliant laughing smile of exulting happiness, the identical expression I had carved and painted on the figurehead. The clear, rich crystal of her voice floated like a caress in the quiet air, "Aye, darling Jamie, I see it in your dear face, yet there's enough of my old sweet rogue to make me twice as happy."

"I don't dare kiss you standing here," I said, "for there'd be no end to it. We've a lifetime of kissing ahead of us." I shouted with pleased laughter. "I was lost—had not the damnedest idea where I was! This is the Isle of Skye, isn't it, and we're standing on your father's old family estate! Oh, you witch, you should be burned at the stake, even though I'm crazy with loving you!"

435

"I've been crazy with loving you for longer than you know," she said. "Aye, this land is where Hector was born and brought up and 'tis named Tir nan Og, which means—"

"I know what it means," I said, caressing her soft cheek with my fingertips. "A dear and wonderful giant of a man told me not long ago, and his friend, very old and wise, sang to me that I'd meet you here."

She surveyed me from head to foot. "Losh, man, look at you—dirty and wet as a shipwrecked tinker!" Taking my arm, she said, "Come, you must change out of those clothes before you catch your death and make me a widow before I'm even a bride. I brought a trunk of your things from London. Your bonny little man Filkins wept with joy to know I'd fetch you home again."

Walking arm in arm with her up the muddy road, I said, "I should know better than to ask how a witch does things, but how in God's name did you keep your gown dry in that cloudburst?"

Silvery laughter rang. "I near broke my neck running back to the house to get out of it and then almost broke it again rushing to the road when it stopped. For the good part of each day for a week past I've come down here in your special green gown, waiting for you to come to me." She looked up at me seriously. "The dream—it had to be ended that way. Ah, Jamie, those dreadful dreams! I could see you, call to you, yet never did you see or hear me in your sorry troubles."

"It damned near frightened me to death at first, seeing it all come to life," I admitted. We were walking, I suddenly discovered when I looked away from her enchanting face, up the driveway of a large graystone manse that looked exactly like Goodowns without the latter's columned porch. "And is your bedchamber here decorated in green, white and touches of gold?"

"I had that done when I arrived," she answered, "because 'twas in the Goodowns room that I first dreamed of you and loving you in that bed. And out of bed, too, of course, but especially in that bed."

We entered the house and it was Goodowns without Brutus and the twins. She came with me upstairs, and in her chamber I opened the London trunk, selected a suit, shirt, stocking and shoes, then stripped to change while she sat and watched me, smiling softly at my nakedness. It was as if we had been married for years. Putting on the dry clothes, I said, "We'll have a grand great wedding in London, but when we sleep together in this house we'll do it in the grace of God."

She nodded. "A Scots marriage. I have the Bible and a ring. After dinner we'll wed." She laughed. "Poor Kirstie MacDonald, our cook, will be a happy woman to see the fine dinner for two that she's been cooking each day for a week eaten by two people at last."

In the duplicate of the familiar Goodowns library we had a drink of fine brandy, settling down to devour each other with hungry eyes. I asked, "How did you know the dream would end here and that I'd come here?"

"Jamie," she answered seriously, "I've always loved you and known you, known you better than I know myself. After I came to live with you and Hector in New York, Hector described this place to me, saying I'd never be a true Mac-Donald till I visited Tir nan Og, and told me that if I came from the mainland I must follow the road north until I came to the trees where there was a road leading toward the benns, the Cuillin Hills. There was a triple fork, he said, right there. After I began sharing your nightmare I came to think it meant we two would come together here where the real triple fork is, you see. When you left New York I told you—it slipped out because I was so near going mad at losing the sight of you—to take the road to the benns when your roving was done."

"It would have helped if you'd explained all that at the time," I commented.

"You know better than that," she admonished me. "I couldn't interfere with what God had planned for you. It was all I could do to keep from bursting into tears when I looked at you and you were always shouting, 'Smile, you damned witch, smile on me, for God's sake!' But I had those dreadful feelings about what lay ahead for you, Jamie, and I loved you more than life itself."

"I was an overgrown spoiled brat," I remarked.

"I'll not argue," she smiled, "yet I loved that wayward child. After you were called dead and I went to Rome the dreaming of you and the roads went on, so I knew you weren't dead. My father wrote about your return and of all those dreadful happenings with Marg and Hector, and of your disappearance again. Hector thought you might have killed yourself and came near doing it himself, Marg told me when I saw her in London."

"So you did what you knew I would do," I said. "You sorted out all the places I could run to and rejected 'em all but Scotland."

"I went straight into your head, Jamie Reid," she said, "aching with the pain you felt, the terrible puzzlement over what was happening to you, and went to your Mr. Bartram and challenged him to deny you went to Scotland. He's an honest and good gentleman and saw what must have been standing out in my eyes. He told me and gave over the care of Little Jimmy to me. Mrs. Grimsby is living in your house and mothering the sweet laddie for us. And you're a man of the west, Jamie. I knew you'd turn your face to the sun and follow it to the sea."

"To the end of the dream," I commented.

"Aye," she smiled. "When I first came here and saw the living place of the dream, I knew, dear God, I knew!" She giggled. "Though before I left London I invited Marg and Hector to our wedding, I was so sure. Will you like that, Jamie? They love you dearly."

"Of course I'll like it," I agreed. "I've a deal to make up to them. Were you ever jealous of Marg when she was my wife?"

"No," she answered shortly, dropping her eyes from mine.

"Here, here, what's this?" I demanded. "Anne, are you lying to me?"

She raised her eyes and I saw with dismay they were glistening with tears. "I was evil, nasty, Jamie. Horrid and sinful. I'm ashamed. No, I couldn't be jealous, darling, because I loved you both and wanted you to be happy. But all the time I was gloating, knowing that if you lived through your trials I'd have you at last. I was greedy and lustful for you, and all the while thought I was being so unselfish and . . . and saintly, damn it! Can you forgive me that, Jamie?"

"Forgive what?" I replied, loving her beyond belief. "For behaving like an honest woman in love?" I chuckled. "Thank God, at last I know my bonny Anne isn't perfect. She has beautiful, adorable, human feet of clay, with splendid chinks in the armor of her perfection. Goddess no more. But a witch, ne'ertheless. Tell me, what does your

438

second sight have to say about us going home to America when the troubles are past over there?"

"My dear lord and master," she answered, her smile blooming again, "whose children do you think I saw playing in the garden on that first day in New York? They looked very like you and me and all had red hair, which I hope you won't mind, except the coppery-skinned one who resembled you alone. The house is still yours, though a good rebel lady friend of mine holds title through a dummy bill of sale we agreed to." The pleasant smell of food and a clatter of plates came from the dining room. "Kirstie has dinner ready." Anne rose, curtsied, and asked demurely, "Will you take my arm and dine with me, Sir James"—the pose broke and her laughter pealed—"then marry and bed me quickly, you dear, sweet scoundrel!"

Laughing together, with her arm decorously on mine, we went to the dining room and, while it may have been only in my mind, I could have sworn I heard, coming from over the mountains, lochs and glens, the music of a small ancient harp beginning the most beautiful song he would ever sing.

Bibliography

A complete bibliography of source books would be too lengthy. However, a partial list of basic references is as follows:

Lee, Henry (Light Horse Harry Lee), and Lee, Robert E., ed. *The American Revolution In The South.* New York: Arno Press, 1969.

Stevens, W. B. *A History of Georgia.* New York: D. Appleton & Co., 1957.

Smith, Paul H. *Loyalists and Redcoats.* Chapel Hill: University of North Carolina Press, 1964.

Callahan, North. *Flight From The Republic.* New York: Bobbs-Merrill Co., Inc., 1967.

Kennedy, Benjamin, ed. and tr. *Muskets, Cannon & Bombs —Nine Narrative Accounts of The Siege of Savannah.* Savannah: Beehive Press, 1974.

Prebble, John. *Culloden.* England: Penguin Books, Ltd., 1967.

Short, Ernest H. *The Painter in History.* London: Hollis & Carter, 1948.

Quiller-Couch, Sir Arthur, ed. *The Oxford Book of English Verse.* New York & Toronto: 1940

Candler, A. D., ed. *The Colonial Records of Georgia.* Atlanta: 1904-1916.

Forbes, Esther. *Paul Revere & The World He Lived In.* Boston: Houghton Mifflin Co., 1942.

MacCana, Proinsias. *Celtic Mythology.* Middlesex, England: Hamlyn House, 1970.

MacLean, Sir Fitzroy. *A Concise History of Scotland.*
New York: Viking Press, Inc., 1970.
Moncreiffe, Sir Iain, Of That Ilk, Albany Herald. *The
Highland Clans.* New York: Clarkson N. Potter, Inc.,
1967.